# THE CON MAN'S
# DAUGHTER

ALSO BY ED DEE

*14 Peck Slip*
*Bronx Angel*
*Little Boy Blue*
*Nightbird*

# THE CON MAN'S DAUGHTER

# ED DEE

**WARNER BOOKS**

NEW YORK   BOSTON

Copyright © 2003 by Ed Dee
All rights reserved. No part of this book may be reproduced in any form or by any electronic or mechanical means, including information storage and retrieval systems, without permission in writing from the publisher, except by a reviewer who may quote brief passages in a review.

*Cover design and art by Tony Greco*

Warner Books

Time Warner Book Group
1271 Avenue of the Americas, New York, NY 10020
Visit our Web site at www.twbookmark.com

Printed in the United States of America

Originally published in hardcover by The Mysterious Press
First Paperback Printing: November 2004

10 9 8 7 6 5 4 3 2 1

*For Lucas, Jesse, Keegan, and Kelsey*

# ACKNOWLEDGMENTS

It took me a long time to get this story on paper and I owe several people for getting me back on track. First, the people at Warner and Mysterious Press: Kristen Weber; and Harvey-Jane Kowal for her infinite patience with my odd cop lingo; and especially Sara Ann Freed whose encouragement and belief meant everything. To Peter Grinenko, a great friend since our days in the NYPD's Auto Crime Division, who guided me through the back streets of Brighton Beach. His knowledge and insight into Russian Organized Crime were invaluable. To my daughters, Brenda and Pat, who were the kind of hilarious rugrats whose wacky exploits provide the heart and joy. Finally, my wife, Nancy, who reads each book more times than anyone should have to read anything, for being crazy enough to live with a cop who became a writer.

# THE CON MAN'S
# DAUGHTER

# CHAPTER

# 1

THE SINS OF EDDIE DUNNE'S PAST returned on a cold
morning in April, more than four years after he'd turned
his life around. The fifty-four-year-old ex-boxer and former cop was walking his granddaughter to school when he
spotted a black BMW moving slowly behind them. Every
few yards, it swung in behind parked cars and waited
while Eddie and Grace strolled a few steps farther down
the steep incline of Roberts Avenue. But the driver was far
too anxious, twice creeping to within a block of them.
Close enough for Eddie to hear the engine tick. Eddie
Dunne knew an amateur tail job when he saw one.

"Knock, knock," Grace said. His granddaughter was
in the middle of her favorite joke, a long, strung-out
knock-knock joke. The longer she could string it out, the
funnier it became. Everything is hilarious to a six-year-
old.

"Who's there?" Eddie said.

"Banana," she said.

Eddie stared straight ahead, following the car's reflection in store windows. The BMW wasn't a total surprise.

Lately, he'd spotted other strange cars skulking through the shadows of his neighborhood. It could be anybody in that car, he thought: jilted lovers, vengeful bartenders, screwed bookmakers, Russian thugs, or cops. It didn't matter. They'd all be looking for someone he used to be.

"Granpop," Grace yelled, her eyes teary with laughter. "I said 'Banana.' "

"Banana who?"

"Knock, knock."

"Who's there?"

"Banana," she said for the fifth time in a row.

Eddie turned up North Broadway toward Christ the King elementary school, climbing another Yonkers hill in a city of hills, where nothing was on the level. He held on tight to Grace's hand. He knew that by the end of this joke she'd be laughing so hard, he'd have to hold her or she'd fall to the ground.

"Banana who?" he said.

"Knock, knock," she said, trailing off in a fit of giggling.

All his instincts told him a cop, someone new to the art of tailing, was driving the BMW. Eddie knew how cops worked. Before the bottom fell out of his life, he'd spent eighteen years in some of the best detective squads in the NYPD. After that came a blur of alcohol-drenched years as courier, chauffeur, and bodyguard for a Russian businessman, whom the FBI considered a crime lord. Lately, he'd heard rumors that the Justice Department had declared war on the Russian mob. The odds said this was about the Russians.

Grace squeezed his hand, prompting him to say his line.

"Who's there?" he said.

"Banana," she said as they cut across the wet grass of the school yard.

He hoped it wasn't the FBI. Feds were the worst. They started working you on the word of a paid informant, some skell who'd been selling them a line of shit about *you* just to stay on the government gravy train. The agents then fed the story to their supervisor, some guy from Horseshit, Nebraska, who thought he was sitting on the next *French Connection*. They'd wind up spending too many man-hours on you, and they'd get nervous. They needed to show results. Feds only knew one result: your name on an indictment. And they always found something. The trick was to stop them before they got their claws into you. No matter who was driving the BMW, he had to put an immediate kibosh on their grand plan.

"Say your part, Granpop," Grace said as she skipped up the steps to the school's blacktopped playground. Eddie took one last glance back. The car hadn't followed them onto North Broadway, but he knew it wasn't gone.

"Okay, here we are, babe," he said. "All your pals are waiting for you."

"First say, 'Banana who?' "

"Banana who?"

"Knock, knock," she said, now laughing so hard, her nose began to run.

"Who's there?" he said.

"Orange."

"Orange who?" he said, knowing the punch line had finally arrived.

"Orange you glad I didn't say banana?" she said, bending over and laughing so hard, she went limp and her backpack slipped down her shoulders. She let it fall to the ground, because that seemed to make the joke funnier than it had been yesterday or the day before. Eddie picked up the heavy backpack.

"I laughed my backpack off, Granpop," she said.

"What have you got in here, a case of beer?" he said, but it was a mistake, because that ignited the laughing again. Eddie didn't understand why this little girl thought he was so funny, or why she loved him so unconditionally. God knows, he didn't deserve it. He knelt down, took a tissue from his pocket, and attacked her runny nose. He'd learned he should always carry a pack of tissues. His face inches from hers, Eddie saw himself in those liquid blue eyes.

"Mommy says I gave my cold to her," Grace said.

"No, you didn't. Your mom works in a hospital. She catches all her colds there."

"Will you take her to the doctor today?"

"Are you kidding?" he said, thinking that Grace's mom, his stubborn daughter, Kate, like every nurse he'd ever known, thought she could diagnose and treat herself better than any doctor. "She'll get some sleep and be better by the time you get home."

Grace kissed him, then ran to join a cluster of girls in burgundy jumpers. The school uniform had changed since the years when Kate attended. Twenty-five years ago, the girls wore dark green tartan, a color that accentuated the striking red hair of his tall, rawboned daughter. Twenty-five years ago, Sister Mary Elizabeth would clang a handbell and Kate and her friends would freeze on the spot, the class clowns twisting into exaggerated poses. On the second bell, they'd line up with their respective classes, two by two. On the third, they'd march to their rooms. All this was accomplished in thirty seconds, in total silence.

Silence had fallen out of style long before the tartan jumpers. These days, the noise level actually rose after the final bell. Eddie waited until his granddaughter and the rest of the first grade meandered into the building; then he turned, planted his foot on the handrail, and tightened the laces on his running shoes. He couldn't see the black BMW. Either it was hidden by the bushes to the south of the school or waiting back on Roberts Avenue.

Eddie leaned against the fence, stretching his hamstrings, taking the extra few seconds to look for heads in the cars parked along the street, making sure there wasn't a backup. The wind off the Hudson carried a hint of a late-season snow, and all he'd worn was a light sweatshirt and a pair of nylon running pants. Normally, he'd start his morning run now, but he needed to get this over with. He needed to confront his trackers, blow whatever fantasy they were concocting.

If the trackers had done their homework, they'd expect to see him running back down the hill. They'd figure he'd stay on North Broadway, straight ahead for three miles north, then come back to Roberts Avenue. Six miles in under fifty minutes. But that wasn't going to happen today. He blew warm breath into his fist, then reached around, pretending to scratch the small of his back. His knuckles brushed the Sig Sauer P228, which rested snugly in the pocket of the elastic bellyband holster.

The number 2 bus, spewing gray smoke, crawled up steep, curving North Broadway, making its return trip from this outpost of aging Yonkers Irishmen. Eddie waited until it passed; then he crossed to the other side of the street to run against traffic. He always ran on the blacktopped road rather than on the concrete sidewalk. Concrete guaranteed knee problems. He began running slowly, giving his body a chance to heat up. The movement felt good, crisp air filling his lungs, his blood flowing. Even in his heavy-drinking days, Eddie had stayed in great shape, working out at least three days a week in the homemade gym below his brother's bar. He could still do sit-ups and push-ups until he got bored.

Eddie coasted down North Broadway, his feet slapping softly on the blacktop. He didn't spot the BMW until he was almost through the intersection. It was halfway down Roberts Avenue, partially hidden by a parked delivery truck. Eddie made a swooping turn through moving traffic, picking up speed as horns blared. His adrenaline kicked in as he hit the corner of Roberts in a full sprint. God help me, he thought, I love a brawl.

A coffee cup flew out of the driver's-side window of the BMW, its contents splashing onto the street. Eddie came on hard, thirty yards back. The driver made a screeching U-turn. Eddie focused on the rear license plates, a New York registration, but he couldn't make out the number. The car lurched forward, its transmission grinding. He was within twenty yards when the engine roared and the driver jumped the light at Palisade Avenue. Sparks flew as the back end bottomed out on the base of the hill when the driver floored it, and the car ate the hill alive, ascending Roberts Avenue as if it had been launched into space. A clean, incredibly quick getaway. Eddie slowed. Nothing he could do without the plate number. Besides, in less than a minute, it would be on the Saw Mill River Parkway.

Then the driver fooled him.

Four blocks ahead, at the crest of the hill, the BMW turned into Bellevue Avenue, Eddie's narrow and curvy little street. It was a move that could only slow down their escape. A move that didn't make sense. Purely stupid. A seasoned wheelman should know the escape route cold and never get trapped on clunky little back roads.

Then a rush of bile flooded the back of Eddie's throat as he realized that it was way too stupid. The driver had turned down the street for a reason. Someone needed to be warned or picked up. Another player was in the game. The BMW wasn't a tail—it was a lookout.

Focusing only on the next few steps ahead, Eddie pumped his legs in short, quick strides. It has to be cops, he thought. Probably feds, the bastards. Best guess was that they were going back to pick up some technician who was attaching a tracking device to his Olds. Standard FBI operating procedure—they used all the toys in the box. The BMW had merely been keeping tabs on him until the tech man had the thing installed. Now they were hustling back to pick him up. They wanted Eddie to lead them to the Russians, to Anatoly Lukin, and they knew they couldn't tail him without electronic help. He put his head down and leaned into the hill.

Eddie's mind clicked through all the possibilities. It wasn't a burglar; burglars wouldn't go to all this trouble. Maybe the tech man was planting a bug in his house. They'd need to break in for that. Most likely, they'd put it in the kitchen, the room with the most conversations. No reason even to look in the bedroom. Kate would sleep through it all. He dug deeper, his lungs burning. He knew damn well she wouldn't sleep through it. A deep, racking wheeze escaped his chest.

Let it be cops, he prayed. Even feds; feds would be fine. They played by the rules. They weren't the worst. He knew the worst. Knew them all too well. The men who populated the dark side of his past were the nightmare scenario. They didn't acknowledge anyone's rules, and they didn't like surprises. Finding his daughter would be a huge surprise.

His pulse thumped in the back of his neck as he reached the crest of the hill. The old neighborhood was filled with huge trees and overgrown hedges. Eddie wouldn't be able to see his own house until he was standing directly in front of it. As he ran toward his house, he heard tires squealing. He pulled his gun from the bellyband holster as the black BMW flew out of his driveway and bounced over the curb. The driver started left, then swerved wide right, away from Eddie. This time, he was close enough to read the plate number. He said it aloud, his voice a hoarse rattle. The car fishtailed on the sharp curve and slid around the corner.

Eddie kept running, no longer aware of pain. His voice became a singsong chant as he repeated the number on the license plate over and over, memorizing a set of digits he knew were the most important numbers of his life. He ran until the car was out of sight and he could no longer see the struggle in the backseat. Until all he could think about was the green flannel shirt his only daughter was wearing, and how it set off her wild red hair, as once did the green of her grammar school tartan.

# CHAPTER

# 2

AN HOUR AND A HALF had passed since Eddie Dunne heard his daughter scream his name from the backseat of the BMW. Not a hint of her since then. Eddie paced the faded tiles of his kitchen floor in the same clothes he'd worn all morning. Detective Barbara Panko of the Yonkers Police Department sat at the table. She'd traced the BMW's registration to an upscale address in Scarsdale. A team of YPD detectives was en route.

"Why don't you jump in the shower," Detective Panko said. "Get some fresh clothes on. I'll hold down the fort."

"Soon as we hear from Scarsdale," Eddie said.

Detective Panko, whom Eddie had called Babsie all her life, flipped through a box filled with Dunne family pictures, looking for a current photo of Kate. It was for the case file. Babsie, from one of the old families of the tight blue-collar community, already knew what Kate looked like.

"When I was a kid," she said, "I wanted red hair in the worst way. Even dyed it once. Remember that disaster? Drove my poor parents crazy."

"You were one hell of an Irish step dancer even without it."

"Yeah, and the only Polack in Mrs. McCrudden's class. God, I hated those short pleated skirts. They made my legs look like tree trunks."

Eddie had grown up with the Pankos. He'd been in their cramped childhood apartment above Panko's Butcher Shop hundreds of times. He'd fought two of her older brothers when the Yonkers CYO still held Wednesday-night smokers. They both were now retired from the Yonkers PD. Babsie, every bit a tough Panko offspring, had spent ten seasons as the star pitcher for the Yonkers PD in the city's fast-pitch softball league. Six months away from retirement, she now watched from the bleachers.

"Your mom doing okay?" Babsie asked, trying to make small talk to keep Eddie calm. She'd given up asking him to sit down. "She's glad she went back to Ireland and all?"

"I guess. Never hear any different."

Uniformed officers from the YPD had scoured the area of Palisade and Roberts, unable to find the coffee cup thrown from the window of the BMW. In Eddie's living room, a tech man installed a tape recorder; the phone trap was already set. Except for Kate's nurse buddies, the phone had been silent. Eddie glanced up at the kitchen clock, which seemed to be standing as still as the world around him. The clock had a farm-scene background— three white chickens in front of a rusted plow. His late wife, Eileen, had collected farm scenes that reminded her of her birthplace in County Kerry. If she were alive, Eileen would be blaming him for this, cursing him, as only the deeply religious can. He looked again at the clock. It occurred to him that little gets accomplished in the time it takes a clock's hands to sweep across three white chickens.

"It takes ten minutes to get to Scarsdale," he said, slamming his hand down on the kitchen counter. "They stop for coffee or what?"

"These guys wouldn't screw around with this, Eddie. They'll call any minute. Come on, let's go through the time line once more. Maybe we missed something."

The detective flipped through the pages of her notebook, then began reading aloud. Earlier that morning, at 0715, Eddie had left home to walk Grace to school. Approximately ten minutes later, Eddie's older brother Kevin, who lived next door, spotted a man in a dark blue jumpsuit and watch cap walking up Eddie's driveway. Eddie's house sat well back off the road, built into the hill. Every house in the old neighborhood sat at its own angle, at the pleasure of the hills. A long driveway wrapped around to the rear of the house. From his kitchen window, Kevin Dunne could see the trunk of his brother's beat-up 1990 Oldsmobile, which was parked behind the house, under the basketball hoop.

"We're talking about only two perps here," Babsie said. "The driver and the guy who broke in. You said you didn't get a decent look at either of them."

"A glance at the driver, only for a split second. Mostly profile. Not good enough to go on record. Male, white, thin . . . I think. He definitely wasn't big. Wearing a watch cap pulled down, dark glasses. Young . . . twenties maybe. Don't put that down; he might turn out to be fifty. The other guy, all I saw was his back. And I saw Kate . . . fighting."

"The guy in the jumpsuit is the guy who broke into the

house," Babsie said. "That's the guy in the backseat, the one holding Kate. Kevin gave me a fair description. I'm hoping he does better with the sketch artist."

The man Kevin saw carried a long black toolbox. Given the jumpsuit and toolbox, Kevin figured the guy was a mechanic coming to work on Eddie's Olds. Normally, Eddie left the Olds out on the street because it bled oil. But Kevin'd had no way of knowing that Kate had used the Olds yesterday because her Toyota was in the shop. She'd parked it behind the house. From his window, Kevin could see part of the Olds, but not Eddie's back door. He couldn't see the guy in the watch cap using a sharp-edged tool to separate the dead bolt from the wooden door frame.

"Tell me again about the BMW," Babsie said. "Anything unusual to identify it—dents, dings, bumper stickers?"

"It looked like a police or government car."

"You're kidding me, Eddie. A BMW cop car? What the hell makes you think *that*? Antennas, emergency lights, what?"

"It was filthy. Looked like it hadn't been washed in months."

"I have a Crown Vic like that outside, but you can't be serious. That's not a reason to assume it's government."

"It looked like the kind of car they seize from drug dealers. You know, the ones that sit in some impound lot while the paperwork is going through. They get this film on them. A grimy film."

"Okay, so going along with that leap in logic, why would law enforcement want you bad enough to break into your house and snatch your daughter?"

"I don't know," he said. "But don't kid yourself,

Babsie. People get caught wrong, they panic. Cops or not, they panic. Cops make bad decisions."

That much he knew for sure. He was the king of bad decisions. Including this morning, when he'd spent too much time trying to catch the BMW that contained his daughter. Then instead of calling the police immediately, he'd spent another ten minutes running back to Christ the King to get Grace. Only after he'd had his granddaughter in his arms did he call the Yonkers PD and give them the plate number. A smart man would have stopped, called the police immediately, then called the school. Instead, Eddie gave his daughter's kidnappers a fifteen-minute head start. This would not have surprised Eileen. She always said he tried to solve all his problems physically, and used his head only for butting against a tavern wall.

"Let's talk about what you heard," Babsie said.

"Heard?" he said, feeling the blood drain from his face. He hadn't mentioned hearing anything.

"Like sounds. Anything unusual from the car? Loose muffler, loud music? Country, rap, or some odd ethnic music?"

"No music. Kate yelled something, but I couldn't understand it," Eddie said, lying. He knew exactly what his daughter had said.

"Tell me again what she was wearing," Babsie said.

"A green-plaid flannel shirt, and she had her hair pulled back. You know, held back by an elastic thing, in like a ponytail, but thicker, wilder."

"What are the chances Kate was the intended target?"

"This wasn't a planned kidnapping, Babsie. No one knew she'd be here. She only decided to stay home from work a few hours ago."

"What about the ex-husband?"

"Asshole."

"That's what I heard. I think he took lessons from my ex. You have a name and address?"

"Scott D'Arcy. Half-assed chef of some kind. Lives in Seattle now, and he could give a shit less about Kate. His address is probably in her book, if you want it."

"No recent contact, no custody battle?"

"He hasn't even sent Grace a birthday card in three years."

"Okay, then, whatta we got?" Babsie said, slapping her notebook on the table. "It's not a custody case, or a jealous husband. It's not a law-enforcement screwup; I'm not buying that. We're left with the obvious, Eddie: These were bad guys looking for something in here. Only possibility. You gotta give us some direction, pal. What's going on here?"

The house had been thoroughly searched. They'd tossed all the closets, emptied dresser drawers. Shelves had been cleared off, pictures taken down, the Dunne family possessions strewn across the floors. Even the basement had been searched with the same focus. Not vandalism—nothing was destroyed. But a manic hunt for something.

"They were looking for something," he said.

"Ya think? Eddie, come on. We're wasting time here. What were they looking for?"

"If I knew that, I'd give it to them. Take every goddamn thing."

Babsie's cell phone rang. She stood and answered it as she walked into the living room. Eddie checked the clock. White chickens stared back. What the hell's the sense? he thought. Just when I get my life together, all hell breaks loose. Guys like me never get off the hook. I was a jerk for thinking I could. At least Grace is safe, next door with Aunt Martha, baking cookies for the cops.

"Scarsdale," Babsie said, slipping the phone back into her pocket. "They say the BMW was stolen. Owners don't even know it's gone."

"How could they not know it's gone?"

"It was taken from a storage facility in Elmsford. The owners have been in Europe for three weeks. Their phone messages were being call-forwarded to the husband's law office in White Plains."

"I'll lay odds the storage place has no idea how long the car's been missing."

"Probably not," she said. "But three weeks of sitting in an auto-storage facility accounts for the car being so grimy."

"Who're the owners?"

"Didn't get their names."

Eddie knew she did, but that she wasn't about to tell him.

"It's time for some deep thinking on your part," Babsie said. "What's your gut telling you? I know your gut is telling you something."

Eddie Dunne believed it was better to think the worst, get ahead of the tragedy. Right now . . . this moment . . . envision something terrible, before it happens, he thought. God doesn't like this, because if He sees you're toughening up, getting ready for the worst, then no way does He let it happen. God is a surprise guy. He rips your heart out with the things you don't anticipate.

"You know I worked for the Russians?" he said.

"I heard you were doing something in Brighton Beach."

"I quit almost four years ago, but for the ten years

prior, I worked for a man named Anatoly Lukin. The FBI and NYPD intelligence have linked him to Russian organized crime."

He spelled Lukin's full name, then told her what she would hear from the FBI.

"You think Lukin is behind this?" she said.

"No. He's just an old man, very sick."

"Then who?"

"Enemies," he said, the idea of it squeezing at the pit of his stomach. "We made a lot of enemies."

"Names, Eddie, names."

"Yuri Borodenko," he said. "Start with that one."

Babsie wrote furiously; it was a name she'd heard. Then she excused herself. Her back to Eddie, she walked into the living room again, talking quietly into her cell phone. He could have told her more, but what good would it do? He took a deep breath and composed himself. He couldn't let emotions interfere now.

Babsie had almost gotten to him with her question about sounds. The last sound he'd heard was Kate's voice. He knew that the sound of her voice at that moment would play in his mind for all the nights of his life. The flickering picture would fade, but her voice, hoarse and desperate, would always be there. She'd screamed one word, and all the failures of his life came out in that word. It was a word he hadn't heard her use since she was a child. He'd been "Dad" since her early teens. But this morning, his tough-minded thirty-four-year-old daughter had called for him. "Daddy," she'd screamed. Just "Daddy."

# CHAPTER
# 3

MONDAY
3:45 P.M.

IT WAS LATE AFTERNOON when Eddie Dunne's Olds swerved around the corner of West Tenth Street in Coney Island. The trip down from Yonkers was a blur in his mind. Eddie couldn't bear sitting in that house any longer. He'd annoyed everyone with his muttering and pacing. He'd kept raising his arms, fists cocked, dying to hit something. Over the objections of Babsie Panko and the FBI, he'd left his brother Kevin to wait by the phone. He needed to get moving. He'd borrowed Kevin's cell phone and, on the way to Brooklyn, called his ex-boss. Not a direct call—Anatoly Lukin never spoke on the phone.

Eddie parked in the shadow of the rickety old roller coaster, the Cyclone. He turned the engine off and waited, studying the cars moving behind him on Surf Avenue. Waves pounded against the shore as he stared at the rearview mirror. After three full minutes, he slammed the car door and walked toward the boardwalk. He was still wearing the frayed sweatshirt and nylon running pants he'd put on that morning.

Anatoly Lukin, like many of his fellow Russian émigrés, loved to spend his afternoons by the ocean. Even on the most frigid days, the boardwalk was packed with beefy men and women in fur hats, reminiscing about Odessa and the icy wind off the Black Sea. Lukin claimed that the Black Sea was much darker than the Atlantic; during severe storms, it churned as black as ink, because there was no animal life, no oxygen below two hundred feet. Eddie turned left on the boardwalk and walked toward Brighton Beach, a half mile to the east. A seagull swooped down to snatch a pizza crust off the splintery planks.

Eddie spotted Lukin's entourage near the Aquarium, walking slowly back toward Brighton. The old man dragged his right leg, the result of a stroke. A pair of bodyguards strolled a few steps behind him. Down on the beach, a white-haired gent in an air force parka scanned the sand with a metal detector. Too old for undercover, Eddie thought, but you never know. The Gotti-fueled decline of the Italian mob in New York had freed investigative resources to work on the nouveau Mafias.

Anatoly Lukin didn't qualify as a member of the new breed. He'd landed in Brooklyn in the mid-1970s, part of the huge influx of Russian Jews allowed to leave the Soviet Union during détente. Many of the new émigrés settled in Brighton Beach, Brooklyn, then turned it into a miniature replica of the motherland with Russian-language movie houses, restaurants, and bathhouses. Most were decent, hardworking people, but Premier Leonid Brezhnev, like Castro with the Mariel boat lift, had opened the prison doors. Anatoly Lukin, forty-two years old at the time, was considered a *vor* by Russian police. The full title was *vor y zakone*, which meant thief-in-law, a title bestowed by fellow thieves on the most feared and respected of outlaws. According to the FBI, Lukin was one of only four *vors* living in the United States.

The wind blew salty spray as Eddie came up behind the bodyguards. He knew they'd spotted him coming, then looked away quickly. He hoped they weren't in the mood for showing off. Today was the wrong day for macho games. But when he was a step behind Lukin, a meaty hand grabbed the collar of his sweatshirt and yanked him back. Eddie spun and slammed a left hook into the bodyguard's ribs. The hook was Eddie's best punch. He kept his balance and rotated his body, bringing the force of his rage behind the blow, like a heavy gate swinging around a hinged post, the whole barn pivoting behind it. The burly Russian coughed out a blast of air and staggered back. Eddie stepped in and snapped a straight right, which landed on the guy's cheekbone. The second punch was half-strength—he didn't want to break his hand—but the guy went down hard, flat on his ass, his leather heels clattering on the wood. The other bodyguard went straight to the hardware. A Beretta M9 pointed at Eddie's face.

Lukin moved between them, murmuring, "No, no, don't let them see this." Lukin assumed he was always being watched. He ordered the bodyguard to put the gun away but kept his huge hand on Eddie's chest until the gun was holstered. A smudge of ink, a Russian prison mark, stained the web of his hand.

"Why you do that bullshit, Eddie?" the standing bodyguard said. "Pavel's just doing his job."

"No, he wasn't," Eddie said. "I know what he was doing."

Pavel's face was ashen. His left eye had already begun to puff up. He pointed up at Eddie and growled something that was clearly a threat in any language. Lukin ordered him to shut his mouth. Still sucking air, Pavel grabbed the wooden rail and pulled himself to his feet.

The goons who surrounded Lukin had always made it clear they didn't like the non-Russian in the organization. But Lukin knew that Russian criminals changed alliances more often than their underwear. It was one of the reasons he'd hired Eddie. He knew that it was loyalty, no matter how misguided, that had forced Eddie out of the NYPD.

Lukin motioned for Eddie to walk with him. They turned around quickly, heading back toward Coney Island. Lukin liked to stay in between Coney and Brighton to cut down on surveillance possibilities. Eddie flexed his right hand, examining the small, brittle bones. He could smell Pavel's cheap cologne on his knuckles.

"No word on your daughter?" the old man asked.

"Nothing," Eddie said.

"And now you've come to find out who you should kill."

Eddie didn't know what to expect from his former boss. The old man didn't owe him anything. Lukin had hired him after his forced resignation from the NYPD and Eileen's cancer diagnosis. These events, and other sins, had become nightmares Eddie could no longer drink away. Becoming Lukin's overpaid courier had given him a solid place to stand.

"First, I'll get my daughter back," Eddie said.

The bodyguards were behind them now, talking angrily in Russian. Eddie checked the back of his neck for blood. Pavel's fingernails had dug into his skin.

"I have no one left to help you fight this animal," said the old man. "These two idiots behind us, maybe six others. He's taken everything else."

"Then it is Borodenko," Eddie said.

"Borodenko is in Moscow, but that means nothing. My sources tell me certain things today. He runs this show one hundred percent."

"You still have sources inside his operation?"

"For what I pay, they should kiss my feet."

Yuri Borodenko was a flashy thug who loved to cruise the Brighton Beach nightclubs, showing off his stunning young wife, a former Russian model. Although in the United States only five years, he'd amassed a fortune through extortion and brutality. He was known to walk into local businesses wielding a cattle prod, announcing he was the new partner. An ethnic Russian, Borodenko got rich by terrorizing his own people.

"Why kidnap my daughter?"

"Snafu," the old man said. "My source is having breakfast with this braggart Lexy, who's telling him Borodenko calls him this morning from Russia. Very pissed off, Mr. Borodenko. This snafu made him cancel this important shipment due to leave today. A woman is involved in this snafu. Lexy says that Borodenko gives him strict orders to find Sergei, his man to fix this special problem. Lexy is an errand boy, but he's bragging. Big man. As if Borodenko is asking *him* to fix this problem."

"This woman is my daughter?"

"This is what I think."

"I know Lexy Petrov, the bartender," Eddie said. "But is he talking about Sergei the Macedonian?"

"No. Sergei Zhukov, a Russian. One of Borodenko's new lunatics. He surrounds himself with people without brains. But how much brains are needed to hit people over the head and say 'Give me your money'?"

"Why would Borodenko's men be searching my house in the first place?"

"Money. What else? There's an old Russian saying, Eddie. In English, it means 'The clock is ticking and the house is burning.' The Russians think you should be making money every second of the day and night."

Lukin offered Eddie a handful of the sunflower seeds that filled his coat pockets.

"Why would Borodenko think I have money?" Eddie said.

"Because you worked for me. Last few months, he's been going after my old friends, some with me from the beginning. In case he finds a loose dollar I'm holding out on him. My fellow Russkie wants everything I have, if I have it or not."

Borodenko made no secret of his ambition to be the most important *vor* in the United States, then the richest man in the world. A former Soviet army officer, he flaunted his solid connections in the Russian black market, particularly those in the military establishment. Soviet weapons of all types were his advertised specialty.

"I read about Ukraine Nicky and Seidler," Eddie said. "The papers said they were robberies. Cash and jewelry stolen both times."

"Robberies, yes. But torture also. Ukraine Nicky . . . big thoughts, but harmless, am I right? Yet someone tortures Ukraine Nicky. Then Seidler, the jeweler. Two old men. Tell me, why torture? Because he is looking for my money is why. He believes I am King Midas."

The old man didn't seem to notice the raw breeze off the ocean. Spring was the worst season at the shore. The ocean took all summer to warm up; then September and October registered the warmest water temperatures. The water stayed warmer than the air until mid-December. But once it got cold, forget about it until July.

"Put a cash offer on the street, Anatoly."

"First, I have already sent word that if your daughter should suddenly appear safe and sound, the situation will end there. No retaliation. It won't work, but we'll try this."

"Whatever it costs," Eddie said. "Ten, twenty grand, fifty grand. I'll get it, whatever it costs."

"A life is what it will cost. Our friend learned from his KGB friends. He kills the weak links, those who talk; this is automatic, no exceptions. Dead men can't enjoy your money. No takers will call."

"Make it worth the chance. Promise more, a million, two million."

"Inhale some ocean air," Lukin said. "Take deep breaths. Calm yourself, or you'll be no good to anyone."

Lukin wore a threadbare cardigan sweater and a dark fur hat he claimed was Russian sable. Whatever he'd done in Russia, Lukin didn't function through violence in America. He was a scam artist, a paper-pusher who preyed on big government and big business. In Eddie's opinion, Lukin was no worse than the Armani-clad conspirators on Wall Street, or the thieves in the ivory towers of most corporations.

"Where should I look for the BMW?" Eddie asked.

"Don't waste the time," Lukin said. "This morning, Mr. Borodenko planned to send a ship with stolen luxury automobiles to Latvia from a dock in New Jersey. Very lucrative operation. They steal automobiles and hide them. When the ship is ready to sail, they put the automobiles inside containers labeled machinery. Customs pays no attention to what is shipped out of the country. He collects two, three times their value."

"The BMW was supposed to be on this ship?"

"Of course. BMW is an expensive automobile. Space on a ship is limited. Expensive automobiles take up the same space as cheap automobiles. Just as easy to steal expensive. Everything is profit margin."

"Do you know what pier, or the ship's name?"

"No, no, no. Don't go running off without your head. Everything was canceled because of this snafu. The car you saw is not on this ship, I am quite sure. That one is probably in the crusher."

"Then who was driving it?"

"My source swears they do not keep such records at his end. All financial arrangements for car thieves are made in Brooklyn. What he tells me is that they were working the last three nights, moving automobiles to the pier. Four BMWs were expected to be delivered to the dock this morning. Only three arrived. The missing automobile was black in color."

Most of the businesses in Coney Island were still closed. Summer businesses were a tough gig. You needed sixteen good weeks to break even, and bad weather killed you. Here and there, a few doors were wedged open, the owners blowing out the musty stink of a seaside winter. One hardy soul slapped mustard-colored paint on his hot dog stand. Only the optimistic entrepreneur who ran the Cockroach Circus had opened for business. The ringmaster stood out front, hawking the attractions inside. Eddie wondered what he was really selling. A precinct cop on a bicycle rumbled over the boards, a female voice squawking in his radio's static.

"See over there," Lukin said, pointing to a clapboard shack with plywood nailed over the windows. "First place I worked in America. Minimum wages." Eddie knew the story, but he believed you should always listen to the stories of old people, no matter how many times they told them. "Sweating my brains out over an outside grill," Lukin said. "Cooking sausage and peppers for sandwiches. Onions, everything smelled like onion. My clothes, my hair. Keep the grill perfect, move the food evenly, that is my secret to grill cooking. Like this, I learned. . . ." The old man demonstrated his grill technique, sliding an imaginary spatula under imaginary food and moving it four times, a quarter turn each. The setting sun spread orange onto the slate blue Atlantic.

"Car thieves are creatures of habit," Eddie said. "They return to places where they're comfortable working. This car was stolen from a gated storage facility in Elmsford. Not every street junkie has the skills to pull that off."

"More than you think," Lukin said. "But I will ask my source to narrow the list. We will find your baby girl safe and sound. Very soon. I have three more days to shake the bushes."

"Three more days?"

"In three days, I am going home," the old man said, the shell of a sunflower seed clinging to his thick lower lip. "I want to be buried in the dirt where I was born."

"Odessa?"

"Not so loud, please. Only you and I can know. Not even my idiot nephew behind us."

"Are you well enough for this?" Eddie asked.

"What is well enough? All I do these days is go to my doctor. Every Tuesday, he says the same thing. 'Eat well, exercise, stop smoking, see you next week, pay cashier, thank you.' It's this Medicare; they keep you going around the revolving door. We should have been doctors. They are the real *moschenniki*."

"The swindlers," Eddie said.

"Doctors swindle the swindlers."

Eddie offered to drive him to the airport, but Lukin said he'd call a taxi. It would be the first time he'd ever ridden in a taxi. The old man stopped and leaned against the wooden rail. A V squadron of geese flew high above the water, following the coastline north.

"If you were me," Eddie said, "what would you be doing now?"

Lukin spit sunflower seeds, which he claimed were the only luxury of his Odessa youth. "You know why they call this Coney Island?"

"Because of ice-cream cones," Eddie said, although he knew the real answer. Lukin had told him this story many times.

The old man kicked feebly at a seagull who swooped down to pick the seeds that had just landed on the board-walk. "Coney Island used to be a real island," he said, "until a storm joined it to the rest of Brooklyn. Nineteenth century this happened. Sand filled in the channels. Before that, the Dutch took boats out to the island to hunt rabbits. The island was full of rabbits. The Dutch word for rabbit is *konijn*. 'Konijn Island,' they called it. 'Coney' it became in the American tongue. Coney Island is Rabbit Island."

"You have a moral here?"

"Simple lesson, Eddie. You are smart like Russian. This is time to think like Russian. The Russian survived because he put his faith in himself, not the police, not the government. My lesson is this: Be the hunter, Eddie, not the rabbit. The rabbit never wins."

# CHAPTER

# 4

MONDAY
5:00 P.M.

AFTER LEAVING LUKIN, Eddie Dunne drove the five minutes to Brighton Beach Avenue. The street was a carbon copy of the Moscow of his imagination. The darkness under the el gave the shopping district a drab, dreary quality. All the signs were written in the Cyrillic alphabet. Women in heavy coats prowled the outdoor markets, speaking in Russian and slinging net shopping bags. Shoving and jostling, these women hunted for each evening's meal as if it were all-out war. Old habits ruled the Brooklyn sidewalks. Hip-to-hip, they fought for position around the fruit and vegetable stands, forcing passersby into the street.

Eddie parked in front of the Sea Lanes of Odessa Bakery. Above the bakery, on the second floor, was the home and business location of Madame Caranina, the Gypsy fortune-teller. Eddie first met her during an investigation of a case where a woman had come to Caranina complaining of stomachaches. The fortune-teller said she had a tumor in her stomach. Caranina told the woman to rub seven thousand dollars in cash over her stomach to draw out the evil, then bring the cash back to her so she could bury it in a grave.

The D train clattered overhead as Eddie called home. Kevin answered on the first ring. Eddie could hear the tension in his brother's voice when he said they had not yet been contacted.

Eddie said, "If they call—I mean, as soon as they call, notify me immediately. If they want to talk to me, give them the number for the cell phone."

"Babsie's shaking her head no," Kevin said.

"Yeah, well. You know what to do, Kev."

Eddie slammed the door as he got out of the Olds, angry at himself for saying "if." He knew that word would be on tape, and what the feds would read into it. He glanced up at the second-floor window. It looked like Madame Caranina was still in business.

Eddie didn't need psychic services. He was looking for Caranina's husband, Parrot. Parrot was a tiny man who wore Hawaiian shirts both winter and summer. He had a huge mane of dyed red hair, swept back in a tidal wave of a greasy pompadour. Eddie didn't remember Parrot's real name. He used so many different names, not even he could keep them straight. The cops in Auto Crime had named him Parrot so there would be no doubt they were referring to the best car thief in New York. His first arrest was for the theft of Reggie Jackson's Bentley from the well-guarded New York Yankees lot. The engineers in Detroit couldn't even imagine a device to stop him. Eddie opened the door and a bell tinkled.

Since fortune-telling was illegal in New York, Caranina described herself as dealing in everything but. Painted on the glass window of her street-level door was a list of services, in descending order: ASTROLOGY, HOROSCOPE, TAROT CARDS, ESP, CRYSTAL, TAROT STONES, RUNES, PALMISTRY, TEA LEAVES, PAST LIFE, READINGS.

The narrow, creaking stairway to the second floor smelled of a combination of rotting wood, spoiled food, and dank carpet. Caranina's door was open. Eddie stepped into the front room of the *ofisa,* the Romany word for a fortune-telling parlor. A vinyl-covered card table and three folding chairs took up the center of the floor. The large windows that overlooked Brighton Beach Avenue and stared directly into the passing el trains were hidden by thick gold drapery lifted from a defunct catering hall. Against the longest wall, an old woman in a flowered babushka sat on a greasy sofa, watching *The Montel Williams Show.* A pair of jumper cables was coiled under the sofa. Eddie asked for Parrot. Without looking up, the old woman rattled something in Romany, that strange Gypsy language that sounds like Greek only because it sounds like nothing else.

The beaded curtain to the back room parted. A dark-eyed young girl in a long velvety skirt and ski sweater appeared. Eddie remembered that her name was Tropicalia, one of the seven daughters of Caranina and Parrot. Tropicalia was twelve, or twenty. Her only education had been in her mother's craft, but lying ran through her blood. She denied knowing anyone named Parrot.

"Your father and I are old friends," Eddie said.

"My father has no *gadje* friends," she said.

Fifty dollars jogged her memory. Tropicalia reached under her sweater, shoved the bill inside the waistband of her skirt, then remembered that her father was away on business with the *baro,* the gypsy patriarch. Eddie remembered an old Russian saying that "Gypsy truth is worse than an Orthodox lie." He told her he needed to see him, that he had a huge business opportunity. He waited a beat, thinking that if Parrot was listening in the back room he'd appear at the hint of big money. Eddie gave Tropicalia a slip of paper with the number of Kevin's cell phone.

"Tell him not to call my home number," he said, then handed her another fifty. For the right price, the Parrot would deliver. Again, he told her how profitable it would be; then he let two more fifties drop to the floor. The bills barely hit the carpet. With the others, they disappeared under the ski sweater and inside the waistband of the long velvety skirt. He wished he'd brought more money.

Back down on the street, Eddie realized he hadn't eaten all day. He stopped at Mrs. Stahl's and bought a potato knish that felt like it weighed five pounds. He took a bottle of springwater from the cooler, then walked back to his car. Sparks from the clackety train above drifted through the permanent half-light under the el. A note was stuck on his windshield. At first, he thought it might be from Parrot, but it was a flyer from a cut-rate travel agency. Budapest—round-trip, eight hundred dollars.

The wise choice would be to go home. Just get in the car and drive to Yonkers. No doubt he should go back and relieve the pressure he'd dumped on his older brother. He should take Grace to Christ the King to light a candle, and on to McDonald's for a Happy Meal. It would be the wise choice. But the wise choice was rarely an option for Eddie Dunne.

Here he was in Brooklyn, eating a knish, while his daughter suffered. There was no reason for her to suffer.

The more he thought about it, the angrier he became. People around him were laughing, enjoying themselves, while he suffocated within. Why should these people be happy? The thought of Yuri Borodenko being comfortable, on vacation, gnawed at him, sent his pulse racing.

People like Borodenko lived the good life because they hired people to inflict pain for them. They paid ordinary thugs for acts of cruelty at their direction. Then it was those thugs who took the weight of revenge. The hirelings bled, while the power brokers, like minstrel-show darkies, flashed immaculate white-gloved hands. But the responsibility was theirs. No matter who had actually been driving the car that stole his daughter from him, Yuri Borodenko's white gloves were on the wheel.

Eddie pulled the gun from his bellyband holster and slid it under the car seat. The anger in him beat faster, in his pulse, in his fingers tapping the steering wheel. His fight manager had always told him, "Use the anger; don't let it use you." With the bottle of springwater between his legs, he ate the hot, mushy knish and drove toward Manhattan Beach. He'd be the hunter, not the rabbit.

Borodenko's Brooklyn neighborhood was an upscale enclave immediately east of Brighton Beach. Manhattan Beach was isolated from the city's bustle, wedged between Sheepshead Bay on the north and the Atlantic Ocean on the south and east. It was mostly a community of single-family homes on twenty-three tree-lined streets, arranged in alphabetical order and named after places and people in England.

Eddie was struck by the amount of new construction, incredibly recent construction. Every street had two or three brand-new homes and another two in the framing stage. Smaller houses were being torn down and replaced by huge brick or stucco structures with columns, corbeled arches, and onion domes. Mother Russia had arrived in the night with hammer and nail.

Yuri Borodenko lived right on the ocean, on a dead-end street named for a famous poet. The only thing separating his house from the beach was a narrow concrete esplanade, badly in need of repair. Austere and window-less, except for the side that faced the ocean, the house was a series of rounded bare concrete walls. From the street, it looked like it could house a military regiment. The only breaks in the white background were a handful of metal boxes for security cameras. Getting in without being noticed would be a challenge. Eddie drove halfway down the block and pulled to the curb.

At the ocean end of the block, an older man in a white T-shirt sprayed Borodenko's beloved Rolls-Royce with a hose. The man had parked the Rolls a good distance from the driveway, not quite under a dogwood tree in full bloom. The tree blocked Eddie's position from Borodenko's cameras, but there was no way to get closer to the house without being on-camera. Even if he could get close, the house looked sealed. Breaking in without being seen seemed a complicated task at best. Keep it simple for now, he reminded himself. The answer will come to you. Eddie made a U-turn and drove away.

On the way back to Brighton Beach, Eddie finished the knish, then dumped the remaining water out the window. At the Amoco on Neptune and Coney Island Avenue, he stopped for gas. Twenty-two dollars and fifty cents filled the Olds. He put another three bucks' worth

in the red gas can in his trunk. Lawn-mower season—
everyone was gassing up. He paid cash.

One more stop before going home: a weedy, debris-
strewn dead end in Coney Island. Gulls screeched overhead as Eddie pissed against the fence protecting the
entrance to the abandoned Parachute Drop. He'd heard rumors that the Parachute Drop was going to reopen; it had
been closed for years. The structure was visible from the
Belt Parkway. People dropping through the air in para-
chutes might draw customers in. Eddie rummaged
through his trunk until he found two old towels he'd used
for waxing his car. He tossed them in the backseat, along
with a faded Yankees hat. Then he filled his water bottle
three quarters full with gasoline and stuffed a dampened
oily rag into the neck.

With the smell of gas on his hands, Eddie returned to
Manhattan Beach. All the tree-lined blocks were quiet,
peaceful, bucolic. Manhattan Beach seemed a great place to
live, the kind of neighborhood people never associated with
Brooklyn. He adjusted the rearview mirror, then glanced
down Yuri Borodenko's dead-end street. He jammed the
Yankees hat down tight on his head, then got out and
quickly wrapped the old towels over his front and rear license plates.

Back behind the wheel, Eddie took one last look in all
directions. Borodenko's block was empty—no drivers,
no pedestrians. The guy who'd been washing Borodenko's
Rolls-Royce was gone, the green hose no longer on the
sidewalk. Eddie put the Olds in reverse and backed down
the block at thirty miles an hour, stopping hard at the
dogwood tree. Pretty pink petals blocked him from
Borodenko's cameras. He opened the door and lit the oily
rag. He held the bottle until the flame was fully engaged.

Then he leaned down and rolled it under Borodenko's beloved Rolls-Royce.

Two blocks away, Eddie heard the first explosion. A second explosion, this one louder, occurred seconds after the first blast. Black smoke rose high above the trees. He stopped by an empty lot to take the towels off his license plates. It was a start.

# CHAPTER

# 5

TWELVE HOURS AFTER his daughter had disappeared, Eddie Dunne sat at his kitchen table, trying to decipher a recipe for angel food cake. He'd taken refuge in the kitchen, far away from the overly reassuring young detectives hovering over the phone in the living room. The cake was his granddaughter's idea. Grace had called it "angel foot cake" when she was a baby, and it always made them laugh. She wanted to have a happy surprise for her mother when she got home.

"The recipe says a tube pan," Eddie said.

"I know which pan."

Grace stood inside the closet-sized pantry, on the kitchen chair she'd dragged in. She was searching the shelves for the pan she'd watched her mother use. Eddie ran his fingers through his hair and read the card again. The steps were complicated, with words like *volume* and *decompression*.

"Do we have a dozen eggs?" he asked.

"Eggs are in the refrigerator, right under your nose."

At that moment, she sounded so much like her mother,

it made his heart pound. Grace hadn't inherited the red hair, but her voice and mannerisms were eerily similar. He remembered when Kate was about Grace's age, sitting on the kitchen floor, sliding little cakes into her Easy-Bake Oven, and somehow getting perfect little pastries out of a forty-watt lightbulb. Eileen had tried to help her, but she wouldn't have any of it. That bossy confidence Eileen always called a Dunne trait would help Kate survive.

"The refrigerator's this big white thing, right?" Eddie said.

The refrigerator held two dozen eggs, neatly stacked in special trays from the Williams-Sonoma catalog. The swanky trays, one of Kate's many kitchen toys, replaced the paper egg cartons in the Dunne fridge. When Kate married Scott D'Arcy, a graduate of the New England Culinary Institute, she threw herself fully into cooking. She took classes, inhaled cookbooks, and ordered pastry brushes and soufflé pans from overpriced catalogs. All they'd ever talked about were things like presentation and "erbs." After Scott landed a job as a sous-chef at the Grand Hyatt in Manhattan, they began stockpiling money for a restaurant of their own. Kate worked double shifts at the hospital until the night Grace was born. But less than two years after that event, Scott took their dreams, and a twenty-two-year-old waitress, to Seattle, where he opened his own bistro.

"Mommy only bakes late at night," Grace said. "When she can't sleep."

"Well, that's when the real bakers work. The union bakers work late at night."

"They can't sleep because they're worried, right? So they bake stuff."

"Right. Union workers are always worried. It's good, though, because they make fresh rolls and cakes and doughnuts for the stores to have in the morning."

"Is nighttime when the union says you're supposed to bake?"

"In this house, you can bake anytime you want."

"The union won't get mad?"

"I know people," Eddie said.

After Scott took off, Kate and Grace moved in with Eddie. But none of her other plans changed. For months, she'd been calling Realtors and scanning the classifieds, trying to get an idea of the total cash required to become a minor restaurateur. Eddie closed the refrigerator door and walked over to the open pantry in time to stop a falling cookie sheet from beaning his granddaughter.

"Hey, chef," he said. "Do you know how to separate the whites of the egg from the yolk?"

"Is the yolt the same as the shell?"

"No, the 'yolt' is the yellow."

"Okay, you just put the yolts on a dish, and the other stuff just goes in a bowl."

Eddie returned to the sink for one more close read. Elbows on the sink, he held the smudged recipe card under the fluorescent light. He'd put the fluorescent light in at the same time he'd installed the bay window over the sink. Installing the bay window had been easier than baking this cake. He'd put the window in for his wife, who had seen all the world she cared to through those panes. In the last years of her life, Eileen went to Mass every morning, stopped at the superette, came home, and that was her day. The more Eddie's life revolved around things outside the house, the more Eileen became its prisoner.

The window needed work. They all probably did. With his finger, he scraped the molding around the window frame. Dried-out caulking chipped off in his hand. He brushed the flakes into the trash as he watched a light-colored Chevy Impala move slowly down the street. The driver had the interior light on, reading something from a notepad. Not to worry. A marked YPD car sat idling across the street. With another two detectives in the living room, there was nothing they couldn't handle.

"This sounds like a lot of eggs," Eddie said. "Are you sure it's not a restaurant recipe?"

"Restaurants don't have recipes, Granpop," Grace said, setting the pan on the counter. "If the cake is too big, I'll just take some next door. Mom says that whenever you make a cake, you're supposed to give a piece to someone. So I'll take a big piece over to Uncle Kev and Aunt Martha."

"That reminds me. You didn't answer my question before. How come you don't want to stay with Uncle Kevin and Aunt Martha?"

"She watches *Oprah*."

"That's a good reason," he said. "Why don't you just go in and watch Uncle Kev's TV?"

"'Cause Uncle Kev only has a little tiny black-and-white TV. Like the kind the baby Jesus had."

Grace had not asked him a single question about Kate. Eddie figured that Aunt Martha, the wife of his brother Kevin, had already told her more than she wanted to know. Aunt Martha didn't believe in coddling. But when Eddie tried to reassure Grace by saying, "Your mom is going to be fine," she simply looked at him and said, "I know."

The white Impala circled the block again. They should

grab him, Eddie thought. But the guy was too obvious to be bad. He was just searching in the dark for a street address on a block where the houses were too old to bother with numbers. He floated past.

Eddie's house, one of the newer ones, had been built in 1927. The nine-room brick Tudor with its odd gables and arched doorways was a handyman's special when they bought it with his biggest fight purse. Those first few years, he did most of the work himself, but he lost interest in the house long before Eileen died. The three most dire needs were a new slate roof, new plumbing, and a new heating system.

Eddie's bank account didn't show nearly enough money to handle all three. His checking account held just enough money to cover a few regular bills: insurance, phone, and electric. Eddie Dunne hated banks, credit cards, and other paper trails. He paid cash every chance he got. At present, his only income came from working nights in his brother's bar, but Eddie lived frugally. He fixed things himself, bought old cars, and dressed as if he were applying for welfare. Since he'd stopped drinking, his only vice was gambling: sports betting with a local bookie, lottery tickets, and a once-a-week trip to Yonkers Raceway.

Grace dragged the chair from the pantry toward the kitchen sink. She wore Kate's old apron, a green one with shamrocks. It said, KISS THE COOK. SHE'S IRISH. It came down to her ankles. She'd found a clear glass cake plate and a yellow-and-green tin cover painted with Pennsylvania Dutch symbols. Eileen had bought it on a trip to the Amish country thirty years ago and then used it for every cake after that.

"Aunt Martha wants to buy a gun for the bar," Grace said.

"A gun in a bar? Oh, that'll turn out good."

"It's because of all that stuff, you know. But Uncle Kev doesn't want to. He says she'll just shoot him in the ass."

The white Impala backed down the street and stopped next to the marked Yonkers police car. It was a short conversation; then the Impala pulled in behind Eddie's Olds.

"We have company," he said

"Aunt Martha and Uncle Kev-o," Grace sang out.

"Wrong-o," he sang back. "Somebody in a car-o."

A tall man in a dark suit got out of the Impala. Under the glare of a single streetlight, he flicked a cigarette on the pavement, then ground it out with his shoe. He was slender, with a full head of hair. From the way his upper body cleared the roof of the car, Eddie figured he was about six four, maybe taller. He leaned back down and picked something off the seat, a cell phone or a pager. As soon as he started coming up the long driveway, Eddie recognized the walk. Walks never change. People get old, get fat, but the way they walk remains a signature. Their guest was Detective Matty Boland, the NYPD's gift to women. During the waning days of Eddie's police career, Boland was a hotshot rookie in the Detective Bureau.

Grace put her finger in the vanilla extract and tasted it. She made a pained face as the front doorbell rang. Eddie had assumed Boland would walk around back. Only people who didn't know them rang the front doorbell. Grace wiped her tongue with her apron.

"Why don't you go watch TV for a while, babe. I have to talk to this guy."

"Is he going to help find Mommy?" she asked softly.

"Absolutely. I just have to fill him in. Then we'll get this cake rolling after that."

"We don't want it rolling, silly," she said.

# CHAPTER

# 6

**MONDAY**
**8:30 P.M.**

BOTH DETECTIVES HUSTLED to the front door as Detective Matty Boland rang the bell again. As he yanked on the antique door, Eddie reassured them he knew the guy. The hand-carved wood, curved on top to fit the arched doorway, swelled up and stuck in damp weather. It was the original door, and he'd been babying it for years, not wanting to think about the hassle of replacing it. Then he wondered what the hell he was worried about. Would it really matter if it crumbled today? He put some muscle into it and it popped open.

"Jesus Christ," Boland said, smiling. "We kicked down steel doors in Harlem faster than that."

"Nobody ever uses this door. I thought you knew that."

"How many years since I was here? I'm supposed to remember doors?"

Eddie had always liked Matty Boland. He was cocky, but not afraid to back it up. His looks and Manhattan social life made him a media darling, but he was a tough street cop. When Eddie was under the IAB microscope,

Boland went out of his way to support him. After Eddie was forced to resign, Boland came up to him and said that if he ever needed anything, he should just call.

"Anything new on your daughter?" Boland asked, as Eddie led him into the kitchen. "Jesus, I can't even imagine—"

"How did you find out?"

"Detective Panko, Yonkers PD, called the office, asking about certain names in the Russian mob."

"She called the Seventeenth squad?"

"No, I'm outta the Seventeenth, be a year in June. I made a move into a federal task force working Russian organized crime."

"Is that why you're here?"

"C'mon, Eddie. I'm being up-front about this. I'm working with the feds on the Russians. What more can I say?"

"Let me guess," Eddie said. "The feds smell an opportunity. They sent you because they think you'll raise my comfort level with whatever deal they're offering."

Boland smiled sadly and looked around the room. His teeth looked like they'd been bleached. He had an upscale haircut, and his handsome features had a pampered glow, like he'd been to a tanning parlor or invested in some expensive skin care.

"I remember this place now," Boland said. "Your wife is a redhead, right?"

"Eileen passed away a few years ago, but you're right, she was a redhead."

"I didn't know that, Eddie. Sorry. Shit, I still sound like an idiot, don't I? I probably should have let someone else do this . . . but I figured I'd look out for a cop better than . . . you know . . . *them*."

Boland gestured toward the living room and a Yonkers

cop he'd assumed was a fed. The fed-hating thing was part of his act. Boland had a charming, bad-boy way that women fell for. Eddie remembered that Eileen, who had never liked any of his cop friends, spoke of Boland for days after she first met him.

"The reason I'm here," he said, "is because the powers that be in the Russian task force want to offer you a deal. It's a quid pro quo arrangement, according to them. They help out on this case, you help them with the Russians."

"We already have an FBI team working solely on the kidnapping. Why can't your task force guys pick up a phone if they hear something about Kate?"

"Because nobody's heard shit," Boland said, taking a seat at the kitchen table. "And we're probably not going to. That's the problem. We know Brighton Beach is stirred up. Things are happening, but we can only watch it from a distance. You follow me?"

"You're not exactly subtle."

"Not for nothing, but what would be the point in subtle? You know what I'm here for. We need eyes and ears inside Borodenko's operation. If we had them in now, we might be kicking doors in tonight. Maybe your daughter is behind one of them."

"If I knew someone inside Borodenko's operation, I'd be all over him myself right now."

"That's exactly what I told them. But you're getting too far ahead here. It would be great if you could hand us Borodenko on a silver platter, but we're realistic. We have other, more immediate goals."

"Let me know when you get to the part about helping my daughter."

Eddie found a lime in the fruit bin and made a gin and tonic for Boland. He knew the drink wouldn't be

Boland's first of the day. He poured himself a club soda, but he didn't add the lime. He wasn't fooling anyone. Club soda is club soda.

"I have an offer," Boland said. "I figured you'd at least want to hear it."

"I can listen."

"First, tell me what this is all about. Why are you so sure that Borodenko's people grabbed your daughter?"

"Money," Eddie said. He knew the money idea would buzz comfortably around Boland's head. The *why* question is always foremost in the minds of cops. Greed is the easiest motive for them to understand. Eddie leaned against the sink and filled him in on Lukin's information: the black BMW, the aborted shipment of stolen cars from a New Jersey pier. He explained Lukin's reasoning—that Borodenko's henchmen had been looting every known Lukin associate. They'd searched Eddie's house for money because Borodenko thought he was holding it for Lukin. Kate had just been in the wrong place, at the worst possible time.

"I can call someone in customs," Boland said. "Have them search any vessel remotely connected to Borodenko."

"I'm indebted to you already."

"Don't be too quick," Boland said. "You know what they say about payback."

Boland's face, almost too pretty years ago, had benefited from some wear and tear. But, with the exception of a little gray, he hadn't changed much at all. The guys who kept working never did; it was the guys who retired who aged badly.

"If they want information on the Russians, I can do that," Eddie said. "If that's your deal."

"It's not my deal. I'm just the messenger on this. If it

was mine, we'd be out there right now, no strings. But the feds want your old boss, Anatoly Lukin, Eddie. If you can deliver him, they'll have the task force make your daughter priority one. Just say the word and they'll start rousting Borodenko's people tonight."

"And all they want is a rat?"

"Did I say rat? Where do you get rat?"

From the living room came the voice of Ricky Ricardo, who was frantically calling for Lucy. The cops had been watching CNN, but Grace took over the clicker, choosing laughter in black and white. Grace loved all the old shows, especially the ones on Nick at Night. Schooled by her mother, she knew all the adventures of the Ricardos by heart.

"Lukin is a sick old man, Matty. He won't live long enough to go to trial."

"They know that. All they want is a quick, easy win. They want the head of a *vor* to hang on the wall at a press conference. It's the feds, man. All PR."

"If I give up Lukin, they start looking for Kate right now?"

"Not just lip service, Eddie, but a serious, pull-out-all-the-stops search. I'll be there to guarantee it."

"Tell the powers-that-be it's a deal," Eddie said.

"Okay," Boland said, hesitating. "Sure you don't want a night to think about it?"

"No. Call your boss now, Matty. I'll give them whatever they want, as long as I get my daughter back."

"You didn't ask about immunity."

"Are they planning to indict me?"

"You never know. Just do me a favor and take a little time to consider asking for immunity. It's easy to talk yourself into a jam with these people."

"Matty, listen to me. Will that jam be worse than the one my daughter is in now?"

"All I'm saying is that if you push a little, they might give you immunity, too."

"Call them now, Matty. Tell them I'll be their dancing rodent. No bag over my head, no disguised voice. I'll testify against Lukin, the whole operation. I'll appear on *Oprah* if they want me to. Just get my daughter back."

Eddie's living room phone rang and he bolted from the kitchen. He let it ring three times, just like they told him to do, then he picked it up as the nervous cop pirouetted around the couch. Grace stared up at him. Eddie put his hand over the mouthpiece and spoke directly to Grace. "It's Edie Porach from the hospital, honey," he said. Grace went back into Lucy Ricardo's world as Eddie thanked Kate's best friend. It was at least the tenth call for Kate that day. When he returned to the kitchen, Matty Boland was putting his cell phone into his pocket.

"We're on for tomorrow," he said.

"I'll get my brother to man the phones here."

"I know you don't care right now," Boland said, "but I hope you don't wind up getting screwed here."

"You hate the feds so much, why do you work for them?"

"Because our job changed, Eddie. More than you can imagine. I've got my twenty in. Something good pops up in the private sector, my papers are in immediately."

Grace stopped suddenly in the doorway; she'd forgotten Boland was there. Eddie had forgotten how Boland transformed around women. Six to sixty, the Boland charm kicked in. Pure reflex. His voice changed, suddenly deeper and softer. That smile and all his attention focused on Grace, as if he were trying to hypnotize her.

Eddie remembered Boland once saying that if he ever decided to pray, he'd pray to the Blessed Virgin Mary, because, as a woman, she'd see things his way. Grace stood there with a wacky smile on her face as he told her she was beautiful enough to be a princess. It was hard to tell who enjoyed the exchange more. Eddie chased Grace back to the living room.

"Think about what I said about immunity," Boland said. "The timing will never be better for you. They need you right now, especially after what happened today."

"What happened today?"

"Somebody firebombed Borodenko's Rolls-Royce. Our intelligence says he thinks it was Lukin's people retaliating for recent hits on some of his people."

Eddie wondered why Boland had held this bit of information to the end. Had he become more clever over the years? Some guys did that. Twenty years later, they became real cops.

"Any witnesses?" Eddie asked.

"One old lady. She says it was a big white guy wearing a Yankees hat. Big black car. Backed down the street like he was Dale Earnhardt in reverse."

People often mistook Eddie's dark blue Olds for black. He'd never thought before that it was a fortunate shade. Eddie went to refill Boland's glass, but the detective stopped him.

Boland lowered his voice conspiratorially. "You didn't hear this from me," he said, "but the Crime Scene Unit found traces of burned hair and human skin inside the Rolls-Royce."

Eddie unconsciously lifted Boland's glass to his lips. He could smell the gin. He'd always loved the smell of gin.

"Human skin?" Eddie said. "Somebody was inside the Rolls?"

"According to CSU."

"Whose skin?"

"Good question. Borodenko's wife—what a gorgeous broad, by the way—says she knows nothing about anybody getting burned. So we got a Russian mystery on our hands."

"Where did they find the skin?"

"Front seat. I should have been more clear about that. You looked worried all of a sudden. You were thinking the trunk, something like that, right? It wasn't Kate, Eddie. All indications are it was a male."

The sound of Grace's laughter came from the living room. Eddie wondered when he'd lost the ability to laugh that pure, uninhibited laugh of a child. He didn't know why he couldn't laugh anymore. Any one of the stupid things he'd done today would be plenty to keep him howling long into the night. He told Matty Boland he'd meet him early the next morning; right now, he had an angel foot cake to bake.

# CHAPTER

# 7

THE PHONE DIDN'T RING AGAIN for the rest of the night. Eddie lay in bed fully dressed, staring at the light shining under the door. Grace, all elbows and knees, slept fitfully next to him. He could hear the cops tiptoeing on the squeaky wooden floors, the toilet flushing, water running, cars coming and going in the driveway, and several times the voice of Babsie Panko. They tried to be quiet, but when you've lived in a house as long as Eddie had, you could tell when its heartbeat became irregular. Not that anyone was keeping him awake. A little before 5:00 A.M., he called Kevin and asked if he and Martha could come over.

Two hours later, in the low-angled sunlight of the morning, Anatoly Lukin and his bodyguards emerged from a newly renovated Art Deco apartment building in the Brighton Beach section of Brooklyn. Watching from a block away, Detective Matty Boland picked up his radio and relayed a brief description to the other members of the team. Lukin wore only a baggy wool suit and the sable hat. Cold weather didn't bother the old man. He'd spent the first forty-two years of his life in the Ukraine, where an average day in spring inflicts more misery than the coldest New York City winter.

"The big shot," Boland said. "Looks like he doesn't have two rubles to rub together."

"*Shkafy,*" said Eddie Dunne, "is the Russian word for big shot."

Boland mouthed the word quietly as he watched from behind the steering wheel of the black Lincoln Town Car he'd borrowed from the federal motor pool. He'd parked to the east of Lukin's building, knowing the glare of the morning sun would camouflage their presence. Even if Lukin's bodyguards spotted the car, its occupants could not be seen. The windows were coated with the darkest tint available.

"The guy in the camel-hair coat is Lukin's nephew, Pavel," Eddie said, nodding at the three men walking. "He runs what's left of the operation, hires the body-guards, gets the old man from place to place."

"You'd think he'd drive him, or grab a cab."

"He's never been in a cab."

Although the old man will make an exception Thursday. His first and last cab ride, straight to JFK. The hell with the rest of them, Eddie thought; it will be a plea-sure to see them in a cell. The Russian trio moved slowly toward Brighton Beach Avenue. Lukin's breath fogged in the damp morning air as he shuffled past cars coated with a thin coat of frost—the price of living next to the Atlantic Ocean in April.

"What's Lukin's purpose here?" Boland said. "Does he actually think that by dressing this way and taking the subway we'll think he's on the balls of his ass?"

"He knows he isn't fooling anyone, Matty. He's just too smart to flaunt money like John Gotti, with his limos and handmade suits. Gotti rubbed it in our faces, and we made a point of getting him."

Eddie gave Boland a rundown on both bodyguards. Pavel ran insurance scams for his uncle. The other goon was strictly a bodyguard. Whatever moonlighting he did involved the breaking of bones. Eddie went back to reading the list of known Borodenko locations. As promised, Boland delivered an FBI list of eighty-seven addresses known to be connected with the Borodenko operation: homes, apartments, garages, warehouses, bars, stores, junkyards, et cetera. The list would lend some organization to Eddie's search.

"Why do they have this list numbered?" Eddie asked.

"Not numbered, prioritized. The computer spits it out like that. It lists locations by the number of observations of Borodenko. The more observations, the higher the priority."

"His home is listed first," Eddie said. "Does anyone think they'd hide her there?"

"Now you see what I'm up against."

The mass door kicking Matty had promised was not going to happen. Not without warrants, and the U.S. attorney said he needed more than the hunches of the victim's father. But a dozen teams from the Russian task force had begun surveillance of known Borodenko locations. Teams had four to seven spots each, depending on proximity. Their instructions were to shuttle between addresses and watch each location for activity consistent with a kidnapping situation. Whatever the hell that meant. Boland apologized, saying he had been led to believe they intended to be more aggressive.

"Let me ask you this," Boland said, adjusting the volume on the police radio. "Lukin ever tap you for bodyguard duty?"

"Occasionally. I was mostly just a courier. I picked up and dropped off packages."

"And you have no idea what was inside those packages."

"I made it a point not to know. Put me on the lie detector."

"Just breaking your balls, Eddie. He ever talk business when you were around?"

"Probably. But he did it in Russian."

Almost twenty-four hours since they'd snatched Kate, and still no ransom call. A cold fear lingered in the back of Eddie's mind. Would this massive police presence force the kidnappers to make Borodenko's problem disappear? The Russians knew a thousand ways to make that happen. Eddie's stomach churned with the realization that he'd put his trust in people more worried about legal niceties than about his daughter. He began making notations, his own priorities. The identity of Borodenko's hatchet man Sergei Zhukov would stay with him for now.

Boland said, "Whatta you figure's Lukin's main source of income?"

"Pump-and-dump scams on Wall Street. Then Medicare, and other insurance scams, staged accidents. Crimes dealing with paper."

"I heard the score on the gasoline-tax scam alone was over a hundred million."

"That was before I worked for him," Eddie said.

He gave Boland a brief rundown on Lukin's rise to criminal power in Brooklyn. Shortly after his arrival in the seventies, Lukin began working for the brutal crime boss Evesi Volshin, who ran gambling, loan-sharking, and extortion rackets in Brighton Beach. Volshin's victims were almost exclusively his own people. When

Lukin arrived, he introduced Volshin to paper scams, including the lucrative gasoline-tax scam. As the money poured in, Volshin became more and more convinced he was invincible. Not a single Russian tear was shed when Volshin was shot to death in a crowded restaurant in 1984, the third time he'd been shot that year. Lukin took over and the focus shifted entirely to paper crimes.

"Tell me how he rips off Medicare," Boland said.

"Easiest way to become a millionaire, according to Lukin. All you need is a doctor's Medicare number and a post office box. He started with fake clinics, generating millions in phony claims. Toward the end, he didn't even bother with the clinic. He just shuffled paper."

"Nobody checks that shit?"

"By the time they get around to checking, he's a few million ahead. All the investigators find is an abandoned post office box."

"What happens if they get lucky and grab someone picking up the checks?"

"That person makes bail, then disappears to the mother country."

Boland picked at the warm loaf of caraway bread Eddie had bought from the bakery on Brighton Beach Avenue. In his left hand, he held a container of coffee, which he balanced on the dashboard. A circle of steam formed on the windshield.

"What do you figure Lukin did with all his money?" Boland said. "Guys like him squeeze a nickel until the buffalo squeals. My guess is he'd be happy just to dump it in a big pit and roll around in it like Scrooge McDuck."

"Yeah, that's probably what he does."

"The word on the street is that he's got a pile of cash hidden somewhere."

"He doesn't pile cash, Matty. His office shelves are lined with about a dozen black binders filled with the paperwork on dummy corporations. It's going to take the government accountants years to figure out where he's hidden it."

The surf pounded steadily behind them. It was just the two of them in the confiscated limo. Boland sipped his coffee as he waited for Lukin to reach the corner. His job was to follow Lukin from his home to the subway, then alert the next segment of the tail. Thanks to Eddie, they knew where he was going.

"Listen," Eddie said. "How about you get me the transcripts of the wiretaps and informant interviews. Maybe I can pick out something your analysts might gloss over."

"The feds frown on that shit, but I'll see what I can sneak out."

Eddie handed him a copy of *Novoye Russkoye Slovo*, the only Russian-language daily newspaper in the United States. It meant *New Russian Word*.

"Start reading this," he said.

"It's in Russian."

"I know, but unless you understand these people, you don't have a prayer. Look in today's obit section. They've got five paragraphs on this thirty-year-old guy. It says 'tragically died.' That means murdered. You can lay money Borodenko was involved. Somebody should be looking into this one."

"How much Russian do you understand?" Matty said.

"Enough to follow the obits."

"But not enough to understand Lukin when he talked about business."

"I didn't want to understand," Eddie said. "You *want* to become the Russian OC expert. Make a point to learn the language."

"The feds got rooms full of interpreters downtown," Boland said.

Intelligence sources predicted Yuri Borodenko would blame Lukin for the firebombing of his Rolls-Royce. He'd retaliate very soon; Borodenko was the patron saint of revenge. With a little luck, the task force hoped to grab someone in the act of murder, then turn him into an informant. Murder one, even the attempt, was a heavy sword to dangle over the head of the average lowlife. But Eddie knew they could never coerce a Russian into cooperating. The only reason a Russian ever spoke to the police was to make fools of them.

"How about drugs?" Boland said. "Lukin invest in a supply route or poppy field somewhere in Afghanistan, or one of those other 'stans?"

"Absolutely not. I'd stake my life on it."

"Cut the shit, Eddie. You're making these guys sound like Damon Runyon characters. This ain't *Guys and Dolls* out here."

"No, it's not. These are very smart people. Don't try to compare them to anyone you ever worked on before. They understand money and documents, they're bilingual, international, and they don't fear our court system. Our jails are like Club Med to them. They're the best white-collar criminals in the world, by far. But I don't see drug dealing and I don't see the violence you're talking about. At least not when I was working for Lukin."

"Well then, I have to bring you up to speed," Boland said. "Guys like Yuri Borodenko are the new, improved Russian *mafiya*. Russian crime exploded worldwide after the breakup of the Soviet Union. These guys are ethnic Russians with serious connections back home. They're using that old country like their personal warehouse. You want a tank, you want a box of grenades, just put your order in. They also control the shipping industry. See, this is why the hell the FBI is jumping in with both feet. They're afraid one of these guys like Borodenko is going to sell the bomb to Saddam, or some other psycho. And for the right price, don't tell me they won't do it."

"Wasn't that a Tom Clancy novel?" Eddie said, now realizing he'd underestimated Matty Boland. It wouldn't happen again.

"I got a lot more stories for Clancy," Boland said. "Two years ago in Florida, we arrested one of Borodenko's people for selling Russian helicopters to the Colombians, the Cali cartel. He even offered them a submarine for drug smuggling. Complete with Russian crew. That's just the tip of the iceberg."

Lukin and his bodyguards turned right on Brighton Beach Avenue. Boland drove slowly to the corner. Like all thoroughfares shaded by elevated train tracks, Brighton Beach Avenue offered both tracker and prey more places to hide. The avenue was almost deserted at this hour. Too early for the crowds of daily shoppers. Too early for the street vendors selling their pastries and *matrioshka* dolls.

"That's why I don't get this mob war," Boland said. "I mean, why? Borodenko has a huge operation with worldwide connections. He doesn't need Lukin's penny-ante scams. So why is he going after this washed-up old sock salesman? The only thing I can figure is that Borodenko knows that Lukin has a humongous pot-o'-cash stashed somewhere."

Boland pulled the car to the curb under the el tracks on Brighton Beach Avenue as Lukin made his usual morning stop, the Stolichny Deli, for tea and blintzes. Boland checked his watch and scrawled notes on times and locations. Slender beams of sunlight in geometric shapes slanted down through the tracks.

"You have anyone up on the platform?" Eddie asked.

"I suggested that," Boland said. "The assistant special agent in charge thought that was overkill. But we have a cop who'll be riding the train. He'll take them to Avenue J. Another team picks them up there and puts them in the doctor's office."

The two bodyguards emerged from the restaurant, followed by Anatoly Lukin, who carried a small brown paper bag. Boland relayed the information over the radio static. Lukin began to climb the stairs to the elevated subway station. A steady file of locals climbed the steps with him. Young women in tight skirts made their way to Manhattan office jobs. An old woman in a brown woolen overcoat pulled herself up the stairs with the help of the railing. Her other hand held tight to the floral babushka knotted under her chin. Unshaven construction workers carried coffee and lunch bags. Looking at these daily subway people, Eddie could see his own immigrant parents seventy years ago, chasing the dream by the sweat of their brow.

"Did they find out who was burned inside the Rolls?" Eddie asked.

"Not that I heard."

In the dappled sunlight under the el, the train roared into the station with a shriek of brakes grinding on steel rails. Out-of-towners wince and cover their ears at the discordant high-pitched sound, but New Yorkers keep right on talking, Eddie thought. Boland spoke of documented deliveries of Russian antiaircraft missiles, submachine guns, assault carbines, plutonium-enriched uranium, and anthrax disappearing into the Muslim pipeline. The train slowed to a stop in the metal-on-metal cacophony they'd heard all their lives. But Eddie thought he caught a faint *pop-pop-pop* right before the train stopped. Maybe he was listening too hard. Boland didn't seem to notice. The train stopped. They both heard the screams.

Boland yanked the gearshift into drive and floored it for the hundred yards to the foot of the station steps. He ordered Eddie to stay in the car, then took the keys with him. Boland scaled the steps quickly, but with a street cop's measure. Never race wildly up the steps. It's too dangerous. You hit the top out of breath, an easy mark.

Eddie sat forward in the car, studying those coming down the stairs. He memorized the wardrobes, trying to separate taste from disguise. He scanned faces. When innocent people run from crime scenes it's usually because they're hiding old sins: deadbeat dads, illegal aliens, bail-jumpers, America's Most Wanted, and lifelong cowards. Eddie watched the eyes for the bright gleam of new sin—eyes too wide open and unblinking, pupils dilated. The eyes are guilt's flashing neon. Or, better yet, examine the people you didn't figure to run. Like the old woman in the babushka who'd gone up behind Lukin. She came down the steps very quickly. Eddie got out of the car.

The woman clutched the babushka tightly over her face as she shoved her way through the stunned crowd. Eddie followed her for a block, trying to get a decent look. She definitely wasn't old. She motored down the sidewalk at a pace far too quick for a grandma. The gray hair had to be a wig. Eddie cut into the street to get a better angle on her face. The woman picked up speed, then turned the corner onto Brighton Eighth.

By the time Eddie reached the corner of Brighton Eighth, the woman was halfway down the block, sprinting like an Olympian. She'd shrugged off her heavy woolen coat. Underneath, she wore rolled-up jeans and a black turtleneck. Eddie scooped the woolen coat off the sidewalk without breaking stride, yet he lost ground. She ran recklessly, like a man, pumping with her arms and shoulders. At the next corner, she made a sharp left—but just before she made the turn, she glanced back over her left shoulder. A split-second look. He saw a dark complexion, big nose, and that was it.

She was almost a full block ahead, crossing Coney Island Avenue. He watched her slice between parked cars and disappear through the entrance to an immense construction site. No chance to catch her in a straight run, but his heart beat faster, because he knew she had to slow down on the rutted moonscape of the lot. She'd hide there, figuring the cops would give up easily. But not him. He had her exactly where he wanted. Far from the eyes of the civil servants.

# CHAPTER
# 8

FOR ALMOST THIRTY MINUTES, Eddie tore through the working chaos of the huge construction site. Material and equipment were strewn helter-skelter, as if scattered by a twister. He climbed in Dumpsters, over huge mounds of bricks, and inside bulldozers, trailers, and portable toilets. He looked behind the skeletal walls of the first ten floors of a high-rise billed as "luxury by the sea." He did the same with its twin sister, only six stories complete. The more he searched, the more he realized that escape was almost too easy; exit holes riddled the fence surrounding the block-long complex. Whoever it was he'd chased had picked the perfect maze in which to disappear. He noted the exact time, then thought through the specifics of the chase, getting ready for Boland's questions. With the discarded woolen overcoat over his shoulder, he headed back toward the avenue.

Tuesday morning had arrived on Brighton Beach Avenue with an uncommon hush. The street directly under the elevated subway station, usually bustling by this time, was silent. Precinct cops had shut down the station, then closed the street immediately below. Only pedestrians with business in the area were allowed past police lines. Apparently, someone had gone under the train. Auto traffic had been detoured so they could search the street for chunks of human body that might have fallen through the tracks. Uniformed cops wearing latex gloves examined the roadway. They carried plastic bags as they scavenged for bits of flesh and bone. One cop sang about the thighbone connecting to the hipbone. Before climbing the el stairs, Eddie glanced up at Madame Caranina's window, wondering if the Parrot had returned from his alleged trip with the *baro*. Dark eyes peered out for an instant before the thick drapery closed.

Up on the subway platform, a balding Transit Authority supervisor in a shapeless burgundy blazer marched back and forth between the lead detective and the uniformed sergeant, trying to get a definite time when his line would be back in service. Technicians from the NYPD Crime Scene Unit and Emergency Services Division had retrieved most of the body of Anatoly Lukin. But a pair of neatniks in blue jumpsuits lingered on the tracks, scraping stubborn pieces of tissue from crevices of wood and steel.

"I'll voucher this and send it to the lab," Detective Howie Danton of Brooklyn South Homicide said as he examined the overcoat Eddie had given him. Several witnesses identified it as the coat the killer had been wearing.

Eddie said, "I think it would be a good idea if I hooked up with a sketch artist as soon as possible. While the face is fresh in my mind."

"Just let me get your part straight," Danton said "What made you chase her in the first place?"

"She looked wrong," he said. "Then she took off."

Precinct detectives interviewed over two dozen witnesses, but the best was a thirteen-year-old Puerto Rican kid who'd been standing in the window of the train's first car as it pulled into the station. He said he clearly saw an old woman in a floral scarf fire a gun into the heads of the two men just as the train was pulling into the station. He saw the muzzle flash twice. She did it quickly: *bang . . . bang*. Then she went after the old man as he tried to stumble away. She pushed him backward. One quick step, then a hard shove. He slammed down onto the tracks seconds before the train. The motorman didn't have a chance to stop. Three other witnesses backed up this basic version, although with much less confidence.

"I don't think it was a woman," Eddie said.

"And that's because . . ."

"She ran like a man."

A few steps farther down the platform, Matty Boland stood against the wall, flirting with a strange-looking blonde leaning from the window of a third-floor apartment. The window was almost eye level with the elevated tracks, but neither she nor the other occupants of the building could have seen the crime, which had occurred beneath the overhang, near the center of the platform. Boland flirted for no reason other than the fact he loved to do it.

"Maybe you're exaggerating the pace," Danton said. "That's a long run for a guy your age."

"How about I race you back to the precinct?" Eddie said. "Then you can make judgments about my age."

Although Eddie had met Howie Danton during his days on the job, Danton, at first, pretended not to remember. Since his departure from police work, Eddie had come to expect a mixture of deference and disdain from the NYPD. It all depended on which version of events they believed.

"Too bad you didn't catch her," Danton said. "Perp grabbed fleeing the scene cuts down on the bullshit alibis. Saves the system time and money. Good try, though."

Please don't patronize me now, Eddie thought. The truth was, he hadn't chased Lukin's killer in the interest of justice. He chased her in the interest of love. If he had caught her in some hidden corner of that construction site, he would have bled her until she pointed him toward Kate. Justice could take its piece after that.

"Whatever happened to your old partner?" Danton said.

"Paul Caruso?" Eddie asked, although he knew exactly whom Danton was talking about.

"Paulie 'the Priest' Caruso. What a crazy bastard."

"Living in Italy, last I heard," Eddie said.

"The job hung you guys out to dry, man," Danton said. "I'm thinking it was over some trumped-up shit about a mob get-together in Howard Beach. Am I right about that?"

"We were at a barbecue at his brother Angelo's house," Eddie said. "They said we were consorting with known members of organized crime."

"Yeah, Paulie's own brother," Danton said. "How the fuck do you keep away from your own brother? But that's the rat squad for you."

Angelo Caruso, Paulie's older brother, was listed as a capo in the Gambino crime family. The NYPD had tried for years to prove that Paulie was aiding the crime family with inside information. On a warm Saturday afternoon in June, Eddie and Paulie had attended a graduation party for Angelo's daughter, Paulie's niece. A handful of made men were in attendance. The story was the vino flowed and time slipped away. Shortly afterward, the FBI turned over surveillance pictures of the party to the NYPD. Internal Affairs filed departmental charges, accusing them of "Conduct Unbecoming: Consorting with Known Members of Organized Crime." Eddie accepted their offer to resign. An offer made only because the city didn't want the embarrassment of having to fire its new Medal of Honor winner.

"The rat squad was gonna get that crazy bastard one way or the other," Danton said. "Every guy who worked in a Brooklyn squad in the seventies got Paulie the Priest stories."

Eddie said, "Listen, Howie, do you have to notify the sketch artist, or do I have to drive downtown, or what? I want to get going."

"They do it by computer now," Danton said. "In the borough, the Six-seven. I'll call, tell them you're on your way. But if we need you later, how do we get in touch?"

"Just call me," Eddie said, pointing to the detective's notebook. "You have my number."

"No protocol involved?" Danton said, glancing at Boland. "Anybody I should check with first? I don't want to step on any FBI toes here."

"You can talk directly to me," Eddie said. "I'm not FBI property."

"Whatever," Danton said with a smirk.

"Is that funny to you?" Eddie said.

"No, no, whatever you say."

"Eddie's daughter was kidnapped," Boland said. "We're looking at Russian involvement."

"I didn't know," Danton said, shrugging. "Whatever I can do, Eddie."

It surprised Eddie that Boland could pay attention to their conversation while exchanging blown kisses with the suicidal blonde hanging out the third-floor window. She kept mouthing invitations and contorting her spiked tongue. Purple eye shadow, black lipstick, pierced everything. It all screamed loco.

"She wants my body," Boland said.

"Yeah, to plunge an ice pick into," Danton said. "No doubt in my mind that crazy bitch has an ice pick under the bed."

"It's the crazy ones," Boland said, "who make life interesting."

Eddie almost gave Boland a piece of advice about crazy women. But he wouldn't listen anyway. And some advice is better left unsaid.

"All these Russians are crazy," Danton said. "This Lukin, for example. Supposed to be like the godfather, a beloved figure, but I don't see any tears. I used to work uniform in the Fifth. If John Gotti or Carlo Gambino had been whacked on Mulberry Street, the screaming and wailing would shatter crystal in Jersey."

Boland said, "The U.S. attorney we're working with says that trying to figure out the Russian mind is like trying to snatch mercury off a countertop."

"So help me out here," Danton said. "You guys were on Lukin. Point me in the right direction. Who the hell am I looking for?"

"It was our first day on him," Boland said. "We don't have shit yet."

"You gotta have something."

If Boland had been with an agent, Howie Danton would never have known they were tailing Lukin in the first place. The feds never liked to get involved in local crime. Boland reacted like a cop, but then he intentionally avoided mentioning the name of Yuri Borodenko. When Danton asked if Lukin's murder could be part of a Russian mob war, Boland did the old soft-shoe routine, everything but sprinkle sand on the platform. He knew the feds were funny about sharing case information with the locals, a hangover from the reign of J. Edgar.

"This guy Lukin's claim to fame is the gas-tax scam, right?" Danton said, going through his mental list of usual suspects, looking for a motive he could buy. "Brooklyn DA indicted a bunch of them. Italians involved, too, weren't they?"

"Three Russians, seven Italians," Boland said. "This could be payback La Cosa Nostra–style."

Not that the gas-tax scam wasn't a big deal; it was still the biggest tax scam in U.S. history. But it was ancient history. The Italians came into it late. When the Gambino crime family got wind of the Russian gold mine, they horned in for a penny a gallon. Then the bubble burst and the Russians offered up a Sicilian sacrifice. The Gambinos never knew how much money they'd gotten screwed out of until the indictments came down. Lukin, the architect, was never touched. You don't kill your moneymaker.

"I wouldn't look too hard at the Italians," Eddie said. "The gas-tax scam happened a long time ago."

"That much money, I don't know," Boland said. "I'd hold a grudge for a long time."

"This doesn't even look like a Mafia hit," Eddie said. "A professional Mafia hit man would have blown Lukin's brains out as he climbed the stairs, not waited until a crowd formed waiting for the train. Or dressed like a woman."

"He's got a point," Danton said.

"The Italians were humiliated by these guys," Boland said, turning to face Eddie. "Don't tell me one of them isn't capable of holding a grudge. Your old partner's brother did time on that case, didn't he?"

"Angelo Caruso," Eddie said. "But he's been out for years. Why now?"

Eddie glanced down at the street. The invasion of police cars and TV news trucks grew as the morning wore on. Reporters circled the scene, each one trying to flaunt his personal street smarts and outflank the competition. All maneuvered to get the front-page angle on a slow news day. An on-camera reporter from NY1 planted herself in front of the Brighton Beach subway sign. Several ambitious cameramen found their way to local roofs and were filming from above.

"Listen, Howie," Eddie said. "Call the borough now. I want to get working on the sketch while I still remember. Guy my age forgets things fast."

"Yeah," Danton said. "I gotta get this crime scene closed before that transit schmuck has a coronary."

Enough good-byes. Eddie left. The others had time to bullshit and flirt—*their* daughter wasn't missing. He ran down the stairs, wondering why he didn't feel any sense of loss for Lukin, the man who'd turned him around at the lowest point in his life. Perhaps he'd come to realize that he hadn't been shown a new road after all, just another highway to hell.

Eddie grabbed a taxi on Coney Island Avenue. "The Six-seven" was all he told the driver. The driver didn't ask for a street address. If a cabdriver knows nothing else, he knows where all the police precincts are located. Eddie'd pick up his Olds after he finished with the sketch artist.

In the back of the cab, he studied the list of Borodenko locations, trying to decide where to start. There had to be some connection between Kate's kidnapping and Lukin's murder. He had two very different pieces of a puzzle: a stolen BMW, and now a quick glimpse of a face. Dark skin, big nose. Probably not even enough for a decent sketch. Boxing was so much easier. In boxing, you knew exactly who to hit, and he could run no farther than the ropes. It all came down to pain, who could inflict and absorb the most. He'd been absorbing more than his share. He needed to hunt this person down. Corner him. Corner her. Either way, it would be over fast. It felt good to think this.

# CHAPTER
# 9

COPS HATE MYSTERIES. Eddie heard the grumbling under his kitchen window as the night tour relieved the day tour. Standing by their cars in Eddie's driveway, cops and FBI agents whispered among themselves. No phone calls, no ransom note—what the hell kind of kidnapping was this? Welcome to the club, Eddie thought. If I had the slightest idea where to go, I'd be there now. But these spoiled bastards, they forget how to investigate. The overwhelming majority of criminal cases are solved for one simple reason: Someone tells the police who did it. A witness plus an informant equals a confession. Case closed. Well, it isn't the formula this time, boyos, so suck it up. Get off your dead asses and goose the case, work something, invent an angle, anything. You never know when you'll get lucky.

"I know winos sleeping in Larkin Plaza who look better than you," Detective Babsie Panko said.

"I'll bet you do," Eddie said.

"Yeah, that's what I get for growing up in an Irish neighborhood."

Early for her twelve-hour shift, Babsie hung her coat on the wall pegs next to the refrigerator and sat down at the kitchen table. The table was strewn with doll clothes from a pink Barbie doll suitcase Grace had emptied out. Grace sat on Eddie's lap, watching him struggle to squeeze the doll's long plastic legs into a pair of red panty hose. Babsie shoved doll clothes aside to make room for her case folder.

"I have the same trouble with my panty hose," the detective said, but it didn't get a smile out of Grace. Eyes down, she ran her fingers over her grandfather's smashed knuckles, gently tracing the consequence of too many fights with poorly taped hands.

"I'm on the phones this shift," Babsie said. "I'm ordering you to get some sleep."

"Tonight," he said, mostly for Grace's benefit. "Tonight I'm home."

After Lukin's murder, he'd spent the rest of the daylight hours in Brooklyn, first putting a face on paper, then driving around searching for its flesh.

"You want to talk about the case?" Babsie asked. She gestured toward Grace, questioning whether it was wise to talk in front of the victim's six-year-old. But Eddie didn't want to send her away; she'd clung to him since the moment he'd arrived. Grace had spent the afternoon with Aunt Martha. Enough to snuff out the brightest candle.

"Okay then, so . . ." Babsie said. "We're making good progress on the case; we're getting close." Then, when Grace wasn't looking, she shook her head no, an emphatic *no*. "We did come up with one guy who looks involved, but, unfortunately, he's in the wind. A twenty-two-year-old Latvian named Mikal Raisky.

Misha, they call him. He worked in that auto-storage place in Elmsford. We can't prove the BMW was snapped up on his shift, but I'd bet on it. This was the fourth auto larceny in the two months he's been working there. Before Misha, the average was less than one a year."

"You check his residence?"

"Gee, I wish I'd thought of that."

"Sorry, Babsie. Does he have an immigration status?"

"He's over here on a four-month student work visa."

"Then he should be easy to find. Those kids are brought over here by private agencies. They call them something like foreign student something agencies."

"Yeah, International Resources in Flushing. What a rip-off that is, by the way. The kids pay them three grand for the privilege of working their asses off for minimum wage. They need to work two and three jobs just to pay them back."

"That's why a few hundred bucks just to leave a gate open is so tempting."

"His listed residence is a Queens address," she said. "Nice old couple said he moved out weeks ago. We got some names of his friends, a couple of vague addresses. The agency gave us his height, weight, a copy of his passport photo, his parents' address in Riga, his university, and—let's see—his work sponsor, Coney Island Amusements."

"There's your Brooklyn connection. Ask Boland to check them out."

"Pretty Boy doesn't have to wrinkle his Armani. We already interviewed Coney Island Amusements. Misha hasn't shown up in two days."

"Phone records?"

"He gave all his employers the phone of his alleged

Queens address. The old couple said he called them every few days to pick up his messages. Apparently, he's got a cell phone, but we can't find any listing under his name."

"This kid knows who took the BMW."

"Yeah, and he's probably running scared," she said. "So we've been floating a sweetheart deal around Brooklyn. Letting his friends know the Westchester DA says she'll let him walk."

"He won't come in voluntarily."

"What the hell has he got to lose? We can protect him for a few months, until he goes back home."

"Home is his problem, Babsie. Borodenko knows where he's from, and the worst part is that, right now, Borodenko can reach his family back home. This kid knows they can assassinate his mother tomorrow morning if they want to."

Home is the thousand-ton hammer guys like Borodenko hold over every single former resident of any former Soviet bloc country. It's why no informant ever comes forward, no matter how courageous or desperate. They know that all it takes is the snap of a finger to wipe out your brothers, sisters, cousins, your children, whomever you love. And no one loses a second of sleep worrying about the law.

"So does the name Raisky ring a bell?" Babsie said. "Maybe you ran across his father or uncle during your Brooklyn days."

"Never heard the name before," he said. "You give this information to Boland?"

"I'm not the one who's afraid to share."

"We need to get his picture to the teams checking Borodenko's locations."

"Speaking of that list, I didn't even know it existed

until a few minutes ago. I guess your pal Boland forgot to fax me a copy."

"Take a look now. See if anything corresponds to your stuff."

Most women hate guys who look like Boland, but he was surprised it bothered Babsie. Babsie was one of those women who did it their way, no matter what. The kind of woman who seemed to get more interesting after forty. She scanned the list quickly, using her finger to run the columns. Bright red nail polish. He wondered if she wore it while winging a softball eighty miles an hour.

"Nothing right on the nose," Babsie said. "Some of the Queens addresses might be close."

As soon as Eddie pulled the panty hose up over the doll's hips, Grace handed him a tiny plaid kilt. The Barbie doll and the clothes had belonged to Kate. The little pink suitcase contained dozens of handmade outfits. Kate had made most of the clothes herself when she was only nine or ten years old, working on a battery-operated toy sewing machine. It always amazed Eddie to see Kate sitting on the kitchen floor in total concentration, turning out tiny dresses and skirts, a few made from remnants of his police uniforms. Grace had never been interested in the doll clothes before, but today she'd dragged it all out of the attic.

"Do me a favor, Babsie: Fax Misha's picture to Boland."

Eddie fumbled as he tried to open the tiny snaps on the plaid doll kilt. He didn't want to pull the snaps out of the wool material by tugging too hard. He recognized the material as the tartan of Kate's old uniforms from Christ the King.

"So what happens now, Eddie?" Babsie said, glancing

again at Grace. "You know . . . with you and the feebs, since Lukin . . . went away?"

"They still want Borodenko."

"Common goals with the feds, that a good thing?" Babsie said, raising her eyebrows. "Who knows, it may work, for the first time in history. But then, you can always count on your old pal Boland, right?"

"He's not that bad."

"Oh no, the guy's the salt of the earth."

"Not someone you'd want dating your daughter, but a good cop."

"What is it with guys sticking up for each other? I'd rather see a three-hundred-pound Hell's Angel at my front door."

That made Grace laugh. She'd put her head against Eddie's chest and closed her eyes, but when Eddie set the kilt aside, she sat right up and handed him another piece of clothing, a denim jacket with two more snaps sewn in as buttons.

"Let me see the picture of Misha," Eddie said.

"It's not the guy your brother saw going into the house," Babsie said, handing him a photocopy of a Polaroid. "This kid's blond, not bad-looking. Kevin said the guy in the jumpsuit was dark-skinned."

"Kevin saw this picture?"

"I stopped by the bar on the way over here," Babsie said. "I wanted to show Kev the finished sketch. We're sending it all over Westchester and the city, most of them going to Brooklyn. And yes, I sent a stack to Boland."

"I'll make sure Boland shares with you," Eddie said.

"Just work product," Babsie said. "Nothing else I want to share with that guy."

Eddie asked to see the sketch Kevin had done. Babsie

pulled a flyer from the case folder. She put it flat on the table and turned it around so Eddie could see it.

"That's the wrong one," Eddie said.

"Don't give me that; I just checked with your brother."

"Can't be," he said. "It's the same one I did."

Eddie tried to put Grace on the floor, but she clutched his shirt. He carried her over to the counter and grabbed the sketch he'd worked on earlier that day in the precinct on Snyder Avenue in Brooklyn. He put it on the table next to the Yonkers PD sketch, then turned them both toward Babsie.

"It's not that close," she said.

"The hell it's not. It's the same face I saw in Brooklyn."

Eddie pushed the two sketches side by side under the bright light that hung over the table. What he could see, which Babsie couldn't, were the things other than ink. Kevin's sketch was more frontal, more defined. Eddie's mind added an olive skin tone, eyes wider in excitement, a mouth slightly more full, and open, breathing hard.

"I can't remember names," Eddie said. "Five minutes after I'm introduced, I'm struggling to remember the name I just heard. But I know faces. This is him."

# CHAPTER

# 10

WEDNESDAY, APRIL 8
12:45 A.M.

EDDIE FELL ASLEEP next to Grace, listening to the murmur of sounds coming from the TV in the living room. He jolted awake less than an hour later, his hair drenched in sweat. He'd heard Kate's voice, a hoarse whisper. Her "allergy voice," they called it. She was saying something he couldn't quite understand. Whispering it. He lay there, listening hard, knowing it was a dream but needing to hear her again, trying desperately to understand what she was saying.

He was still awake when something rang. The sound confused him at first. He fumbled around on the floor, under the bed, looking for the source of the strange music. Then he remembered: It was in his jacket pocket. Kevin's cell phone, ringing to the tune of "When Irish Eyes Are Smiling."

The caller had a French accent; the Parrot could do them all. "In front of Nedick's in an hour, and bring five large," the faux Frenchman said. Within ten minutes, Eddie had dressed, asked Babsie to stay with Grace, and dug ten thousand dollars out of a metal box hidden in the

tiles of his bedroom ceiling. The voice of Sinatra filled
the Olds as he backed down the long driveway. He was
going like hell down the Saw Mill River Parkway before
Frank finished "Nancy with the Laughing Face."

It always amazed Eddie how quickly you could get
around the city of New York in the wee small hours. The
West Side Highway was wide-open, but the Third World
surface played hell with the Oldsmobile's shocks. Twenty-
two minutes: Yonkers to the Brooklyn Battery Tunnel to the
Belt Parkway. He slowed only for the tolls, where he paid
cash. His built-in paranoia would never allow him to have
his movements electronically recorded by the E-ZPass system.

The roads were empty; the only danger was getting
caught speeding. In his pocket, just in case, he had an
NYPD detective shield. It was a copy of his old shield, an
imperceptible sixteenth of an inch smaller. The sixteenth
of an inch made it a souvenir, not criminal impersonation.
Eddie owned two; the other was pinned to an old uniform, stuck in the back of his closet. Most cops used the
fake shield in order to avoid the ten-day fine for losing
the real one. The real one sat in a safety-deposit box until
the day they retired. It was the first lesson of police work:
that nothing is what it appears to be.

Nedick's really meant Nathan's. Nedick's, once a
ubiquitous New York chain, specialized in the odd combination of hot dogs and orange drink. It served as short-
hand for Parrot's old meeting spot. The Parrot always
screwed up the two hot dog stands, and it became a joke,
then a code. Eddie knew Parrot would wait up in the subway station across from Nathan's, checking to see if
they'd been followed. For a guy whose clothes screamed
"Look at me," Parrot knew how to hide.

Eddie knew that nobody hides like a Gypsy. They exist without birth certificates, school records, Social Security numbers, telephone numbers, credit cards, and bank accounts. Certain males get a driver's license, but no more than necessary. They have no insurance—hospital or life—no Medicare. Most have no records on paper. They intentionally avoid any assimilation into the culture for fear of "pollution." No one has a clue as to how many Gypsies move through the world.

A heavy mist off the ocean dampened the streets of Coney Island. Eddie cruised the corner, past Nathan's, down to the boardwalk. He made a U-turn and parked next to a cotton-candy stand. Not long ago, hookers and junkies had ruled the streets at this hour, but then Comstat changed the way the NYPD attacked recurring street crimes. In April, it was now quiet enough to hear the surf. Eddie waited until traffic ceased, then walked to the corner to let Parrot see him. He stepped back behind a ten-foot pile of black trash bags and checked his Sig Sauer. A rat startled him as it scurried from under the black bags and disappeared into an alley.

Across the street, under the el, a boarded-up social club had once been a summer hangout for members of the Gambino crime family. Eddie's old partner, Paulie "the Priest" Caruso, had told him that in Coney Island's heyday they called it the "goombahs' beach embassy." Years later, it became a Puerto Rican after-hours spot. The sign above the door read NO GUNS, NO KNIVES, NO SNEAKERS.

A commercial van went by, tires hissing on the wet pavement. It was a Ford, painted with just a coat of primer, its windows blackened. The name SAMMY SOSA was spray-painted on the side, above the flag of the

Dominican Republic. Eddie didn't think a Gypsy would drive anything with a flag, but it probably rendered the van theft-proof. It turned down the dead-end street and stopped behind Eddie's car. The left blinker flashed, then the right. Eddie stuffed the Sig Sauer in his jacket pocket and walked back toward the van. He opened the door on the passenger's side and got in.

"Eddie Dunne, come back to life," the Parrot said.

"You thought I was dead?"

"Caranina saw it."

A heavy canvas curtain hung behind the front seat, blocking any view behind them. Eddie yanked it aside. The back of the van was carpeted ceiling to floor. Heavily taped cardboard boxes littered the floor. They were marked, and labeled with a variety of shipping labels: UPS, FedEx, USPS.

"You've been down South," Eddie said.

"Land of Dixie." The Parrot wore a white satin waiter's jacket over a yellow Hawaiian shirt, which seemed to glow in the glare of street light. His hair, dyed a bright orange, was dulled by the grease needed to lacquer it back.

"Miscellaneous jewelry and electronic devices," Eddie said, gesturing toward the packages in the back.

"From my cousins, for when they return to New York."

They were all cousins. These particular cousins were mobile con men who spent the winter driving through the South, preying on the ignorant and elderly. They posed as housepainters, home repairmen, or driveway blacktoppers. None of the work was ever done right: a watery coat of paint on a house, or oil sprayed on a driveway to make the old blacktop shine. The point was to grab the money and run: on to the next county, the next state. Eddie knew the boxes in the back of the Parrot's van contained items stolen from the "clients'" homes. Gypsy women were always fainting, needing a glass of water. In the confusion, someone slipped into the bedroom. They mailed the swag north to avoid getting caught holding stolen property.

"You gotta help me," Eddie said. "I don't care what it costs."

"For my friend, I bleed to death, right here," the Parrot said. He grabbed a box cutter from a console tray and held it to his wrist. A thin red line appeared before Eddie could stop him.

"Whatever we say between us," Eddie said, "will never be spoken of again. I haven't seen or heard from you in years."

The Parrot blotted his wrist with a napkin and put his feet up on the dashboard. His shoes were black patent leather. He lit a cigarillo, then dabbed at his wrist.

"Who took your daughter?" Parrot said. "This is our question."

"Borodenko is our answer," Eddie said.

"I thought he was in Russia."

"He is. Who runs the show when he isn't here?"

"Nobody," Parrot said, shrugging.

"Ever hear of a guy named Sergei Zhukov?"

"Crazy Sergei. Breaks heads for Borodenko."

"Tell me what he looks like."

"Shorter than me, but wide, like a truck. Tattoos all over—both hands, on his neck, and on his brain, I think. Also, I hear his girlfriend's name is tattooed on his dick."

"How romantic."

Parrot said the tattoo on Sergei's neck was a spiderweb that appeared to be growing up out of his collar. Eddie knew that was a common Russian prison tattoo for junkies.

Eddie handed him two sketches, his and Kevin's version of the same face.

"You know this guy?" Eddie said.

Parrot bent over, holding the sketch at an angle to catch the beam of a streetlight coming through the windshield. A gust of wind rocked the van. From across the street came the sound of the B, D, or F train screeching to the last stop on the Sixth Avenue line.

"The face looks like it's Arab, or something Mideastern," Parrot said. "You sure it's Russian?"

Eddie knew this wouldn't be easy. The Parrot was a businessman first; he was not going to make this seem easy. "I have the five grand."

"Money is not important here. Important is you get your daughter back. You know my love for all children. Nothing else is more important to me. You know that."

"Ten grand," Eddie said.

"I would like to take your ten grand, but I don't know this guy. The face doesn't look right. I don't think this is a Russian. A Palestinian, a Syrian maybe. Something very different, my friend."

"I can go higher," Eddie said.

"Not higher, please, between old friends. This one kidnapped your daughter. I will work without sleep, without food until I find him."

"He also stole a BMW from a storage garage in Elmsford."

"I don't know Elmsford."

"In Westchester County, near White Plains. It's a hike from Brooklyn. That's why I think not too many people qualify here."

"In the days when I stole cars," Parrot said, "I would never use a closed storage spot."

"You quit stealing cars?"

"Special occasion only," he said.

"This car was a black BMW. Supposed to be delivered to a pier in New Jersey on Monday. That shipment was canceled."

"Postponed one week," Parrot said.

"Was it a special occasion?"

"Mercedes-Benz occasion," Parrot said. Then, changing the subject, he added, "You see, the trouble with closed storage, especially outside the city, is that you risk the added charge of burglary. Besides, it's too much trouble, unless you have someone inside."

"This is the someone inside," Eddie said as he showed him the picture of Misha.

"Here I can help you, my friend. I know this one. Young Latvian boy. Blond hair, six foot, well built. Works for Coney Island Amusements."

"How do I find him?" Eddie said.

"Follow the junkies."

"He's a junkie?"

"Club drugs," Parrot said. "Ecstasy, and like that. When he first got here, no drugs. Then he tried to work more jobs. Four months is short, and they see the money. Money, money, money with the Russian kids. This one started a job in Borodenko's club, as a busboy or dishwasher. Now he rocks around the clock."

"Which club?"

"Not the Brighton Beach clubs," Parrot said. "The Eurobar. Big-money club in Manhattan. Fancy women, ten-dollar drinks."

Eddie took the stack of bills from his inside jacket

pocket and handed it to the Parrot. The Gypsy flipped through it and took about half. He returned the other half to Eddie.

"I will take the rest when I find this one in the picture," he said. "When I find your daughter, I will take your ten grand."

"Find my daughter and we'll make it twenty," Eddie said.

# CHAPTER

# 11

CAR HORNS BLARED in the standstill traffic as Eddie
Dunne crossed the street in front of the hottest club in
Manhattan. The line outside the Eurobar stretched around
the corner—club freaks, hustlers, and wanna-bes, all
shivering in the damp night air. At the front of the line, a
bottle blonde in a red rubber skirt sex-talked a bouncer,
scheming to get past the velvet rope, while security boss
Richie Costa stood in the doorway, looking for the money
people, the ones he whisked right in. Costa was trying
to ignore a drunken Yuppie, when he spotted a face he
recognized. He yelled to Eddie Dunne and waved him
over.

"That's bullshit," the drunken Yuppie yelled. "You let
*him* in. What the hell am I, some putz from Jersey?"

Eddie had been prepared to flash his phony detective
shield in the doorman's face, growl "Squad," and walk in
like he owned the joint. But he had history with Costa;
his presence at the door made that impossible. Eddie
stepped over the rope and heard somebody in the crowd
whisper the name of an aging movie star.

"That's not Eastwood," the drunken Yuppie said. "I know Eastwood. This guy's nobody."

"Someone is asking for a beating," Eddie said.

"Tell me about it. I want to hit him so bad, my arm is twitching."

"Want me to do it?"

"I don't want him dead right here, Eddie. I've been hit by you, remember?"

"Important thing is *you* remember," Eddie said.

Costa's father was a bookmaker who used his connections to get Richie under the tutelage of Eddie's former trainer. The kid came into the gym looking like he'd spent his youth in some East Cupcake Jack La Lanne, working on his pecs and lats. But Irish Eddie Dunne's ring years had taught him that rippled muscle had nothing to do with fighting. In fact, most bodybuilders were slow, laboring, one-punch wonders. If they didn't take you out with the first shot, they became human punching bags. All Richie Costa needed was a chain to hang him from the ceiling.

"I'm surprised to find you here," Eddie said. "I thought Russians owned this place."

"Nah, this Jewish guy, Kleinman from Hoboken, owns it."

"Kleinman's a front," Eddie said. "He fronted places for Lukin."

It came back to Eddie, the key to fighting Richie Costa. He always remembered what worked against certain boxers. He could recall knockout punches the way baseball players remembered home runs: the date, time, the pitcher who threw a low slider on a three-and-one count, even the temperature that day. Start this guy off with a short left hook, Eddie thought, snap it into that six-pack midsection. Richie always kept his forearms up, protecting his face. Hit him up high and all you wound up with were sore hands. But one to the gut and his elbows dropped.

Eddie said, "You're not on the outs with the Bronx crew, are you?"

"No, no, I still work for the same people. The Eurobar is a joint venture we have with this Russian business-man."

"A joint venture? With Yuri Borodenko?"

Eddie considered how much he should tell Richie. But if he could get inside, he wouldn't need him. He could find Misha on his own.

"What can I tell you," Costa said, "the guy knows how to make money. We never been prejudiced against mak-ing money."

"Keep an eye on the cash flow."

"We ain't stupid, either, Eddie. We got a guy checks the books every night. I go in every so often, count the house, have a pop, then drift back out. I actually like it better out here. You'd be amazed how much these bobos will slip you just to get in this shithole."

"Not to mention the women," Eddie said.

"You wouldn't fucking believe it. Pussy gets thrown in your face out here like it's falling from the sky. Broads, they practically offer to go down on you right here if you'll let them in."

"Sleep all day, score all night. My kinda job."

"Yeah, that would be sweet, but I got a day job now, too. Stock market stuff. Going around with a suit and an attaché case, talking to stockbrokers, persuading them in regards to the merits of certain stocks. My wife thinks I'm Bill Fucking Gates."

Eddie wondered what Richie carried in the attaché case. Either a prosciutto and provolone hero or brass knuckles, but he didn't need documents for his end of the investment business. Yuri Borodenko had taken over Lukin's old partnership with the Italians in pump-and-dump schemes on Wall Street. The Russians handled the business end. They touted a certain stock until it became overvalued, then sold their shares, and the bottom fell out. The role of Richie Costa's crew was to "persuade" stockbrokers not to sell a stock the mob wanted only to be bought. Persuasion in one recent case had included a vicious beating right on the floor of the Stock Exchange.

"What brings you out at this hour anyway?" Richie asked. "These broads in here are way, way too young for you. Your fucking heart will explode if you get one of these young broads in the sack."

"Thanks, I'll be careful of that. Actually, I'm just doing a little PI work."

"Nothing to do with wise guys, right?"

"Missing Russian kid," Eddie said. "His parents hired me to find him. He's underage, but if he's in here, I'll keep it quiet for an old friend. Tell them I grabbed him on the street."

"Appreciate it, amigo," Richie said.

"You can't have too many old friends, my old partner used to say. It certainly worked for him. I'm back taking these shit jobs while Paulie is living large in Italy."

Eddie hadn't heard from Paulie in years, but he knew when to drop his name.

"I forgot Paulie was your partner," Richie said. "He's my godfather, you know that? Fucking wild man, Paulie 'the Priest' Caruso. He could make you laugh your ass off."

"Now he thinks he's Marcello Mastroianni. Strutting around the plazas in a white linen suit."

"What a pisser, that guy," Richie said. "Marcello Mastroianni, that's good."

"I could buy and sell both you assholes," the drunken Yuppie yelled, finally getting the point that he was wasting his time. On busy nights, the doormen at the hot clubs always ignored the guys wearing business suits. They figured they'd been drinking since they left the office eight hours earlier and that all they were going to do was puke or fight.

"You want to take a look inside for this kid?" Richie said. "Come on, I'll take care of it."

Eddie decided on asking Richie for no more than entrée. He couldn't be trusted with knowledge. He'd tell his boss, and the boss would tell Borodenko. The mafiosi thing would never permit Richie to help an Irish ex-cop. Richie wasn't even a made man, and probably never would be, but he was the type who believed that whole Don Corleone fantasy. He'd bought the myth of mob life: hook, line, and blood oath. Richie Costa was destined to follow in his old man's cement shoes.

The club was cavernous, the ceiling at least twenty feet high. It must have taken up half the block belowground. The main part of the club was three floors below street level and was broken up into several large rooms. Wide-load Richie led the way down the superwide flight of stairs into the shriek of two hundred drunken voices battling the pumped-up music. On the way in, Eddie heard accents that were clearly Soviet bloc. Much of the crowd appeared to be Mideastern, with a smattering of Asians.

Before he went back to the street, Richie set Eddie up

at the best table in the house: a raised booth in a corner opposite the bar, with a RESERVED sign. Then he told the bartender that Eddie's drinks were on the house. Nobody ever paid for drinks in that booth. Eddie had planned to be less conspicuous, but the view from the wise guys' table might work. From the leather-tufted perch, Eddie could see the bar, the dance floor, and most of a large room set up like a hotel lobby with couches and coffee tables.

Only problem was the lighting. The dance floor was lit by strobes, the faces illuminated in flickering orange or nuclear green. Staring made his stomach flip-flop. The hotel-style lobby area had only dim lighting, and the bar was a cave with shadows swooping across the wall. Eddie sipped club soda and scanned the place, thinking he'd made a mistake not showing Misha's picture to Richie. He'd never find him alone.

But he wasn't alone for long. A young woman appeared, talking as if she were finishing a conversation they'd started earlier.

"Very important gentleman, this must be," she said, sliding into the booth. "Maybe very important gentleman buy Tatiana a cosmopolitan, and she'll tell him a story. Tatiana tells interesting stories."

Tatiana wore a short gold lamé dress, and he could only describe her long, straight hair as gunmetal red. Eddie signaled the bartender, wondering if his free ride at the bar included a passenger.

"I bet I can guess the ending," he said.

"Happy ending," she said. "Always happy ending."

But Tatiana told a sad tale of her Russian childhood, saying how her overdeveloped figure had caused the boys to lust after her body, and the other girls to die of jealousy. Too much "problem" for a simple girl who liked simple pleasure, and complicated pleasure as well, darling. This is why she preferred older, very important gentlemen. She talked nonstop, not permitting an interruption until her hand was on his thigh.

The bartender brought Tatiana's drink. Eddie looked for a flash of recognition, but it wasn't there. No eye contact at all. Tatiana was a regular, a pro. The bartender overdid it by not looking at her.

After the story, Tatiana was all questions, no answers. Who was he? What did he do to become a very important gentleman? A famous doctor, or lawyer, no? He figured she was in her late twenties but had already lived forever.

Eddie Dunne had his own well-rehearsed bar act. He introduced himself as Desmond Shanahan of Dublin, an importer of artichokes, on a buying trip in the States.

"You bullshit me, no?" she said.

"Artichokes aren't bullshit."

"Everything is bullshit."

"Everything but money," he said.

"So, Mr. Desmond Shanahan," she said, working her way up his thigh, "tell me. I'm your pupil who wants to learn, so how can Tatiana make some no bullshit money?"

Eddie showed her the picture of Misha. She took her hand off his leg.

"What is reason for this picture?" she said.

"How much would it cost not to give you a reason?"

"Without a reason, five hundred."

"You know who he is?"

"Maybe."

"Now who's bullshitting?"

"Tatiana never bullshits when money is speaking. This

one is cute, but broke. He's new person in the club. Last few weeks, frequently he's here. I don't know his name."

"Is he here tonight?"

"Possible. Yes, is possible."

"Just tell me where he is. That's all you have to do. Two hundred bucks."

"Tatiana never works for less than five hundred."

Final figure: $250. Tatiana wanted it all up front, then half up front. She got nothing up front. She took her cosmopolitan and left to search for Misha, weaving through the crowd, her ass undulating in the tight dress, as if to show Eddie what he was missing. Paulie the Priest would have said her ass looked like two pigs trying to fight their way out of a sack. A gold lamé sack.

For a half hour, Eddie waited. Forty-five minutes. In the strange world three floors below the street, the only song he recognized was from a Dave Matthews album Kate owned. He thought about an old movie filmed in New York where people descended into hell from a freight elevator that opened up on a Manhattan sidewalk. But if this was hell, he was home. The booze, the noise, the laughter, the music, ice tinkling in glasses, the smell of perfume—he loved it all, always had. He didn't know where heaven was, but hell was only a short elevator trip down from the sidewalks of New York, and that was fine with him.

"Your lover is in the VIP room," Tatiana said. "Three hundred you owe me."

"This is guaranteed?" Eddie said.

"Like everything in America."

Eddie peeled $250 from the roll he'd brought for the Parrot. Tatiana shoved the bills into her small gold purse. She told him the way to the VIP room, which was on the second floor, on the other side of the building, past the kitchen, up a back stairway. She blew him a kiss and went in search of another very important gentleman. He noticed then that her shoes were also gold.

Eddie knew all the big clubs kept a VIP room to draw some hot rock band or movie star, who, in turn, would get the place mentioned on Page Six of the *New York Post*—the kind of publicity money couldn't buy. The back stairway was farther than Eddie thought. He passed the smells of the kitchen and the *whoomf, whoomf* of swinging doors. No more carpet back here. The floors were rough concrete, the halls dimly lit. Garbage cans and beer kegs had been stacked inside the door to the alley. The area smelled of rotting vegetables. A standing ashtray was wedged in a corner, a squadron of butts facedown in the sand.

Eddie came out of the stairway into a well-lit hallway. From the opposite end of the second floor, the clamor from the dance floor was a dull roar. He could hear the sound of a TV, an NBA game, the announcer talking about Kobe and Shaq. No chance to get by without being spotted. He wondered how Tatiana had done it. Better to try to schmooze his way in first, rather than get caught sneaking past. He poked his head in the door of the security office. A huge black man in a short-sleeved white shirt sat behind a desk.

"The Knicks are wasting their time," Eddie said. "If Shaq wants to win it, nobody gonna stop him."

"You got that right," the man said a little warily.

Eddie smoothed it out. Introduced himself as a friend of Richie Costa and a retired NYPD detective. In five minutes, Lester and Eddie were asshole buddies. Eddie joked about how the room reminded him of his old squad room. Coffee cups and food wrappers littered the floor of a room jammed with six metal lockers, three unmatched couches, and a wooden desk Goodwill would refuse. A huge marked-up calendar hung on the wall. The smell of Tatiana's perfume lingered in the room.

"Nice system you got up there," Eddie said, pointing at the bank of TV monitors. Eddie told Lester he was out looking for security ideas. He was in the process of setting up a system for a new club. Lester ran down all the locations covered by their cameras. Eddie recognized some of the areas under observation: the dance floor, the bar, and the street. The kitchen was shown shutting down for the evening; another camera focused on a private office, where a uniformed cleaning woman slow-danced an upright Hoover.

"You guys have a VIP room?" Eddie said.

"Don't put in a VIP room, if you know what's good for you. They are one king-size pain in the ass."

"I figured, but the owners want one, draw all the big celeb muckety-mucks."

"I'm telling you, Eddie. Worst part of this job is dealing with those arrogant bastards. Scum of the earth. They piss on the floor, break lamps, glasses, all kinds of shit. One guy shit on the couch, then covered it with the cushions. Some nights we find condoms, needles, drug crap all over the place."

"What the hell is TAFKAP?" Eddie asked, looking at a notation on the wall calendar.

"The Artist Formerly Known as Prince," Lester said. "Can you believe it? His manager gave us a list of demands a mile long. Plus, he wants us to guarantee no press, no cameras, and then he'll honor us with his presence."

"Then he'll be pissed if the press isn't here," Eddie said. "You can't please these bastards."

"Amen, brother."

"Mind if I take a quick peek in the VIP room, Lester? See what it looks like?"

"It's right down the hall," the guard said, looking up at the bank of cameras. "Just let me check one thing. It should be empty by now. Hold on a sec; let's turn this camera on. One of the managers has a habit of sneaking his ladies in there. Don't want to embarrass anyone." He reached up and turned on camera three. The room came slowly into focus. The picture was dark. He could make out three people sitting around. "Nah, they're still there."

"Any big stars?" Eddie said, getting close to the TV screen. At first, the only big star he recognized was Richie Costa, standing with his back to the door. A young light-haired kid sat on a stuffed chair, across from a squat older guy in a dark sports jacket with wide lapels. The squat guy jabbed his finger in the kid's face.

"Is that Sergei Zhukov, the one with the tattoo on his neck?" Eddie asked, pointing to the guy with the wide lapels.

"You know Sergei?" Lester said.

"Some piece of work," Eddie replied.

"One of a kind, thank God," Lester said. "My panel here shows they got the door locked. Some kind of meeting, looks like. Maybe we better hold off, do it some other night."

"No problem," Eddie said. "Next time, I'll bring doughnuts. Is there a back way out of here?"

"The side door, but that's another sore point with me, Eddie. They lock all the exits. It's a fire violation, but they don't give a shit. You saw that garbage all sitting there, right? It's more important to them to make sure no uncool people sneak in. Until closing, only way out is the stairs you just came up, and out the front door."

No problemo. Eddie let the door to the stairway slam hard. He danced down the stairs, his leather shoes tapping the metal edges, the Gene Kelly of noisy exits. The kid being intimidated by Sergei was Misha. The kid was Borodenko's problem, and guys like Sergei knew only one solution. Eddie needed to get to him before Sergei got bored.

He went back to the swinging kitchen doors and peeked through the glass. Scrub-down was in progress. Eddie felt the ledge above the door. Kitchen help were always smokers. Paulie the Priest used to say the only difference between chefs and cooks was that chefs didn't have tattoos. Real cooks, forced to smoke out in stairways, left cigarettes and matches above door ledges, or wedged in a doorjamb. He found matches, then hit the garbage cans for a discarded copy of the *Daily News*.

Eddie crept back up the stairs, then climbed one flight above the VIP room and the security office. The hallway was dark. He had barely enough light to find the smoke detector. He took the newspaper and rolled it into a funnel shape. He lit the paper, waited until it was fully engulfed, and then held it directly under the smoke detector. It went off, a loud, piercing siren. Eddie dropped the paper in a burning pile on the concrete floor. He ran to the stairway and positioned himself so he could see the door below.

Lester came through the door first, clomping down the stairs on his way to open the exit door. Apparently, their state-of-the-art system couldn't tell which smoke alarm had been set off. Costa came next, followed by Misha and Sergei.

They never heard Eddie behind them. He swung up on the railing and kicked Sergei square in the back. The Russian rocketed forward, pulling Misha down with him to the landing below. Eddie ran down and planted a second footprint on Sergei's sports jacket as he pulled Misha to his feet. The kid was already drenched in sweat. Eddie jammed his Sig Sauer into Misha's cheek, hard enough to imprint the shape. With his mouth right against the kid's ear, he made a point to use his nickname.

"Misha, who stole the black BMW?"

The kid stammered something in Russian. Sergei tried to get up; Eddie put both feet, all his weight, on the center of his back.

"I need a name now, Misha."

Beyond the stairway door, he could hear the stampede of a drunken fire drill. Eddie held tight to Misha's shirt. "You little fuck," he said. "You'll die right here."

"Please," Misha said. "She'll kill me."

Eddie towered over the kid. He wrapped his forearm tighter around his throat and forced the gun into his mouth, the barrel clicking off the kid's teeth. He told him to believe he was about to die.

"Who is she?" Eddie yelled. "I need a name, asshole. She took the black BMW? She who? A name. Give me a name."

The stairway door opened. Richie Costa poked his face in.

Eddie squeezed tighter on Misha's neck. "Who the fuck is 'she'?"

Eddie had both arms wrapped around the whimpering kid. Richie Costa swung from the side, a pure sucker punch. Eddie went to his knees, crumbling on top of the kid, both of them on top of Sergei in the crowded stairway. Eddie screamed at Misha, "Give me a name." Costa punched him again. Somebody kept yelling to get the kid out of there. The stairway door stayed open; security goons jammed the doorway. Lester yanked Misha up, pulling him under his arms. Eddie made it hard for him, holding on to the kid's soaked shirt. Costa tried to loosen Eddie's grip but couldn't. They tore Misha's shirt off. Eddie grabbed his belt. Then a lead pipe or a nightstick came down repeatedly on Eddie's forearms and wrists. At some point, he let go.

# CHAPTER

# 12

SOUTHBOUND TRAFFIC on the West Side Highway, always jammed during rush hour, crawled more deliberately in the early-morning fog. The steady blur of oncoming headlights flickered like processional candles in the gloom. Eddie Dunne's swollen right eye enhanced the surreal haze as his northbound traffic lane moved freely, leaving Manhattan. Most of his life, he'd made his exit at this time, before the sun and normalcy arrived.

This particular morning, Eddie owed his freedom to Russian practicality. The business manager of the Eurobar, rousted from his bed, didn't want any official reports of a scuffle gumming up a spate of license applications he had before the city government. He wouldn't press arson charges if Eddie was willing to walk away quietly. A sweetheart deal, too good to pass up. Live to fight another day.

Eddie squinted, trying to maintain a distance from the taillights ahead of him. He didn't need a car accident on top of everything else. After passing the entrance to the George Washington Bridge, the escaping traffic thinned to a handful of nocturnal misfits. He took the Saw Mill River Parkway, then went over the hill of Roberts Avenue. Eddie had called Babsie and arranged a breakfast meeting, but he had nothing to report. He'd lost the Battle of Eurobar, beaten by a sucker punch from Richie Costa. In the confusion, he'd lost his gun, and the best chance of finding his daughter.

The Eurobar's business manager had told Eddie he'd hired Misha as weekend kitchen help. The confrontation in the VIP room that Eddie had witnessed resulted from the security people catching Misha dealing drugs in the men's room. Sergei Zhukov, whose management duties seemed undefined, was merely in the process of banning him from the Eurobar. The Russians never cared whether or not you believed their lies; they just told the story and stuck to it.

The only good thing that came out of the incident was that if Eddie had ever had any doubts Borodenko was involved, they were gone now. He'd been approaching this all wrong. He needed to forget about the stolen car and go after Borodenko at a higher level, start taking down some of his key associates. Misha, even if he had confessed, might not know what had happened to Kate. And "she," whoever "she" was, probably didn't know, either. Too low-level for the big secrets.

An old boxing truism says that if you attack the body, the head will die. He'd been attacking the body. Now he realized he didn't have time for that strategy. After a nap, some food, he'd be ready to hunt for the head. He parked his Olds in back of Christ the King school.

The Yonkers neighborhood where the Dunne brothers were born and raised was known as "the End of the Line." The "End" got its name when it was the northernmost trolley stop in the city of Yonkers. The Yonkers trolley line took local residents to and from their jobs in New York City, connecting them with the subway station at West 242nd Street in the Bronx. In the early fifties, the Yonkers trolleys were replaced by buses, and the burnished steel tracks had been paved over with blacktop. Kieran Dunne, father of Eddie and Kevin, was one of several old trolley motormen who never got the hang of driving a bus. Out of work, he took the next step in Irish logic. He bought a bar.

The North End Tavern was located just steps from that last bus stop. Every evening, dozens of workers coming off the bus from their "city" jobs stopped in for "just one" before going home to face the bride. For three decades, Kieran Dunne's North End was the social center of the neighborhood's bustling business district, a two-block thoroughfare on Palisade and Roberts avenues. But times changed. Kids went to college, then moved to tonier parts of the county, old-timers died, or retired to the Sun Belt. The neighborhood hung tough, but fewer and fewer people piled off the bus each evening.

Almost all the stores were still mom-and-pop concerns, many of them remaining in the same family for generations—among them a pharmacy, a small supermarket, a barbershop/beauty shop, and two bars. The glory days of the North End Tavern were in the past, but the new owners, Kevin and Martha Dunne, had somehow managed to keep the place afloat.

With all his heart, Kevin Dunne believed the city of Yonkers would rise from the ashes. The waterfront alone was too valuable to leave dormant for long. The City of Gracious Living had beautiful treed hills sloping down to the Hudson, and a fabulous view of the Palisades of New Jersey. Yonkers was an easier commute to Manhattan than Staten or Long Island, and closer than most of Brooklyn and Queens. Just ask Uncle Kev-o.

It was after 9:00 A.M. when Eddie Dunne walked through the open doors of his brother's bar. The front doors of the North End stood open until noon in all but the worst weather to allow the night's accumulation of smoke and stale beer to escape. Eddie paused to allow his pulse to slow down and let his eyes adjust to the dark. A trio of elderly men sat together in the far corner of the bar, each reading his own newspaper. The TV above them was set to CNBC, the financial channel, the stock market ticker tape running nonstop. Their father, Kieran Dunne, had never allowed the television on unless it was boxing, the World Series, or a NASA space shot. Behind the bar, a full-figured brunette washed glasses.

"I'll get some ice for that eye," Martha Dunne said. Steam rose from the low sink as Eddie's sister-in-law dried her hands on a bar towel.

"I don't need ice," Eddie said. "Is my brother here?"

"You should get yourself up to St. John's and have that looked at."

"I'm glad you're concerned about my eye, but right now I'm looking for Kevin."

Martha had a gravelly voice and long brown hair that hung in bangs, almost covering her eyes. Some said she had the sexy manner reminiscent of an actress filmed only in black and white. Eddie thought they mistook cunning for sexy.

"Then how about coffee?" she said. "I've made fresh coffee."

"Martha. Where is he?"

"At the market, squeezing the tomatoes, or so he'll tell us. A regular comedian, your brother."

"Why didn't you tell me Scott's sister was here?"

"Is that how it's going to be, Eddie? No chitchat, get right to the fighting."

"You know damn well you should have called me."

"I thought Grace would tell you."

"She didn't. She hardly said anything last night. But you definitely should have."

"It was too late when I got home," she whispered, trying to keep the volume down.

"Nine o'clock is too late? You knew that son of a bitch sent her here, and you didn't think it was important enough to call me?"

"Kevin and I needed our sleep, and I didn't want you to frighten Grace. I knew you'd be furious, flying out the door. I thought it could wait until morning."

"You decided that on your own."

"At least we all got a night's sleep."

"Kevin didn't know, did he?" Eddie said. "You didn't tell him last night because you knew he would have called me."

"I saved you both a night of lunacy."

A chin-high wooden partition separated the bar from the back room. The back room consisted of half a dozen wooden booths hidden along the far wall. At night, they were used only by sleeping drunks and cheating spouses, but Martha and Kevin had been building a respectable lunch trade, and the booths were now getting some daytime use. He could see Babsie Panko's blondish gray hair in a back booth.

"You going to tell me what my ex-son-in-law wanted?" Eddie said. "Or do I have to ask Grace?"

"Your ex-son-in-law wasn't here," Martha said. "His sister was. And if you ask me, she's a nice person. Scott asked her to find out how Kate was, and that's what she did."

"Suddenly, he's concerned."

"Grace is still his daughter."

"Jesus Christ, whose side are you on?"

Eddie's voice hung in the sudden quiet of the bar. A scraggly brown mutt named James Joyce padded through the door and flopped down near the heat register. Eddie knew his brother wasn't far behind.

"I'm on Grace's side," Martha said softly. "One of us has to be realistic . . . for her sake. I think the average person would agree that the father has his rights, too."

Eddie wanted to lean across the bar and shake his brother's wife until a sense of family loyalty filtered into her head. He hated when Martha cited her personal opinion of what the "average person" would do as unarguable evidence for her narrow-minded views. He knew deep down that Martha was worried that the responsibility of caring for Grace might fall to her. Eddie told her he'd wait for his brother in the back booth.

"I heard it all," Babsie said. "When did you find this out?"

"I stopped at school before I came over here. Father Qualters said he saw her talking to Martha. Makes me wonder how the hell Scott found out in the first place."

"Yonkers is still a small town, Eddie. Besides, it's in the paper today."

She showed him a copy of the *Westchester News Journal*. The story was on page one. A new picture of their house, and an old one of Eddie in boxing trunks— a posed shot taken when he was barely twenty years old. Inside, a group photo of Kate's nursing class, a circle around the face of his daughter.

"You were a little hard on Martha," Babsie said. "It wasn't your most attractive moment."

Coming from a huge clan, Babsie understood family politics, but she didn't know Martha that well. Whatever had happened to Martha, she seemed unable to find joy in anything. Eddie's personal gripe with her stemmed from his belief that Martha had turned Eileen into the same rigid, unforgiving "good" Catholic she was. Kevin blamed it all on Martha's hysterectomy, and the marked change in her after the doctors "didn't put me back together right."

"That eye looks ripe," Babsie said. "But I should see the other guy, right?"

Eddie touched it gingerly. "No. Actually, he escaped untouched."

Scar tissue had permanently thinned the skin above his eyes and left it fragile. Many nights, he'd find blood spots on his pillow for no reason.

"Maybe you're just too old for the club scene," Babsie said.

He knew Babsie had noticed the welts on his hands and arms from where they'd beaten him when he was holding on to Misha. But she'd said enough about his injuries. She seemed to know the right things to say, and not to say. Eddie gave her a decent play-by-play of his night in the Eurobar, including the lost gun. He didn't mention paying money to the Parrot or the bar pro Tatiana. He told her that he'd found Misha and that he'd said a "she" forced his participation in the theft of the BMW.

"Who's 'she'?" Babsie said. "I went over Borodenko's associates list pretty good. I didn't see a woman on there, and I notice things like that."

"Women in Russia rarely have power. It's a cultural

thing. I never heard of a woman in any of the Russian crime organizations. Certainly not in Lukin's operation. Not even in a minor role."

"The FBI list is based mostly on reports from Immigration," Babsie said. "She might be local talent."

"They don't like American men on the inside. I definitely don't see any Russian man taking orders from an American woman."

"What about Borodenko's wife, the model?"

"From everything I've heard, Yuri doesn't trust her to balance the checkbook. She spends her time shopping or drunk, or both."

Kevin Dunne arrived, all fuss and bluster. He was breathing hard and lugging two bags of groceries. The polar opposite of his squared-off younger brother, Kevin was the round and jolly Dunne. Kevin had inherited their father's big Irish personality, as well as the uncommon jet black hair and pale white complexion. Martha pulled Kevin into the kitchen to get her side of the story across first.

"We did have one interesting call last night," Babsie said. "About five in the morning. A guy speaking in Russian. He talked for about two seconds."

"You're sure it was Russian?"

"I made a copy and played it over the phone for the FBI translator. I can't pronounce it, but I wrote it down for you." Babsie turned her notebook around for Eddie. The words in Russian were *"Prishli mne kapustu."* Eddie knew more Russian by ear than in writing. "The translator said it literally means 'Send me the cabbage.' She says it's what you say when someone owes you money."

Babsie handed him the extra tape.

"Somebody is playing games, Babsie. When I hear the

voice on the tape, maybe I can figure it out. In the meantime, let's concentrate on finding Misha."

"You're being straight with us about the money?"

"I do not have Anatoly Lukin's money, Babsie. Or Yuri Borodenko's. Get a search warrant if you want."

"I believe you. Just don't get your hopes up about finding this Latvian kid. He's a corpse looking for a place to lie down. Let's start thinking outside the box. What about an old PD case? Think back. Some scumbag from your past who thinks he has a score to settle."

For two nights, Eddie had done little else but think about old cases. There were a hundred possibilities: guys he'd collared, guys he'd embarrassed or beaten up, those he'd screwed out of money, or their women. He couldn't even come up with a short list. The old faces all ran together. He'd been an equal-opportunity bastard.

"The only people I can think of who might have a reason to hurt me this bad are dead."

"I guess someone came back to life," she said.

# CHAPTER

# 13

EDDIE'S OLD PARTNER, Paulie "the Priest" Caruso, said his brother Angelo, a capo in the Gambino crime family, once told him this story about being in a restaurant on Mulberry Street one midweek afternoon with a bunch of young goodfellas from the neighborhood. They'd been sitting there for several hours sipping vino, picking at the antipasto, and arguing about why bartenders always put exactly three coffee beans in the sambuca. Joking around, they asked the waitress for her opinion. The waitress was an attractive young girl from the Midwest, working her way through NYU. She didn't have a clue, but she was enjoying herself. Everything was flirty and fun, and both the girl and the wise guys were enjoying the banter. The girl finally worked up the courage to ask if they were in the mob.

"The mob?" said Angelo, shocked. "Why do you say that?" The girl said, "Well, I just figured: a group of young guys sitting around all afternoon on a Tuesday, with nothing to do, nowhere to be. What kind of job would let you do that?" Angelo looked at her and said, "We could be cops."

None of the wise guys were laughing when ex-cop Eddie Dunne parked in the bus stop outside the Bronx Knights Social Club. Eight or nine of the locals were hanging around out front, some of them on folding chairs they'd dragged out of the club to check out the spring parade of women young enough to be their granddaughters. Eddie reached under the seat and pulled a purple velveteen bag from the springs. The logo of Seagram's Crown Royal dressed up the front of the bag; inside was a Smith & Wesson .38 Special, Eddie's old NYPD service revolver. In the NYPD, you bought your own gun; he'd kept his and gotten a gun license when he resigned. Eddie shoved the gun in his waistband, slammed the car door, and walked toward the club. A pair of older thugs who recognized him wandered off, as if a lime gelato had suddenly beckoned them from the corner bistro. A young guy in a Yankees jacket stood up and put his hand on Eddie's chest.

"Whoa, where you going, pal?"

For his trouble, the baseball fan wound up on his ass, taking two folding chairs down with him. Across the street, old women in housedresses stopped hanging wet clothes on the squeaky pulley lines that crisscrossed between buildings. Arms folded, they leaned on the window ledges of third- and fourth-floor apartments. The neighborhood, accustomed to violent men in the social club, tuned in.

Quick and graceful, Eddie weaved his way through the mismatched tables and chairs in the front bar area. None of the club members had a chance to warn Richie Costa, who was stretched out in the barber chair in the back room, getting his Wednesday facial and trim. Eddie flashed the S&W, then grabbed Richie by the hair and yanked him out of the chair, back through the bar, and out into the street, his white barber's cape flying like the flag of surrender. Eddie wanted the stadium audience outside: the old ladies across the street, the schoolgirls walking home, the packed city bus going by. If he decided not to kill him, at least he wanted to humiliate him on his home turf.

From a window across the street, Sinatra sang "Fly Me to the Moon." Eddie stuck the gun back in his pocket. He stood still on the sidewalk and let Richie throw the first punch. A roundhouse right, the stupid bastard. Eddie blocked it two feet away from his head, then threw a pair of low combinations. Bim, bam, bim, bam. Then high, a right hook. Blood shot out of Richie's mouth. Bad gums, Eddie remembered. Richie had always had bad gums. He rested a beat, then allowed Richie another free punch. A piss-poor off-balance right hook. Hadn't he learned anything? Eddie went low, low, low, high, low, high. Still fast and rhythmic. The last one a brutal overhand right flush on the left temple. Down went Richie. He rolled on his side, pretending he wanted to drag his fat ass up and fight, but then he decided to work on just keeping his eyes open. Eddie turned to the goombah chorus behind him. The guys lounging against the wall stopped jingling their change.

"You want to know why I'm pissed?" Eddie said. "Anyone want to know?" In the yard next to the club, a German shepherd chained to a picnic table began to whine and claw at the hard-packed dirt. "Yuri Borodenko kidnapped my daughter," he said. "My only daughter . . . and this guy here . . . this scumbag . . . is helping him. I thought you people didn't hurt families. Where the hell is the 'honor' you're always bragging about? Snatching kids now. You should be ashamed of yourselves, acting like low-life bastards. Richie, this low-life bastard here, should tell me everything, right? He should tell me where my daughter is. Anyone disagree with that?"

Eddie leaned over Richie.

"They want you to tell me," he said.

"I only got business with those people, Eddie. I didn't even know about your daughter. That's the truth. I swear on my mother."

"Your mother would spit in your face, Richie. Last night, you stopped me from grabbing the kid who knew where she was. You helped him get away."

"How the fuck was I supposed to know that?" he said, spraying blood on the sidewalk.

With a fistful of hair and a fistful of shirt collar, Eddie pulled Richie to his feet. Blood dribbled down his chin. Richie leaned back against a car. Eddie moved around him, shuffling playfully, his fist raised, measuring Richie. He knew no one would call the police.

"How about the 'she' the kid mentioned?" Eddie said. "Who is the 'she' that steals cars?"

"I don't know what the fuck you're talking about, man."

The smell of garlic wafted from an open kitchen window.

"Left jab, right hook," Eddie said, then hit him twice. Richie's knees buckled. Eddie propped him up against a parked car. "I'm calling my shots, Richie. Making it easy for you."

"I didn't know about your daughter, I swear."

"Where's my gun?" Eddie said. "The Sig Sauer. I know you took it."

"Sergei has it. That crazy fuck Sergei. Last I saw him, he had your gun and the kid."

"Left jab," Eddie said, but he threw a sharp right cross to Richie's face. The sound of cartilage snapping. "Oops, I lied," Eddie said. "I guess it's catching." Richie's nose would need work; that much was true.

But not as true as the next straight left jab. Richie went down face-first. He caught himself with his hands, but his arms buckled like rubber bands. He fell forward, cracking his chin on the sidewalk.

"Get me some answers or we do this again tomorrow," Eddie said. He grabbed Richie's barber cape and rubbed most of the blood off his hands.

As soon as Eddie went to his car, the guys on the folding chairs jumped up, flew into action, dancing around like they were in the rumble scene in *West Side Story.* On his knees, Richie Costa held his face, blood oozing through his fingers. His friends helped him to his feet. Step by baby step, they pulled him toward the club. Eddie started the car, then took one last look. The part of Richie's face not covered with blood was whiter than the sheets on the third-floor clothesline, snapping in the afternoon breeze.


Eddie stopped at a Burger King across from the southern border of Fordham University, washed up, and bought two large cups of ice. He rummaged through the trunk of his Olds until he found two old running T-shirts. He wrapped the ice in the shirts and tied them around his knuckles. Old scar tissue caused his hands to swell up quickly. Every year, he could feel his hands stiffening more, aching in particular when he had to do something small and delicate, like putting panty hose on a Barbie doll.

The cell phone rang just before the toll on the Whitestone Bridge. "When Irish Eyes Are Smiling." With swollen hands, he managed to hit the wrong button. He lost the call. The toll collector was a woman. Her hair was in cornrows and she was wearing gold hoop earrings bigger than her head. He handed her a fifty, the first bill he managed to pull off the roll. No way he was digging around for exact change. The radio in her booth was playing the same song he'd recognized last night in the Eurobar.

"Dave Matthews," he said.

"Who are you, Dick muthafuckin' Clark?" she said. She slapped the change into his ice-wrapped hand, acting as if it were something she saw all the time. Coins hit the pavement, but Eddie took off. He was halfway over the bridge when the phone rang again; this time, he punched the right button. It was Boland. They'd found his gun. Next to the body of Misha Raisky.

The Sheepshead Bay Marina was a mile east of Brighton Beach and directly north of Manhattan Beach. The number of sailboats that called Brooklyn home always amazed Eddie. The row of masts ran forever alongside busy Emmons Avenue. He parked behind Boland's car in the marina parking lot and took the ice off his hands.

"I thought the pros knew how to duck," Boland said. "That eye looks like it hurts like hell."

"I've had worse," he said. "You sure it's Misha?"

"He had a picture ID from a foreign student immigration service. Name: Mikal Raisky. They called some old man from Queens, guy he used to live with. He's the ID at this point."

The Crime Scene Unit had finished and departed. Both the body and Eddie's gun were gone, as well. All that remained was yellow tape and a series of bloodstains shaped like a chain of islands. Misha's head had come to rest on the big island, near slip number 17, which was stenciled in white paint. They'd found Eddie's Sig Sauer next to his hand, as if the killer'd had a last-minute brainstorm and decided to concoct a suicide scenario. Five entrance wounds, three in the back, isn't even covered in *Suicide for Dummies*. Boland said he identified Eddie's Sig Sauer by the serial number he'd given him earlier.

"Was it a dump job?" Eddie asked.

"Just barely. We figure the shooting went down over there in the parking lot. Although it baffles me why they didn't leave him there, rather then take the time to drag him across the grass to this spot. I mean, what's the point?"

"Does this shit ever have a point?"

Boland said they'd picked up shell casings in the parking lot off Emmons Avenue. The CSU had found blood splatter on the blacktop and on the side of a broken-down pickup truck. The killer or killers had apparently dragged Misha about seventy feet from the parking lot to the wooden walkway that bordered the boat slips. It was evident from the scattered blood spots that he'd tried to crawl away across the walkway. The killer fired one more shot for good luck as Misha lay facedown on the boards. The CSU dug the bullet out of the wood, but the shell casing had probably bounced into the water.

"Broad daylight, busy street, apartment building across the street," Eddie said. "Pretty ballsy."

"Does that surprise you, with the Russians?"

A caretaker named Toby Davis had found the shirtless

body shortly before 8:00 A.M. He insisted it wasn't there when he'd arrived for work two hours earlier.

"What time you last see him?" Boland asked Eddie.

"Four A.M. Give or take a few minutes. I didn't see him or my gun again after the scuffle in the stairway."

Eddie had filled Boland in on the happenings in the Eurobar, including a recap of the fight in the stairway.

"Sergei left with your gun and the kid?"

"According to Richie Costa. I wasn't sure who took my gun. But I stopped by the Bronx Knights on the way over. Richie Costa told me the last time he saw the Sig Sauer, it was in Sergei's hands."

"How the hell did you manage to get that out of him?"

"You don't want to know."

"I assume that's Costa's blood on your shirt?" Boland said. "Am I going to find him in a body bag somewhere?"

"Not by my hand, although I was tempted."

Without being asked, Eddie took his bloody shirt off and handed it to the detective.

"Jesus, your hands are cold," Boland said, pushing the shirt back to him. "I believe you didn't kill Costa, Eddie. And nobody thinks you killed this kid. Howie Danton caught the case. He knows it's nothing but a piss-poor setup. We have to go through the motions. You know that."

"So go through the motions."

"Okay. It's a safe bet ballistics will confirm your gun is the murder weapon. The squad is going to ask you where you were between six and eight this morning."

"In the Eurobar, being quizzed by the manager. I left a little before seven. Drove home up the West Side Highway."

"You stop by somewhere for breakfast, or make an impression on anyone?"

"I was in my granddaughter's school around eight-fif-teen. Nobody can get from Sheepshead Bay to Yonkers that fast in the morning without a helicopter. I can get five nuns to swear I was there."

"Four nuns, I would have a problem, but five, I'm sold."

Eddie filled in more parts of the Eurobar story. He told Boland what the kid had said about a "she." Boland checked his list of known Borodenko cronies and found no mention of a woman. Eddie said that Babsie was checking the staff and management at the Elmsford auto-storage garage for female possibilities.

"Danton wants me to get the owners of the boats in this section," Boland said. "See if any names cross-check with our list."

"See Toby. He's been here forever."

"You're on a first-name basis with the caretaker?" Boland said.

"I worked in the squad here, remember?" Eddie replied. "Paulie Caruso kept a boat here for years."

"I remember the boat. Thirty-five-foot Grand Banks. Nice."

" 'Sleeps four, fucks eight,' Paulie used to say. I'd sleep in it when I had an early court appearance or was too shit-faced to drive home."

"I always wondered where you crashed. I figured you had to have someplace to stay. From here to Yonkers every day is a pain in the ass of a commute."

"Paulie said I spent enough nights on that boat to qual-ify for a merchant seaman's license."

"Where was it tied up?" Boland asked.

"Slip ninety-one," Eddie said, pointing west. "Way down past the trees, near that pulley setup. He didn't want a place you could see easily from the street. You know, for those rare occasions when we partied on duty."

"Yeah. I heard all about you guys and your wild boat parties. Never invited me."

"You were into your career then."

The wind changed direction and came off the ocean. The temperature seemed to drop ten degrees in a matter of seconds. "An onshore breeze," Paulie had called it. Onshore because it was coming from off the water. Eddie always argued it should be called an offshore breeze, since it was coming from the ocean. It was a stupid argument, one best played out when they were bombed. One of many. Old friends replayed stupid arguments all their lives. Only quarrels over women were fatal. Eddie felt the chill coming off the Atlantic, which was still bitterly cold from the long winter.

# CHAPTER
# 14

**WEDNESDAY**
**4:45 P.M.**

EDDIE LEFT HIS CAR at the marina and drove with Matty
Boland to Brighton Beach. They parked on Coney Island
Avenue, near the entrance to the construction site where,
thirty-four hours earlier, Eddie had lost Lukin's killer.
The only thing he knew to do at this point was find Sergei
Zhukov, and he needed help. He needed the feds fully in
the mix. But finding Sergei would be the easy part. Eddie
understood the futility of trying to get a hardened Russian
criminal to confess. The word *hardened* didn't do these
guys justice. Decades of frigid weather, deprivation, and
sanctioned cruelty had forced them to develop a level of
toughness and cunning beyond anyone's ability to understand.

"The biggest mistake you can make," Eddie said as
they walked down Brighton Beach Avenue, "is to under-
estimate how smart Russians are. You've never gone up
against people this slick. If you don't understand that,
they'll play you like a mandolin."

Eddie set the pace on the crowded street, eating up
sidewalk like a man on a mission. He realized Boland

claimed he was trying to find Kate, but his eyes were on a different prize. Boland wanted to talk about the big picture: cartels, wiretaps, and worldwide crime. He needed to concentrate on finding a single redhead in a twenty-block haystack.

"Where the hell are we going in such a hurry?" Boland said.

"Part of our bargain. We're going to school."

"This must be gym class," Boland said. "But seriously, I don't need any more education."

"You want an informant? Then keep up with me."

The clock was coming up on sixty hours since Kate had disappeared. Eddie had no idea if the FBI task force had held up their part of the bargain. They said that every known home, business, and vodka joint connected with Borodenko had been checked out. Checked out how? Eddie wanted to know. A drive-by with the window rolled up? Eddie needed to do something to keep their hearts and heads in the game. He knew that if they lost direction, they'd drift back to working whatever case they'd abandoned sixty hours ago. If he got them someone on the inside, they'd owe him those hearts and heads.

"Say you were a car thief in Moscow," Eddie said. "You steal a brand-new car. How do you make money on it?"

"My first day in class, a quiz already. Okay, probably can't ship it out of the country. I'll say you cut it up and sell the parts. Weather that bad, parts business has to be good."

"Forget parts."

"So I'll find a buyer. Some guy's yak dies and he needs dependable transportation. I sell him the stolen car."

"Wrong again. In a country where people wait for years for a car, you'd never get it by the apparat. The government will know it's stolen."

"I give up. What's the answer?"

"You ransom it back to the owner," Eddie said.

"Ransom the car back. Like a kidnapping."

"Exactly. Kidnapping of cars and people is far more commonplace in Russia than it is over here. My point is this: You need to think differently. These people find angles and ways to make money you can't even imagine."

They pushed their way through the crowds bargaining with street merchants under the peeling brown paint of the el tracks' supports. Past the Payless shoe store, the Primorski Restaurant, and the KFC.

"I'll give you the key to understanding all this," Eddie said. "The one thing you definitely need to know: The Russians are all about money. Stop the money, you stop them."

"Sounds like the American way."

"I'm not talking about the honest buck. *Vorovskoi mir* means it's a thieves' world. Many of these people understand no other concept of earning. Maybe in another two generations, but not yet. They don't trust anyone but themselves. Not our government, our legal system, or our business practices."

"They trust it enough to steal from it," Boland said.

"That's right. They understand that: not invest in it, but steal from it. Okay, I already told you the answer to this one. What's the easiest way to become a millionaire in this country today?"

"Marry a Republican fund-raiser."

"The answer is to rip off Medicare or the insurance companies. See that Laundromat over there? They have hundreds of mailboxes for rent. Brighton Beach has more rental mailboxes than any neighborhood in the city. You'll find rental mailboxes in restaurants, grocery stores, and gas stations. Anonymous mailboxes are the lifeblood of the scam artist."

"I don't have to open a clinic?" Boland said.

"You don't even have to buy an aspirin. It's simple. All you need to acquire is the Medicare ID number of a doctor who's going into research, or abroad for an extended period. Not a big problem—all you need is an administrative contact in any hospital. Next, you write Medicare, requesting a change of address for that doctor. You change it to one of these post office boxes that you've rented. After that, it's easy to get the Medicare numbers of a few hundred senior citizens. Offer a free chest X ray, or free blood pressure screenings. Free anything. Once you have those numbers, then you can proceed with the bogus billing. You never see another patient, and the millions start to flow. It will take them six months to a year to send an investigator around. By then, you're back in Russia, set for life."

"Look for me out in the Hamptons."

"And we haven't begun to scratch the surface yet," Eddie said. "Ever hear the word *hidtrost*?"

Boland repeated the word and asked if it was Russian street slang. Eddie didn't know if it was slang or not.

"The Russians refer to *hidtrost* as a secondary intelligence. It's the con man's intelligence. It's not common sense, or education. It's the way the scam artist's mind works. The ability to read between the lines. It's more respected than traditional intelligence among the Russian criminal element. In the old country, ripping off the government is a badge of honor. The only way to make a buck. They grow up seeing con men and hustlers making big money."

"Plus, it fits neatly into your contention that the Russian criminals are harmless schemers."

"Not harmless," Eddie said. "I never said harmless. My complaint with your approach—excuse me, the FBI's approach—is that you want to emphasize the Russian *mafiya*, the *organizatsiya*. You want a hierarchy you can put on a chart on the wall. That's wasting everyone's time; it doesn't exist. These people don't trust any big organization. They're not going to form one."

"You're wrong there, Eddie. They're a hell of a lot more organized than you think."

They walked past the crowds swarming the fruit stands, and the people selling pastries and sweaters.

"See that woman in the doorway?" Eddie said. "Old woman, with the backpack. She's selling prescription drugs."

"Prescription drugs?" Boland said.

As they passed the woman, she could be heard whispering to passersby, in a raspy voice, *"Lekarstvo, komu, lekarstvo?"*

"She's saying, 'Medicine, who wants medicine?' " Eddie said. "The supply varies. They usually have some antibiotics, Valium, kidney medicines; OxyContin is big now. Dilaudid. Viagra is always a seller. Twenty-five codeine-laced aspirin will cost you around five bucks."

"Stolen prescription drugs."

"Not stolen. Mostly smuggled in from Russia, Bulgaria, Switzerland, wherever they can get it in bulk. That old woman works for a guy I'll point out to you. He usually hangs around the travel agency, recruiting people, or he's in the Samovar sucking up the vodka."

"How about heroin or coke?"

"I don't know that firsthand. What I do know is that they've been bringing ecstasy in by the trunkful. This same guy who hangs out in the Samovar also recruits Hasidic Jews to smuggle ecstasy. He tells them they're carrying diamonds."

Eddie looked in the window of the travel agency. It was covered with handwritten posters, mostly in the Cyrillic alphabet. English signs listed fares to London and Berlin. Out of place was a poster of a tanned couple on the beach in Jamaica.

"He's not here," Eddie said. "He's in the Samovar. One thing before we go in. The legitimate businessmen are not going to go against Borodenko. You're going to have to hold their feet to a big fire. Borodenko is their *krysha*. *Krysha* means 'roof,' their protection. Like the old mob protection rackets. Same thing, only in Russian."

Eddie led Boland into a bar where a gaudy chandelier dominated the center of a room it was way too big for. The decor was a dingy glitz, the woodwork trimmed in peeling gold paint. The place was more than half-filled in the late afternoon. The heavy-lidded bartender took his time getting down to them. He was too busy admiring his unshaven profile in the mirror behind the bar, a cigarette with the filter torn off dangling from his lips. Only death deters tough guys from smoking, Eddie thought.

"Lexy," Eddie said to the bartender. "Meet my friend Desmond Shanahan from the FBI." Lexy grunted and gave a minimum nod. "From this day forward, Lexy Petrov will say that happy hour doesn't start until Eddie Dunne and Desmond Shanahan come through the door."

Eddie ordered a diet cola for himself and a Stoli on the rocks for Boland. Boland raised his eyebrows at Eddie, wondering why the hell he was talking so loudly and who Desmond Shanahan was. Eddie called Lexy over and whispered to him. Lexy whispered back, then turned away.

"What did you ask him?" Boland said.

"I gave him a chance to help me find my daughter. He told me to go fuck myself. Now the prick is fair game."

Lexy set their drinks down. Small bowls of caraway and sunflower seeds were spread around the bar.

"Lexy Petrov and I used to be friends," Eddie said, speaking a little louder. A few heads at the bar turned his way. "Lexy once told me he has ten occupations. Isn't that interesting, Desmond? Busy, busy man, our Lexy. He told me many things in the days when we drank together as friends."

The tables were half-filled. Eddie recognized most of the customers' faces. He knew the waitress Ludmilla very well.

"I don't know all ten of Lexy's occupations," Eddie said. "I do know he's a part-time leg breaker for a loan shark; plus, he sets up phony car accidents for insurance purposes. Oh, and he acts as a go-between in kidnapping cases. Some gangs in Russia specialize in kidnapping the families of wealthy Russian-Americans. Like the mother of that hockey star a few years ago. Lexy was the go-between. Little work, big profit. Lexy is going to be my go-between and help get my daughter back. And he will not even charge me. He'll do it because he loves me. And if he gets her back safely, I will not kill him."

Boland laughed nervously. "Cool down," he said.

"Cool your ass," Eddie said.

"Show them the sketch you made of the guy who killed Lukin," Boland said.

Eddie ignored him. He'd already realized the sketch

was useless. The only way the sketch would work was if they came across a desperate junkie, a scorned woman, or a cop who knew him. The Russians wouldn't turn in one of their own to the police. As far as the Russians were concerned, all the sketch would do was alert the bad guy that someone had seen his face.

"Help me out here, Lexy," Eddie said. "Tell me why someone would kidnap my daughter. I have no big money. It must be something personal. Desmond points out it may have been someone I offended. I don't know. If I offended you, Lexy, how would you handle it?"

"I'd come after you," Lexy said, taking a quick check in the mirror.

"Exactly, that's what a man does. So it must be true what you told me . . . that Yuri Borodenko is a faggot. We're talking about a faggot here."

"That's subtle," Boland said.

"Viktor," Eddie said, looking down the end of the bar. "Viktor, Lexy says Borodenko is a faggot. You agree? By the way, I was telling my FBI friend about your imported-drug business. Lexy explained to me how it works. Incidentally, your girlfriend, outside there, needs a new backpack. Little pills are falling out."

"Let me pay for these drinks, and then we'll hit the bricks," Boland said.

Eddie snatched Boland's money off the bar and shoved it in his shirt pocket.

"We are among friends, Desmond," Eddie said. "We do not pay for anything in here, right, Ludmilla?"

"You're being an asshole," the waitress said. "No wonder someone punched you in the eye."

"Pretty, Ludmilla. Worried about my eye. Ludmilla means 'loved by all,' and she lives up to that name. Lexy told me she is the queen of the bait and switch. Ludmilla puts on her worst clothes and heaviest accent, then goes around to little independent jewelers and tries to get them to buy a necklace she claims was in her family for generations. I don't know where the hell she got it, but it is valuable. She tells them some story about it belonging to Anastasia—remember that movie with Ingrid Bergman? But the jewelers can see that the necklace is valuable, and poor Ludmilla doesn't know its value. She says that she desperately needs the money to get back to Russia. The jewelers are greedy; Ludmilla always laughs about that later. Greedy bastards, serves them right, trying to screw her with their lowball deal. Poor Ludmilla accepts the deal; she has no choice. Always for cash. Then she screws them with an imitation. My friend Lexy Petrov told me all about it."

"Why don't you get the fuck out of here," Lexy said.

"Why don't you throw me out?" Eddie snapped.

"Easy, easy," Boland whispered.

"How's the vodka?" Eddie said.

"I could have used a triple," Boland said.

"Lexy," Eddie yelled. "Another vodka for Desmond. Another vodka I won't pay for. Hey, speaking of vodka, what's the name of that fat guy who comes in here? You know, you told me he buys grain alcohol from some distillery in Missouri, then smuggles it into Russia in bottles labeled as witch hazel, and then he relabels it and sells it as vodka. What a great scheme. I'll think of his name later. So many fine entrepreneurs drink in this fine bar."

The fine bar was emptying out quickly. More stools were empty than occupied now. People in the dining area began putting their coats on. Plates of thin potato pancakes, others with Russian herring, and bowls of cold borscht were abandoned. Someone turned the sound system way up.

Eddie put his arm around the man on the stool next to him, a balding young man with a Fu Manchu mustache. "I always forget your name, my friend," Eddie said. "I'm sorry for that. But I would vote you as the top new scam artist on the scene." The young man drained his glass quickly and stood up. "He's being shy, Desmond. Lexy told me all about this young man. He smuggles Russians across the Canadian border into Maine. When someone contacts him, wanting to be brought to this country, he and his pals go into Canada through the woods of Maine. They meet the family, then lead them across the border, through the same woods. But here's the funny part: When they bring the family in, they are armed to the teeth, automatic weapons, extra ammunition, grenades, gas masks. Why such heavy weapons, you ask, when one could sneak across that border armed with nothing more dangerous than a pirogi? That's the point. It's all showbiz. All an act, so they can charge their fellow countryman the high rate—ten thousand dollars apiece—for a stroll through the woods."

The restaurant door opened and closed at a faster rate. Eddie had succeeded in clearing the place out. He turned around and saw the table in the corner had suddenly been abandoned.

"Come over here, Desmond," Eddie said. "Let me show you this beautiful hand-painted mural of Saint Petersburg. Hand-painted when Evesi Volshin owned this restaurant. But see these dark spots here? If you look closely, you'll see they're not windows; they're bullet holes. Bullets that went through Evesi's body when he sat right in this chair. Isn't that right, Lexy?"

"No one cries for Evesi," Lexy said.

"That's right," Eddie said. "Evesi deserved to die. Evesi was a scumbag kidnapper. In fact, the night of the shooting, shell casings were everywhere. People eating their dinner moved their chairs so the shooters could pick them up. Evesi was scum, like Borodenko. Isn't that right, Lexy? You were here that night, Lexy. Or couldn't you see through your mask?"

"Plenty more bullets in the store," Lexy said.

"Is that a threat? Right in front of Desmond Shanahan of the FBI?"

"It is whatever you see in your nightmares."

"What is that, Lexy, an example of Russian mystery? Some inscrutable phrase supposed to strike fear into my heart? Oooh, I see the smoke of the cossack fire."

Eddie walked toward the bar. Lexy stepped back. Eddie stood on the rail, reached over, and pulled a metal club from underneath.

"Eddie," Boland said.

"You're good at telling stories, Lexy. Deliver this message for me. Tell whoever it is to be a man, let my daughter go, and come after me."

Eddie looked carefully at the metal bar. One end was wrapped in black electrical tape. He reached over and smashed the mirror. Shards of glass fell onto the shelves of bottles and on the floor behind the bar.

"I'm taking this with me," Eddie said. "If anything happens to my daughter, our next meeting will be your nightmare."

# CHAPTER

# 15

8:00 P.M.

"WHY DID THE MAN attackle you?" Grace asked, gently daubing Eddie's eye with a damp washcloth. "Because you were looking for Mommy?"

He wasn't sure where Grace had found her mother's first-aid kit. He watched her carefully, not entirely sure what chemical she was doctoring him with. Kate could reel off the names of drugs Eddie had never heard of.

"He *attackled* me because he's crazy," Eddie said. "The police took him away to jail so he can't hurt anyone else."

They were sitting around the kitchen table, finishing the "angel foot cake." Kevin had brought franks and beans, Grace's favorite, from the restaurant. The house was quieter than it had been. The Yonkers Police Department had moved the plant location to their Fourth Precinct, two miles away, on Shonnard Place. The phone would still be tapped, and the FBI still involved. Eddie guessed they must have figured that since he wasn't sitting there, they shouldn't have to, either. Uniformed officers would still maintain a presence in the neighborhood, checking his house at least once an hour.

"Not all mentally ill people deserve to be in jail, honey," Martha said. "Some people are sick and should be in hospitals."

"When I see him again," Eddie said, "I will make sure he goes to a hospital."

"So much for turning the other cheek," Martha said.

"Martha," Kevin said sternly.

When Eddie got home, Grace had told him that Babsie Panko'd helped her fix up an old pink dollhouse of Kate's. Grace had dragged it out of the attic and onto the front lawn. He remembered the dollhouse; he and Eileen had put it together one Christmas Eve.

"God came into our class today," Grace said.

"His spirit is always with you, sweetie," Martha said. "It's with you now."

"I asked Him to help Mommy."

"I pray to Him every day, too," Martha said.

"I see Him every day," Grace said

"You don't really see God," Martha said. "But you feel His presence and know He's always there for you."

"I see Him every day," Grace said, her voice getting louder. "Today, He said, 'Good morning, class.'"

"Oh, honey, I don't think so," Martha said.

"What does God look like?" Kevin asked.

"He's bald and he wears a black suit."

"That's Father Qualters," Kevin said. "He only thinks he's God. You ought to play golf with him sometime."

Eddie winced from laughing. Grace thought she'd hurt him, and her eyes welled up. Eddie pulled her to him and kissed her neck until she giggled.

"Well, Uncle Kevin has a whoopee cushion," Grace said, trying to retaliate. "He puts it under the chair cushion, and when you sit down, it sounds like a fart."

"Don't say that word, Gracie," Martha said.

Eddie looked up at the clock and wondered where Babsie had gone. He wanted to fill her in on Misha and find out what progress she had made. But it was more than that. He liked the fact she was there, looking out for Grace. Babsie had a calmness about her. And an openness that made her comfortable to be around. He had no doubt that Babsie Panko could handle anything.

"Listen, Eddie," Kevin said. "Next time you go into one of those Russian places, call me. Promise me that. Call me before you do something like this again."

"Eddie doesn't need your help," Martha said.

"You'll be the first guy I call, Kev."

"Do the police have anything promising?" Martha asked. "Any kind of leads at all? I ask Babsie Panko, and God knows I love her, but she doesn't exactly inspire confidence. That may be my opinion, but . . ."

"She's funny, like Granpop," Grace said.

"And that's good enough for me," Eddie said. "Us jokesters have to stick together."

Eddie still wondered how his former son-in-law had found out about Kate so quickly, before it even appeared in the paper. He didn't want to think Martha had called him. He needed Martha now to look after Grace when he was gone. Kevin would be around, too. But Kevin, God bless him, thought Martha was the greatest thing ever created.

"I have some good news," Kevin said.

"Please, honey, it's not the time."

"We need something good to talk about, right, Eddie?" Kevin said, sipping gingerly from a steaming cup of coffee Martha had pushed into his hands. The look on his face said it all; he had news that couldn't wait. "I heard something yesterday. McGrath, the electrician. You know who I mean?"

McGrath's Electric Shop had been next door to the North End Tavern for over thirty years.

"Everybody here knows the McGraths," Martha said, gesturing for him to pick up the pace.

"Yeah, but I bet you didn't know this: He's retiring."

"He says that every year," Martha said.

"He's already got a buyer for his house on Douglas Avenue," Kevin said. "I was in Food Mart and heard about it, so I went right over to him and asked him point-blank. He's moving to Naples, Florida. He bought a condo there last winter. He says he's had it with working his ass off eleven months a year."

"What is he doing with the shop?" Eddie asked.

"That's part of my idea," Kevin said. "You're going to love it, Eddie."

Kevin always had an idea, some big wacky idea. Invariably, too big for Martha's tastes. She apparently knew what was coming next. The look on her face predicted she didn't like Kevin's latest brainstorm.

"He's not in Florida yet," Martha said.

"I was thinking," Kevin said, his eyes wide, his waving hands drawing the floor plans of his big idea. "We should rent the space for Kate."

"Don't mind him, Eddie. He means well."

"C'mon. It would make a perfect little restaurant for her," Kevin said. "She's been looking and looking. This place is perfect. We could knock out the wall between us. Put a small service bar in her place that connects to our bar. We could join the kitchens. She could do all the food, the fancy dinners. We'd handle the drinks, the burger crowd."

"It sounds perfect," Eddie said.

"Let's not be getting our hopes too high," Martha said.

"Let's do it," Grace yelled.

Kevin Dunne never had a plan that couldn't work. The caption under his picture in his high school yearbook read "No prob-lemo."

"It's all settled then," Kevin said. "I'll put a deposit down tomorrow."

Later that night, Eddie Dunne sat alone in his kitchen, wondering when the other shoe would drop. Unlike his brother, Eddie did not believe that everything always works out. He knew the more time that passed, Kate's chances diminished. If the worst happened to Kate, he'd lose Grace, as well. Scott had not sent his sister into enemy territory just to check the condition of a woman he claimed to hate; he had another motive.

Eddie needed a lawyer to get the proper documents drawn up, legal guardian, whatever he needed on paper to protect Grace. Not that he was putting his trust in the system. Not by a long shot. He knew the system well enough to know it never did anything for guys like him. Rolling around in the back of his brain was the start of plan B. Guys like Eddie needed to have a plan B.

He sipped a cup of tea as he looked into his granddaughter's bedroom. The old radiator clanked as steam rose. He'd planned for years to modernize but had never gotten around to it. In those bad old days, so many things had called him away. Things that Eileen, who'd called him the Hell-Raiser of the Western World, had listed under one simple heading: "Nightlife."

When he was honest with himself, Eddie could admit

he'd been wrong. Maybe Eileen would have been different if he had grown up sooner. For too many years, he'd wasted his quality time in bars, being the last guy to go home after a night out carousing. His was a lifetime of booze and recklessness, which had provoked his forced resignation from the NYPD, and culminated in the death of Eileen. The doctors said cancer, but that ugly word didn't even begin to touch his guilt. He had no doubt that the stress of living with him had triggered her disease. Now, because he'd tried to make it up, because he'd grabbed his last chance to be a father, and a priceless shot at being a grandfather, they were going to take it all away.

Grace stirred, kicking the pink bedspread farther down the bed. Her bedroom, the one nearest to the kitchen, had been Kate's when she was a child. He felt sick when he thought about all the arguments Kate had heard, all the sad scenes playing out just a few feet down the hall. In the amber glow of a Hello Kitty night-light, he stood there watching the little girl, who, for no reason he could understand, loved him so much. He was constantly amazed that Grace thought he was so hilarious, so much fun. The one thing in life he was sure of was that no one would ever love him this much again. He couldn't lose her.

A full moon illuminated the quiet street. Eddie noticed a small red sticker on the bedroom window. Eileen had put it there when Kate was a baby. It was meant to alert firemen that a child slept there. Unfortunately, it alerted everyone that a child slept there. He began to peel it off, wondering if he'd blown this surprising and priceless gift just when he'd come to understand it.

Headlights flashed across the bedroom wall as a big

vehicle turned into their street. Eddie squinted, trying to see if he recognized the car. He wondered if it was the YPD making its hourly drive-by. A dark SUV, one of the king-size models, towered over his neighbors' Hondas and Tauruses. Brake lights painted the street with a red glow. The bass thump of music reverberated. A little too loud for police work.

Maybe it was a wrong address, some yo-yo looking for his bimbette. Nothing to do with him. Kids, probably. Kids with a case of beer iced down in a cooler on the floor behind them. Probably just driving around, looking for a girl who lived on the hill. She won't do it, but her sister will. But then the big tires bounced softly up onto the curb, bright lights pointed at the house. Eddie put his big silhouette in the center of the window, hoping it would scare them off. On the lawn, near the edge of the driveway, Eddie noticed the small pink doll-house Grace had dragged out there earlier. He still remembered the argument that Christmas Eve when he and Eileen had put it together. The SUV stopped halfway up the driveway.

Please back off, he whispered. Eddie's nature begged him to run outside, but he knew he couldn't abandon Grace. Disappearing had been his old act. He looked back at Grace, who was sound asleep, zonked-out. Maybe she'd sleep through this.

The engine growled as the driver seemed to search for the right gear—reverse, Eddie hoped. He had a bad feeling; the guy was too ballsy. Either drunk or crazy. He prayed for drunk as the music got louder, thumping in his chest. Grace moaned something, half-asleep. Call the cops, he thought. That's what a good citizen would do. The SUV made a sudden hard left onto the lawn, then went right across it, tire tracks cutting deep in the soft grass and aiming directly at the pink dollhouse. The cracking of plastic echoed in the quiet neighborhood as the big tires crushed it.

Eddie raced down the hall and grabbed the Smith & Wesson from his bedroom closet. He didn't care who the hell it was, or how many. He could feel his arms reaching into the SUV, yanking whoever it was out of that car. His hand was on the doorknob when Grace cried out from the bedroom.

"I'll be right back, babe," he yelled. "Everything is okay."

She called him again.

"Just a second, honey," he yelled.

Something hit the front of the house, slamming off the ancient door. Grace cried, "Granpop."

So he ran to her and held her and watched from the pink bedroom as the SUV backed down the driveway. The driver peeled out, tires screeching. Bits of mud and stones pinged off the sides of parked cars. Grace, her voice thick with sleep, asked what was happening, unsure whether or not she was in a bad dream. He held her and said it was just a dumb driver who got lost and that she'd always be safe with him.


Three marked patrol cars from the Yonkers Fourth Precinct responded. In the swirl of light on the lawn, Eddie let Martha snatch Grace from his arms and take her to her house. He told the cops he didn't get a plate number but that even if he had, he was sure the vehicle had been stolen. He led them to the other evidence, a gray canvas bag that had been thrown against the door—the door that no friend ever used. Detectives examined tire marks and photographed the bag. He asked the detectives to contact Babsie Panko and tell her about the canvas bag and its contents. Stenciled on the side was U.S. MAIL. Inside was a human head.

CHAPTER

# 16

THURSDAY, APRIL 9
1:00 A.M.

FOR THE SECOND TIME in four days, a yellow crime-scene
tape stretched across Eddie Dunne's driveway. Bits of
pink plastic dollhouse were scattered across the lawn.
Tiny dresses and miniature chairs and tables clung to
clumps of grass around deep, swirling wheel ruts. CSU
techs dug up chunks of turf for tire-tread comparison.
Standard operating procedure, but a waste of time in this
case. It might reassure the victim when you went through
the evidence-collection motions, but both the techies and
Eddie knew the SUV had already been transformed into
a metal block and stacked with other metal blocks in
some junkyard in the borough of Brooklyn or Queens.

At this point, an unidentified human head was all the
Yonkers PD had to work with. Until the location where
the crime actually occurred could be determined, investigative responsibility fell to the jurisdiction where the
head was found. Along with Kate's kidnapping, Babsie
Panko had inherited a possible homicide. She volun-
teered to take the case because in all likelihood it was re-
lated to the kidnapping. The canvas bag and its decaying

contents were on the way to the medical examiner's office in White Plains. Babsie put the head on the seat next to her and took off.

Babsie Panko said that so far that year, more serious crime had occurred on Eddie Dunne's lawn than in the rest of the entire Fourth Precinct. She told him she didn't know how he had the guts to look inside the bag. He said it was easy; he had to know. At first, he didn't think it was real, just something you see on the shelves in Wal-Mart on the days before Halloween. But it had weight to it. He'd reached in and turned the spongy skull around. It wasn't trick or treat. He'd taken only a quick look. Enough to know it wasn't his daughter.

The sun rose before the police cleared the scene. They were slowed by curious neighbors in bathrobes and slippers, who added their individual two cents and then shuffled home. Despite Martha's objections, Eddie insisted that Grace go to school. He wanted her life as normal as possible, and he'd fight Martha daily on that. Babsie Panko arranged for a plainclothes cop to be assigned to Christ the King. After Eddie got her to school and met the cop, he went home, showered and dressed, then drove to Brighton Beach. More than five hours early for his meeting with Matty Boland.

The skies were gray; heavy low clouds hung over the skyscrapers of Manhattan. A constant pain drummed above Eddie's eyes as he rode down the West Side Highway. He always got a headache before the rain. Staring at every face in every car made it worse. But he thought that if he could only look into every single vehicle, every single room, sooner or later he'd find the face of his daughter. He wouldn't miss that wild red hair. Then all hell would break loose as he slammed across lanes of traffic or through walls. Kate would expect nothing less of him.

When she was young, Kate hated her red hair almost as much as her freckles. He would hold her and kiss each freckle on her nose until she giggled, then screamed, "Daaaad" in frustration. In grade school, the kids had called her "Howdy Doody." It had infuriated her, and punches were thrown. Eileen, feeling guilty over passing those physical traits along, had claimed Kate was just another "fighting" Dunne. But by the time she got to high school, the freckles had disappeared. She grew tall and straight. Her figure filled in, even curvier than Eileen's. She never heard those taunts again. And somewhere along the line, he'd stopped kissing her on the nose.

Eddie knew Kate was alive. If they'd killed her, it would have been her head in the bag last night. That would have been a final gesture, he thought. That would have been the move that meant nothing else mattered. If that had happened, he'd be turning Yuri Borodenko's mansion on the Atlantic into a mausoleum. Borodenko would hear the news in Russia, and misery would enter his life.

Today, there were no cars in front of Borodenko's for him to blow up. Eddie parked halfway down the block, wondering where to begin. They'd cut down the dogwood tree; the scorched logs sat stacked near the curb. All around the stump, grass, blacktop, and sidewalk were blackened in a circle twice the size of a Rolls-Royce. The black circle made the house seem even more of a white stone fortress.

The borough would have Borodenko's building permit on file. He'd go from there. Find the builder and grab the plans. Buy them or steal them. The builder would be listed, a Russian, for sure. Stealing was the only option. And that would take time, valuable time, and maybe not worth it. Borodenko was too smart to leave a security flaw that an Eddie Dunne could exploit. Too smart to keep a tattooed psycho or kidnapped woman inside his house. So where, then? He wondered where the feds were. Why weren't they watching this house?

It didn't make sense that they were doing this to him. As bad a life as he'd led, he'd rarely hurt anyone other than his family and himself. And that was in the past. Four years ago, thirty years too late, he'd become the person he always could have been, and he'd spent the nights since regretting every moment away from his family, and every drink that had unfairly shouldered the blame for his weakness. But in that continuous reel of regrets that played in his head, he never saw anyone who hated him enough to torture him this way. No one who wanted him twisting in the wind like this. Maybe he didn't give the Russian criminals enough credit. He never imagined they would make the effort to hurt him this deeply.

If not revenge, why were they doing this? They were keeping her alive for a reason. If it had been money, there would have been ransom notes, or calls. There had been only one call. He'd listened to the tape. The voice sounded put-on, like a bad audition for the Actors Studio. Someone trying to mimic a deep gangster growl. The caller said, *"Prishli mne kapustu."* "Send me the cabbage." Melodramatic gangster talk for "Send me the money." Send who the money? No follow-up call, no specific amount, no details. The call was phony. Designed to make him think that this was about money.

Shortly past noon, he caught a glimpse of motion near the house—the garage door rising. The house had a garage underneath. A steeply inclined driveway led down to it. From where he sat, he could see only the top panels of the garage door as they slid upward, disappearing back into the garage. When it was all the way up, the nose of a dark car appeared. A black Mercedes, one of the big ones. It paused at the top of the driveway, the nose angled upward. The garage door closed behind it. Eddie slumped down in the Olds and waited. They had only one way to go—toward him.

The car bounced heavily onto the roadway. He could see two occupants. They came slowly. Two women. The driver was dark-skinned, her dark hair shoulder-length. The passenger, sitting up front, was Mrs. Borodenko, but he almost didn't recognize her with short hair. At the wedding in the Mazurka, she had big curly blond hair. What romance writers would call "tresses." Eddie stayed down in the seat as he watched them in his rearview mirror. They stopped at the stop sign, then turned right. He waited a beat, then made a quick U-turn. Within five minutes, he was settled in behind them on the Belt Parkway, going toward Manhattan.

Shopping trip, Eddie figured. Saks, Bloomies, or some Italian designer with live models on a runway. Perhaps Mrs. Borodenko keeping touch with her old fashion contacts. But they weren't going to Manhattan. The Mercedes moved right and went up the approach to the Verrazano-Narrows Bridge, going to Staten Island. It definitely wasn't a fashion run.

Eddie hung back through the tollbooth, then turned onto Hylan Boulevard. He kept driving as they pulled into the parking lot of a restaurant called Jimmy's Bistro. He went a full block, made another U-turn, and parked across the street.

He watched through binoculars as they got out of the Mercedes. They acted like old pals. The dark-haired driver seemed happier, more relaxed. She was obviously telling Mrs. Borodenko something funny, placing her hand on her shoulder like an obnoxious salesman. Mrs. Borodenko was tinier than he remembered, but he and Lukin had been seated so far back at her Mazurka wedding, he hadn't gotten a good look. He zoomed in on her face. Against the backdrop of dark gray clouds, she looked as if she were made of porcelain.

He waited until they entered the restaurant, then gave them another ten minutes to get a table. And another ten, in case they were meeting someone who was late. Then he went in. The place had a Mulberry Street ambience. Everything under bent-nose control. Finding them wasn't easy. They were at a table so hidden, it had to be reserved for customers in the witness protection program. A small fountain separated them from the other diners. He saw them sitting opposite each other in the high-backed leather booth, laughing with the waiter. Like regulars. He'd wasted his entire morning tailing women to lunch.

# CHAPTER

# 17

**THURSDAY**
4:30 P.M.

THE TWO WOMEN in Jimmy's Bistro were already on their second bottle of wine when Eddie left. He drove like a madman, speeding back over the Verrazano to Brooklyn, late for his meeting with Boland. Weaving in and out of traffic on the Belt Parkway, he started to call Babsie, but he put the phone back down because he didn't want to start depending on that. Breathe, he told himself, just keep breathing. Wait for the opening. Sooner or later, they always give you an opening.

Matty Boland was dressed to impress—a dark blue suit, a white shirt, and a burgundy tie with small polka dots. He didn't seem to notice that Eddie was late. All he wanted to talk about were the events of the previous night, and the severed head.

"You piss ice water, man," Matty Boland said. "No way would I have had the balls to look inside that bag. Just the idea it might be your daughter . . ."

They took the Lincoln Town Car, heading toward JFK. The traffic to the airport seemed unusually light. As they passed the entrance to Marine Park, Eddie thought about the shooting fourteen years earlier. In moments like last night, or that shooting, he seemed to be able to stand outside himself, a spectator to the slow-motion chaos around him. In the ring, it had been the same thing; there were times when he couldn't even hear the crowd, or feel his own body, and all that existed was the enemy before him. In Marine Park all those years ago, he and Paulie Caruso had walked shoulder-to-shoulder into a barrage of gunfire, calmly killing two local punks who'd just committed a double murder.

"That shit takes a piece out of you," Boland said, shivering. "If you want to talk about last night, I can listen. That's what I'm trying to say."

"Just take care of them," Eddie said. "I'll be fine."

For the first time in his adult life, Eddie had asked for help. He couldn't let anything else happen to Grace. He'd called Boland and offered to do whatever he could to help them nail Borodenko, providing the feds protected his family twenty-four hours a day. They even worked a deal with the Yonkers PD to have a policewoman assigned full-time to stay with Grace.

"Sick guy, this Russian bastard," Boland said.

"You have no idea, Matty. There's a story floating around Brighton Beach that Yuri Borodenko caught someone listening in on a private conversation. He cut the guy's ears off and made him eat them."

At JFK, Boland tinned his way past the security people and drove right onto the tarmac. He parked on an angle, facing a red-white-and-blue Boeing 767. Fifty yards away, workers tossed luggage onto the conveyor. Eddie watched the crew preparing the plane, trying to figure out why he was here. Boland had gone through a lot of trouble just to park near the belly of a departing jumbo jet.

"So who belongs to this head?" Boland asked, adjusting his seat backward and stretching out. "Somebody's gotta be missing it by now."

"You'd think," Eddie said. "Babsie Panko canvassed the hospitals, morgues, and the cemeteries in the metropolitan area. Some of the older, filled up cemeteries have no phone numbers. She has all the local police departments checking their jurisdictions."

"You didn't recognize it," Boland said.

"I didn't look that close. It appeared to be male. Very little hair. Babsie Panko says it's elderly. The face was dark, very swollen and distorted. My guess is that he'd been dead over a week."

"Just a spare head somebody had sitting around?"

"Or dug up for the occasion."

It might not even be Borodenko's people this time, Eddie thought. It could have been any one of the people he'd humiliated in the Samovar yesterday. Or any old acquaintance pissed off and sick enough to dig up a human head and throw it at his door. When this was all over, when Kate was safely home, maybe they'd laugh about it. Some of his old cop pals would have made it a drinking event. Eddie Dunne's annual skull toss. Closest to the door wins.

"Everybody in the task force has Sergei Zhukov's picture," Boland said. "We're going to find him soon."

"I figured he was flying out today and that's why we came here."

"No, Sergei's not flying anywhere. We have a hold on his passport. If he goes, he's swimming."

"Borodenko flying in?"

Boland shook his head no. Lights began popping on in the gloomy afternoon. Activity around the plane quickened. A steady stream of luggage and boxes flowed up the conveyor belt.

"Okay, I give up," Eddie said. "What the hell are we doing here?"

"Watching the money plane."

It was almost 5:00 P.M. when a cream-colored armored car pulled up. Two armed guards joined the baggage handlers and began putting large white canvas bags on the conveyor belt. Seconds later, another armored car pulled up.

"You wanted me to see guys loading money bags," Eddie said.

"The powers downtown want you to understand what we're up against."

"Like I don't?" Eddie said. What he did understand was the reason for Boland's power suit. The city detective trying to impress him with the invincibility of the almighty federal government.

Boland said, "Downtown says all you talk about is minor schemes. They think you underplay it. They want you to be aware that these guys are more than a handful of local grifters. If they're going to make a big investment in you, they want you to understand exactly how dangerous this situation really is."

"Okay, so you showed me the money plane," Eddie said. "And where is all this cash going?"

"Nonstop to Moscow. The guards are loading twenty-three hundred pounds of crisp, brand-new American one-hundred-dollar bills. Just off the printing press. Over one hundred million dollars on this flight. And this goes on at least once a week."

"A hundred million," Eddie said. "Apparently, it's not federal aid going to the Russian government. We wouldn't be here if it were that simple."

"It's mob money," Boland said. "Stacks of fresh hundreds going into various Russian banks either controlled by or directly owned by Russian organized crime. A hundred mil, still in the Federal Reserve wrapper. Brand-new and already going through the laundry. You can almost smell the soapsuds."

"And they want our money because the ruble buys shit."

"They need dollars to operate worldwide, Eddie. The Russian *mafiya* now owns over eighty percent of the banks in Russia. Over two thousand new banks in just a few years. Most of them way undercapitalized. After the breakup of the Soviet Union, whatever state control there was evaporated. No rules, no regulations. Convicted felons own banks over there. They're using these banks to launder an incredible amount of illegal money."

"Why rob a bank when you can own one?"

"Exactly," Boland said. "Criminals everywhere are getting in on this. Now the Russians have brought the Colombians on board. They're well on their way to being the World Bank for illegal drugs."

"All right," Eddie said. "This money we're looking at now starts out as street money, right? From the sale of drugs or guns, I assume. How does it wind up here, in this plane, as brand-new money?"

Boland gave Eddie a quick lesson in the rules of money laundering: First, ownership must be concealed. Second, the money must change form; three million dollars in twenties cannot come back as three million in twenties. Third, the process must be obscured—the whole point of money laundering is that the trail cannot be followed; and fourth, control must be maintained.

"It's all done through bank transfers," Eddie said. "I know that much from Lukin."

"Almost always," Boland said. "Let's say Borodenko acquires an amount of dirty money. From the sale of any contraband. Like you said, drugs, guns, stolen oil, gasoline, bombs, anything. Say fifty million dollars. They wire the dirty fifty million through several front companies and eventually into a London Eurodollar account. Then a Russian mob–controlled bank orders fifty million in one-hundred-dollar bills from a New York bank. Simultaneously, the London bank wires the fifty million, plus commission, to the same New York bank. That bank then buys fifty million in uncirculated hundreds from the U.S. Treasury. They load it on this flight and it goes directly to the Russian bank."

"Investigate our banks," Eddie said. "We have control over our own banks."

"Been there, done that. They're operating legally."

"Monitor overseas wire transfers."

"Sounds easy, but there are over seven hundred thousand of them daily."

"Well, I told you they were smart," Eddie said. "Lukin always said the worst thing that happened to the United States was the breakup of the Soviet Union."

"That's the problem," Boland said. "It allowed these people to travel the world freely. The KGB already had spy networks set up throughout the world. When the Soviet Union fell apart, those networks almost instantly morphed into ones run by organized crime. The world was their oyster."

"Borodenko had KGB connections."

"And that spells organization. This is where it gets worse. I know you don't like to use that word, but this is spread out all over the world. We have information they are trying to pull Mideastern terrorist organizations into the fold. This money you see here being loaded on this plane might be cash flow to buy Russian nuclear, chemical, or biological weaponry. And that means any Saddam wanna-be who can scare up enough oil cash is in the game. The potential for harm here is enormous and frightening."

"One question: If this brand-new money comes directly from the Federal Reserve, why the hell is the government letting it go on?"

"A lot of this money will never come back here. It costs our government only four cents to make one of these hundreds. For every hundred-dollar bill that disappears into the black hole of the Third World, the government makes ninety-nine dollars and ninety-six cents. That adds up fast."

"Okay," Eddie said. "I'm softened up, ready for the kill."

"Obviously, we have to take Borodenko down. We need a serious informant, someone with firsthand knowledge about Borodenko's operation. We want to put bugs in as many locations as possible. I know you tried to hand us Lexy Petrov, but my bosses don't think all those little scams are enough to make him cooperate. They figure you got someone else in your pocket."

"Will this court order cover Kate's kidnapping?"

"Eddie, we need your commitment, no matter what."

"You didn't answer my question. Will the court order cover the kidnapping?"

"I'll do all I can to get it added. If not, I'll get the word out informally. The more bugs we get in, the better the chances we hear something about Kate or Sergei. As soon as anything is said that even hints of the kidnapping, we'll amend the warrant immediately. If one word about her is uttered, we'll be all over it."

"We're talking about right now. Not six weeks from now."

"Soon as I can get the affidavit typed up."

"Drive me back to my car," Eddie said.

On the way back to Brooklyn, Eddie again gave them Lexy Petrov, his old friend and bartender. He told Boland he had a tape recording of a drunken Lexy confessing to the murder of Evesi Volshin. Volshin was still alive on the floor of the Samovar when Lexy walked over and beat his skull with a lead pipe. Some nights, in a vodka haze, Lexy liked to brag about killing Volshin. He'd reach under the bar and pull out a lead pipe, then show the bits of Evesi's blood and hair embedded in the black electrical tape that wrapped around the pipe. This pipe was now in Eddie's trunk.

"Lexy knows everything," Eddie said. "And he'll roll over."

"We'll pick him up tonight," Boland said as his cell phone rang.

Screw Lexy, Eddie thought. He'd given him the chance to show his friendship yesterday. Maybe he didn't know about Kate, but Eddie had no doubt he knew something about Sergei. Eddie heard Boland say, "You're shittin' me!" He put the phone down, grinning and shaking his head.

"They identified the head they threw on your lawn," Boland said.

"Fast work."

"Extensive dental work made it easy," he said, still grinning in amazement. "The guy had top-notch reconstructive work by some famous dentist to the stars in Manhattan. Just a few years ago. Luckily, it stayed pretty much intact, considering all the trauma to his face. This guy took a hell of a beating before they sliced his head off."

"Anybody I should know?"

"Actually, yeah," Boland said. "It's Paul Caruso, Eddie. Your ex-partner, Paulie the Priest."

# CHAPTER
# 18

DUST ROSE from the dirt floor of the basement of the North End Tavern. The floor had been a dirt one since Kieran Dunne first bought the place in the 1950s. Kevin talked about pouring concrete but never got around to it. It didn't matter to Eddie, who spent more time down there than anyone else. He liked the dank, beery smell; it seemed to fit the raw sport he loved. The sweet science, although not sweet tonight. Viciously, he pounded away on the duct-taped heavy bag that hung from the ceiling's center beam, trying to exorcise all that haunted him. He punished the seventy-pound canvas bag, manhandling it as if it were a feather pillow.

"I remember the first time I saw you hit somebody," Babsie Panko said. She was sitting on an empty beer keg.

"Who did I hit?"

"My brother Gus. At my niece's christening. You were both drunk. Gus got mad and threw a punch. You hit him back. He fell and knocked over the pot of kielbasa. Daddy threw you both out."

Eddie barely remembered. He'd gotten drunk at a dozen

Panko christenings, weddings, or wakes. He'd usually gotten an early start because he helped Babsie's older brothers carry chairs they'd borrowed from the Brelesky Brothers funeral home. They'd carried two dozen folding chairs ten blocks, from the funeral parlor through the streets of Yonkers to their apartment above the butcher shop.

"That was the first time you danced with me," she said.

"Probably why Gus punched me."

"You were a senior, eighteen, I think. I was a freshman, just turned fourteen."

"No wonder he hit me," Eddie said.

Eddie shuffled, working with the bag's movement, throwing hooks when it swung side to side, straight punches when it swung toward him. He remembered Richie Costa breaking his wrist the first time he worked out on the heavy bag. The trick was to hit it with the front of your fist, no angles. Hit in the middle of its horizontal axis and it wouldn't spin.

"We have to talk about your old partner, Eddie. Even you have to agree now that all this has something to do with an old case, or something you guys did together. Throwing his head on your lawn is a message even Irish guys should be able to understand."

Grace, skipping rope inside the ring, was far enough away that they could talk. The ring was only a foot off the ground. Kieran had bought the canvas and ring ropes at a CYO auction. The Dunnes drove spikes in the dirt and hammered out a wooden frame made from sections of two-by-fours Kieran had salvaged from the old P. Ballantine and Sons Brewery. The basement, like much of the bar, was salvage. Kieran liked to brag he'd never bought a new piece of wood in his life.

"They have a cause of death?" Eddie asked.

"The ME might not be able to determine an exact cause of death as it is now, but timewise, she thinks five to ten days, minimum. She says he was brutally beaten before he died; that much is sure."

"I didn't even know he was in New York."

"He wasn't," Babsie said. "At least customs can't find how or where he entered the country."

Babsie asked Eddie to tell her about Paulie Caruso. Talking in short bursts of air, punctuated by grunts and the thump of his fists against canvas, he started with his nickname. Paulie first started being known as "the Priest" when he was working undercover on prostitution. The undercover cop's job was to allow a street hooker to make an offer of sex for money, then signal the wagon to pick her up. Eventually, the street girls would begin to recognize the same undercover cops and run. Disguises were called for. Paul Caruso had one brother in the priesthood and one in the mob. The good died young, and Paulie inherited a closetful of black suits and white collars, plus a collection of vestments in colors to match the many moods of the Catholic church. Paulie began wearing the black suit and backward collar on Eighth Avenue. It was a surefire act. Girls propositioned him every step of the way. The van would drive along behind him and scoop up the hot-pants crowd like they were lost souls at a tent revival. The archdiocese finally heard about it and stopped it. But Paulie still became a man of the cloth whenever the spirit hit him. It was the least of his sins. Paulie the Priest was instant insanity . . . just add alcohol and stir. He danced the tarantella . . . straddling the fragile line between heaven and hell.

"Any truth to the rumor he was working for the Gambino family?" Babsie said.

"He probably told his brother some things. But he didn't work at it."

Eddie's friendship with Paulie the Priest was one of many bad choices he had made in those days. The Priest had been in the Coney Island squad for five years when Eddie arrived. At that time, the precinct was a dumping ground for detectives on the verge of losing the gold shield. The new police commissioner failed to see the wisdom of throwing all those fallen angels into the same pit. He set out to change the practice, infusing the old dumping-grounds precincts with top-notch detectives. The Priest welcomed Eddie to Coney Island with an extended tour of local watering holes. Eddie's career went downhill from there.

"So, any case stand out in your mind?" she said. "Any one thing you and Caruso did together that might be coming back to haunt you?"

"How long have you been a cop?" Eddie said, breathing hard. He stopped throwing punches and held the heavy bag from swaying.

"Almost twenty," she said.

"Then you know this could be from one small confrontation that happened years ago. A traffic ticket, or a domestic dispute where the husband blames you for humiliating him in front of his wife. You forget about it ten minutes after you leave the apartment, but for the next ten years, he plots to kill you."

"Why don't we just focus on the Russians and the years you worked them with Paul Caruso. I'm betting there's something hinky buried in there somewhere."

"He was the best cop I ever worked with."

"Funny," she said. "I heard he was a no-good thieving bastard."

"That, too."

The Priest was almost too good a cop. Eddie always said that if his life was in danger, he'd want him on the case. The Priest not only saw through every lowlife's con, but knew how much swag they had in their pockets, and when it would be his. But everything he did, he did to excess; one drink was too many, a thousand not enough. He lived his life with a kamikaze recklessness, as if trying to guarantee an obit listing every cause of death known to modern man. Although beheading would not have been on Eddie's list of predictions.

"Boland said the reason you resigned is because IAB asked you to wear a wire to bring down Caruso."

"In those days, you didn't entrap your partner," Eddie said.

"What I get from you is, He's my partner, right or wrong."

"I didn't say that."

"They had a picture of his villa in Sicily in the *Daily News* today. Right on the water. Worth over a million dollars. Sounds dirty to me, Eddie."

Grace moved from the ring to a line of beer kegs, making noise just to hear it. She played some kind of clanging song with an old rusted hammer. Pipes ran from the kegs up to the taps at the bar. Kevin had put some of the kegs into a refrigerated locker—mostly for the younger crowd, the light-beer lovers. The old-timers didn't like their beer that cold, so Kevin let a few kegs sit out. Kevin claimed that tap beer was better years ago, the heads fuller, when you had to pump the lines by hand. Now with compressed-air systems, it came out flat. The new nitrogen and $CO_2$ combination tanks were hard to keep in balance. Clean the lines often and wash the glasses in hot soapy water, that was Kevin's simple rule. Either way, the basement still smelled like a brewery.

"What do you want me to say?" Eddie said, stopping for breath. "Paulie was a guy who would take a hot stove and the kitchen sink. And maybe he did work for the Gambino family. The bottom line is, I don't care. All I care about is getting Kate back."

"That's all I want, too, Eddie. But Paulie Caruso *is* the bottom line. Paulie and you. What's happened here is not coincidence."

"I know that. I've thought through all the old cases. We pissed a lot of people off. But we're talking about fourteen years ago." Eddie grabbed a towel and wiped the sweat out of his eyes. "You know anyone in customs?" he asked.

"Don't change the subject."

"I'm not. You mentioned customs before and it got me thinking. You know anyone who could expedite a passport?"

"Why do you need a passport?"

"I don't," he said, pointing a gloved hand at Grace. "I have a passport, but I've been thinking about a trip to Ireland this summer. My mother has never seen Grace. We've got a slew of cousins over there."

After she sold the bar to Kevin, Teresa Dunne took the proceeds and her Social Security checks back to Ireland, where she bought a drafty two-story stone house in Dungarvan, County Waterford, the town of her birth. Always content alone, Teresa now spent her days walking among her ancestors in the windswept St. Mary's graveyard and staring out at the Irish Sea.

"This came up suddenly," Babsie said. "Some people are going to think the wrong thing. Like maybe, say, your son-in-law makes a move to gain custody. You're planning to whisk her out of the country."

"Who cares what they think?"

"I know somebody," Babsie said. "But you gotta promise me you won't do anything stupid."

"Stupid was dancing with you when you were fourteen years old. We didn't do any Irish dancing, did we?"

"Are you kidding? In my father's house? No, it was a slow dance. Johnny Mathis, 'The Twelfth of Never.' "

"Jesus. Your brother should have shot me."

# CHAPTER
# 19

FRIDAY, APRIL 10
9:00 A.M.

CITY COPS BROUGHT their own coffee into the FBI building, even though they knew the rich kids had everything.
Eddie Dunne found Matty Boland at the dingy lunch
wagon wedged under the approach to the Brooklyn
Bridge, directly behind NYPD headquarters at One
Police Plaza. They were both due at the FBI's New York
headquarters for a hastily called meeting of the joint task
force investigating Russian organized crime in the United
States.

"Why the hell are we here?" Eddie asked. "Why aren't
we out knocking on doors?"

"Buyer's remorse," Boland said. "It's the whole thing
with Paulie Caruso, Eddie. Guys like the Priest make
them nervous."

The sudden appearance of the severed head of Eddie's
old partner had injected doubt into the task force's plans to
use him as the foundation of their assault on the Russian
*mafiya* in New York. He couldn't blame them for being
careful; the feds didn't need another embarrassment. But
shouldn't his daughter's life outweigh their anxiety?

Eddie bought a container of black coffee and a buttered bagel at the wagon. Today, they'd run a hard-nosed Q&A, "give him a scare," as Paulie the Priest used to say. Then, he hoped, it would be back to the business of finding his daughter. The caffeine jolt would help him stay sharp through the barrage of fedspeak he was sure to hear.

"Maybe you should give some serious thought to calling a lawyer," Boland said. "They're going to screw you around up there. I don't have to tell you the horror stories; you know them as well as I do."

"I need these people to help me, Matty. I'm willing to listen to what they have to say."

"I *know* what they're going to say. They're going to put this case on hold until they can figure out exactly how you and the Priest are involved. The feds are great for holding off and hoping the problem goes away. And remember . . ." Boland put his hand to his ear in the universal sign for a phone call.

"They're already tapping my phone," Eddie said.

"Then check your house for bugs. They're going to protect their own asses. That's priority one with the high-level feds. By the time they jump back in this case, the Russians will have sold the Lincoln Tunnel to the Iranians. We'll be swimming to Jersey."

"I'll swim to Jersey. Just find Kate."

Eddie had parked his Olds in the underground public garage at Madison Street and the Avenue of the Finest. The garage was located directly underneath NYPD headquarters. Uniformed cops stood at the entrance, checking for car bombs. Eddie wound up parking three levels below the building. It marked the closest he'd been to headquarters since the day a civilian clerk had flipped his

detective shield into a cardboard box containing the
badges of the recently quit, fired, retired, or dead. The
guy just tossed it on the anonymous pile with dozens of
numbered metal pieces engraved with the seal of the city
of New York. *Clink,* it's over. Finality bestowed by some
overweight desk jockey treating each shield as if it were
a meaningless chunk of tin. The lazy bastard couldn't
have cared less that each one of those shields had spent
the last few decades pinned to some cop's breast pocket
and was therefore witness to the unspeakable. Each could
tell a million stories. He should have genuflected in their
presence.

"The guy who called this meeting is a pretentious bastard," Boland said. "Last month, we were at the Ninth
Precinct with the two uniformed cops who locked up that
diplomat's kid. We needed to get downtown quick for a
press conference, so we grab the subway. We get to the platform and this guy hears the *bing-bong*—you know, the signal that they're closing the subway doors. He tells everyone
that the *bing-bong* is a descending major third—like an E
to a C—like the beginning of Beethoven's Fifth. The cops
looked at him like he was a Martian or a stone fag. I was
embarrassed to be with the guy."

It was a five-minute walk across Foley Square from
One Police Plaza to 26 Federal Plaza. On weekdays, the
square was populated by jurors, bored civil servants,
tourists looking for Little Italy or Chinatown, and film
crews using the steps of the Federal Courthouse for background. Sometimes, when they were shooting a movie
scene, you'd have to walk around police barriers. It was
still only a five-minute walk. Boland was stalling.

"I can't believe you remembered 'a descending major
third,' " Eddie said.

"My mother was a music teacher. But my point is, I wouldn't say that in front of cops."

"You have something you want to say to *me*, Matty?"

"Yeah, I was just going to tell you. Internal Affairs is sending a courier with your file and the Caruso file. I offered to bring them, save them the trip—that way, you'd get a peek. But no dice."

"You'd probably get a hernia lugging those files."

"I just want to warn you that IAB will be there dredging up the past. I know you're out a long time and all. But at this stage of my career, I don't need anyone thinking I'm part of some rat squad ambush."

"Don't worry about it," Eddie said. "I have a high pain threshold. I don't care what the hell they dredge up, as long as they keep looking."

On the corner of Worth Street, familiar faces gathered in the early stages of a small demonstration. The same core group had manned every antigovernment rally for the past twenty years. Yellow signs stood ready, stacked against a pole. The slogans demanded freedom for the manipulative and articulate killer of a Philadelphia cop.

"I gotta ask," Boland said. "How come you refused to testify against the Priest? You could have saved your own ass."

"It was a bullshit case; they were trying to nail him for other things."

"I heard he was a very dirty cop."

"It depends on what you mean by 'dirty.' The Priest was a dinosaur. He never saw anything wrong with accepting a free meal or a free cup of coffee."

"Free hotel rooms, free cars, free trips to Puerto Rico," Boland added.

"Probably a lot more than that in his early days. He

slowed down after the Knapp Commission, but he was a stubborn bastard. He should have seen the handwriting on the wall and retired."

"They got you guys for consorting with known criminals," Boland said.

"At his niece's graduation party. He'd been consorting with those people all his life. He couldn't've avoided them if he'd wanted to."

"Story I heard is that half the Gambino family was there. That's what bothers me, Eddie. You had to have known that someone would be taking pictures. The feds or the rat squad, somebody. I can't believe you just walked into that."

"It was during my Johnnie Walker Black period. All I cared about was the next glass in my hand."

The view from the small conference room on the twenty-eighth floor of 26 Federal Plaza was spectacular. The confluence of the Hudson and East rivers at the tip of the narrow island gave a clear perspective on the amount of water surrounding and bisecting the boroughs. But like most natives, Eddie Dunne was more interested in the brick and mortar than the coastline. He looked for roofs he'd made love on, roofs he'd caught homicides on. He had to amuse himself somehow; thus far, they'd excluded him from the meeting.

Eddie had finished his coffee and bagel and read all he wanted of the *New York Post*. He started looking around the room, trying to figure out where they'd hidden the camera and mike. The FBI tech men were much better than in the days when they wired a mike into a TV set, then sat it dead center in the middle of the room. The only thing in the center of this room was an odd-shaped chunk of polished brown granite in the center of a small table. On it was a brass plaque that read ALFRED P. MURRAH FEDERAL BUILDING, APRIL 19, 1995.

No goddamn reason for making me wait this long, he thought. Arrogant bastards couldn't find a junkie in Harlem without guys like me. Eddie walked over to a large mirror and placed his fingernail against it. There was no gap between his fingernail and the image of it in the mirror. It was a two-way mirror. If it had been a real mirror, there would have been a space between his nail and its image.

After ninety minutes, he heard the sound of heels clicking on the tile floor. Special Agent Stacey Powers, a young woman with a Southern accent, led him two turns down the hallway, then into a conference room that faced uptown. She pointed out a seat at the end of a long, polished table, next to a grim-faced Matty Boland. Yellow pads and pencils were stacked in the center of the table. Powers introduced seven nonsmiling males, agents or attorneys, all crisp and buttoned-down. Then she went straight to the first question: When was the last time he'd seen Paul Caruso?

"Fourteen years ago at a party in Queens," Eddie said. "I never saw him again after that."

"Any correspondence between you since he moved to Sicily?"

"None."

"Do you know if Detective Caruso ever returned home to the United States again after that?"

"If he did, he didn't call me," Eddie said. "Ask his brother."

"We spoke to Mr. Caruso," Powers said.

Agent Powers gave Eddie a quick, annoyed glance, then said there was no record of him ever returning, not even this time. Friends and neighbors thought he was traveling in Europe again. Local police considered Paul Caruso an international playboy, jetting off to Amsterdam or the French Riviera on a whim. No one had any idea how his skull had arrived in New York, or where the rest of his body might be hiding.

Agent Powers said, "According to your department's records, you had a fistfight with Detective Paul Caruso at a graduation party in June of 1984, in the backyard of Angelo Caruso's house."

"It wasn't a real fight."

"He needed extensive dental work following the encounter."

"Paulie liked to do Robert De Niro imitations," Eddie said. "He was doing De Niro playing Jake La Motta in *Raging Bull*. I was supposed to be Sugar Ray Robinson. He'd had a little too much to drink and stepped into a punch."

"I understand that was the last time he spoke to you."

"That's true."

"Tell us about Marvin Rosenfeld," a new questioner said from behind them.

All heads turned to a man sitting in one of the four leather chairs that surrounded a glass coffee table. French cuffs, blue shirt with a white collar. He'd come in after the introductions, carrying a teacup, complete with saucer.

"Marvin Rosenfeld started out as a tax attorney," Eddie said, addressing his answer across the table to Agent Powers. "He had an office on Remsen Street in the seventies. Then he started working as a financial adviser for a scumbag Russian crime boss named Evesi Volshin."

"Rosenfeld lived in Manhattan Beach," French Cuffs said.

"And he died there," Eddie added.

Eddie figured French Cuffs was the assistant special agent in charge. The one who claimed to know the musical roots of the subway *bing-bong*. He had no yellow pad of his own. Eddie figured the conversation was being recorded. Agent Powers took notes for effect.

"Rosenfeld was murdered at home in March of 1984," French Cuffs said. "Tell me about that homicide and the Marine Park shooting that followed it."

"Nineteen eighty-four was a long time ago. Agent Powers has the files in front of her."

"Humor me," French Cuffs said. "Tell me about that day."

Eddie told him that he and Detective Paul Caruso were working off the detective chart, investigating a rash of burglaries in upscale Manhattan Beach. They spotted a souped-up Dodge Charger parked in the driveway of the expensive home of local attorney Marvin Rosenfeld. They figured Rosenfeld wasn't the muscle-car type. Detective Caruso drove around the block once more. On the second pass, they saw two men they knew to be Brooklyn thugs tossing black plastic trash bags into the Charger. It didn't look like trash removal or anything legitimate. It looked purely wrong. Caruso parked half a block away. A few minutes later, the Charger backed out of the driveway. They followed it a short distance east on the Belt Parkway to a deserted employee parking area in Marine Park. The Charger pulled behind a park storage building, where the two men had apparently hidden a second vehicle. When they began transferring the bags to the second vehicle, the two detectives moved in. They came up on them quickly, guns drawn, loudly identifying themselves: "Police! Freeze!" The two thugs began firing. The detectives returned fire, killing both men. Eddie pointed out that both he and the Priest won the Medal of Honor for this incident, the highest decoration awarded by the NYPD.

"You just happened to be there," French Cuffs said.

"It's called police work."

"You didn't call for backup?" he asked.

"No radio. Not all detective cars had radios in those days. We always signed out the cars that didn't."

"Why was that?"

"If you had a radio, they always called you back into the house for annoying errands: Pick up lunch, coffee, booze, drive the boss to a meeting. Things like that."

"The guys who did the robbery, Santo Vestri and Ray Nuñez, who were they?"

"Two half-assed wanna-be gangsters," Eddie said. "Consignment guys, mostly. They'd get rid of hijacked loads for a percentage: TVs, fur coats, drugstore supplies, anything."

"Two small-time punks who died in a police shootout," French Cuffs said. "Who the hell cared, right?"

"Not even their mothers," Eddie said, turning to look at him. "These guys murdered both Marvin Rosenfeld and his wife, Svetlana, while their little girl sat right there. They shot the parents to death right in front of her."

"But you didn't know this at the time of your encounter in Marine Park."

"If we had, we wouldn't have gone so easy on them."

"Were you outraged enough to follow up on the shooting, Mr. Dunne? What happened to the child?"

"The wife's parents moved back to Russia, took the

little girl. She drowned a year or two later. Fell into an icy lake."

"My report says hypothermia," Agent Powers said.

"The record indicates you recovered a lot of money from the trunk of that Dodge Charger."

"Front page of the *Daily News* said four point two million," Eddie said.

"Four point two million," French Cuffs said. "How did a small-time lawyer like Rosenfeld come to have so much cash?"

"I'm sure that's also in that file Agent Powers is holding."

"I read it," French Cuffs said. "It says that in the early 1980s, Marvin Rosenfeld was a money launderer who worked for the man you mentioned. Evesi Volshin was *the* major Russian crime boss in Brighton Beach up until that week. The four point two million was Volshin's money, believed to be from the lucrative gasoline-tax scam, waiting to be laundered. The money was coming in so fast, they had a hard time getting it all out. Hundreds of millions, if you believe the rumors."

"I'm sure all the rumors are in the FBI report," Eddie said.

"The report also mentions that Anatoly Lukin, your former employer, was the real mastermind of the gas-tax scam. Or was that only a rumor?"

"Evesi Volshin was an idiot; I'm sure someone else was the brains. Lukin would be my guess, too."

"Volshin himself was murdered a few days after Rosenfeld," French Cuffs said. "Anatoly Lukin then took over the Russian mob. Isn't that correct?"

"And your next question," Eddie said, "is about my relationship with Anatoly Lukin."

"No sense in me asking, then, is there?"

Eddie said, "First, let me tell you that Evesi Volshin was a vicious bastard who preyed on his own people. Russian people in Brooklyn started celebrating in the street the minute they heard he was dead. He was shot and beaten to death in a crowded restaurant. No witnesses. A hundred people have taken credit for his murder."

"So you agree that Anatoly Lukin took over his operation on that day?"

"Common knowledge," Eddie said. "But what you're leading up to is the fact that shortly after those murders, Anatoly Lukin hired me. And that makes you think I had something to do with the murders."

"It doesn't matter what I think," French Cuffs said. "It's an investigative dead end. You're the only witness left alive."

"Mr. Dunne," Agent Powers said. "Last Tuesday, you told Detective Boland about several black binders that Anatoly Lukin kept in his office. You said they contained dummy corporations. Where did they come from?"

"From Marvin Rosenfeld. The guy was an expert in dummy corporations before it was fashionable. He made them up in advance. Dozens of phony corporations at a time. He kept them in black binders and sold them to any interested party."

"How did the binders move from Rosenfeld's possession into Lukin's?" she asked. "The Brooklyn DA never took those binders into evidence on the day of the murders."

Eddie stood and nodded to the silent group around the table. For all he knew, they'd had their tongues clipped in Quantico.

"Mr. Dunne," Agent Powers said. "The binders are

missing. Apparently, someone stole them from Lukin's apartment shortly after he was shoved under the train."

"I don't have them."

"You disappeared for almost an hour after Lukin's death," French Cuffs said.

Eddie glared across the table at Matty Boland. He'd chased Lukin's killer to a construction site and come back with the coat. But that didn't prove anything to them. Witnesses identified the coat as the killer's, but the feds always saw Machiavellian plots when city cops were involved.

Eddie stood up and walked to the door.

Agent Powers said, "We have a duty to protect the reputation of the United States government, Mr. Dunne. This doesn't mean we'll stop looking for your daughter. We want you to understand that."

"If I were you, I wouldn't do anything foolish," French Cuffs said.

"Actually," Eddie said, "this is the smartest thing I've done in a long time."

# CHAPTER
# 20

### FRIDAY
### 11:00 A.M.

EDDIE'S PULSE SLOWED in the cool darkness of the
Brooklyn-Battery Tunnel. The more he thought about it,
the more he understood what had happened. He'd been
around bosses like French Cuffs before. Public service
was invented for them. One of the many ways they
avoided taking action was by suggesting the possibility
of some serpentine scheme that would undermine the
plan's success. Take no chances. This ensured the
longevity of the mediocre. Eddie couldn't prove he'd
chased the woman in the wool coat, so French Cuffs
hinted at his possible duplicity. God forbid they embarrass the Bureau. Careerwise, it was always safer to do
nothing. Paulie the Priest had called it "empty-suit disease."

All Eddie had learned in 26 Federal Plaza was from
Boland as he chased him across the plaza. Boland said
that Sergei Zhukov lived in Rego Park. They had agents
sitting on his house, as well as the Eurobar and a restaurant he frequented in Queens named the Registan. Other
agents were interviewing friends of Misha. Boland told

him he needed to calm down. Eddie said he'd calm down when someone besides Babsie Panko came up with a decent lead. He told him to concentrate on Sergei. Find him and all would be forgiven.

Out of the tunnel, in the sunlight again, Eddie squinted to find the sign for the Belt Parkway. He could think like French Cuffs, too. His own natural paranoia had already created a dozen scenarios, some involving the FBI in the kidnapping. But they were all too complicated. Answers are always simpler than that. Keep it simple, he reminded himself, or you'll wind up with your head up your ass, like Special Agent French Cuffs.

The Howard Beach Boccie Club sat on a quiet street of one- and two-family homes, surrounded and shaded by old trees. There were no signs outside. Those inside knew who they were and why they belonged. Behind the trees, the club was protected by an eight-foot chain-link fence and the reputation of its members.

Eddie pushed the gate open. A quartet of old men in flowered shirts and dark pants had congregated under a gazebo near the far corner. Eddie waited as they spoke softly in a lyrical Italian. Sotto voce. They spoke softly in English, as well. In fact, these men had spent their lives in hushed conversations. Eddie waited for Angelo Caruso to acknowledge him. It was Angelo's move. After a minute, three men stood up and walked away.

"How ya doin', champ?" one of them said as he bobbed and weaved in a fighter's stance, feinting short slow-motion jabs at Eddie. Eddie still got this every now and then, despite the fact that his fight career had ended over thirty years ago. Guys like Ali and Frazier must get it all the time, he thought. People dancing around them, throwing punches. He wondered if they were tempted to reach out and smack them down. He bet nobody tried this with Mike Tyson.

Angelo called Eddie over and welcomed him with an affectionate hug.

"The court looks good," Eddie said. "New scoreboard, ball holders, the works."

"Looks ain't everything," Angelo said. "It still don't drain right. Every time it rains, we sweep puddles. Cost us twelve grand for this, and we're bowling through mud half the time. Is it asking too much to slope a piece of ground so it drains? It's not rocket science, is it?"

In his early seventies now, Angelo had just begun to look as old as his younger brother had—the last time Eddie saw Paulie the Priest, that is. The mob guy had led a healthier life than the cop. The Priest used to say that for every five years Angelo spent in prison, he came out looking ten years younger. A ring of white hair circled the well-tanned bald head. Silver-framed glasses sat on an aquiline nose.

"I heard about your daughter. I have people sniffing around about this. It's not right, this kidnapping thing the Russians do. Fucking animals, if you ask me."

"Richie Costa is working on it, too," Eddie said.

"Richie is off-limits to you now, Eddie. I heard all about it, and interceded on your behalf. I can understand one time, your emotions all jumbled. Our kids make us crazy, and this situation is a heartache. But once is all we can forgive. *Capisce?*"

Angelo picked up an unlabeled gallon jug of red wine. He filled a pair of clear plastic cups two-thirds full. He handed one to Eddie and held his up in a toast.

"To Paulie," he said.

Without drinking to his ex-partner, Eddie put the cup back down on the table. "What the hell is going on, Ange?"

"I should ask you that question. They threw his head at your door, not mine."

"Was Paulie in business with the Russians?"

"I should know? Paulie was Paulie. Nobody could predict my brother. Not even when he was a little baby. Paulie lived like he wanted to. Caution to the wind. You know that, the shit he pulled with you."

They both turned to watch a white-haired man in a Panama hat as he tossed a small natural-colored ball, the *pallina,* or "little nut," down the other end of the clay court. There would be no serious play today, in deference to the death in the family. They were playing only to take the focus off the conversation between the ex-cop and the old mob boss.

"Sunday is the service," Angelo said. "Our Lady of Consolation, two o'clock. I didn't think they would do it on a Sunday, but the priest was kind enough to allow a small Mass for my brother."

"I'm sure you'll be generous."

"We must do all we can for the One Holy Catholic and Apostolic Church, Eddie. No burial ceremony, though. We'll add his name to the stone, underneath his brother's. If his body turns up later, we'll cremate. They let you cremate now, as long as you promise not to throw the ashes."

"Paulie always said he wanted his ashes spread in Vegas," Eddie said.

"The Mirage, that's right. He loved the Mirage. Maybe I can make a call."

"Why did he leave Sicily?" Eddie asked.

"Who knew he left? Three weeks ago, I talked to him; he was home. Maybe a little more than three, but everyone thought he was in Sicily. My sister talked after I did, a few days maybe."

"He got over here somehow," Eddie said.

"You figure that out all by yourself?"

I figured out more than you can imagine, Eddie thought. Partners spend a lot of long hours together. Eddie knew a few Caruso family secrets.

"Was he using other identities?" Eddie asked. "There's no record of him leaving Sicily. Any other name he might have on a bogus passport?"

"I think he was dead when he got here, Eddie. I know some people in Sicily—they went over and looked at his house. His villa was wrecked, his safe emptied. They said there was blood all over the place."

"This safe," Eddie said, measuring his words. "What did Paulie have in it?"

Angelo smiled. Eddie held his arms out as if inviting Angelo to search him for a wire.

"My brother should have been more like you," Angelo said. "He was not careful."

"Too many people are careless, Ange. That's why there's so much trouble in the world."

"I don't know what he kept in his safe," Angelo said, blowing a smoke ring. "Maybe the panties of his old girl-friends." Eddie noticed the stump of his little finger. Angelo bragged that it had been chopped off by a hit man from Calabria. Paulie told him it was a woodworking accident in his garage.

Eddie said, "Did Paulie ever mention a set of black loose-leaf binders that belonged to Marvin Rosenfeld? They contained phony corporations."

"Yeah, Paulie sold them to Anatoly Lukin. Why the hell do you think Lukin hired you? I thought partners told each other everything."

"We know different about Paulie, don't we, Ange?"

"Let's not speak ill of the dead, my friend."

Wooden balls rolled across the deep red clay. A red ball close to the *pallina* was knocked away by the green ball. The old man in the Panama hat slapped dust off his hands, pleased with himself.

Angelo said, "You ever see Paulie's villa?"

"Never had the pleasure."

"You never went, really?"

Eddie took a deep breath and looked away. A breeze blew, shuffling papers on the tabletop: a *Racing Form,* a copy of the *New York Post* Eddie had read from cover to cover in the FBI office a few hours earlier. Angelo took a metal tape measure and used it as a paperweight on the *Racing Form.*

"My brother, the ex-cop," Angelo said, "he builds a house that should have been on *Lifestyles of the Rich and Famous.* I tried to talk to him, but he never listened. He thinks because he's in Italy he can spend like a drunken sailor and no one will notice. Called attention to himself, that's what he did."

"Paulie keep a lot of money in the safe?" Eddie asked.

Angelo laughed and shook his head.

"If the motive was robbery," Eddie said, "why did they throw his head at my house?"

"Because someone knows more than they should, my friend."

"Knows what?" Eddie asked.

"My brother is dead. Stop playing games, Eddie."

"If there was some secret to know," Eddie said, "how would these people who killed Paulie hear about it?"

"Maybe Paulie told them. They beat him, tortured him, and he told them."

"How would they know enough to ask Paulie the question in the first place?"

"It has been my experience over the years," Angelo said, "the bigger the secret, the shorter its life."

"I would think the opposite."

"You are some piece of work," Angelo said, "you know that? I remember the first time my brother brought you to my house. You had the balls to tell that joke about a little kid playing with shit in the street. Remember that? A kid making a statue with shit. When someone asked him what he was doing, he said he was making a statue of an Italian cop. At first, I thought my friends were going to throw you on the barbecue pit. I said to Paulie, 'Who is this stupid Irish bastard telling guinea jokes here, of all places?' "

"They didn't."

"I know. You got their attention, got it good, and then you delivered the punch line: The person asked the little kid why he didn't make an Irish cop instead. The kid said he was going to but he didn't have enough shit."

Angelo laughed; the joke still had a bite for him. Eddie was struck by the peacefulness of all the sounds. The soft breeze through the leaves of the trees, the wooden boccie balls rolling, a rake combing lines in the copper-colored clay, the voices.

"So I shouldn't be surprised," Angelo said, "you have the balls to come here and accuse me of being a rat."

"I'm not accusing you of anything, Angelo. I'm trying to figure out how many eyes I should keep open at night."

"Keep them all open, Eddie. Just like I do. And stay away from Richie Costa. That's your last warning."

# CHAPTER

# 21

**FRIDAY**
**3:00 P.M.**

THE AFTERNOON TURNED into one of those warm spring days when you can smell the new grass. Eddie threw his raincoat in the backseat. He'd worn a sports jacket for the FBI meeting. He should have arrived in a ripped T-shirt. That would have been the wardrobe they expected. If Eddie despised one thing in his life, it was bullies. His rules were simple: He hated people who hurt other people. It didn't matter whether it was physically, emotionally, or financially. French Cuffs had used the FBI's muscle in a heartless, cowardly way. At a time when Eddie was desperate, this arrogant bastard had decided to play tough guy. With an innocent woman's life in the balance. There'll come a day, Eddie thought. There'll come a day.

Warm weather had lured the denizens of the Bronx into the streets. Jump ropes snapped, Rollerblades whirred, and boom boxes confirmed that rap now ruled. Eddie parked at a meter in front of the bakery on East 187th Street. He put his S&W in the purple Crown Royal bag and wedged it in the seat springs. Ten minutes later, he came through the door of the Bronx Knights Social Club with both hands raised above his head. He held a flat white box in the air.

"Peace," he yelled to a dozen gun barrels pointed his way.

"Just do a one-eighty, Eddie," Lino Terra said. "Don't let the door hit you in the ass on the way out."

"Cannolis from Ferrara's," Eddie said. "An offer you can't refuse." He put the box on the table and opened it. He stepped back, held his jacket open to show he was unarmed.

"Stick those up your ass," Richie Costa said. Richie's face was half-covered by a white bandage. He looked like the Phantom of the Opera.

"I just left Angelo Caruso," Eddie said. "He said I could talk to Richie for five minutes as long as I behaved myself."

"I don't give a shit about Angelo Caruso," Richie said. "You get your ass outta here, and take your fucking pastries with you."

"Angelo said we're all family men," Eddie said. "His brother and I were family. He said you guys would understand."

"We understood one time," Lino Terra said. "You don't get away with that shit twice."

"I'm not here to hit anyone," Eddie said.

"Good-bye," Lino said.

"Most of you guys have kids," Eddie said. "Lino, back me up here. If someone snatched your beautiful little girl Marissa from Saint Anthony's one morning, you'd understand then, right? A bunch of you guys have kids; I know that. Or maybe I'm wrong here. Maybe you can't know until it happens to you. How helpless you feel, how desperate."

"Is that a threat, you crazy fuck?" Lino said.

"Somebody shoot this mick cocksucker," someone yelled.

"Do something for me," Eddie said. "This is all I ask. When you tuck your kids in tonight, give them a kiss for me. I would never want any of you guys to feel the pain I'm going through right now. That's from the bottom of my heart."

"You always go too far, Eddie," Lino said.

"How far would you go, Lino? All I'm asking is one simple thing: I want to talk to Richie for five minutes. Come on . . . you can't give me five minutes?"

The ticking of a ceiling fan was the only noise. The TV above the bar had the sound turned down. They were watching CNBC; the stock market ticker ran across the screen. Like the micks from Yonkers, the bent-nose guys from the Bronx Knights were into their portfolios. Lino Terra patted Eddie down. They gave him five minutes with Richie, out of earshot, but they'd be watching.

"Make this quick, asshole," Richie said.

Eddie gently touched Richie's shoulder. He could feel him trembling.

"You are my last hope," Eddie said softly. "Without you, my daughter dies."

"Don't put that weight on me, you cocksucker. I had nothing to do with it and I don't know what the fuck is going on."

"I need to find Sergei Zhukov."

"Oh, like I know where the Russkies hang out."

"Don't make me beg here, Richie. I'm not good at it. I'm serious. I need you to be serious. Listen to me: If you don't help me here, I will kidnap Lino's daughter. Then I'll get the others. And they'll all know it's because of you, because that's exactly what I'll tell them before I leave here."

"Don't put me in the barrel like this. If I knew anything, I'd tell you. You gotta believe that. Only thing I know is that he lives in Queens. I went drinking with him a coupla times, after we closed the Eurobar."

"He lives in Rego Park. Where did you drink with him?"

"Always Russian clubs. One place in Manhattan, on Fifty-second Street, but mostly Brighton Beach joints. And poker games—the guy is a heavy-duty cardhead. One of the worst degenerate gamblers I ever saw. He'd bet on stupid shit, like two cabs pulling away from a light, old ladies running for a bus. Shit like that."

"Tell me about the card games," Eddie said.

"We hit a little game in one of the clubs, but the guy loves high stakes. He goes for ten, twenty grand without batting an eye. Every Friday night, he goes to this game. I went with him once. But it sucked. All Russian guys talking gibberish. You don't know if they're fucking you or laughing at you, or what."

"Where is the game?"

"You'll never find it. When I played, it was in an apartment on Avenue U. But it moves every week. They got these fucking psycho luggers."

"Where did you meet the luggers?"

"Parking lot on Brighton Eighth, near the beach. You park your car and they have luggers drive you to the game."

"How good are the luggers?"

"In-fucking-credible," Richie said. "Best wheelmen I ever saw. No way can you tail them. It's impossible. They go down one-way streets, make a U-turn, and come back

at you. Then they drive down another one-way street the
wrong way all the way. Red lights mean nothing. They
drive over the sidewalk. The guy we had drove through a
fucking park, across the softball field, a fucking city
park."

"Better than your dad's luggers?

"Better and way crazier. These mutts don't give a shit
about losing their licenses. They just get a new one sent
from Russia with a different name, then take it to Motor
Vehicles and get another New York license. No problem."

"Who else was at the game?"

"All Russian guys. I couldn't remember even if you
tortured me. I went to that one game. Miserable. I remember the food sucked. All this greasy shit, little white
fish that looked like that Jewish shit. All kinds of greasy
white sauces I never saw in my life. Some guy in a lab
coat delivered it. Sergei was bragging about the food. He
said they get it catered from some big deli in Brighton
Beach."

"M and I International?" Eddie said.

"Could be. Don't hold me to it."

Richie jumped when Eddie went to shake his hand.
Richie wasn't accepting apologies. The Bronx Knights
were never going to forget that beating, so Eddie grabbed
the cannolis, said, "Ciao," and left.

# CHAPTER

# 22

FRIDAY
6:00 P.M.

BIG STAKES CARD GAMES are all-night affairs. Eddie knew he wouldn't get to bed before dawn. He had a few hours before the start of his high-roller hunt for Sergei Zhukov, so he drove to Yonkers to touch base with the people who loved him, win or lose, his little cheering section from the hill. Friday nights, he knew exactly where they'd be.

It had taken Kevin Dunne several years to unearth the hidden character of the North End Tavern. He took all the credit because he and Eddie had done most of the work themselves. The art of renovation, Kevin claimed, was in knowing what not to change. Except for a steam cleaning, the old tin ceiling remained untouched, as did most of the original woodwork. They'd sanded and refinished the oak floors and replaced the bar with a classic mahogany horseshoe-style one they'd bought from a Connecticut salvage yard. The biggest visual difference came when they stripped the plaster walls away to expose the old brick, a move that sent the bar regulars home clucking about the latest Dunne brainstorm.

Kevin hoped the step back in time would help lure back

several decades' worth of Yonkers kids who'd moved up-state, the majority of them less than an hour away. Nostalgia was the hook. Kevin scoured the city, collecting old street signs and photographs of the city: the trolleys, Getty Square, the Schoolboys' Race, the Sacred Heart High School Bagpipe Band, the Yonkers Marathon, dozens of high school sports photographs, and Eddie Dunne's face on the cover of *Ring Magazine*. Every time you looked at the walls, a new black-framed remembrance stared back at you. Most of the former Yonkersites who appreciated these images were in or near retirement. Kevin's goal was to trade regular trips down memory lane for some of their discretionary income.

The plan included a series of special nights: Gorton High School night on the second Thursday of every month; Sacred Heart on the third Tuesday; Yonkers Fire Department and PD retirees, and so on. "Mini-reunions," he called them. All he had to do was contact the alumni associations and word of mouth would be all the advertising they'd need.

The limited menu presented the biggest problem. The present limit was one dish a night, and Martha was adamant about sticking to that. "The customers are family," she said. "Family members do not get a menu." On Sunday, the lone entrée was pot roast, mashed potatoes, and string beans. The same vegetables came with the entrées all week long. Occasionally, a seasonal vegetable would replace the string beans. Monday brought roast chicken; Tuesday, liver and onions; Wednesday, franks and beans; Thursday, beef stew; flounder on Friday; and Saturday was burger night. For the hard to please, burgers and fries were available every night except Friday. Saint Martha would not sell any meat on Friday, no matter what the old men in Rome decreed. But one Friday night, Kevin let a regular customer run to the corner to pick up a pizza for his fish-hating kids. Martha said, "There you go; the floodgates are open."

The usual Friday crowd surrounded the bar when Eddie walked in with a pizza and a box of cannolis. The subject at the bar was the latest plot of bartender B. J. Harrington. At issue was the wisdom of the deceptively tough Harrington's ongoing public effort to engage Britain's Prince Charles in a boxing match to decide possession of Northern Ireland. B.J. was attempting to have a crown he had purchased at a theater auction declared the official crown of the king of Ireland. Possession of the official crown, he figured, would give him legal standing to challenge the Brits. Although he was twenty years older than the prince, B.J. was confident. He'd lined Eddie up to train him. Five rounds, winner take all. Registered letters were flying back and forth across the pond.

Babsie Panko and Grace waited for Eddie in a back booth. For him, it had been a day of carrying white boxes. Babsie grabbed the cannolis and put them on her side of the booth. "Dessert for later," she told Grace.

"Don't let Aunt Martha see the pepperoni," Grace said.

Babsie opened the pizza box and cut slices all the way through. She scooped them out one at a time and put them on the rose-trimmed plates Kevin had bought from a wholesaler on the Bowery. The restaurant had been all Kevin's doing. Their father, Kieran Dunne, had not emphasized food in his thirty years in the bar business.

"You look beat," Babsie said.

"I'm fine," Eddie said. "I'll go see if Kevin wants a slice."

"Your brother is putting new ice in the urinals," Babsie said.

"Why does he do that?" Grace asked.

"It's a guy thing," Babsie told her.

"It's stupid," Grace said.

"God, you're getting more like me every day," said Babsie.

Grace ate half a slice, then went to the jukebox to press numbers. The Wurlitzer played only songs from the fifties, mostly doo-wop and Elvis. You didn't need quarters; Kevin kept it on free play. An Irish bar without music, he claimed, was just another wake.

"What happened with the feds today?" Babsie said.

"Nothing helpful. How's Kate's bedroom working out for you?"

"It's fine."

"If I haven't said it before, Babsie, I really appreciate your moving in. I mean it."

"Expressing gratitude is an effective way of changing the subject. It forces a polite Polish Catholic girl like me to say, 'You're welcome.' I said it. Now, let's try to remember that I'm not the baby-sitter; I'm the lead detective. Tell me about the meeting."

"They wanted to rehash the Rosenfeld case."

"That's your claim to fame, right? You and Paul Caruso. The shoot-out in Marine Park. You recovered a couple million dollars."

"Money that Rosenfeld had been laundering for Evesi Volshin from the gas-tax scam."

"Remind me how that worked," Babsie said.

Like all great rip-offs, the gas-tax scam was simple. A handful of gasoline distributorships were responsible for paying the twenty-eight-cents-a-gallon tax. Anatoly

Lukin, who worked for Evesi Volshin at the time, had front men buy wholesale gasoline for their distributorship. They then moved it, on paper, through a series of bogus corporations. The gas was sold to independent retailers at cut-rate prices. The retailers received a forged invoice stamped "All taxes paid." Of course, the taxes were never paid. Lukin always designated one of the corporations in the daisy chain as the "burn" corporation, the one required to pay the taxes. For years, nobody missed the tax money, but then investigators finally discovered the "burn" corporation was nothing more than a post office box in a dry cleaner's. The corporate principal was an elderly Russian émigré, who suddenly disappeared.

"It's easy to believe the big money estimates," Babsie said. "Ripping off the government for twenty-eight cents for every gallon, and this went on for years. Boland said the money was coming in so fast, Rosenfeld had trouble washing it all. That's why he had it in his safe at home. He kept it there until he could move it."

"You talked to Boland?"

"He called me after you walked out of the meeting."

Babsie was wearing jeans and had her shoulder-length gray hair held back in a ponytail. Each time one of them took a slice of pizza, she closed the box and put the napkin holder on top to hold it down.

Eddie said, "They think that I took these black binders that contain the paperwork for a slew of phony corporations."

"Boland told me someone removed the binders from Rosenfeld's house after the double homicide and that they wound up in Lukin's possession. Now they're missing again. You're the natural suspect."

"I don't know where they are now, Babsie. But apparently, my partner sold them to Lukin after the Rosenfeld murder. I saw his brother Angelo today; he said that Paulie told Lukin I was in on it. I wasn't."

"I believe you. Your partner is another matter. He sold those black binders without you knowing it; no telling what else he did behind your back."

Kevin was hustling from one table to the next. Grace was telling him to "bend a leg." Eddie figured she meant "shake a leg." He loved the way the kids today were comfortable around adults. It wasn't like that when he was growing up. But it was a trade-off. In his day, the kids from the North End learned discipline and were pushed by the nuns and priests at St. Joseph's and Sacred Heart, and all the now-closed Catholic grade schools in every parish in Yonkers. Even the street kids, like the Dunnes and Pankos, came away with a great education.

"I have no idea why Paulie's head wound up at my door, Babsie."

"I don't doubt that for a second," she said. "But you gotta understand: Nobody trusted your partner, so they're gonna assume you're the same kind of guy."

"Paulie liked living large," Eddie said. "But he wasn't a money vacuum. It was more about the thrill of the scam. He was a guy who'd drive ten miles out of his way to buy a pack of untaxed cigarettes."

Eddie told her about the first time he met Paulie Caruso. It was in the squad room in the Coney Island precinct. Paulie took him out drinking. They left the precinct in a late-model Cadillac Seville. At some point during the evening, Eddie found a green NYPD property voucher above the visor. When he read it, he realized they were cruising around in a car used in a homicide two years earlier. It was seized as evidence by Detective Paul Caruso, and he'd been examining it for 23,000 miles.

"People think money was skimmed from the Rosenfeld robbery," she said.

"I know. It was all we heard from cops for months after that. But you know how cops are. Any time someone turns in a lot of money, his brother officers say the same thing: 'I wonder how much was really there.' "

"I read the reports," she said. "I think he grabbed the money in the park that day, and someone knows."

Immediately after the shooting, Eddie drove to find a telephone to call it in. Paulie the Priest waited at the scene. Eddie found a phone near the service road. Like he told IAB, he couldn't see the Dodge Charger, and he lost sight of Paulie. They knew all this anyway; they'd checked the phone he'd used. But he was positive no one else had entered or left the lot while he was gone; he returned less than ten minutes later. He'd been able to see the entrance to the lot the whole time.

"Okay," she said. "Where do we go from here?"

Babsie meant with the case, but he hesitated, thinking she'd read his mind. He'd been thinking about her. What was the state of Babsie Panko's social life? He knew she'd been divorced for years. She hadn't mentioned boyfriends.

"To look for Sergei Zhukov," he said.

"You know where to look?"

"Richie Costa gave me some good hints."

"After he sucker punched you, he helps you out. He must have had some change of heart. I wonder what happened to make him suddenly see the light."

"I don't remember you being this sarcastic," Eddie said.

"It's become my best quality," she replied. "When are you going to follow up on Richie's good hints?"

"Tonight."

"I'll get someone to watch Grace and go with you."

"You can't, Babsie. What I'm doing isn't exactly legal."

Grace played "Earth Angel" and was dancing around, hugging an imaginary partner, assaulting him with a very theatrical smooch. Eddie imitated her, so she exaggerated even more.

"Roughly, how illegal?"

"I've answered questions all day, Babsie. Can we change the subject?"

"Okay, how about this: Is Kevin making money with this place? The neighborhood isn't what it used to be, to put it mildly."

"He's doing good now—especially since B.J. came here. Bartenders make or break your place."

For whatever reason, people were drifting back to the North End Tavern. Nights were solid and afternoons, especially Saturday, were drawing more guys, some stopping in after golf somewhere. Old faces were showing up after a spin through the old neighborhood. Most of them hadn't been on the block in twenty years.

"B.J.'s a legend," Eddie said. "He brought a following."

"And what about your following?" Babsie said. "All those fifty-year-old ex–prom queens who show up nights you're behind the stick. I hear they're cashing their alimony checks at the bar."

"Yeah, but they fall asleep by eleven."

"Granpop," Grace yelled. She stood on a wobbly chair next to a posed picture of Eddie in boxing trunks. He struck the pose for her from his seat. She put up her fists and made a valiant attempt at a game face.

"She's a great kid, Eddie. She really loves you."

"I know. She thinks I can do anything. What happens when I can't find her mother?"

"We're going to find her. If you ever let anybody help you."

"Not tonight," he said, looking up at the clock. "Tonight, I can't."

Eddie wondered why he'd never really looked closely at Babsie Panko before. Since his last drink, he'd come to think of himself as a man who'd had amnesia. The beauty of it was that the life he discovered had always been his.

"How do you think they got Paulie's head over here?" Babsie said.

"I'm thinking it either came by ship or was mailed to one of the private boxes in Brighton Beach."

"I can't get my mailman to walk up five steps," she said. "But heads they deliver."

# CHAPTER
# 23

SERGEI ZHUKOV'S CADILLAC sat at a meter in the parking lot on Brighton Eighth. The cars around it ran the high-roller gamut from world-class rides to death traps. Almost every car contained a *Racing Form,* a newspaper turned to the sports page, or some new casino rag with an article on the latest foolproof system. The high rollers always find the action, Eddie thought. Sitting under a streetlight with the motor running was a black Mercedes. The driver wore a Yankees hat that fit his oversized skull like a blue stocking. He flipped the pages of a magazine and looked up every now and then to check for newly arrived players. He was Eddie's backup plan. If what Richie Costa had said about the luggers was true, plan A needed to work.

Thirty minutes prior to closing, Eddie entered M & I International Foods. He asked for the catering manager, then walked the aisles while they hunted her down. Display cases loomed on both sides of him, food piled shoulder-high. Blinis, dumplings, cheeses, and stuffed cabbage stretched to the back of the store, where you turned into a larger room with counters for the cooked foods. Russian émigrés who remembered long bread-lines and meatless months under seven decades of Soviet rule had to be overwhelmed in the M & I. Right there, on Brighton Beach Avenue, were two floors of meats, sausages, chickens, prepared foods, caviar, chocolate, and breads. It must have seemed like a dream.

During his years working for Lukin, Eddie often accompanied him on trips to M & I. The old man loved to force-feed him samples of dozens of different smoked fish, endless shish kebabs, specialties like Georgian eggplant caviar, and brined cabbage turned a ruby red with beets. "Look at this bounty, Russian bounty," Lukin would say. He once told Eddie that one thing the Russian *mafiya* had in common with American cops was that they both hated the Communists. The bastards deprived the Russian people of the right to enjoy their own food. Then he'd hand Eddie a spoonful of *smetana,* a thick Russian sour cream ladled out of vats, or some lethal Russian mustard or horseradish.

The women who worked the counters and cash registers all wore starched white uniforms and lace caps. So when Eddie saw a hatchet-faced woman in a tweed business suit marching toward him, he knew she was management.

"Hi, I'm Desmond Shanahan," Eddie said. He apologized for not having brought his business cards, then explained he was a business rep for an international artichoke dealer. His company was trying to break into the Russian market and had invited a group of Russian businessmen to discuss the possibilities. They wanted to impress a maximum of thirty guests with a feast of M &

I's best, delivered to the hotel conference room. Money was no object.

She walked Eddie through the aisles, suggesting various options. He told her the exact menu could be worked out later. He had a budget of ten thousand dollars but could go higher. Only one problem: The delivery would have to be late. What would be the latest they could deliver? She said special arrangements could be made for an order that substantial. "Select the best," he said, encouraging her; "do not cut corners."

He asked if they often did late deliveries. "In fact," she said, "we have one going out later tonight."

"I know I'm accused of being too thorough," Eddie said, "but could I see the vehicle you use for these deliveries?"

She looked puzzled, but she took him out behind the store and pointed to a fairly late-model white Dodge van with the company logo on the side. It was the only delivery vehicle, and it was cleaned on a daily basis. Then Eddie gave her his usual Desmond Shanahan Manhattan phone number, which he knew would ring endlessly on some desk in the office of the New York City Employee Benefits Programs on Church Street. He took her card and assured her he'd be in contact on Monday.

Patience, Eddie knew, was the keystone of the surveillance arts. He sat in his Olds until almost midnight, at which point the back door of the M & I opened and a white-coated man loaded five covered trays into the back of the van. Someone locked the door behind him.

The tail was easy. Eddie stayed a block behind the Dodge van, but he could have been on the guy's bumper. No one expects you to follow the food, he thought. They went down Coney Island Avenue to Fort

Hamilton Parkway, where the van stopped at a small frame house that faced the BMT yards and backed up on Greenwood Cemetery. A broad-backed man helped the driver carry the trays into the house. From the way the guy checked out the street, Eddie knew he had the right place.

When the van pulled away, Eddie got out and approached the house. He came at a side angle, trying to see if he could get near a window. The blinds were shut. He didn't know what room or even what floor the game was on. Getting closer wasn't worth the risk. "Trust your instincts," the Priest had always said.

Only one car was parked in the driveway, but five trays of Russian food had just gone in. No doubt this was the game. If Sergei was as sick as Richie Costa had said, he'd be at some game. Gamblers are the worst junkies; they will not rest until they find action. And they can't get their fix on just any corner.

Eddie took a quick drive around the neighborhood. He knew the players would be on their own as far as transportation back to their cars. Most would call for a cab and have it meet them a block or two away, probably New Utrecht Avenue. Chances were good that Sergei would make an early exit on a Friday night. He had to keep tabs on the Eurobar. If he didn't protect his own interests, some snot-nosed bastard would jump right in his shoes.

Eddie sat back, settling in for the long haul. He dismantled the car's interior light, then checked his equipment: rope, tape, and stolen handcuffs. He wore a carpenter's pouch tied around his waist. The Smith & Wesson .38 rested in the small of his back, sitting in a stiff leather holster he'd bought behind police headquarters on Centre Street when Wagner was mayor. He took a sip of the soda bought from the M & I. It had a picture of a tiger on the can, but he had no idea what the flavor was. Maybe cream, but he wouldn't swear to it.

His old partner had hated the waiting. Paulie had always tried to spook the quarry by any means possible. If the Priest were here now, he'd be sending a bouquet of flowers to the door, then an ambulance, or an undertaker. All would be asking for the subject by name. His idea was to make it too uncomfortable for the suspect to stay inside for long. Bad guys were always antsy. Sooner or later, the suspect would bolt, and then he'd be theirs.

It was almost 2:00 A.M. when the first player walked out the door. Eddie focused the binoculars on the doorway, hoping to use the available light. Too tall for Sergei, but light was going to be a problem. The cops today probably had night-vision goggles. They had a lot of advantages today. The cell phone being the biggest, in his opinion.

Technology, however, was no match for luck, and this was Eddie's lucky day. Twenty minutes later, a pissed-off Sergei Zhukov slammed the door behind him. No doubt it was Sergei. The height, the weight, the hairstyle, the waddling walk. A little drunk, but it was him. Eddie let him walk to the corner before he started the Olds.

With his headlights off, Eddie moved to the intersection. He watched Sergei waddle to the next block, going toward New Utrecht. Eddie opened the car door a crack and held it with his left hand. He waited a few beats more, until Sergei was in the middle of the dark stretch opposite the subway yards; then he turned his bright

lights on and drove right at him. Sergei glanced over his
shoulder, but too late. At thirty miles an hour, Eddie held
the door as a battering ram and slammed into the
Russian. Briefly airborne, Sergei slammed to the ground,
tumbling over. Eddie jumped out, holding the rope in his
teeth. Sergei was on his hands and knees. Eddie grabbed
his legs and dragged him back until they were both hidden by the Olds; then he rode him until he was flat, facedown. He pulled the stunned Russian's arms behind him
and handcuffed him quickly. Eddie took the rope from
his teeth and began tying Zhukov's legs, like a rodeo
cowboy working against the clock. A car's lights swept
over them. Sergei started yelling. Eddie pushed his face
to the ground. All he needed was a patrol car; no way his
timing could be worse. But it wasn't a cop; it was a taxi,
probably looking for Sergei. Eddie yelled, "He's fine,
just a little drunk." The taxi pulled away. The lettering
on the door said BAY RIDGE LIMOS, not GOOD SAMARI-
TANS, INC.

Eddie took a roll of duct tape from his pocket and ran
it one time around Sergei's face, but he held his mouth
wide-open and the tape went inside. Eddie kept rolling
tape, winding it five or six times around Sergei's head, as
if his skull were a maypole. The hard object Eddie
thought was a gun in Sergei's pocket turned out to be a
pint of vodka. He yanked the Russian to his knees, then
to his feet. He wrapped his arms around him and carried
him to the back of the Olds, bent him over his open trunk,
then stuffed him inside and slammed it shut.

Sergei kicked for the length of time it took Bruce
Springsteen to sing "Born in the USA." The more he
kicked, the louder the music. Finally, he stopped. Eddie
drove to the parking lot in Marine Park, the same park

where he and the Priest had killed the crazy bastards who murdered Marvin Rosenfeld and his beautiful wife, Svetlana. He parked at the far end and turned the Olds around to face the entrance. He walked around back and opened the trunk. He didn't need to take out the bulb; Sergei had broken it with his feet.

"Fuck you" was the first thing Sergei said when Eddie took the tape off his mouth. Some skin and a fair amount of black hair came with it. Eddie shoved the old tape in the carpenter's pouch.

"You want my money, take my money," Sergei said. "Stupid fucking American slob. Go ahead, look in my pockets. Ten thousand dollars, more money than you'll make in your stupid fuckin' life. Go ahead, take it."

"Look at me," Eddie said. He waited until he saw the slow recognition cross Sergei's face.

"The cop," he said.

"Not a cop anymore, so it doesn't matter what the hell I do to you."

"Oh, Mr. Tough Cop, look, I'm shaking at your scariness. You think you can fucking scare me, American pussy? You don't know shit about me. I'll rip your heart out of your chest and eat it like Big Mac. Untie me, go ahead. If you are a man, go ahead."

"I'll untie you," Eddie said. "Tell me where my daughter is and I'll untie you."

"Your daughter?" he said. "Your daughter is in Brooklyn."

"How do you know that?"

"I saw her when I fucked her. I fucked her in the ass."

Eddie hit him so hard, the back of Sergei's head dented the metal wheel well. He closed the trunk and walked away, pacing back and forth in the darkened parking lot.

When he opened it again, the Russian was breathing hard, as if he'd run a distance. But he had enough wind to laugh. Eddie hit him again, then pulled back, regretting it. He needed him conscious.

"You can hit no harder than that?" Sergei said. "My mother hits harder than that."

"Where in Brooklyn is my daughter?"

"In my bed. I left her in my bed."

"You're a lying piece of shit," Eddie said as he pulled Sergei's legs out of the trunk. "Tell me where she is."

"Check my dick," he said. "See if your daughter is there."

Eddie took Sergei's wallet, keys, vodka, and cell phone. He stuffed them in the carpenter's pouch. The roll of bills was thicker than Eddie's wrist. Ten grand might be close. He held Sergei's leg away from the car and put the barrel against the Russian's left foot. Once again, he asked him about Kate.

"On the bed, I told you, waiting for me to fuck her again."

Eddie fired; the muzzle illuminated the dark corner of the parking lot. Sergei grunted, blew air out through his nose. The bullet had ripped through the upper leather and exited the sole, a jagged, nearly round hole. At least one toe was gone. Sergei growled in Russian, his face shining now with sweat.

"Where did you last see her?"

"On my Russian dick," he said, his voice gravelly, coming from deep inside him.

Eddie fired again. Son of a bitch, he thought, this isn't helping anything. But the scumbag in his trunk deserved everything coming to him. Next, I'll shoot his Russian dick off, see how tough he is. Why these bastards play this game, I'll never know. It must be something in the way they live—something horrible—that makes them care so little about life. Live or die, it's all the same to them as long as they're big men. "Russian ego," Lukin had said, "is their downfall."

"So this is what makes a Russian a man," Eddie said. "Raping a little girl like my daughter, only twelve years old."

"Old enough to bleed, old enough for butcher," he said. "I like young ones, virgins like your daughter."

"I bet you loved her straight black hair," Eddie said.

"I wipe my ass with her black hair," Sergei said.

Sergei knew nothing about Kate, beyond the fact she'd been kidnapped. Stupid son of a bitch, why didn't he just admit he didn't know where she was? It was more important to him to play the Russian tough guy. Screw him. Eddie put the gun back in the holster. He had to get out before someone called the cops. He'd wasted hours tracking Sergei Zhukov, and it had taken only five minutes to discover he'd abducted an idiot. Psycho bastard. They were all psychos. He rewrapped Sergei's mouth, not sparing the duct tape. He poured the bottle of vodka over Sergei's wounded toes, then hit him one more time before slamming the trunk down.

The lights on the Belt Parkway reflected off the water of Gravesend Bay. Tankers sat out in the middle of the bay, waiting to enter New York Harbor. On the concrete path that ran along the water, a jogger's reflective gear bounced along, yellow and red. He or she was moving at a decent pace, well under eight-minute miles. Eddie hadn't run since Monday, and already he could feel the loss of conditioning. It evaporates quickly at this age, he thought. A man my age should be working out, trying to maintain his strength as long as possible. A man my age should be doing anything other than driving around Brooklyn at this hour of the morning with a bleeding Russian psychopath in his trunk. Now what the hell do I do with this idiot?

# CHAPTER
# 24

THE BARS IN BRIGHTON BEACH were closing when Eddie knocked on the Parrot's door. He heard them jabbering inside . . . then quiet. But Eddie Dunne was not to be denied. He kept pounding and yelling out all the names he knew. It sounded like a casting call for an old Disney cartoon: "Parrot, Tropicalia, Madame Caranina."

Finally, the rough-voiced Caranina said, "Who's this?"

"It's Eddie Dunne," he said. "I need to see your husband."

"He's away on business."

"I saw his van downstairs," Eddie said, sliding a hundred dollars of Sergei's ten grand under the door. "I need someone to help me with my car. Anyone can do it. The battery's run down and I need a jump start. There's another two hundred in it for whoever wants it."

"You have cable?" Caranina said.

"No, I need his cables, and the keys to the van."

Five minutes later, Eddie heard keys jingling. Tropicalia opened the door but left the chain on. She peeked through, checking him out. Eddie stood back from the door, not wanting to scare them off. He noticed Tropicalia now wore a head scarf, the sign of a married Gypsy woman. She opened the door just enough to reach her hand through to drop the cables and keys on the floor, but Eddie moved quickly, slamming into it with his full weight. The chain lock tore away from the old wooden frame as he bulled his way in. He charged through the *ofisa,* then through the beaded curtains. The floor of the back room was covered with mattresses; you couldn't tell where one stopped and another began. The apartment was overly warm and pungent. Eddie heard the bathroom door lock. He walked across the mattresses, stepping over women and children. Eddie raised his leg and kicked the door just above the knob. The door flew back. Parrot, sitting on the toilet, acted surprised.

"I have the flu," Parrot said.

"Dress," Eddie said.

"It's going around, the flu; everyone is sick."

"Wear these," Eddie said, throwing a pair of powder blue tuxedo pants at him.

"Tropicalia can do the cables," Parrot said.

"You want me to pull you off that thing?"

Grease from cooking covered the inside of the front windows. Packages of Yankee Doodles and Devil Dogs sat on the small table. The family bickered in Romany. Tropicalia was the loudest, Caranina the angriest, banging her finger into Parrot's chest. Eddie knew he was the *gadje* bastard, the non-Gypsy subject of the squabble, and neither woman was saying good things about him.

Except for Parrot in his red briefs, they all wore too many clothes. The adult women wore long nightgowns, as they did long skirts, to cover the "unclean" parts of their bodies. A guy he didn't know, late teens, remained on a mattress, lying under the covers. Probably Tropicalia's new husband. Eddie told him to stand against the wall, where he could watch him. Someone on one of the kids' mattresses began to cry. Another adult female, fifteen or fifty, crawled over to tend the sobbing child.

"We don't work like this, you and me," Parrot said, slipping into a pair of patent-leather loafers. "We work like gentlemen, not like this."

"Come on," Eddie said. "The sooner we get started, the sooner we get finished."

A box of wax likenesses of Madame Caranina sat open on the floor. She sold them to customers so they could meditate over them. Eddie handed Sergei's money to everyone, including the kids. The family argument escalated. Only Caranina and Tropicalia appeared to have a voice in whatever was being discussed. Parrot handed a pack of cigarettes to Tropicalia's apparent new husband. Then he threw a white silk scarf around his neck, and he was ready.

"You have made a dead man," Parrot said as they crossed Brighton Beach Avenue.

"It's four o'clock in the morning. No one will see us."

"They see everything. All day, all night."

Eddie remembered that Lukin always said, "If you cut the Gypsy into ten pieces, you have not killed him; you have only made ten Gypsies." The Parrot would survive.

Eddie had parked on Coney Island Avenue, next to the construction site where he'd lost Lukin's murderer on Tuesday. It was away from potential eyes in inhabited buildings. People always avoided parking near construction sites because of loose nails and screws. But Eddie's daughter had been missing for almost five days. He didn't care about flat tires any more than he cared about the problems of the Gypsy.

"You have no car emergency," Parrot said.

"In a way I do," Eddie said.

In the second-floor window above the Sea Lanes of Odessa Bakery, the stolen drapes were pulled aside as dark eyes watched Eddie and Parrot reappear from under the el. They got into Eddie's car together. Eddie tossed the carpenter's pouch into the backseat. He started the car and turned the radio on. Those watching from the second-floor window knew there was no *gadje* car problem.

"Have you delivered that Mercedes to Jersey yet?" Eddie asked.

"Maybe tomorrow."

"We're going tonight," Eddie said. "I'll go with you. Get it over with."

"No way, Eddie. Not tonight. Sunday afternoon is the best time to drive a stolen Mercedes to Jersey. Then I fit in with the Pakistani doctors going to Grandma's for dinner. Cops see me in that car tonight, I'm an automatic stop."

Eddie pulled out Sergei's money.

"I have almost ten grand here," he said. "It's yours if we deliver it tonight."

Parrot counted the money. A sound came from the trunk. Parrot looked around, but the noise stopped. Eddie turned the radio up.

"Short three eighty-five," he said.

"I gave it to your kids," Eddie said. "This is all you're getting."

"Ten grand buys twenty grand of trouble. What if I say no? You going to shoot me, Eddie?"

"I would, but I don't have to," Eddie said. "Come with me; I'll show you why."

A hint of dawn was beginning to light the eastern end of Coney Island Avenue. Eddie walked Parrot around to the back of the Olds. He opened the trunk.

Sergei shot straight up like an insane jack-in-the-box. Parrot stumbled back over a piece of rebar and fell on his ass. Eddie grabbed the growling Russian by the shoulders and tried to wrestle him back down. Somehow, he'd rolled over onto his knees. Grunting like a wounded moose, Sergei tried to dive face-first to the roadway. Eddie used his legs for leverage, pushing off the curb, stuffing Sergei back in his box, but not before allowing him to make eye contact with Parrot. Eddie flipped Sergei over on his back. Sergei kicked at him, even with both legs taped together. Eddie banged the trunk lid down on his legs. Only the bloody feet protruded.

"Now you're screwed," Eddie said; then he cemented the deal by wrapping Parrot's silk scarf around Sergei's right foot. He crammed his legs back in and slammed the trunk shut.

Parrot dusted off his blue tuxedo pants and got back in the car. He asked to use Eddie's cell phone. Then he told him where he'd hidden the Mercedes 450 SL. Before they got to the corner of Brighton Beach Avenue, Eddie saw the Ford with its coat of primer and SAMMY SOSA scrawled on the side. Caranina and Tropicalia were loading all their worldly possessions into Parrot's van. He knew they'd pack only some clothes and all the mattresses, with the money sewn inside. In thirty minutes, they'd be traveling.

"Ever been to a Gypsy funeral?" Parrot said.

"I'll make a point to go to yours."

"You will dance and have the best time in your life. Big party, three days long, everyone gets drunk. They throw things in your casket, things that will make you happy. Magazines, whiskey, smokes. Then six weeks later, they have tribute. Tribute is a big banquet table filled with food. Women serve the men. Someone stands for you—he acts for you. Your friends buy you a new suit of clothes and Cuban cigars, give you money. They say toasts, calling your name, as if you were there. I stood in for my uncle Bebo. Top-shelf. Nothing but the best."

"That's why you gave that kid your cigarettes."

"Jimmy, my daughter's new husband. He will be me, so he needs to smoke Marlboros."

The Mercedes was hidden in plain sight in the DOC-TORS ONLY section of a parking lot at Coney Island Hospital. Eddie used his own slim jim to pop the lock. He slid the thin, flat piece of steel between the glass and the weather stripping. He wiggled it gently until he felt the notch grab the lock rod, then pulled it up until the lock flipped over. From under the hood, Parrot complained he needed his tools. Eddie dumped Sergei in the big Mercedes trunk.

"I'll drive your Olds," Parrot said. The Mercedes was so quiet, Eddie didn't know it was running.

"No you won't. You'll just take off and I'll never see you again. I need you to get the Mercedes onto the dock. We'll ride together, then take a cab back."

"I don't do homicides."

"I'm not killing him," Eddie said. "I'm deporting him. I fined him; now I'm deporting him."

"They won't open this trunk until it reaches Odessa. He's dead by then."

"That's his problem."

Eddie drove. The Mercedes rode like a jet aircraft, smooth and powerful. The sun rose at their backs as they crossed the Verrazano Narrows. Eddie set cruise control to seven miles over the limit. It would be too suspicious to keep the speed right on the money at this hour. Parrot turned the heat on, then the radio. Diana Krall sang "Peel Me a Grape," the bass thumping softly in Eddie's throat. Parrot went back to counting money.

"You're paying for the cab back to Brooklyn," Eddie said.

"I'm not going back to Brooklyn."

"Good thinking," Eddie said. "Listen to the Gypsy in your soul."

"I have cousins in Queens."

"Go south, for God's sake, Parrot. Go where the weather suits your clothes."

"Talking in old songs is funny to you. You think this is funny?"

"No, I don't. I'd rather see you leave New York alive and happy, but dead is fine, too. Your choice, Parrot. But before you make the choice, you're going to tell me everything you know about my daughter. If you don't, I'll tell Borodenko that you did."

Not even the Mercedes could keep out the trash smell from Fresh Kills; it was the drawback of taking the Outerbridge Crossing to Elizabeth, New Jersey. Eddie turned the heat down; it was starting to make him sleepy. Parrot stared out the window.

"Don't protect these people," Eddie said. "They hate you, and you know it."

"You're the one who got me in this position."

"Borodenko would have come down on you sooner or later. He'd become a partner in Caranina's business. If you missed a payment, he'd have someone beat the shit out of you, and Caranina. They'd rape Tropicalia. You're a Gypsy; you're shit to him. He'd take or destroy everything you love."

"So you did me a favor," he said.

"I'm the only *gadje* friend you have."

"So my friend is next to me, what I need enemies for?"

"This is about my daughter," Eddie said. "I'll do whatever I have to. I thought you'd understand that."

The docks smelled more of the oil refineries than anything remotely nautical. Eddie stopped on an oil-soaked semicircular patch of dirt, a U-turn spot for big rigs. Across the street was a truck stop advertising hot showers and a breakfast special. Eddie hadn't heard any noise from the trunk since they'd left the Belt Parkway.

Parrot said, "If I was you, Eddie, I'd look in Coney."

"What am I looking for?"

"Remember that picture you showed me a few nights ago? You said it was a guy, and I didn't think about it, because it didn't look like any guy I know. But then I got thinking. The face reminded me of Zina. I don't know her last name. She's a lesbo, used to steal cars. Pretty good, too."

"She doesn't steal cars anymore?"

"I don't know, since she started working for Borodenko."

"You don't know where in Coney?"

"Near the boardwalk. She takes care of Freddie, a retard who works for Borodenko, too. They both live over there somewhere. She drives a silver Firebird, flames on the side. You can't miss it."

"You don't know what street."

"Across from where Luna Park was, one of those streets."

"Freddie?"

"Yeah, he's a retard. He's the guy who got burned when the Rolls blew up."

"They said nobody was in the Rolls."

"This guy was. He got burns on his face and arms. This guy eats at the El Greco diner, three times a day, seven days a week. Breakfast, lunch, and dinner. Other day, I asked this waitress I know, 'Where's Freddie?' because I always say something to him—you know, some bullshit. Nothing too funny, because he ain't right. She says he got burned when the car blew up and hasn't been in all week."

Eddie got out of the car. Parrot stretched his leg over the console and pulled himself across. He adjusted the driver's seat forward so he could reach the pedals. Standing in the chill of the morning, Eddie motioned for Parrot to roll down the window. The air was so thick with exhaust, he could feel himself breathing in the particles. With his back to the big rigs pulling in and out of the truck stop, he leaned into the Mercedes.

"What happens to this car now?" Eddie asked.

"I'll find a man in the trailer. He'll point, and I'll drive this into a container. I hope it is one with a car already in there. Then they'll lock it up."

"How much do they pay you for this?" Eddie said.

"For this car, two grand. But not here; I have to go to Brooklyn. So I give up two grand for you."

"Don't go back for the money."

"You fixed that already," he said.

Parrot made a U-turn and cruised toward the gate. He'll be fine, Eddie thought. The Parrot was indestructible.

# CHAPTER

# 25

THE TRUCKER DINER was half-empty, the long-haul guys long gone. Eddie called five cab companies before he got one that would take him from the truck stop in Elizabeth, New Jersey, back to Brooklyn. While he waited, he had a fried egg sandwich, heavy on the catsup. He saw Parrot's van go past the window, heading toward the dock. The women had already loaded up their lives. They'd been in Brooklyn too long anyway. Gypsies are supposed to be on the move.

He called Babsie and asked her to check the FBI list for any Borodenko real estate holdings on the ocean block in Coney Island. He gave her the names Zina and Freddie and told her everything he knew, which consisted only of what Parrot had said. Babsie said she was cooking breakfast and then they were going to sign Grace up for the soccer league in Lennon Park. Grace yelled that Babsie had been teaching her how to handle the ball. Sitting at a table near the clatter of a truck stop kitchen, he realized how much he cared for Babsie. He told her he might have to beat up her brother again, because he definitely owed her a slow dance.

"Just get your sorry ass home," she said.

Back in Brooklyn, Eddie counted what he had left. Breakfast at the Elizabeth truck stop had cost him five bucks, including tip. The ride back to Brooklyn went for ninety-six, but at least he'd gotten a chance to close his eyes. Counting tolls and the parking ticket he found on his Olds, the night had been costly. He'd also been way too generous with Sergei's money. The hundreds he gave Parrot's kids had been stupid. He could use that money now, a little spread-around cash to get his foot through the doors of Borodenko's businesses.

Worst of all, he'd lost time, wasting too much of it on Sergei Zhukov. Maybe finding the burned guy named Freddie wouldn't be too difficult. Find Freddie, you find Zina. He wondered if Zina could be the "she" the late Misha Raisky had talked about.

On Brighton Eighth, Sergei Zhukov's car yielded nothing more than half a box of condoms, an unopened pint of Popov vodka, and a copy of *Hustler.* The Cadillac was brand-new but filthy. It reeked of an eye-watering cologne and spoiled food. Eddie donned Sergei's calfskin gloves for the search. The floor of the backseat served as a repository for fast-food bags, chocolate wrappers, assorted drug paraphernalia, and a pair of red thong panties. No day planner, no Palm Pilot, no address books. Eddie checked every scrap of paper for a name or an address. Most of the writing was in Russian and the pieces of paper appeared to be betting slips.

Babsie called while Eddie was still in Sergei's car. No doubt it was the first time "When Irish Eyes Are Smiling" had been heard in the Russian's Caddy. Babsie said Yuri Borodenko legally owned or quietly had his hands on nine properties near the ocean in Coney Island. Seven were commercial. Among them, a small arcade specializing in video games, and a T-shirt store. He also owned two co-op apartments. She said there was no mention of any women on the associates list, and only one Freddie, but he died three years ago.

Armed with Babsie's list, Eddie posed as Detective Desmond Shanahan from the INS task force. He began with the business owners, hoping they hadn't heard of his performance in the Samovar. After flashing his bogus shield, Eddie said this location had been identified by a confidential informant as a hideout for a very tall Chinese female involved in smuggling aliens from Asia. "Look anywhere you want, Officer." Cooperation all around. Eddie inspected every nook and cranny, every cabinet and cardboard box. Most were far too small, even for a midsize Chinese smuggler. He thanked the managers, faked a notation on an index card. Then he said, "One more question, please," and asked about Zina and Freddie, who'd been burned. Several people knew the two he was talking about, but no one admitted to knowing any more than Parrot.

It was late afternoon when he got to the two co-op apartments owned by Borodenko. Fatigue and melancholy had already set in when a middle-aged woman in a paisley housedress opened the door to the first apartment. Eddie felt his eyes well up as he tried to play the game and couldn't.

"My daughter was kidnapped," he blurted out. He told her the Gypsy's story about the lesbian and the burned man. Before he finished, she pulled him inside. She poured a glass of tea and handed it to him while he apologized.

"Shush, shush," she said. "This is your baby. Of course you must look everywhere."

Eddie tried to leave, but she wouldn't hear of it. She took him by the hand and showed him through her home. In closets, under the beds, behind the shower curtain. She promised she would call all of her friends and tell them of Kate's plight. When he left, she shoved a handful of gingerbread cookies wrapped in a cloth napkin into his pocket. Then she kissed his hand.

The second apartment seemed vaguely familiar. He knew he'd been in the building before, working a case or doing something for Lukin. When he arrived at the door, the tenant, a waitress, was just leaving for work.

"I forgot you lived here," Eddie said.

"Oh, you forgot," Ludmilla said. "I thought you came here to apologize. I thought it was sweet you should do that. But you forgot I lived here."

"I've got a lot on my mind right now."

"Where is your friend the FBI agent? When will he arrest me?"

"No one is going to arrest you, Ludmilla. Listen, why don't we get out of the hallway?"

"You worry because I'm talking, but you talked too loud in the Samovar. Everyone I work with thinks that I'm a thief. My manager, the customers, they all know. The bait-and-switch queen. Where does that leave me now?"

"I overdid it, Ludmilla."

"Tell me why am I working in the Samovar if I'm making so much money selling fake jewels? For fun? You think I do this for fun?"

"No, I don't."

"You always remembered where I lived when you were too drunk to go home to your wife. Ludmilla was special to you then."

"That was a long time ago."

"I'm not even a memory to you. I'm a thief to you now."

"That's not true."

"What kind of man are you? You forget making love in this apartment, but you remember fake jewelry, when I was just a young girl."

"I'm a man who's looking for his daughter, Ludmilla."

"So now you think I kidnap your daughter. Okay, okay," she said. Her hands shaking, she fumbled with her keys and opened the door. She flung it wide-open. "Go ahead, look," she said. "Look, look, look."

Eddie went in and looked—carefully.


Eddie barely remembered the ride home. He kept the windows down, the radio volume up. One minute he was singing to the joggers along the FDR in Manhattan, the next he was in the Bronx and he could smell anise from cookies baking in the Stella D'Oro plant. When he got out of the car, his legs ached from the stiffness. His right hand was badly swollen.

Grace filled him in on their day while he ate leftover macaroni and cheese casserole Babsie had fixed. They'd signed up for soccer, gone food shopping, picked up a movie, and still had had time to make five o'clock Mass at Sacred Heart.

"Granpop, I taught Babsie how to play chicken foot."

"I wasn't very good," Babsie said.

"Yes you were," Grace said. "For your first time playing dominoes."

The second hand on the electric clock above the sink swept past the three white chickens near the rusted plow.

Eddie tried to calculate the hours since his daughter's disappearance.

"Babsie wants to know why Mommy has that pogo stick in her room," Grace said. "I told her you gave it to her."

"It was hers when she was a kid," Eddie said. "I found it in the garage and gave it to her for her birthday . . . as a joke."

"Tell her the funny part, Granpop."

Eddie told her the story about Kate. When she was about Grace's age, he'd bought her a spring-driven pogo stick. Kate jumped endlessly in their driveway. *Ka-ching, ka-ching* for hours and hours. Eddie said he was working late tours and he heard that noise in his sleep all summer. All the neighborhood boys came over and tried to outdo her. They didn't have a prayer. The first week, Kate set her first goal at one hundred jumps without falling, then two hundred, then a thousand. She wore out the pogo stick's rubber tips by the dozen. "Call the *Guinness Book*," she'd yell up to the house. *Ka-ching, ka-ching* all day long.

"See, she never gives up," Babsie said.

"My mom never gives up," Grace said.

Later, Eddie fell asleep in the chair as Grace read *The Polar Express* to him. She laughed because Eddie called her Kate. At nine o'clock, he went to bed while Babsie and Grace watched a movie.

When you've been awake far too long, the first moment of falling asleep is like dropping off a cliff. It's a fall so sudden, so quick and violent, it jolts you awake, your body shivering while drops of sweat bead on your forehead. Eddie didn't know the scientific explanation, but he knew the rest of the night never got much better, as your sleep-deprived brain spliced your fears and dreams and ran them endlessly like a cheap rock video. All you could do was grab on and try to save yourself.

"Eddie, Eddie," he heard Babsie whisper. "You're setting the world's record for nightmares."

She knelt down next to the bed. He knew time had passed, for Babsie was in her nightgown and the house was dark and quiet.

"What time is it?" he asked.

"A little after three."

"I wake everyone up?"

"She's still sleeping, but you were getting loud."

"Sorry."

"Jesus, you're freezing," she said. "Scooch over."

Babsie slid in bed next to him. She rolled on her left side and put her arm across his chest. He could feel her against him, her warmth.

"You have to stop thinking, Eddie. Just for a few minutes."

Babsie buried her head in his shoulder. Her hair smelled clean, but not one of those fruity shampoos. He was sure that Babsie's experiment with red hair in high school was the last time she'd ever colored her hair. Gray, shoulder-length, it suited her. Everything was real about Babsie. She didn't know any other way.

"You want me to leave, just say so," she said.

"No . . . please."

"I don't know if I should, you know. You stood me up once. After graduation, you called me. You said we'd go to a movie, then to Frank and Joe's to grab a pizza, but you never showed up."

"I stopped in the North End for a beer," he said. "I never got out of the place."

"I'm surprised you remember."

"Kevin said it was the biggest mistake of my life."

She leaned over and kissed him.

"I always wanted to do that," she said.

Her breasts felt plump and firm. He rolled over and faced her. She held him with a strength he'd never known in a woman. Her lips were plush, fuller than Eileen's. She reached down and felt him.

"Don't think about anything," she said as she rose to her knees and pulled the nightgown over her head. Her nipples were erect, her stomach not flat, but firm. She straddled his legs and guided him into her. In the yellowish haze of light filtering through the blinds, he watched her outline, the curves, the square shoulders. Babsie was not a fragile girl. He held her hips as she moved, her body wanting to gallop. "Slowly," he whispered. "Slowly." He wanted to savor each second, each subtle movement of her body. Holding herself up with her hands, she leaned down until her mouth was on his, her breasts grazing his chest. And they moved in rhythm, together, as if they'd been there before.

# CHAPTER

# 26

*KA-CHING, KA-CHING.* Eddie's eyes snapped open at the sound. It came from the driveway, someone on the pogo stick. Three steps to the window, but he couldn't see anyone. He dug his underwear out of the sheets and ran to the kitchen window. Babsie was dressed and on the phone. She stood at the window watching Grace, her hair still wet from the shower. Bacon sizzled.

"That thing is rusty, Eddie," Babsie said, hanging up the phone while writing notes on a pad.

"What thing?"

"The pogo stick," she said, a wide grin starting. "The pogo stick needs oil. What the hell did you think I meant?"

Grace bounded across the driveway, tilting left and right. Five jumps and down. But she got back up, holding on to Babsie's car.

"Kids are amazing," Babsie said. "They deal with stuff."

The clothes dryer buzzed; she'd been up long enough to do laundry. Eddie went over and put his arms around her. Maybe it was so easy because they'd known each other all their lives.

"Your husband was a bus driver, wasn't he?" Eddie said.

"Yeah, Philly drove the number seven. He left me for a bus driver groupie from the Hollow."

"There are really bus driver groupies?"

"Strange little women," Babsie said. "But Philly was a magnet for strange. He was a guy who actually believed that they had special erasers that could erase the clothes off women in photographs. I'd always catch him with the center section of the *Daily News,* trying to rub the bikini off some Australian babe."

In the driveway, Grace climbed back on the pogo stick. Six jumps and down she went again. Eddie regretted the story about how persistent Kate had been. He didn't want Grace to get hurt trying to set a record.

"I'll find something to lubricate that pogo stick," Eddie said.

"Put your pants on first. Then sit down and eat. I have some news about the case."

Babsie had filled a metal serving bowl with scrambled eggs. She put three slices of bacon on a plate, then poured a glass of orange juice for him. Eddie knew she'd brought the bacon with her. Kate wouldn't allow it in the house.

"When you called me yesterday," Babsie said, "you said that Parrot told you this Zina and a Freddie lived near the boardwalk in Coney Island. I looked up Borodenko properties in the area."

"Right."

"Then I thought I'd take a different angle," she said. "You told me Parrot said that Freddie was the guy who got burned in the Rolls-Royce. I knew the cops'd checked the city hospitals but never pursued it further because they didn't have a victim or a complainant. So I called Edie Porach at St. John's and asked her how I could check on all burn cases that were reported since last Monday in a hundred-mile radius of New York City. I gave her the name Freddie. She called around and got back to me just now. The Burn Center at Stony Brook out in Suffolk County treated this guy the evening of Monday the sixth, a few hours after the Rolls blew up. He claimed he'd had an accident with a barbecue grill."

Babsie turned her notebook around for Eddie to read. The name she'd circled was Fredek Dolgev.

"It was cold that day," Eddie said.

"Forty-two degrees was the high. Not exactly barbecuing weather for me, but a lot of people do it. The nurse said this guy was a little on the slow side. A young butch-looking woman brought him in. No insurance—she used a credit card to pay. Her name was Zina Rabinovich. Now check out his home address."

"West Nineteenth Street, Brooklyn. Coney Island."

"They drove a long way in an emergency, didn't they?"

"They wanted a hospital out of the city," Eddie said. "This home address is right at the boardwalk."

"I know. What the hell else do you need?"

"Jesus, you are amazing," Eddie said.

"Yeah, I hear that all the time," she said.

Eddie didn't shower or shave; plenty of time for that after Kate was safe. He dressed in ten minutes. Martha was sitting on the front step, watching Grace. Babsie pulled the YPD car to the back door. Eddie knew he couldn't get away without her, but he did talk her into taking his Olds. He noticed that she was wearing a dressy blouse, which was made of a shiny black material. And blush, a faint touch of blush on her cheeks.

"Watch the road, Romeo," she said.

Forty minutes later, they made the Cropsey Avenue exit off the Belt Parkway. They parked on West Twentieth, on the ocean block, a block west of the two-story building that housed Coney Custards. Coney Custards faced the boardwalk. On the second floor were two small apartments. The entrance faced the side street.

"I don't know how the hell you made that commute every day," Babsie said. "All that traffic every night would make me nuts."

"I didn't come home every night."

"That explains a lot."

Eddie and Babsie had a direct sight line across an open lot and a blacktopped parking area to the apartment entrance. The building's outside walls were covered with mismatched strips of aluminum siding, some painted with a redbrick-colored primer. The entire place looked ripe for flattening by the winds of the next nor'easter or the big bad wolf.

"Trash bag at the curb," Eddie said. "Somebody is living there. Is this entrance the only way in or out?"

"Gotta be a fire escape on the back side."

"I'm going to check it out."

"Don't do anything stupid, Eddie. We need a warrant."

"First I'll get my daughter; then I'll worry about the Supreme Court."

"I'll call Boland," she said. "Have him meet us here with a warrant. If someone comes out before then, we'll move on him."

"We don't have enough for a warrant," he said, then added, "Okay, tell him I said Parrot told me he'd seen a woman who looked like my daughter being dragged into this building."

"What's his real name? We can't call him Parrot."

Eddie made up a name; then, while Babsie was on the phone, he put on his Yankees hat and sunglasses and took a stroll down the boardwalk. The interior floor of Coney Custards was raised so the counter crew in their orange-and-blue golf shirts looked down on the customers. Huge silver cylinders behind them spun out soft ice cream. Two old ladies sat on a bench, licking a peach-colored concoction from sugar cones. Eddie walked fifty yards past to see the opposite side. Fire escape—Babsie was right.

On the way back, Eddie turned down the side street. The first door on the right opened into a very narrow hallway. One flight up was as far as you could go. Apartment A to the left, apartment B to the right. Neither of the two mailboxes had names on them. He could hear the hum of a motor, probably coming from inside Coney Custards. Otherwise, quiet. He went back to the car.

"Kick the door in yet?" Babsie asked.

"Not yet, but it's too quiet in there."

"Boland is on his way to Queens. He says he'll get someone working on the warrant, although he's not optimistic."

"Call him back," Eddie said. "Tell him to make it for both apartments, A and B."

"That's not gonna help our cause; we don't even know which apartment."

"This isn't going to happen, is it, Babsie? The warrant, I mean."

"The feds always find a sweetheart judge."

"Not on Sunday," he said. "Okay. Make a note that

you ordered me to wait for the warrant. If I'm not back in five minutes, come in and arrest me."

"Yeah, right," she said.

Babsie went around to the boardwalk side. She stood on an angle so she could watch both the fire escape and the front window of Coney Custards. They didn't know if there was an entrance from the apartments into the back room of Coney Custards. Eddie entered the claustrophobic hallway. The stairs were so narrow, two bulimics couldn't have squeezed past each other. He knocked on both doors. Nobody home in either place. So he went to the picks.

Apartment A had a new French-made lock. Big bucks. He didn't even try. He could hear voices, but he couldn't tell if they were coming from Coney Custards. Apartment B had an older lock, the tumblers worn from use. They turned easily, one by one. In less than thirty seconds, he was inside.

The apartment faced the ocean and boardwalk. It smelled musty, everything damp to the touch. The carpet was gritty with sand, but fresh tracks from a vacuum cleaner crisscrossed the floor. An attempt at cleaning had been made. The living room was sparsely furnished, but what was there seemed out of place. Too good for the venue. Dark-wood antiques and overstuffed chairs didn't fit the grimy apartment. In a corner was a straight-backed chair with a cane seat that belonged in the room about as much as a Steinway. Not a single picture of any kind hung on the wood-paneled walls.

"I smell Lysol," Babsie said.

"You shouldn't be in here."

"Oh, like they invited you."

The only windows looked out over the beach and the

Atlantic. Yellowing water stains lined the window ledge. He went to the window and lifted the thin curtain. It felt moldy, as if rotted from the dampness. Only the antiques raised it above a flophouse rating. No frames, no flowers, no frills. Spartan, to say the least. He checked the closet—men's work clothes, two pairs of boots, no dress shoes or sneakers. The smell of mothballs.

"At least it has location," Babsie said.

"Try sleeping here in the summer. Ice-cream machine going day and night. All you hear is people yelling and fighting on the boardwalk."

"Sounds like you've been here before."

"Rooms like it," Eddie said.

Babsie began looking through drawers in the kitchen. The old refrigerator smelled of leaking gas. The freezer was completely empty. The fridge held an open quart of whole milk and nine bottles of Guinness stout. She noted a phone number near the spot on the kitchen wall where the telephone should have been.

"Someone did a half-assed cleaning job," Babsie said.

"Nobody knew about this except us. Parrot," Eddie said. "Parrot might have sold me out."

They could feel the floor vibrating beneath them when the custard machine ran. Babsie crawled on her hands and knees across the living room floor, looking under everything. Eddie went into the bedroom. A queen-size mattress sat directly on the floor. Eddie picked up the pillow and put it to his face.

"Smell this pillow," he said.

"Sour milk," she said. "From downstairs—all those ice-cream workers smell like sour milk at the end of the night. One of them slept here."

"You don't smell perfume?"

"What do you want me to say, Eddie? I don't smell perfume, but check this out." She showed him a quarter-size piece of a torn photograph. "I found this under the convertible sofa. The vacuum must have missed it. It seems strange . . . not one picture in the entire apartment and someone rips up a photograph."

"I can't believe you don't smell perfume."

"My point is, why rip it up?" she said. "I'm going outside to check the trash. I'll give you five more minutes. Then lock the door."

After she left, Eddie dropped to his hands and knees on the bedroom floor. He ran his fingers through the carpet, looking for anything, an earring or a fingernail painted dark red. He tore the bed apart, reached inside the pillowcase, then under the sheets. He picked up the mattress and checked under it. When he had the mattress raised, he saw something green. It was a piece of green cloth that had been shoved down under one corner. Eddie pulled it out and his heart began to pound.

He stared at it, knowing exactly what it was, a circular piece of green cloth covering an elastic band. A "scrunchy," the kids called it. Both Kate and Grace used them in their hair. Kate wore them around her wrist until she was ready to put her hair up in a ponytail. It couldn't have fallen there by itself. Someone had stuffed it down there. Eddie held it up to the window. In the glare of light off the ocean, he could see strands of red hair.

# CHAPTER

# 27

BABSIE PANKO SNATCHED two black trash bags off the Coney Island sidewalk and carried them to Eddie's car. She'd found other pieces of a torn photograph in one of the bags. She didn't know whether or not they were all pieces of the same picture, but it bugged her that there was not a single photograph in the apartment. It had to mean something. She needed time to find whatever else was in those bags. At this point, it was garbage, not evidence, so screw jurisdiction. She wasn't even going to ask. The kidnapping was her case; she'd take any damned garbage she felt like. She slammed the trunk of the Olds just as Matty Boland, followed by the sector car from the Sixtieth Precinct, pulled into the block.

"I thought you were going to Queens," Eddie said.

"I am," Boland said. "As soon as I figure out what the hell you two are doing to me."

"Doing to you?" Babsie said. "Is everything about you?"

"You have our warrant?" Eddie said.

"On what basis, Eddie, a hunch?" Boland said. Then in

a lower voice, he added, "I'm not getting roped into some bullshit illegal search. It's my case; I'll say when we apply for a search warrant."

"This is *not* your case," Babsie said.

"Borodenko is my case, and we're making serious progress right now. Let's not screw it up with some cowboy move."

"Will this serious progress get Kate back?" Babsie said.

"Possibly, very possibly."

"Kate was in that apartment," Eddie said. "That's definite, very definite. Either you get a warrant or I go in without it."

The uniformed cop had come alone in a white Crown Victoria with COURTESY, PROFESSIONALISM, RESPECT written on the side. His partner was in the station house with the paperwork from a four-car accident on the Belt Parkway. He'd been sent to meet a female Yonkers detective but was reluctant to approach them when they were still arguing. He figured he'd let the suits work the problem out between themselves. They'd call him when they were ready. As long as the discussion remained heated, he figured he'd sit in the car and get his memo book caught up.

"You don't know she was in there," Boland said.

"Parrot told me he saw a redhead being dragged in here last Monday."

"Saw it where, in a crystal ball? Let's get his ass out here. I want to hear this story from his lips."

Boland strode over to the radio car and asked the uniformed cop to go to Brighton Beach and bring Parrot back. Every cop knew the Parrot. Sensing the urgency, the cop made a squealing U-turn.

"Who lives here anyway?" Boland asked Eddie.

Eddie's quick lie to Boland made him realize he didn't fully trust him. Boland seemed to have adopted the feds' tough-love approach. He'll come around, Eddie thought; he's a cop. But this was too important for loyalty tests. With the clock running and one lie under his belt, Eddie told Boland a true story and a fantasy. He explained how Parrot had identified the sketch of the person who kidnapped Kate as a woman named Zina. Babsie had traced a burn victim named Fredek Dolgev and a Zina Rabinovich to this address. Both worked for Borodenko. The odds were that it was Dolgev who had been burned in the Rolls-Royce explosion. When Babsie came to interview them, she found the door to apartment B open. Eddie said they didn't go in but that he could smell Kate's perfume.

"Who are you bullshitting?" Boland said. "You were in the apartment already."

"What is it with you, Boland?" Babsie said. "You're more interested in covering your ass than in finding Kate. Here's a cop you worked with, tells you he knows his daughter was in there. He gives you a perfectly logical explanation, and you want to pick him apart."

"If that's logic, I'm fucking Einstein."

"Shut up for a second, will you, you selfish bastard," she said. "Listen to him. Eddie isn't telling you he was in there. But he knows his daughter was. Read between the lines and let it go at that. Do the right thing for once in your self-centered life."

"I'm the one who has to sign the affidavit, not you, Babsie."

It struck Eddie that if Kate had been here and was now gone, she might be dead. They might have panicked

when he was getting close. He could feel the weakness
in his legs. But then he realized they didn't want her
dead. It was about torturing him. As long as he writhed
in the shackles, they'd let her live. Her death would be
the endgame. The radio car screeched around the corner.
The driver was still alone. Boland went over to him; he
didn't even let the driver get out.

"Parrot's flown the coop," the uniformed cop said.
"Just a few pieces of shitty furniture left. All Caranina's
hocus-pocus shit is gone. People in the bakery said they
split Friday night."

"So how do we get the warrant now?" Boland said.
"The victim's father ID's a whiff of perfume?"

"Which apartment we talking about?" the uniformed
cop asked. "I know these people."

He introduced himself as Carlos. Babsie explained she
was working on the kidnapping of Eddie's daughter.
Looking for an edge, she told Carlos that Eddie was a former NYPD detective. Carlos knew about the kidnapping.

"Sorry about your daughter, man," Carlos said.
"We've been doing some serious looking. Especially
since, you know, you being on the job and all."

"We need your help, Carlos," Babsie said. "We came
here to interview someone in connection with this case
and found the door wide-open. No sign of violence we
can see, but we thought the precinct should check it out."

Carlos picked up the radio and told the dispatcher that
Six-oh Charlie would need no further assistance at this
location. It was the first radio car Eddie had looked
closely at in years. The dashboard and front-center console contained more technology than he'd ever seen. The
picture of Kate that Babsie had submitted to all Brooklyn
precincts was stuck in the visor on the passenger side.

"The apartment on the right belongs to Freddie," Carlos said. "Freddie probably forgot to lock the door. It's not the first time."

"Fredek Dolgev," Babsie said.

"Freddie's all I know him as."

Carlos described Freddie as a large, broad-backed man with thinning white hair. Probably in his early fifties. A Russian with very little English at his command.

"Burned skin on his face and arms?" Eddie said.

"Is that what it is, burned skin? I just noticed it this week."

"It happened Monday," Babsie said. "He told the hospital it was an accident with a barbecue grill. He squirted the fluid and it flared up in his face."

"No shit? He had his face bandaged, but I never asked. He's not one of our talkers. A lot of the Russians will come up and talk to me rather than to the Anglo cops. Because I'm Hispanic. I guess they figure I'm non-American, too, but I was born in Brooklyn."

"Ever see him barbecue anything?" Babsie asked.

"No, but that doesn't mean much. He could barbecue on the other side of Coney Custards. They got a little dirt patch out there."

"Does that seem plausible to you?"

"I could see that happening to Freddie, yeah. He's not all there, you know," Carlos said, pointing to his head.

"What do you mean, 'not all there'?" Boland said.

"Slow, I guess. Slightly retarded. But not drooling or anything. The guy has a job; he works somewhere toward Brighton Beach. I see him walking to work every morning. He walks down the boardwalk, no matter how bad the weather is."

"Does he work for Yuri Borodenko?" Boland asked.

"Doing what?" Carlos said. "Sweeping the sidewalk? That's all I can see Freddie doing for Borodenko."

The radio dispatcher sent Six-oh David to a traffic accident on Neptune Avenue. The female dispatcher, a rarity in Eddie's day, had a Caribbean accent.

"So he does this occasionally?" Babsie said. "He forgets to close the door."

"Not that often, but every now and then."

"How do you handle it?" Babsie said.

"We go in, look around for him. If he's not there, we close it."

"Ever have a problem with him?" Eddie asked. "Is he violent, or a drunk, anything like that?"

"Not with me. But I can check with the other teams who work the sector. If you're looking at him for a kidnapping, I'd be shocked. This guy doesn't have the smarts to pull off a dognapping."

"Carlos," Babsie said, "does anybody come by and help him with complicated things, like paying bills, that kind of thing?"

"Zina. She probably helps him out. She lives across the hall."

"What's their relationship?" Boland asked.

"Relationship?" Carlos laughed. "You never met Zina. Zina is a dyke, with a capital *D*. You'll see what I'm talking about when she pulls in."

"Rather than hang around and wait for Zina, why don't we do this," Babsie said. "Carlos goes in and looks for Freddie. In case of foul play, illness, whatever. We go in as a safety factor, being his partner's not here. If nothing is there, we'll just close the door and leave."

"Eddie stays out," Boland said. "Just active police officers."

"Good enough," Babsie said, and glanced at Eddie, who appeared nervous, running his fingers through his hair. It was more than a glance. Serious eye contact between friends.

Babsie entered behind Carlos and went right to the bedroom. Carlos walked around, calling Freddie's name. Boland stuck to his own agenda, looking for an address book or telephone numbers. On her hands and knees, Babsie focused on the area around the mattress as if she was looking for a lost contact lens. She checked every inch of the mattress until she found the green cloth. She called for Boland.

"It's a scrunchy," she said. "For your hair. I have a couple myself."

Boland frowned until Babsie pointed out the red hairs clinging to it. She put it in a small plastic bag she carried in her pocket. They went outside and showed it to Eddie.

"I know this is Kate's," Eddie said. "She was wearing it that morning."

"Hope this works out," Boland said.

"Just call the CSU to vacuum this place," Babsie said. "I'll call the Westchester DA, see if she can get a search warrant rolling."

Boland said, "We also need Parrot to sign an affidavit about seeing a redhead being carried in here. I'll get a better description from Carlos and we'll pick up Dolgev. He's probably at work. Then see where we go from there, but I think we're on thin ice with the courts. This search has bogus written all over it."

Babsie waved the scrunchy in his face, as if trying to remind him of the important thing. Babsie knew guys like Boland needed constant reminding.

"Okay," he said, the attitude slipping away. "I'll call

the CSU. They'll fingerprint the shit out of this place. I'll ask them to scrape the sinks, drains, and vacuum around the mattress, anywhere else that looks promising. It's a defense lawyer's dream, but maybe we'll get something out of it."

"Kate will be enough," Babsie said, handing the plastic bag with the green scrunchy to Boland.

"I'll drop this off at the lab," Boland said. "But they're going to need a hair sample for comparison."

"A hairbrush," Babsie said. "She has three or four on her dresser."

"Perfect, but get them later," Boland said. "Right now, Babsie can stay here with Carlos and wait for CSU. Eddie's going to show me something in Queens."

"Show you what in Queens?" Eddie said.

"A short cut," Boland said. "To your old friend's house. Your old pal, Angelo Caruso. Somebody whacked him and his wife."

# CHAPTER

# 28

## SUNDAY
## 3:00 P.M.

ANGELO AND ANN MARIE CARUSO lived in the shadow of
Aqueduct Race Track in a two-story redbrick home on a
Queens street of identical homes. Angelo could have af-
forded a bigger home in a swankier locale, but Ann Marie
refused to leave the neighbors she'd known since she was
a young bride. In the Carusos' small front yard, the grotto
of the Blessed Virgin ruled center stage. A white tin
awning covered the front step. Folding chairs lined the
narrow, sloping driveway. Underwear, white T-shirts, and
socks were draped across the chairs, drying in the sun.
Every day for the fifty-five years of her marriage, Ann
Marie had washed clothes by hand and dried them this
way. Paulie the Priest had told Eddie that his sister-in-law
rarely used the washer and dryer. She'd never used the
oven upstairs. Upstairs was for company, for special occasions. The downstairs was set up like a separate apartment. They cooked, ate, watched TV, and died in the
basement.

Eddie led Boland down the driveway. Eddie hadn't
been in the Caruso home since June of 1984, when

Angelo and Ann Marie threw a high school graduation party for their niece. It was held in the backyard, where Angelo showed off an immense barbecue grill he'd built from bricks salvaged from the demolished tenement in which he was born. Angelo roasted a sixty-pound pig that day. And the event had been immortalized on film by the FBI from a van across the street.

They entered the basement through the garage. A young uniformed cop sat at Angelo's workbench, where Angelo'd accidentally cut off a finger he later credited to a battle with a brutal *pistola* from the old country. The young cop said the house had been torn apart by intruders looking for money and jewelry. He expounded on how some burglars read the obituaries printed in the newspaper; the obits told them exactly when a family would be at church. Grieving people are distracted: They leave doors open, money lying around. The Carusos had probably arrived home early from the service at Our Lady of Consolation. They'd surprised the burglars and lost their lives. Paulie the Priest would have told this cop that he didn't know his ass from a hole in the ground.

Ann Marie had been shot once in the head. She lay next to her stove, covered by a sheet, the victim not of a burglar but of a poor choice in men. Angelo, her chosen, lay in the exact center of the room on a circular multicolored rug that Ann Marie had woven from loose scraps of cloth. Angelo had been strategically placed, as if he were the room's centerpiece. His mouth was stuffed with U.S. currency. He'd choked to death on money.

"Any thoughts?" Boland said.

"I always liked Ann Marie," Eddie said

"When was the last time you saw them?"

"Ann Marie, fourteen years ago. I saw Angelo on Friday at the Howard Beach Boccie Club. First time in about five or six years."

"Who initiated that meeting?"

"I did. I wanted to find out what he knew about Paulie. He said he thought his brother was still in Sicily."

After conferring with the detectives from the 106th Precinct, Boland said the Carusos came straight home after the service for Paulie. They were probably moving in order to prepare for the company that would follow. The first couple arrived not more than twenty minutes after the Carusos themselves. Whoever killed them had been waiting, and it all happened fast.

"If they all left the church around the same time," Eddie said, "why did it take the friends twenty minutes longer?"

"Food," Boland said. "They went to their own houses first to pick up whatever covered dish they'd made."

The floor above groaned with the weight of a few dozen of the Carusos' family and friends. Eddie wondered if their murderers had desecrated Ann Marie's living room. Eddie had never set foot beyond the velvet rope that declared the pristine parlor off-limits. He'd only viewed it from a distance: the plastic-covered white sofa, the tasseled velvet pillows, fringed brocade lamp shades, and the gilt-framed reproduction of the Mona Lisa. If they'd defiled her pride and joy, Ann Marie would find a way to curse them from the grave.

Boland said, "Angelo have any theories on how or why Paulie's head arrived unannounced?"

"If he did, he didn't tell me."

"He seem worried about anything?"

"Angelo always seemed worried."

"So what happened here today?" Boland said "It doesn't look like a mob hit to me."

"No," Eddie agreed. "The Italians wouldn't have done it like this. Not at home, and they wouldn't have destroyed the house. They'd know Angelo wouldn't keep money here. And they definitely wouldn't have killed Ann Marie."

"Russians?"

"That's my guess," Eddie said.

"Money jammed down his throat is saying something. Angelo get a little greedy maybe? He worked with the Russians a long time, didn't he? Going back to the seventies and the gas-tax scam."

Eddie told him how Angelo Caruso had originally struck a bargain with Evesi Volshin. Caruso had heard about the humongous windfall of the Russians' gas-tax scam. He demanded the Gambino crime family be cut in for a penny a gallon. At the time, the tax was twenty-eight cents on the gallon. The Russians were keeping it all, but they convinced Angelo they were paying part of it. After Volshin was gunned down in the Samovar, Lukin took over. The partnership continued, with Caruso now getting two cents a gallon. It all fell apart when the indictments came down and the Italians took the brunt of the fall.

"Angelo have anything to do with Evesi Volshin's murder?" Boland said.

"That's a safe bet."

"Maybe what goes around comes around," Boland said.

Eddie told him that Angelo'd sworn he'd never work with the Russians again. But the young Italian mafiosi had formed alliances with the new Russkie in town, Yuri

Borodenko. Richie Costa and the Bronx Knights, for example, doing stock pump-and-dump jobs with Borodenko's crew. As well as the partnership in the Eurobar. The Russians do the thinking and organization; the Italians provide the muscle and connections.

"This is a current beef," Eddie said. "Possibly Borodenko sending a message. He wants to be the American Stalin."

"I'm not sure I know what the hell that means," Boland said. "But I don't have a better answer, not yet anyway."

"Read Solzhenitsyn. Other than that, I don't know what to tell you."

"Borodenko is still in Russia," Boland said. "We'll talk to him the second he lands on American soil."

"Yuri Borodenko is going to stay overseas until this is over."

"You mean it's not over?" Boland said. "Who's left—you?"

Eddie hated it when guys like Matty played the tough guy. It came off as false. Tough guy lines were best understated. He didn't have to say, "Who's left?" It was obvious. The fact that Paulie Caruso's head had wound up on Eddie's lawn linked him to any scenario imaginable. The only reason they hadn't come after him already was because they knew cops and FBI were hanging around his house, working the kidnapping.

"I'm going home to have dinner with my granddaughter," Eddie said. "Then I'm going to look for Freddie Dolgev. Call me if you find him first."

"Dead or alive?"

"That depends on who finds him."

\*       \*       \*

You could stay away from the North End Tavern for twenty years, and then the moment you stepped through the door, B. J. Harrington would start mixing your favorite drink. B.J. never forgot an old friend or a cocktail. He gave Babsie a 7&7 because that was the same drink he'd given her on her eighteenth birthday. After five decades of bartending in Yonkers, B.J. knew all the secrets, where all the bodies were buried. Dressed in his usual V-necked sweater over a starched white shirt and black tie, he held court as much as served drinks.

"The sister of your ex-son-in-law was nosing around again today, Eddie," B.J. said. "I didn't give her the time of day."

"I'm going to need a lawyer for this," Eddie said.

"I thought you'd never ask," he said. He took a card from his pocket and handed it to Eddie. "Best guy in family court," B.J. said. "Mention my name. He's owed me a favor for thirty years." He then turned toward the end of the bar, where Grace was reaching over, trying to turn up the volume on the jukebox. "Gracie," he said, never raising his voice, "get down from my bar or I'll have the police haul you away."

When the Sunday dinner crowd started to thin, Eddie and Babsie grabbed a booth. She'd already filled him in on the NYPD Crime Scene Unit's search of Dolgev's apartment. Nothing definitive had been recovered that would nail down Kate's presence. Prints needed to be checked, other evidence analyzed. The CSU guys said they'd send Boland the results. For now, he didn't want to tell anyone about finding the scrunchy. Too much talk spooked the angels.

"I have an appointment at One Police Plaza in the morning to look through your personnel file," Babsie said.

"You could just ask me."

"Might be a few too many things rattling around in your head that you haven't put together, or that you forgot."

"Like what?"

"You know what I mean, Eddie. Everything seems to be coming back to the relationship between you and the Caruso brothers—the now-deceased Caruso brothers."

"Fourteen years ago," Eddie said.

"Fourteen is an odd number to remember. Most people say ten or twenty. You have the exact number on the tip of your tongue. See, it seems that the past keeps raising its ugly head here, and that worries me. I want to read Paul Caruso's file, your file, and I want to read up on the Rosenfeld case."

"You know the Medal of Honor we won for that case was actually twenty-two-karat gold," Eddie said. "The Priest had his melted down, then had a cheap fake made to replace it."

"What happened to yours?"

"The real one? Last I remember, some barmaid had it around her neck."

"That's what I mean," she said. "Maybe you blanked on a few wacky moments from your Wild Irish Rover days."

The chatter of the Sunday crowd was now a softer buzz. B.J. kept the jukebox lower on Sunday. It was a day for families to talk, he said. Kevin brought the pot roast to the tables. All you could eat for $7.95. Martha tended to the kitchen. They'd originally tried it the other way around, but Kevin's personality worked better in the dining room.

"Look," Babsie said, leaning close to him. "Tomorrow is a week, and not a word. We keep calling it a kidnapping, but it's really not. This is something else, some old vendetta, and you and I both know it."

"You think I'm lying?"

"Absolutely not."

"What else is wrong?" he said.

Babsie shook the ice cubes in her empty 7&7, looking into the glass as if for answers. Eddie could have told her that never worked.

"Okay," Babsie said. "You don't allow yourself to think the worst, but what happens if we find the worst?"

"She's going to be fine."

"I know, I know. But the thing I fear now, no matter what happens, is that every time you look at me for the rest of your life, all you're going to see is Kate calling you from the back of that car."

"I liked it better when you were calling me a liar."

"We have to talk about it sometime."

"Not tonight," he said.

He didn't want to think about this right now. Whatever was happening between them, it was all he had to hold on to. It seemed as if his whole life depended on her, a child, and a few red hairs clinging to a piece of green cloth.

"Okay," she said. "Tell me about those two hoods again, the two guys who killed the Rosenfelds."

"Santo Vestri and Ray Nuñez," Eddie said. "Idiots who spent most of their lives in the system."

"But yet they stumble across a four-million-dollar score."

"Four point two."

"It seems weird for two reasons. One, that they knew Rosenfeld would have that much money; and two, that Rosenfeld didn't have a bodyguard with that kind of cash sitting around."

"I seriously doubt these guys had any clue that there was that much money on hand. And I don't have an idea why Rosenfeld wouldn't have had some kind of security. But then again, I remember he worked for Evesi Volshin, one of the most arrogant people on the face of the earth. This guy thought he was the king of the world. No one would dare rip him off."

"And you think there's no way the murder of Angelo Caruso and his wife is connected to that incident?"

"I gave my best guess to Boland. The past is the past. I think it's a brand-new world and all the new roads lead to Yuri Borodenko. Maybe he's getting rid of all the tough old birds. Then there'll be no doubt who's in charge. I remember reading in *The Gulag Archipelago* that the KGB would watch the crowd cheering during a rally for Stalin. The people would stand there applauding and yelling for hours and hours. But then someone would realize the stupidity of this and sit down. Then a few others. Then they'd all sit down. The KGB would make a note of who sat down first. They'd have those people eliminated. They knew that any independent thinking was dangerous. Borodenko is doing away with the independent thinkers."

"Are you an independent thinker?" she said.

Eddie reached across the table and held her hand. Her hands were cold.

"I want you to know that no matter how this turns out,

I know that I brought this on myself. You are the good that's come out of it."

Eddie's phone rang. Kevin looked over, recognizing his signature Irish tune. It was Matty Boland. They'd found Freddie Dolgev.

# CHAPTER

# 29

---

**SUNDAY**
**10:00 P.M.**

FREDEK DOLGEV'S MENTAL RETARDATION was more severe than they'd imagined. By the time Eddie got to the
Coney Island precinct, the interview was over. Boland
doubted that anything the maintenance man said could be
held reliable. Eddie said he didn't care about reliability,
that he'd take whatever truth Dolgev's fevered brain
could conjure up.

"He's got the mind of a ten-year-old," Boland said. "It
wasn't much of an interview."

Freddie's lawyer had called and insisted the questioning of his client cease. The lawyer arrived about ten minutes later. He'd been on the phone ever since. Boland said
that after the lawyer called, they didn't push any further.
It wasn't worth jeopardizing the search of his apartment
for such a small prospect of a return. Plus, as Boland said,
it didn't hurt to get a little goodwill on the legal ledger.
Who gives a shit about goodwill? Eddie thought. Give
me five good minutes. I'd have him pissing blood in half
that time.

"Where did you find him?" Eddie asked.

"Uniform picked him up. Somebody told them about a guy hiding under the boardwalk, talking to himself in Russian. He wasn't far from his house. Apparently, he came home, saw the cops, and freaked out."

Eddie had dropped Kate's hairbrush off at the NYPD lab on Jamaica Avenue before going to his old precinct. It felt strange walking up those steps. The squad room was essentially how Eddie remembered it, disheveled and disorganized. The paint job, a shade of brown, rather than the two-tone green in his day. Computer screens blinked where old Remingtons had once rested. A plastic tower with CD-ROMs had replaced the stack of phone books.

"Can you hold him until we get the lab analysis on the hair?"

"Not on the word of a Gypsy we can't find," Boland said. "The boss is kicking him. I asked him to stall until you got here. At least you could eyeball him."

"He say anything at all?" Eddie said.

"'*Nyet, nyet*' is about the extent of it. We used that Russian interpreter from the DA's office—the heavyset woman. Sometimes I wonder whose side she's on. Whenever we showed him the picture of Kate and asked questions about her, the interpreter told us he answered 'No,' although it sounded different every time to me. But it was clear he knows something. The guy is scared. He's in there stinking up the room."

From behind the two-way glass of the observation room, they watched Fredek Dolgev pace the floor, muttering. He was alone in the interview room. The right side of his face, where it could be seen above the bandages, looked like a deep red birthmark. His thin gray hair was singed; both eyebrows had been burned off. His right shirtsleeve was tight from the bandages. But the burns didn't seem to bother him. The guy was clearly agitated about something. His face contorted in some internal argument. The back of his shirt was stained with sweat. A huge set of keys hung from his belt.

"Somewhere in that hellhole of a mind, he knows he's part of something wrong," Eddie said.

"He'll never say it, though. The only thing he knows is to shut up. We could beat this guy until morning and he wouldn't give up the people he depends on."

Boland said he'd started with simple questions, trying to get Freddie to relax, but that didn't happen. At first, he was careful to avoid any direct questions about the kidnapping of Kate. He tried to talk about Freddie's background, figuring everybody is comfortable telling their own story. Then he'd swing back around to questions about Kate, and Freddie would go into his shell.

"You get a background check?" Eddie asked.

"Yeah, Immigration finally started keeping somebody there on weekends."

Fredek Dolgev came to the United States from Russia three years ago. He was sponsored by his cousin Yuri Borodenko. Dolgev had worked for Borodenko in Moscow for many years, shoveling snow and keeping wood in the fire. Borodenko brought him over to the States as a hardship case after his father died. He was currently employed as part of Borodenko's personal staff, doing repair and maintenance work.

"Did he say how he got burned?"

"Yeah, he admitted being in the Rolls-Royce," Boland said. "He said he ran because he thought he'd set the car on fire, cleaning under the dash. He didn't know which hospital they took him to, or why they went so far out of their way."

"Zina took him," Eddie said. "Her name is on the form."

"I asked him about Zina. I asked him several different ways. He kept repeating that Zina is his friend."

"We know any more about her?"

Boland said several of the squad detectives knew her. According to them, Zina Rabinovich was a tough, streetwise Russian Bukharan Jew, the first in her family not born in Russia, but in the borough of Brooklyn. She'd worked in numerous junkyards, managing the used-parts business. She was in her twenties, slender but well muscled, with shoulder-length brown hair. And the word *tomboy* didn't do her justice. She walked with an exaggerated street punk's bounce, all head bop and shoulder flex. No one had ever seen her wear anything but work boots, jeans, a T-shirt, and a leather motorcycle jacket. Zina was a girl who could take a car apart blindfolded. She could spit, curse, scratch, smoke, and throw better than most guys. About a year ago, she began working for Borodenko as a chauffeur and bodyguard for his wife.

"She hangs out in a dyke joint off Stillwell called Alice B's," Boland said. "Don't go there; you ain't tough enough to drink in that place."

Zina's arrest record included a few assaults, all upon males. The rest were car thefts, starting as a teenager and including her high school principal's Honda. She lasted only two months into her senior year, then went to work in the junkyards.

"I bet she still steals cars," Eddie said.

"You're thinking she stole the black BMW?"

"Parrot said it's her face on both sketches. I also think she broke into my house, and killed Lukin."

"Let's find a reason to bring her in. Maybe she's more than just a chauffeur."

Eddie kept quiet on the fact he'd tailed Mrs. Borodenko and a slender dark-haired female to lunch on Staten Island. Although he never got a good look, he was sure now that the other female was Zina. For the few minutes he was able to see both of them clearly, he'd focused on Mrs. Borodenko.

"Do you have a booking photo of Zina?" Eddie asked.

"Yeah, but don't look at it yet. You're an eyewitness. We'll need you to be a virgin, so give me a chance to put together a decent photo lineup."

Eddie kept hearing a jangle as Freddie wore out the floor in the interview room. The noise came from a huge ring of keys clipped to Freddie's belt loop. At least fifty keys. Eddie got closer to the window. It looked like each key had a piece of tape with a notation, probably an address.

"Look at all those *keys,*" Eddie said slowly, emphasizing the last word. "I bet he has a *key* into everything that Borodenko owns."

Boland took a step closer, his nose almost against the glass. "Holy shit," he said. "I gotta get my hands on those keys."

"Hold him overnight."

"I smell an immigration violation coming on," Boland said. "He'll be out in the morning, but it'll give me enough time to find out if we need a warrant to copy keys."

"Screw the warrant; just copy them."

While Boland was on the phone, the squad lieutenant

entered the observation room and told them he'd cut
Freddie loose. Boland immediately hung up the phone
and chased the boss back to his office. The lawyer picked
up his briefcase and thanked them for their considerate
treatment of his client. Eddie watched from the doorway
as Freddie Dolgev stared down at the tiles. Then Boland
dropped the news that unless they came up with Freddie's green card, he was going to be held on his ques-
tionable immigration status.

"That's pathetic," the lawyer said. "That's low even
for you people."

"Show us he's legal," Boland said, "and then he's a
free man."

"It's harassment, pure and simple," the lawyer said.
"You guys are dying to spend a week in civil court."

While Boland and the lawyer chest-bumped, Eddie
stood in front of Fredek Dolgev, trying to force him to
look up. The Russian appeared intent on memorizing
the floor tiles. Eddie grabbed his scorched chin and
raised his head. Dolgev jumped back, his eyes wide and
locked on Eddie Dunne. He began pointing and yelling,
*"Razborka, razborka."* Then he leaped at Eddie, reaching for his throat. Eddie stood his ground, but a young
squad detective swiveled in his chair and wrapped his
arms around the charging Russian. The other cops
jumped in. They staggered back between desks. Eddie
kept whispering, "Let him go, let him go." Files and
desk lamps hit the floor. Eddie edged closer, inviting the
man to choke him. They all went down in a pile.
Somebody yelled, "Watch your weapons." When it
ended, Eddie made it plain that he wanted Mr. Dolgev
arrested for assault.

"He never touched you," the lawyer said.

"He attacked me," Eddie said. "Everyone here is a witness. I never saw him before in my life, and he threatened me."

"You inflamed him," the lawyer said.

"I never said a word."

"He knows you," said the female interpreter from the DA's office. "*Razborka* means an account that needs to be settled. A judgment on you. He knows you."

"This is patently wrong," the lawyer said. "This is an unfair stunt pulled on a man with diminished mental capacities. I won't stand for it; the courts won't stand for it."

The lawyer stormed out, but not before taking everything Fredek Dolgev had on him—his money, his wallet, and his keys. With the keys gone, it didn't really matter what happened to Freddie.

"Those keys would have made all the difference in the world," Boland said. "The keys to Yuri's kingdom. We could have gotten every single bug installed in one night."

In the letdown that followed, Eddie talked to a young detective about the old-timers: who'd retired and who'd died in Florida. He pulled names out of his memory. The cop didn't have much history in the precinct. Squads turned over more quickly these days. He kept typing an arrest report as the radio on his desk blared rap music. The cleaning crew dumped trash cans and swung a damp string mop over floors of a forgotten color. Eddie sat sipping the strongest black coffee he'd had in years and realizing how much he missed it all. With Boland gone, he asked the young detective if he could look around.

Eddie strolled around reading WANTED posters,

Detective Division memos, and personnel orders. Then, when the cop went into the boss's office to drop the typed form in his in box, Eddie lifted a booking photo of Zina Rabinovich and put it in his pocket. He didn't need any lineup. This was the face.

# CHAPTER
# 30

**MONDAY, APRIL 13**
**1:00 A.M.**

EXCEPT FOR THE FACT that every patron was female, Alice B's could have been any neighborhood bar in town. It had once been a raucous Coney Island beer joint, and the new owners apparently liked the blue-collar ambience, as very little appeared to have changed. Centered on the wooden frame above the bar was a piece of stained glass too lovely to remove. Embedded in the glass was the image of a harp, the national symbol of the Emerald Isle, and the name of the previous owner: O'Gorman. Eddie took a stool in the corner, far away from the other drinkers. His back was against the wall, cop-style. At that angle, he could see everyone in the place.

Midnight on Sunday finds most New York bars dozing. Alice B's had that hushed feel, everyone whispering but not knowing why. Even though he wasn't drinking anymore, Eddie still liked the calm of gin mill Sunday nights. It was a time for the bar's family to reconnect, for the bartenders and waitresses to sip the owner's good stuff and trade dirty jokes. The obnoxious weekend crowd was gone, so the regulars finally got the attention they deserved. Eddie figured the people in Alice B's tonight were regulars. So when he walked in, he interrupted not only girl talk but family hour.

The attractive slender woman behind the bar wore leather pants and a black turtleneck sweater. She didn't rush right down to Eddie, waiting a few beats instead, hoping he'd figure things out on his own. When he didn't, she sighed and made a big show of schlepping down to his end of the bar. Most bartenders slap a coaster down in front of you, then invite you to name your poison. This one did neither.

"I think you picked the wrong place, pal," she said. "Try Nevin's, down the block. I think you'll feel more comfortable there."

"Club soda," Eddie said. "Twist of lime, if you have it."

"Look around, big guy. The diddly-diddly crowd ain't here anymore."

"Forget the lime if it's a problem."

"You didn't hear me."

"I heard you," Eddie said.

Eddie watched to make sure she didn't play games with his drink. He put his money down on the bar; there was no way she was going to let him run a tab. As his eyes got used to the light, he could see there were four women at the bar, another half dozen at tables, and two moving slowly across the dance floor. One of the dancers was a redhead. Her hair, full and wild, made him look twice, but she was much shorter than Kate. Eddie took out the photograph of Zina and leaned it against his club soda.

You rarely see a smiling mug shot. Zina was not pretty, but she had a great wide smile, full lips, and a complexion that wasn't suffocated by makeup. Her nose was big and slightly off center, but it made you focus on those immense dark eyes. Oddly enough, her hair looked clean and shiny. A neat trick for someone who supposedly lived under the hood of a car.

Eddie took his time studying each woman who might possibly be Zina. Most were too fat, too thin, or too Barbie. The nearest drinker at the bar was a big-boned woman with a GI buzz cut. She was wearing a sleeveless denim vest. On her right biceps was a large tattoo of a leopard holding a banner in its teeth. He couldn't read the words on the banner. His eyes kept drifting back to the redhead on the dance floor as the jukebox played a slow country-and-western song. The couple swayed, barely moving. The C&W surprised Eddie. He didn't think this would be a Nashville crowd.

The bartender sat on a cooler, her legs tucked up under her, as she talked to a small blonde at the bar. Eddie waited, sipping his club soda. He wanted them to get used to him for a few minutes. Let them realize he wasn't a self-loathing drunk out searching for a beating, or a lesbo watcher looking to get his jollies. The bartender and the blonde were facing in his direction but were looking at the TV above his head. He could see in the mirror's reflection that they were watching a *Law and Order* rerun. With the sound off, they read the closed captions.

"Bartender," Eddie finally said. He knew better than to refer to her as miss, or think of her as a bar*maid*.

She said something out of the side of her mouth, which got a few laughs, then walked down.

"Do you know this woman?" he asked, showing her the picture of Zina. He held his thumb partially over the B number under her chin, but still letting her see it.

"I figured you gotta be a cop," she said. "Ballsy attitude and all. My friend says it's not balls, that it's something kinkier, but I'll give you the benefit of the doubt."

She took a quick look at the photo, not long enough to tell anything. Her answer was prepared and practiced.

"Never saw her before."

"Look again," he said. "She comes in here all the time."

"I told you: I don't know her."

"Sure you do. Her name is Zina Rabinovich."

"If you know who she is, why the hell you asking me?"

"I need to find her."

"Sorry, can't help you."

"Then I'll ask your friends," he said, starting to get off the stool.

"Wait, wait, wait," she said. "What's so important that you need to find her tonight?"

"Because a friend of hers just got arrested. A retarded guy named Freddie Dolgev. He lives across the hall from her. He wanted me to find her."

"If you know where she lives, go there."

"I did. She's not home."

"Okay, just show me some identification before I let you go around interrogating my customers."

Eddie took out the small leather case that contained the replica of his old detective shield. The tattered case looked like it had been around the block. He'd carried it since he'd first made detective. The emblem and numbers had embedded in the leather. It couldn't have looked more authentic. His ID card was another matter. Retired cops got to keep their ID; it was merely stamped "Retired." No such perk if you resigned. Before turning in his ID on his last day as a cop, he'd color-copied and laminated it. It looked official-enough, sitting behind the yellowed plastic sleeve in the case.

"Give me a minute," the bartender said.

Her leather pants squeaked as she went back to the other end to confer with the small blonde. The big bare-armed woman, muttering to herself, slapped the bar hard with the palm of her hand; then she stood up and walked out. As she turned to throw an ugly glare at Eddie, he saw that the tattooed banner read DEATH BEFORE DISHONOR. A minute later, the small blonde pulled up the stool next to him. She wore a navy blazer over faded jeans and could have been a suburban soccer mom.

"I never saw you around here before," she said after she asked to see his identification.

"I'm on special assignment."

"Where do you normally work?"

"The Four-eight in the Bronx."

"You know Kevin Moroney?"

Eddie did know Kevin Moroney. But he also knew the blonde was a cop and that she had his number.

"It was the ID, right?" Eddie said.

"The whole department changed years ago. We use an upright card now, and it's red, white, and blue. Only retired cops carry these old maroon cards."

"I should get it changed."

"If you're going to pull this stunt again, you'd better. There's one thing I want you to remember: Don't ever pull this shit in here again or I'm going to lock your ass up. You're not an active cop. You can't play like you're one. That's impersonating. It's a crime. Good try, but you can't do this. We understand each other?"

"Yeah," Eddie said. "But how about Zina?"

"Don't worry about Zina. Someone will get word to her that Freddie is jammed up. Is he in the Six-oh?"

The couple on the dance floor clung together during another slow tune, a twangy female vocalist who had it bad and that ain't good. All other eyes were focused on him.

"Listen," Eddie said, leaning over so he could speak softly. "You seem like a nice young woman. So I have a little advice for you. Don't get on the wrong side of this. If Zina has anything to do with kidnapping my daughter, you don't want to come out of this as a lesbian cop who obstructed justice."

The little blonde sat back and gave him a look that said, Okay, now I've got it. "I know who you are," she said, nodding her head. "I heard the story. Tough thing, tough goddamn thing. I want you to know that if Zina had anything to do with it, I'll be the first one to put cuffs on her. Okay? We see eye-to-eye on that, right? Like I said, I feel bad for what happened. Hurting your family is bullshit, but that doesn't give you the right to come in here and threaten me. All that does is piss me off. "

"I wish all I felt now was pissed-off," Eddie said.

"Get the fuck out of here," she said. "Before we have to call an ambulance."

In the quiet, the regulars picked up on the tension in the blonde's voice. Eddie nodded toward her and scooped all but a buck off the bar. Nothing to be gained in forcing the issue. On the way out, he stopped to read the posted softball schedule. The Brooklyn Adult Women's Fast-Pitch Softball League. Six teams total, a few in Queens. Alice B's played Dietrich's for the season opener on May 1. Eddie snatched the schedule off the wall. It gave him five more places to look. One called Lady's was close by, in Bay Ridge, ten minutes away. He had enough time before closing to hit a few of them.

A damp, cold Coney Island chill hung in the night air. The streets were empty, but as soon as he took three steps from the bar, he could see something was wrong. The entire driver's side of his Olds tilted toward the road. He had a flat tire and no spare. There would be no tour of lesbian bars tonight. Then as he got closer . . . double that problem. Two flats. Both tires had been slashed.

Sunday night was always a bitch in Brooklyn. Auto mechanics in the borough were never informed that Brooklyn was part of a town called "the city that never sleeps." Just try to get a tire fixed on Sunday night. Eddie took both tires off, then eventually found an off-duty cabdriver willing to make two hundred bucks. He tossed the tires in the trunk and the driver took him to the spot his garage used. He bought two retreads from Northey's Discount Tire, got them mounted, and paid another two hundred for the ride back.

By the time he got there, a hint of a sunrise had begun to lighten the sky. Stillwell Avenue was so quiet, he could hear the ocean churning. A few early birds hustled toward the el station. Eddie jacked up the front end of the Olds and slid the wheel on, only hand-tightening the lugs. Then he went to the back wheel. He heard another car nearby, the engine idling roughly. Looking in his side-view mirror, he saw a dark blue muscle car, either a Camaro or a Firebird, parked in front of the coffee shop across from Nathan's. The car vibrated from a badly tuned engine. The glass was tinted black. A stream of cigarette smoke rose from the crack above the window on the driver's side. Eddie tightened the lug nuts on the back wheel. He didn't bother with the hubcap; he tossed it in the trunk for now. Then he went back to the front wheel.

With two lugs to go, Eddie worked faster. He needed a shower, something to eat, and a chance to talk to someone who loved him. He pressed his cheek against the front fender and leaned into it. Then something hit the car. He heard it at the same moment he felt the impact. It hit the roof, something solid, a heavy, rolling bang. At first, he thought it was a rock, maybe a baseball or pool ball. Rolling . . . from the roof . . . rolling down to the hood. It bounced off the hood, hit the pavement, and rolled against the curb right in front of him.

Nobody had to yell "Grenade." Despite stiff knees, he moved quickly, three steps to the back of the Olds. He hit the ground and rolled under an SUV parked behind him. He saw the muscle car peel out, but he only heard rubber squealing for a moment. Then the explosion.

The aftermath was worse than the boom. His ears rang as if he had a burglar alarm in his head. The SUV still shook. Dirt and grit that had fallen from the undercarriage of the SUV when it was rocked by the blast filled his mouth, eyes, and hair. Eddie pushed himself out, then to his feet. He could feel the smashed safety glass in his palms. The air was full of rising dust and dirt and the smell of explosives. And the ringing car alarms, burglar alarms.

Then another ring, the wail of sirens. On Stillwell Avenue, people in bathrobes came from apartments he didn't know existed. They were out pointing at him. Cops were on the way. Eddie knew they'd be uniformed precinct cops finishing up a midnight tour. Looking to get home and crawl in the sack with mama still warm from the night. He knew the cops had just finished checking the business glass in their sectors, ready for morning coffee and a hard roll. They were thinking, Can't this bullshit wait for the day tour? It never did. He also knew what the Coney Island cops would say after the mop-up and the paperwork were done. They'd say what Paulie the Priest always said: "Just another day at the beach."

# CHAPTER

# 31

THE BOMB SQUAD dug small chunks of metal out of car fenders and wood-framed buildings and identified the weapon as a Russian RGO fragmentation grenade. RGOs sold for five bucks apiece on the worldwide stolen-weapons network. The fuses often varied in length by as much as seven seconds. Eddie'd been lucky to get a slow burner.

His ears weren't as lucky—he could still hear the ringing. His skin felt tight and drawn, as if freshly sun-burned, and he'd inhaled and swallowed a pound of grit. Otherwise, he was fine.

No stitches, no broken bones. The biggest victim was the Olds. After the CSU went over it, they towed it to the precinct, but it was history. "Junk it," Matty Boland told him. "Your insurance won't cover acts of God or hand grenades."

Although he was hurting, Eddie felt surprisingly at peace. It was the same feeling he'd always had in the days after a tough fight. Pain and exhaustion were strangely comforting. Boland drove him home the long way. A quiet

ride up the Major Deegan past the white stone facade of
Yankee Stadium, the home of the Bronx Bombers, a name
that had taken on a new significance. The Baltimore
Orioles were due to get blasted at 8:10 P.M. He closed his
eyes in the morning sun as they drove past Yonkers
Raceway, where the suckers arrived at 7:30.

Boland dropped Eddie at his back door and left. The
house was empty except for a cop looking for a book on
Eddie's shelves. The Yonkers Police Department had sta-
tioned a uniformed cop at the house after the incident
with the head on the lawn. Maybe the grenade incident
would keep them around awhile longer.

Less than an hour after the explosion, Eddie had called
Kevin from Brooklyn. He didn't want them hearing it on
the news. Yelling into the phone, Eddie told him that he
never got touched. That was the same line he'd used
when he called his father after every fight. By the time
the family saw the bruises, the swelling, and his sewn-up
eyelids, the anxiety level would have diminished. They
never knew how often he pissed blood, or bit off chunks
of his tongue.

More than ever before, Eddie wanted his family to go
about their business. Act normal, so Grace wouldn't
sense the fear. That's why the house was quiet. Grace was
in school, Kevin and Martha in the bar. Business as usual.
Except for Kate. And Babsie, who was down at One
Police Plaza, poring over Eddie's personnel file, searching for a fourteen-year-old smoking gun.

Eddie slid leftover pizza into the microwave, box and
all. He knew the crust would be tough and chewy, but
speed was all that mattered. Two minutes later, he sat
there listening to his kitchen clock and washing a slice
down with a diet cola. Diet belonged to Babsie. Eddie

didn't drink diet and Kate didn't drink cola. He couldn't taste it, but it soothed his parched throat. He had another one, refilling the cup with ice. No way he could handle more coffee. He'd had three cups before Matty Boland arrived at the Six-oh with a Starbucks Grande for the trip home. The only negative thing Boland said was that he didn't feel sorry for him; he'd warned him not to go to Alice B's. Now he was going to have to live with the label of being the first known victim of a lesbian hand grenade.

In the shower, pieces of stone and glass washed down from his hair and ears. He easily located the head abrasions the EMT had told him were there. The technician figured the SUV he'd hidden under bounced from the grenade's concussion and hammered his head into the pavement. Hot water stung his skin. The good news was that his ears were improving. The ringing burglar alarm seemed to be less audible as the hours passed. Hopefully, the distance to his daughter was now shorter. He'd struck a nerve today. Apparently, the mere mention of the name Zina Rabinovich brought fireworks.

After he got out of the shower, Eddie hunted down the keys to Kate's Toyota Camry. Martha had picked it up from the shop; he knew she would have stuck the keys in some odd place, not on the rack in the kitchen, where everyone else left them. He found them in Kate's top dresser drawer. It was the first time he'd been in her room since she'd disappeared, a full week ago.

On the wall above Kate's dresser was a small crucifix. On the dresser were pictures of Grace, him, and Eileen, and a small silver statue of the Blessed Virgin Mary she'd bought with her lunch money in second grade at Christ the King. Kate had a love-hate relationship with the

Catholic church. More and more, she'd been speaking out, always shocking her aunt Martha. Kate believed that if the church would let women be priests, or allow the male priests to marry, it could solve the priest shortage tomorrow. "A bunch of old fogies hold us back," she claimed, "out of touch with reality, and driving the church straight to hell."

To Eddie, religion was a private matter. He couldn't care less what the robed politicos did; he'd find his own spirituality. He'd never been happy with the new Catholic church anyway, all the handshakes and Protestant singing. Kate's old fogies even screwed up the Mass itself. They took away the Latin and destroyed the mystery. Mystery demands faith, and religion is about nothing except faith, Eddie thought. The words are a drone anyway, so what's the difference? Bring back the Latin; turn the priests around.

His head buzzed with coffee and worry as he tried to fall asleep. He'd reached a point in his life where he wanted desperately to believe in God, and especially that big reunion in the sweet hereafter. Only that belief made growing old bearable. Eddie wanted a chance to apologize to those he'd hurt for no reason, and to connect with those he'd ignored because he was too stupid to see their goodness. He wanted to inhale the incense and believe it all, but so much evidence pointed at a random, uncaring deity. If that's a wrong idea, then why does a child suffer while so many scumbags, as many as you can possibly imagine, walk free? Don't even try to explain it to me. Not now.

Eddie had been drifting in and out of sleep when he heard Babsie's voice in the living room. She was talking to Kevin about the hand grenade. Kevin told her about

Eddie yelling into the phone, then an old story about their dad. Whenever the smoke alarm had gone off in the restaurant, Kieran, going deaf at the time, paid no attention to it. When one of the customers at the bar mentioned that maybe Kieran should look into it, he would say he assumed it was just the battery on his hearing aid going bad. Listening to Kevin and Babsie talk, Eddie felt removed, outside of himself. They both seemed to be amazed that someone would throw a hand grenade. He wasn't. Maybe that was Eddie's problem: Nothing ever surprised him. Nobody was ever more evil than he expected them to be.

Babsie came by his room as he was starting to pull on his pants, but a back spasm flopped him back on the bed.

"What are you doing?" she said.

"Getting up."

"Looked more like a twisting half gainer."

"What time is it?"

"Early. You've got time. Grab another hour or so."

Babsie had dressed for the trip to NYPD headquarters. Her grayish blond hair was back in a ponytail, all business. She wore a black pantsuit that had a short waist-length jacket. She even wore lipstick.

"Thomas Edison used to doze in a chair, holding a pencil," Eddie said, struggling with his pants. "When the pencil fell out of his hand, he'd get up and go back to work."

"Nobody was throwing grenades at Edison," she said.

"Is Grace here?" Eddie asked, squinting at the clock. He knew he'd slept too long.

Babsie said she'd picked Grace up from school, and now she was over at Kevin's house, jumping on the pogo stick.

"She's coming over for dinner in a few minutes. If

you're getting up, fix your pants. I don't want Martha coming in and seeing this. She'll be calling me a Polack whore."

With Babsie's help, Eddie got to his feet. The repercussions of rolling around Stillwell Avenue had set in. A pain shot from his hip down his right leg. Babsie said it was probably sciatica. Her brother had it from jumping off the bleachers after a softball game. Eddie managed to get his pants up, but then reaching for his shoes was a challenge.

"I need to talk to you before they come over," she said. "I saw your personnel folder today."

"And you weren't struck blind?"

"What the hell happened? You had a great career going. Came on the job in 1966, made detective in only three years. That's damn fast for the NYPD. Couple of years in the best detective squads in Manhattan. Rated number one in the thirteenth precinct squad. I read all those glowing evaluations. I could see all the commendations in your file. Then comes 1974 and you get transferred to Brooklyn. It's like you fell off the face of the earth."

"Coney Island," Eddie said. "The Irish always get burned at the beach."

"You got scorched. Mostly petty IAB bullshit, at first. Then you got serious. Three serious rips for drinking on duty. You still made some good collars, but in between was party time. Despite that, you somehow hung in there and survived for ten years. Then you went down in flames in 1984. Right after the Rosenfeld case. I can't help it, Eddie, everything circles back around to that case."

Eddie knew he couldn't avoid rehashing the Rosenfeld homicide. He told her again how the couple were murdered in their home by Ray Nuñez and Santo Vestri, who stole over four million dollars in cash from them. He was getting sick of repeating this story; he should have cards printed. He told her again that Rosenfeld was a lawyer whose expertise was in setting up phony corporations and moving money through them. He moved millions for Evesi Volshin, a Russian criminal. The cash was dirty, mostly from the gasoline-tax scheme. Nuñez and Vestri entered the Rosenfeld house in Manhattan Beach, killed the couple in front of their little girl, and took off with the cash. Eddie and the Priest spotted them leaving, followed them to a nearby park, where a gun battle broke out. Nuñez and Vestri were both killed.

"I called around," Babsie said. "They have old rosters stored in Queens. I got a few names of old Brooklyn squad detectives. Some of them are working big jobs in private security. I got pointed to this former squad boss, Jack Ferguson."

"I know 'Tomato Juice' Jack."

"He lives in Palm Beach, Florida now. He tells me that Nuñez and Vestri were shitbird junkies."

"I told you that."

"Not exactly. But forget that. Did you know that six weeks before the Rosenfeld murders, Nuñez and Vestri were suspected of ripping off the wedding of one of Angelo Caruso's nieces? They grabbed the cash bag right out of the bride's hands as she was leaving the reception. Four radio cars responded and the Six-oh is pretty specific. They estimated that over twenty grand was taken. Ferguson said they knew it was Nuñez and Vestri, but they were never arrested. The complainant, one Angelo Caruso, later denied the robbery'd ever happened, said it was all a big misunderstanding."

"How much did you take in at *your* wedding?"

"Not enough to pay for the booze. I had to go and marry into the only cheap Italian family in New York. But that's not the point."

"I get the point. Somebody dropped the complaint, most likely because they made some other deal with Nuñez and Vestri. Maybe Angelo Caruso takes these guys aside and tells them if they want to live, they had to do a job for him. The Rosenfelds were that job."

"Sounds like you've thought about this before, Eddie."

"It's easier than thinking about my own problems."

"I figure Nuñez and Vestri weren't supposed to kill the Rosenfelds, but it got out of hand."

"Why think that?" Eddie said. "Maybe the murder was intentional. Part of the plan. Marvin Rosenfeld was a smart guy. He could link Nuñez and Vestri back to Angelo. Makes sense they had to kill him."

"So you agree with me that Nuñez and Vestri were hired by Angelo Caruso?"

"Walking dead men. And the Priest and I executed them, leaving no witnesses."

"You're being a jerk now. If you knew it was set up, you wouldn't have turned all that money in. You would have known the Rosenfelds were already dead, and there'd be no one to say how much money was stolen. Guys like Paulie the Priest don't let four million dollars slip through their fingers that easily."

He could see Grace and Martha walking across the lawn. They both were laughing. No one else but Grace could get a laugh out of Martha.

Babsie's phone rang as Grace came through the bedroom door. She'd tiptoed down the hall and peeked into the room. When she saw him sitting on the bed, she ran and jumped into his arms, wrapping her legs around his waist. The first thing she said was that someone named Roberto had to go to the principal's office for using bad words.

"You want to know which ones?" she said.

My God, he thought holding her close, has anyone ever missed out on more of his life than I have? He looked over at Babsie, who'd put her phone away and was standing there staring at him, eyes moist.

"Bad?" he asked.

"The lab compared the hair samples," she said. "It's a match."

# CHAPTER

# 32

EDDIE DUNNE FELT the hairs on the back of his neck rise as he pulled into the parking lot of the El Greco diner. For the first time in a week, he had a real shot at finding his daughter. Fredek Dolgev had been released from custody earlier that afternoon. His lawyer posted bail before the NYPD lab identified the red hair found in Dolgev's boardwalk apartment as belonging to Kate. Eddie was betting the attorney still didn't know. In fact, he was counting on it. The minute that knowledge reached Borodenko, the maintenance man would become a liability.

The El Greco was a large sixties-style Brooklyn diner. Square and flat-roofed, it was wrapped in enough shiny metal to replate both the *Monitor* and the *Merrimac*. The street-side chrome was pocked with hundreds of dings and dents from car bumpers. Eddie parked against the rear fence, facing front, so he could watch both the street and the entrance to the diner. One last check of the other cars in the parking lot, then he climbed the four steps up to the diner.

He had no doubt that as soon as Dolgev was released, he'd immediately returned to the comfort of routine. Anyone who ate in the same restaurant three times a day, every day, could be considered a sure thing. This guy was like clockwork. The clock said he should have entered the diner ten minutes ago. He'd be sitting alone in a booth, looking out at Sheepshead Bay.

Neither Boland nor Babsie knew of Dolgev's methodical eating habits. Eddie had kept it to himself. He didn't want any civil servant using phrases like "diminished mental capacity" in the middle of the beating Eddie was prepared to inflict. Kidnappers got no special disability exemption. Dolgev was not the innocent here. He'd tell what he knew, period. Nothing more, nothing less. A week's worth of Eddie's pent-up rage would open the Russian's mouth—no matter how long it took. Brutality, like beauty, was in the eye of the beholder.

Inside the diner, all seating revolved around the kitchen. A counter and chrome stools faced the kitchen. Behind that, loose tables for four, which could be pulled together for larger groups. Red vinyl booths lined the windows. The floor was carpeted in a dark burgundy. Eddie told the hostess he was meeting a friend. He said he'd scout around first, see if he'd arrived.

At 6:50, the El Greco was a madhouse. Conversations shouted over clattering plates and silverware boosted the noise to prison-riot levels. At a table near the door, a little girl colored on the restaurant's place mat— an outdated outline of the nations of Europe. She carefully kept between the borders as her mother made secret arrangements for a cake with candles. The mother spoke in English with a common Russian accent, but her clothes were upscale. "Hold the cake until after dinner," she told the hostess, "or she'll never eat her vegetables."

Fredek Dolgev sat in his booth, oblivious. Head down, fist wrapped around a fork, he shoveled food into his mouth. Eddie stayed on the opposite side. His plan was not to approach him here, but to follow him home. He didn't think he'd lead him to his daughter, but he might lead him to Zina. Eddie thought he'd tail Freddie until he saw him reaching for his keys, about to enter a building. Then he'd snatch this Russian off the street, as he had another Russian, Sergei. Among the trees of Marine Park, Freddie Dolgev would tell him where to find Kate.

Eddie checked faces hidden behind partitions and fake plants, looking for detectives, off-duty cops, old girlfriends, anyone who could complicate the scenario. Mirrored walls were the tailman's friend. He checked all sides of the restaurant perimeter, looking to see if any of Borodenko's hired guns lurked nearby. Not that the Russians needed to worry about Freddie. He had enough IQ to understand that American cops weren't going to yank out his fingernails. He wouldn't utter a word to them. But Freddie's loyalty didn't matter. If he weren't Borodenko's cousin, he'd be dead already.

After he was satisfied, Eddie returned to Kate's Camry in the parking lot and tried to get comfortable. He didn't really like the Camry. It had a tight, responsive quickness to it, but it seemed hard-riding and tiring to drive. And there was something miniature about it he didn't like. The cloth seat covers, made of a suedelike material, acted like Velcro, preventing any sliding across the bucket seats. The rough cloth of the headrest felt like sandpaper against the skin abrasions from the lesbian grenade. Eddie preferred bench seats. He preferred the cushy Olds, every bit as quick, and yet as comfortable as your living room sofa. The Camry's reclining seats were a plus, however. He angled the seat back so he could watch the diner's front steps and back kitchen door at the same time. He stayed in the passenger seat, as if waiting for the driver.

Eddie called the North End Tavern and asked for Kevin. B. J. Harrington told him he was missing out on the roast chicken, which was as grand as it was every Monday. Then he told him that Kevin was in the back, and he asked if Eddie wanted to speak to his lovely sister-in-law instead. Eddie was about to relent, when he noticed a black Lincoln Town Car pull into the parking lot and make a quick U-turn. The U-turn piqued his interest. The driver pulled the Lincoln right up to the door of the diner and waited at the front steps with the engine running, forcing other cars to go around him. Eddie clicked the phone off.

The Lincoln parked at the foot of the diner steps, facing the street, motor running, poised for the getaway. This wasn't about a cheeseburger takeout. It reeked of muscle. Either a stickup or vig collection. The passenger door swung open and a guy wearing a black leather car coat got out. About five ten, wide-bodied, he was a refrigerator of a man. Eddie sat up straight as the man limped around the front of the Lincoln. He knew that head. A big gangster dome with sparse, close-cropped stubble, sitting neckless on a stocky body. Eddie knew exactly who it was. Somehow Sergei Zhukov was not in a car trunk on his way to Russia, but entering the El Greco diner. Sergei grabbed the rail and pulled himself up the four steps and into the diner.

By the time Eddie ran up the diner steps, Sergei had

managed to evaporate. Eddie stood near the front table, trying to spot the black leather car coat. The chat level in the restaurant had decreased several notches as people studied their salads. It was as if a thick blanket had muffled the restaurant noise, smothering all the tables as it rolled from front to back. He could see Dolgev at his window booth, squeezing a white mug in his big hands, the world forever tuned out.

Afraid to blink, Eddie scanned all sides. Still no Sergei. A sharp intake of breath came from the birthday girl as the cake arrived from the kitchen, its candles burning. The waitress and the mom and dad began to sing as Sergei suddenly appeared in the aisle. He came straight up behind Dolgev and put the gun against his ear. The blast from the first shot sucked the air out of the room.

"Sergei," Eddie screamed as he pulled his old service revolver and circled around to the left, but there was no way to get an angle. It was a reflex action, a mistake on Eddie's part; he had no way to keep a single breathing soul out of the line of fire. Sergei saw him coming and knew he had the advantage. They pivoted around each other, guns drawn, face-to-face. People dived to the floor, holding their heads. Sergei backed toward the door, smiling, moving slowly, his halting gait that of a man with fewer toes. Eddie edged toward him.

Then, for no reason Eddie understood, Sergei stopped by the birthday girl, reached down, and grabbed the mother by the hair. He yanked her to her feet.

"Sergei," Eddie said. "She has nothing to do with this."

"*Mussor,*" Sergei said. Garbage, a Russian punk's word for cop. "She dies for you."

"Go, just go," Eddie said. "No one will follow you."

Eddie put his gun away and waved his empty hands. Sergei didn't release the woman. He kept her in front of him as he hobbled backward out the door.

"Come on," Eddie yelled. "Let her go. I'm not following you!"

The Lincoln turned left on Emmons and accelerated out of sight. Eddie didn't get a good look at the driver. On the way out, he took charge of the restaurant, ordering the hostess to call 911 and say shots had been fired, people injured. He told her to ask for two ambulances. Dolgev was dead; Eddie didn't bother with him. The mother of the birthday girl lay on the blacktop parking lot, two bullets in her face. A total of three shots had been fired, the police said later, as if it were important to count such things.

When the first radio car arrived, Eddie left the mother to the uniformed cops. He shoved his way back through the crowd leaving the diner. The birthday girl sat in the arms of a waitress. Alone in his booth, Fredek Dolgev slumped facedown on the table, still holding tightly to his coffee cup. Blood and bits of brain and bone stuck to the window that looked out onto the sailboats on Sheepshead Bay. Eddie reached around the body and unhooked the keys from Freddie's belt.


It was after eleven when Eddie looked into Grace's bedroom. She'd kicked off the covers and now lay at an angle, facing the foot of the bed. Like Kate as a child, Grace always seemed red-faced and overheated. She ran around barefoot, dressed in only shorts and a T-shirt on days when it was definitely not warm enough to do so.

Kate never told her to put more clothes on. She said she was raising her to make her own decisions; that when she got cold, she'd put something on. Eileen wouldn't have approved of this liberal parenting, but Eddie liked the results. Grace made a puffing noise and laughed in her sleep, having a good dream. He prayed to God to always keep her dreams happy, and asked Him to do whatever He could for the dreams of the birthday girl.

"Matty Boland called," Babsie said. "He wants you to call him."

Babsie sat at the kitchen table, wearing a flannel robe and pink furry slippers. On the table was an empty wooden chessboard angled against the Yonkers phone book. Loose scraps of a torn photograph were pinned to the board like the start of a jigsaw puzzle.

"Bad scene?" she said.

"Thanks to me. I jump in . . . people die because of it."

"You didn't kill anybody, Eddie. There's a bastard out there who did, but you didn't kill anybody."

"Maybe a hundred years from now, I'll think that, too. Right now, the lesson is: Everyone who comes near me dies."

"I thought this guy Sergei was in the wind."

Eddie told her the truth about what had happened to Sergei. He needed to start telling someone the truth or suffocate in a maze of half-truths and omissions. He realized he was putting her in a tough spot, but he had to open up to this woman. He told her how he blew off Sergei's toes and stuck him in the trunk of a Mercedes bound for Russia. All the Parrot had to do was drive the car a couple hundred yards down a dock and whisper bon voyage. Gypsies should be good at that, he figured.

"Remind me not to piss you off," Babsie said.

"You would have done the same thing if you'd heard the way he talked about Kate."

"He said he saw Kate?"

"He said it, but it was bullshit."

"Well, at least you didn't kill him," she said. "You don't have that to worry about."

The only remorse Eddie felt was that he'd failed to kill the Russian. It made him sick that he'd gotten too cute with it. Fining and deporting him was playing the same glib, facile game that had gotten him in trouble as a cop. The fact that he'd shot Sergei in the foot rather than the head wound up destroying the lives of a family.

"I guess your Gypsy friend really did sell you out," she said.

"Looks that way."

It surprised him that the Parrot had sold him out. Not because he expected the Gypsy's loyalty. If the price was right, he'd understand it. Expect it. But this was going to be a hard payoff to collect. Borodenko would sooner kill him than pay a Gypsy. Maybe Madame Caranina talked him into it. Caranina liked money. Men always make their best and worst decisions on the advice of women.

On the floor next to Babsie was a plastic trash can filled with scraps of paper.

"What is that stuff?" Eddie asked.

"In the trash can? Those're the bits of photograph I found in that black garbage bag outside West Nineteenth Street."

"Is that all one picture?"

"I don't know; I just started. Bigger than I first thought. Looks like a nine-by-twelve, something like that. So far, I got a couple of legs done. But there're at least two people. Guy in white shorts, then a woman's legs. Long legs."

"Good luck," he said.

"Listen, Eddie, if you want to talk about what happened today . . . I'm comfortable sitting here in my fuzzy slippers."

Eddie had already told her about shooting Sergei and she hadn't flinched. He wondered what else he could release from his nightmare vault. Oddly, what he remembered most about the El Greco diner was the smell of the cologne from the father of the birthday girl. After the Lincoln took off, he pushed Eddie out of the way and lay down on his wife, as if the mere pressing of his body against hers could stop the life from leaking out of her. Eddie understood this. He loved her, and he was desperate. She was still breathing at that time. Her eyes were open but gazing blankly. Eddie could see one exit wound behind her ear. It was then he noticed the strong cologne, that overpowering chemical smell that seemed common to so many men who, because of their jobs or personalities, had a need to impress. His old partner had worn cologne like that. Every once in a while when Eddie caught a whiff of overripe cologne, he'd turn around and look for Paulie the Priest.

Eddie said, "This guy shoots an innocent woman in the face for no reason. He watches her drop to the ground. Then he puts his gun away, buttons his coat, and gets in the car. In front of a hundred witnesses."

"People are evil, Eddie. One thing about being a cop is that we don't have any ambiguous feelings about that fact."

"I was surprised he didn't grab the little girl. But she was probably too small for him to hide behind. I kept thinking about Kate, how these guys have no regard for human life."

"That's why we have to put an end to it. We're going to get Kate back and stop these bastards."

Eddie couldn't believe he'd come to care so deeply for Babsie in such a short time. Eileen had always said that Eddie's parents had taught him how to fight but not how to love. If that were true, why did this seem such an easy fit?

"Now, I've got some bad news for you," Babsie said. "Scott filed a petition for custody with Westchester County Family Court. He's going to ask for temporary custody of Grace, to remove her from a possibly dangerous situation."

"What danger? She's the most protected kid in the country."

"A lot about you in the petition, Eddie. Not good stuff."

"How much time do I have?"

"I don't know. I heard this from my brother's wife, who works at Con Ed with Scott's sister. You better get your ass in gear on this."

"I'm calling B.J.'s friend tomorrow. We'll fight it, slow the process up. By the time it goes to court, Kate will be back."

"Yeah," she said.

"She *will* be back, Babsie."

"I'm agreeing with you. We'll find her."

"If she was dead, they wouldn't have killed Freddie. The only thing Freddie could have told us is where she is."

Babsie nodded. Eddie knew she had the decency not to point out the flaw in his logic: that Freddie's knowledge of Kate's kidnapping, or where she was now, didn't mean she was alive.

"Now we have to find Zina," Babsie said.

This was what cops did every day. It was what most people only learned in the midst of the worst moments of their lives. You simply grasp at the next straw. Zina was the next straw. She would surely know something about Kate. This time, the magic door would open. Zina would show him the way.

"Why did Matty Boland call?" Eddie said.

"He wants Freddie Dolgev's keys," she replied.

# CHAPTER
# 33

EDDIE TRIED TO CALL Matty Boland at home, then on his cell phone. Boland answered, but static cut out most of what he said, except something about a fucking tunnel. Eddie stayed on the line until he cleared whatever tunnel he was in. First thing Boland brought up was Dolgev's keys.

"What keys?" Eddie said.

He played that game until Boland stopped playing his game and admitted the reason he needed them. The FBI task force had obtained a warrant for installing an electronic eavesdropping device in a garish nightclub on the edge of Brighton Beach, a place called Mazurka. A new informant had revealed that Yuri Borodenko held high-level meetings to discuss his criminal enterprise in an office in the rear of the Mazurka nightclub.

"If I had such a set of keys . . ." Eddie said.

"Let's not string this out. What do you want?"

Although telephone wiretaps could be set up from outside, a bug was essentially an open microphone, and thus the installer somehow had to get inside the place.

Although locks could be picked, having the keys was always better. Fredek Dolgev's keys would make their entrance quick and simple. The less time on the street, the better. "Tonight's the night," Boland said. A judge had signed the warrant three days ago; therefore, the clock was running.

"I want to go in with you," Eddie said.

"Jesus Christ," Boland said, then added, "Okay, okay."

The FBI warrant would be amended to include the use of other "expertise necessary to gain access," meaning Eddie Dunne and his keys. Eddie grabbed almost ninety minutes' sleep before meeting Boland, the FBI's lock man, and a Russian interpreter in the back of a van parked near the handball courts in Coney Island.

It was just after 2:00 A.M. when Eddie handed the keys to the FBI lock man. They were sitting around a circular table two feet in diameter in the custom-built surveillance van. The lock man compared the keys with the notes he'd taken on existing locks. The interpreter tried to match the notations taped on each key to a specific location. They were certain the two odd-shaped keys would match the Mazurka's high-priced outer locks. Advertised as impossible to pick, the French-made locks had thus far thwarted the lock man. Now the only question concerned the inner office. How many inside locks would they face?

"This is the third try," Boland said as he and Eddie stepped outside to piss against a wall of the handball court. Boland said the FBI's lock man was amazing at his workbench in the office. In there, he could pick any lock known to man. The guy was Houdini in the right setting. In the field, however, in the bowels of Brooklyn in the dead of night, was a different story. Hands started sweating; the heart ticked louder. "I told him I was bringing a brick with me tonight," Boland said. "If he didn't get it in ten minutes, I was going to break a goddamned window."

"What about alarms?" Eddie asked.

"That's the easy part."

"The alarm guy is a federal stool, right?"

"You didn't hear me say that."

Boland decided it was a good thing they'd brought Eddie along. He was the only member of the team who had actually been inside the Mazurka. Shortly before he left Lukin's employ, Eddie had accompanied the old man to the lavish wedding reception Yuri Borodenko threw for his new teenaged Russian wife. This was a bash rumored to have cost in excess of fifty thousand dollars. But they'd put Lukin's party at a table so far back, Eddie had barely been able to see Yuri and the baby bride. Lukin's placement at the party was a clear insult, and a sign of things to come.

The rumor at that time was that Borodenko was the undisclosed owner of the Mazurka and had sunk over half a million dollars into the place simply because his fashion model wanted a nice place to go. Now Eddie sketched out on a legal pad a floor plan of what he remembered of the nightclub. The huge brown metal doors were heavy and etched in Russian design. The inside foyer had mirrored walls, a floor of black-and-brown Italian marble, and a two-headed eagle, the symbol of Russia before the revolution. A hand-painted mural of the Saint Petersburg skyline pointed the way to the cavernous nightclub.

Eddie said he'd never forget the night he was there. Bowls of borscht and frosted bottles of vodka everywhere. The tables were covered with pink tablecloths. Russian men in suits bought at Barneys "Gangster Room" danced across the inlaid-wood dance floor with their voluptuous blondes. Eddie doodled on the inlaid squares of his pen-cil-sketch dance floor as he tried to picture the place in his mind. Multicolored lasers crisscrossing the room. A black woman crooning Russian love songs on an elevated stage in front of the dance floor. To the left of the stage was the kitchen. Waiters in tuxedos rushing around with skewers of beef. To the right of the stage were the rest rooms and private offices.

At 4:00 A.M., the task force moved. It went quickly; seven of nine people were inside the place in less than thirty seconds. Two stayed outside in the van. The job was always easier when you had the keys. They knew there were no guard dogs. Even the best-trained guard dogs would make the place smell like dog shit.

Inside the darkened club, every investigator had a spe-cific responsibility. Computer expert, records expert, et cetera. Matty Boland's job was to make sure everything was put back exactly as it had been when they entered. Eddie had no assignment, but Boland handed him a pair of latex gloves. Eddie had asked to watch the records per-son, who'd be going through files, address books, and all other paper records. He wanted to find something on Zina.

Although no outside windows were noted, light was kept to a minimum. Radio contact was limited to emer-gencies. Working off pinpoint flashlights, the team turned right at the dance floor. The lock man dropped to his knees in front of a door that said EXECUTIVE OFFICES. With the flashlight held in his mouth, he slipped into the lock a small curved metal pick that looked like a dental tool. Eddie could hear the tumblers flipping one by one. Thirty seconds ticked away before the lock man stood up; his gloved hand turned the knob.

The Executive Offices were far from any exterior walls. Boland turned the light on, revealing a nicely decorated reception room with a leather couch and one metal filing cabinet. Two more doors. One was a private bathroom with a shower stall. The other was the inner office they were looking for. Jackpot in less than two minutes. No problemo, as Kevin Dunne would say.

The tech men had already decided on a power system for the bug. They ordered a new telephone line for the Mazurka, billable to a third party under their control. They found the connection and ran the wire in the ceiling above the manager's desk. They wanted the microphone set directly above the desk.

Boland watched as a tech man put a cloth down on the desk to avoid footprints. He made a note of everything they moved. Ceiling panels were raised to find the telephone wire. The tech man near the wall, standing on a stepladder, pushed a wire across the ceiling to the man standing on the desk. The guy on the desk had the important job: He attached the microphone to the phone wire. When the tech man nodded, Boland notified the agent in the plant in lower Manhattan to call the new phone number. The tech man clicked the microphone, opening the line. The guy in Manhattan could hear everything. Thus began a one-way phone conversation that would last for twenty-seven more days, unless evidence of new crimes extended the warrant.

The tech men carefully replaced the ceiling panels. Boland put his finger to his lips, reminding them that everything they said could be heard downtown. While this was going on, Eddie Dunne looked inside every folder in the file cabinet. He looked through the employee files, the manager's appointment calendar, and the

Rolodex. He found Fredek Dolgev's file, although not one single notation regarding Zina. Then he found her name on that month's pay sheet. Zina Rabinovich . . . with a line drawn through the name, the word *terminated*, and the initials Y.B. The date was April 6, the day Kate was kidnapped. Borodenko was in Russia on April 6. He'd fired her from Russia.

In under fifty minutes, the members of the task force were walking out of the club one by one. They waited until the street was empty and then hustled into the waiting vans. It was done smoothly and efficiently. Eddie might have to take back some of the nasty things he'd said about the feds.

There were four in the van as they rode back to the underground Queens garage they called "the bat cave." Matty Boland lit a big Cuban cigar and talked about the importance of what they'd just done. If the bug turned out to be as good as it seemed at this point, it would strike a death blow to the Borodenko operation. Boland was flush with his success.

"If this goes right," Boland said, "I've got First Grade detective in the bag. No way they can't promote me."

Human nature, Eddie thought, it comes down to thinking about number one. *Numero Uno.* He'd once read that people expend by far the most energy on the preservation and enhancement of their self-image. We see ourselves in splendor. Perhaps this is why we are so devastated when tragedy hits home. How can God do this to *me?* The great *me.* But deep inside, you know exactly why.

# CHAPTER
# 34

EDDIE STUMBLED INTO THE KITCHEN, limping almost as much as the psycho Sergei Zhukov. That shooting pain that Babsie called sciatica came and went for no reason he could understand. Every day, more of his life seemed to be breaking down. He felt old for the first time, his breath sour, skin dry and itchy. Just another unshaven old man scuffing through the corridors of some rest home. Babsie sat at the kitchen table, a magnifying glass up to her face.

"I put this photograph together," she said. Detective Barbara Panko never wasted any time with "Good morning" or "What's with the limp?" She went straight to the heart of the matter.

The house was quiet, the weather too warm for the clank of steam in the pipes. Grace was at school, no TV, no radio. Eileen had always had to have the TV on; silence made her antsy. Just the two of them now. Babsie had worked out a schedule with the Yonkers PD wherein they only watched the house when she wasn't there. But every single school day, a uniformed cop sat outside Christ the King.

"What photograph?" Eddie said.

"The one from the trash at Freddie Dolgev's house."

It had been after 5:00 A.M. when he'd gotten home from Brooklyn. The fluorescent light over the stove had led him to a note written in big block letters. It was signed by Babsie and Grace, but one signer had written her name too large and too near the end of the page. She'd had to slide the "ce" under the "Gra." It said that a piece of "angel foot cake" was waiting for him under the cake tin. It was signed "Love." He hadn't been hungry, but he'd poured a glass of milk and finished the cake. Then he'd collapsed into bed, hoping not to dream.

"Grab some coffee and come over here and look at this picture, will you?" Babsie said.

"Soon as I get my eyes open."

He'd slept miserably. The first time he woke up, the morning sun was angled low in his bedroom window. Loud voices and the rumble of heavy equipment shattered the usual early-morning peace—a city road crew getting an early jump on resurfacing the street. First time in twenty years, and they chose now to do it.

"How did you make out last night?" Babsie asked.

"The Mazurka is wired."

"Another feather in Boland's cap, thanks to you."

"Can't hurt. They might pick up a mention of Kate's name."

"They won't say anything to you; it might jeopardize their almighty case."

"They'll tell us, Babsie. Good bunch of guys on the task force."

"A few maybe, and that's only because Louie Freeh dumped that stupid lawyer or accountant requirement and brought some cops and street kids aboard."

The second time he woke up that morning, he'd heard Babsie sliding the glass pot back into the Mr. Coffee. A kitchen chair squeaking against the tile floor; a cup set down on the table. Grace's voice complaining about school. He'd thought about Kate, how loud she was in the morning, banging pots and pans. Over a week had gone by, but Eddie had no doubts that his daughter was alive. Not that he believed in ESP or any of that occult crap, but a parent and child must be able to tune in on the same wavelength. So much is genetic, he thought, why not a common wavelength?

"Come over here," Babsie said. "This picture is really interesting."

In his mind, Eddie saw Kate tied up and blindfolded. He tried to imagine the room. Sense it as she was doing. They'd have to tie and blindfold her because she'd be fighting and cursing like the tough pain in the ass he'd raised her to be. No one doubted that. She could be a pain in the ass. God bless her. Amid all this going on, it made no sense that these people outside woke up today, showered, went out to blacktop some curvy, hilly little side street, thinking only of their own lives: dinner, sex, golf, the weekend, whatever. It wasn't right.

"Hey, Dunne," Babsie said. "Get your ass over here and look at this picture."

"All right, all right," he said, carefully lowering himself into the chair. He'd decided that sciatica made sitting worse than standing.

Working on an old wooden chessboard, Babsie had connected the pieces of the torn photograph she'd found outside the apartment in Coney Island. Last time Eddie saw it, she'd had pins in the pieces. Now they were glued down with a white gooey stuff she insisted wouldn't stick permanently. With more patience than Eddie could imagine, she'd turned and twisted dozens of small pieces of a black-and-white photograph until they made sense. She turned it around so Eddie could see.

"A regular puzzle whiz," he said. "I can't believe you did this."

"Recognize anyone?"

Although it was obvious the picture had been ripped to shreds, you could make out what the photographer first saw staring up at him through the developing fluid. Three people: two men and a woman, standing on a dock in front of a powerboat. The woman was in the middle. They had their arms around one another and were smiling broadly. Eddie was squinting into the sun.

"You look so young here," Babsie said, pointing to the man on the right. She'd pointed to a slender man in jeans and T-shirt, taller than the others. His hair appeared darker than it did in real life, as it did in all his old pictures. His eyebrows looked bushier than they did now.

"I hardly remember this," he said.

"I'm guessing the other guy is your partner."

"The one and only Paul Caruso," he said.

Eddie couldn't remember the picture being taken or who took it. Another woman probably. Some Brooklyn divorcée Paulie'd brought along for him. Paulie'd had an endless supply of gum-popping Donnas and Dianes he knew from the days before he fell madly in love.

"You remember where this was taken?" Babsie asked.

"Sheepshead Bay Marina."

"How about the year?"

"Early eighties. That's Paulie's boat behind us. Two big staterooms. He loved to brag about those staterooms."

"Was this a special occasion?"

"I have no idea. But, yeah, that's his boat. The *Bright Star.*"

"He name it himself? Seems a little . . . I don't know . . . gay . . . from what I know of Paul Caruso."

"He took a lot of shit over that name. Guys figured he'd give it some obscene name. *Goombah Mama,* one cop suggested. *Pussy Galore*—you know, from James Bond. We had a lot of good times on that boat."

"You guys don't exactly look like sailors to me."

"Not me, but Paulie knew what he was doing. A little anyway. He really loved the big inboard diesel engines. He talked more about horsepower than he did about anything to do with the sea. It was all about speed for him. Faster the better."

"Who is the woman?"

"Paulie's girlfriend, Lana."

"Good-looking lady."

Eddie fixed cereal for himself while Babsie sipped coffee and stared at the photo. He sliced a banana, poured the milk, and sat down across from her. He'd have breakfast, then get back to Brighton Beach. Eddie had asked Boland to steer him in the right direction as far as finding Zina. Zina had not returned to her apartment on West Nineteenth. She had to be sleeping somewhere. He realized Boland couldn't officially reveal the contents of any transcript from the Mazurka bug. But he could find a back door, a wink, or a nudge. Maybe accidentally leave a coffee stain next to a specific location on the list of Borodenko's locations. Just point him in the right direction.

"Are you going to make me ask the obvious question?" Babsie said.

"What question?"

"How the hell did this picture find its way into the apartment of Fredek Dolgev?"

"They probably got it from Paulie somehow. Angelo said they tore his house apart in Sicily."

"But why take this picture from Sicily in the first place? Then rip it up on West Nineteenth Street in Coney Island?"

"I wish I knew that myself."

"But you see what I'm trying to say. You have to admit this all comes down to your connection with the Caruso brothers. You yourself said you always wondered about the Rosenfeld shooting. It sounds like a setup, right?"

"No doubt about it."

"Maybe I should talk to this Lana," Babsie said.

"Good idea, but she's dead."

"The bottom line here, Eddie, is that somebody thinks you have the missing money from the gas-tax scam. Maybe Paulie told them. I don't know."

"It was fourteen years ago. Why did it take them so long to come after it?"

"I can't answer that, but think about who's dead: Lukin and both Caruso brothers. You're the only possible conspirator left."

"Oh, now I'm a possible conspirator."

"It's the only thing that makes sense. The reason they haven't come back here is because cops have been all over this place."

"They already searched my house."

"What about Paulie's boat?"

"He sold it before he went to Sicily," Eddie said. "But boats have VIN numbers, like cars. It's traceable. The marina might have old records."

"Didn't they find Misha's body dumped in this same marina?"

"Yeah, but quite a distance from where ours was kept."

"Ours?"

"Well, it wasn't mine, but I probably spent more time on it than Paulie did. I told you that I slept on it many nights when I was too tired or too drunk to drive home."

Babsie made notes on the boat. The picture didn't show the registration number. It did show the slip number.

"Is that a ninety-one or a sixteen?" Babsie asked.

"It's a ninety-one. The slip numbers were stenciled on the dock, facing the boat."

"Where did they dump Misha's body?"

"On seventeen."

"But he crawled there from sixteen. The bloodstains started on sixteen. They thought it was ninety-one."

"You've been watching too much *Columbo*."

Eddie remembered the boat far better than anything else that had occurred during those years. Sitting on a dock, twenty yards from traffic on Emmons Avenue, it seemed like another world—a world too good to last.

"I'll stop by and check the marina tonight," he said.

"You're going back to Brighton Beach already?"

"I never finished all the lesbian bars. Sooner or later, I'll find Zina in one of them."

"Yeah, well, you won't have that much time to chat with the girls tonight. Matty Boland called again. They have another big operation going. They want us at One Police Plaza. Two A.M."

"Both of us?"

"Don't worry, I'll drive my own car. You go do your dyke-trolling thing. Just meet me at police headquarters."

"Two a.m.?"

"Two a.m.," she said. "I'll bet it's another operation generated off information from you. Boland is using you like a trust fund. You'd think the guy would spend at least one day working on Kate. He pretends he's Mr. Concerned, but he's nothing but a self-absorbed prick."

Eddie turned the picture around. He looked closely at Caruso, and for the first time he saw a heavy-lidded, brooding face. When he'd first met Paulie, Eddie envied him as a person capable of living in the moment. The change came later; the anger followed. Time and circumstance changed you in ways you could never imagine. Or maybe they brought out the real you. Shafts of light filtering through the oak trees streaked the kitchen floor.

# CHAPTER
# 35

BECAUSE OF THE BRAZEN MURDER of two people in the El Greco diner, an elite group of law-enforcement officers gathered without fanfare in the early hours of Wednesday at NYPD headquarters in One Police Plaza. Press and TV crews remained camped in Brooklyn, bemoaning the lack of investigative progress while focusing their cameras on the bloodstains at the foot of the diner's steps. The entire city seemed stunned by the callous nature of the crime: A mother singing "Happy Birthday" to her daughter had been brutally murdered in front of her family. Eddie Dunne, referred to as an "unnamed eyewitness," provided a face to the tragedy. The scowl of the madman Sergei Zhukov terrified viewers of every newscast in the tristate area. The city of New York, riding the crest of the largest homicide reduction in its history, was not about to allow one incident to trigger a backslide.

"How did they treat you in the dyke bars tonight?" Detective Babsie Panko asked.

Since early afternoon, Eddie Dunne had been visiting

every known lesbian bar in the city. His source was a free magazine he'd picked up in Manhattan.

"Mostly, they were nice," he said. "Too nice. That's what worries me. They knew about me, and treated me like some sad old uncle, down on his luck. They took my card and promised they'd call if they heard anything about Kate or Zina. They were sweet, sympathetic. I think I liked it better when they were throwing hand grenades."

Babsie and Eddie took seats in the back of the auditorium. The auditorium, on the first floor of One Police Plaza, was an odd mixture of brick and Danish-style wooden slats, but it was well capable of handling a force of over one hundred. The walls on opposite sides of the room were lined with large pieces of cardboard displaying hand-drawn numbers. The numbers corresponded to the teams that would be handed separate assignments. They caught Matty Boland hustling toward the stage.

"What's my role here?" Eddie asked.

"Finger man," Boland said. "We can depend on you to pick Sergei Zhukov out of a roomful of Russkies. Babsie's here as a courtesy, mostly. Intersecting cases and all. You're both riding with me."

"Lucky us," Babsie said.

The bulk of the manpower had been drawn from the vast pool of the NYPD, forty thousand strong. Officers had been pulled from a variety of different specialties, and most didn't know one another. Each team consisted of at least one member of the FBI's Joint Russian Task Force, two investigators and one supervisor from the Organized Crime Control Bureau, plus two uniformed and heavily armed members of the NYPD Emergency Services Unit. At the briefing, names would be read aloud and squad numbers assigned. They'd be told to meet with fellow squad members under the posted number on the wall, make the introductions short, and get on the road. A cadre of technicians and specialists, including a dozen cops from the Auto Crime Division, had been handpicked by Detective Matty Boland. As soon as Eddie saw all the Auto Crime cops, he knew it had to be a junkyard.

"How did you find him?" Eddie said.

"Sources," Boland said, winking. "We have solid intelligence reports that he's in Flushing Salvage, waiting on a ship going east. Let's leave it at that."

Because he knew how the NYPD worked, Eddie knew Boland's information couldn't have come through intelligence channels. The desk jockeys on the upper floors of the Puzzle Palace tended to milk their exposure to an operation this big, enhancing their visibility. This had all happened too quickly. It had to be hot off the bug they'd just put inside the Mazurka. Info snatched from a fresh conversation held deep inside the Russian nightclub.

Boland then told them that Yuri Borodenko, owner of Flushing Salvage, had buried a single-width two-bedroom mobile home on the property. Entrance to the underground trailer was down through a new metal storage building in the center of the huge junkyard. Word was they used the buried trailer as a central processing location for cash and contraband.

"Our problem," Boland said, "is they've been digging tunnels from the trailer out. The tunnels end beneath the shacks across the street. Exactly how many, we don't know. Minimum, three. That's why we needed so many teams. We've absolutely got to cover all possible escape routes."

"Hit fast and hard."

"No shit," Boland said. "But the whole block needs to be totally surrounded long before we hit the gate."

"Entrée courtesy of Freddie Dolgev's keys?"

"No keys this time. Bolt cutters and battering rams all the way. Noisy as hell, but it doesn't matter. Their dogs will be going apeshit anyway."

"This underground trailer would be a good place to hide someone else," Babsie said, reminding Boland they had a kidnapping investigation going, as well.

"I didn't mean to gloss over that," he said. "I tried to put Kate's picture in all the packets, but the attorneys nixed it. They don't want it to appear like a fishing expedition; Kate's not the subject of the warrant, and we have no evidence that she's in there. But if she is, you'll have her home tonight."

Eddie's pulse fluttered for a moment when Boland said "tonight." But tonight? No way. The favorite saying of his doomsday Irish mother was "Don't get your hopes up." He wasn't about to. But Babsie was right: The buried mobile home would be a great spot to hide Kate. The tunnels provided easy entrance and escape routes for the kidnappers, but the size and intensity of this operation would contain any quick exit. No matter how many *baklany* were inside, the punks from Brighton Beach would just throw up their hands when they saw this army. Eddie knew that under ordinary circumstances there was no way a search of this size would ever have been put together. He owed it all to the mother of a birthday girl, who'd died because he hadn't used his head.

"Okay, I understand they don't want it to appear like a fishing expedition," Eddie said, trying to clear up a loose end. "That means the entire focus is on Sergei, the subject of the arrest warrant."

"Correct."

"And you know he's in there?"

"As of an hour ago. We have people sitting on the place as we speak."

"But no one from Homicide is here?"

"Howie Danton is here, along with his partner," Boland said.

"Only two of them, and all these FBI agents, including wire men?"

Boland shrugged. "No sense wasting a golden opportunity."

Boland handed Eddie a handwritten working copy of his affidavit for the court order. He read down to where a registered confidential informant had told them that located in the trailer was a set of black binders containing the papers for dummy corporations used to funnel criminally obtained U.S. currency into offshore banking institutions.

"These are the binders I'm supposed to have stolen," Eddie said.

Boland shrugged. "Our informant claims he saw them in the trailer."

The informant also told them that meetings were held in the trailer to discuss disbursement of monies from illegal enterprises, such as the sale of Russian military equipment, including nuclear weapons. The affidavit pled the usual case that all other means of obtaining evidence had been exhausted. But Eddie knew that once the words "nuclear weapons" appeared in a warrant application, no judge would refuse to sign.

"Everything always works out good for you, Matty," Babsie said.

"So this isn't really about Sergei," Eddie said.

"We want Borodenko to think it is. But as long as we're in there . . ."

Immediately after the briefing, the squads formed, decided on vehicles, and headed for Queens. Eddie had been on a few of these large raids in his career. He'd always hated them. The mere size of the force gave everyone the feeling they were invincible. The worst was the mass arrests of the Thirteenth Division cops in the seventies. It was a hastily organized mass raid, just like this. The target was a Brooklyn plainclothes division on the take. Dozens of cops had been indicted. When word of the indictments leaked out, the commanding officer, one of those named in the indictment, rented a room in a hotel near the courthouse and blew his brains out. Fearing a rash of suicides, the upper echelon ordered everyone to be picked up immediately. In the middle of a nice afternoon, Eddie was pulled in from a Manhattan squad to arrest a young plainclothesman. He walked into the house of a cop he'd never met, and while his pregnant wife sobbed, he waited while the young cop took his guns from a box in a bedroom closet and handed them to Eddie. After they left, he could hear the wife crying for blocks.

"The thing that surprises me most about Sergei," Boland said, "is that he never came after you."

"I wish he had," Eddie said. "I wish they all had. What they're doing to me now is worse."

Boland took the Town Car. They drove over the cobblestones of the Fulton Fish Market, which was jumping with activity in the middle of the night. Truckers from all over the East Coast unloaded crates of crab, cod, halibut, and lobster while buyers from local restaurants and supermarkets moved from stall to stall, inspecting the catch. At the tip of the island of Manhattan, the almost-full moon lit New York Harbor. In the crisp, clear night, the Statue of Liberty appeared small and distant. Eddie liked the view better in bad weather. There was something about a haze, the way the torch would shine through the fog, that made her loom larger.

"Eddie, you have to stay in the car tonight," Boland said as the silent convoy left the Belt Parkway. "Too much brass on this caper. They see you marching in with us, the shit will hit the fan. I'll come back and get you if we need you to identify Sergei. Or if we have good news. You can count on that."

The Queens County they rode through was not Archie Bunker's neighborhood. The streets around the junkyard loomed as surreal as a moonscape. An eight-foot chain-link fence topped with razor wire encircled the huge lot. Across from the junkyard sat a collection of phantom factories, sandwich shops, and uninhabitable mystery shacks. The roadway, sidewalks, and grass were painted black with oil. No lights, no signs, no civilization. Packs of wild dogs owned the night. Skeletons of cannibalized cars were scattered about the streets like the abandoned caissons of a retreating army.

Boland donned his vest and a blue nylon jacket with NYPD in Day-Glo letters, then grabbed a portable copy machine from the trunk. He left the car running. The police radios had been set to a special frequency so they could hear the play-by-play. The commander of Emergency Services was running the show. They'd be the guys going through the door first.

"They don't need me in there," Babsie said.

"You don't have to baby-sit," Eddie said.

"Like you can afford my baby-sitting fee," she said.

"I'm just pissed at Boland. He should have given us a heads-up, so we knew how to dress. No way I'm getting grease on this new jacket. But I am a little surprised you didn't fight him. I thought for sure you'd want in on the door-kicking party."

"They'd keep me so far in the background, my ass would still be in Brooklyn."

"Yeah," she said, not quite buying his story. "They got enough bodies here to invade the Kremlin."

From where they were parked, Eddie could barely see the front gate. The barking dogs behind the fence, however, could be heard for miles. A heavily protected Emergency Services cop lumbered up to the gate and aimed a tranquilizer gun through the chain-link fence. One pop, then a howl. Yard-long bolt cutters snipped the chain as if it were strung popcorn. Another dog bit the dust. The cops yanked the chain through and tossed it to the ground. They swung the gate open and went in. One more dog barked pitifully, and then there were none.

The NYPD believed in the strategy of overkill. Always bring more cops to the party than you need. Four teams followed the ESU through the front gate. In the pitch-blackness, wavering flashlight beams were the only show as the cops moved around the stacks of front ends and quarter panels, past the mounds of tires, wheels, and hubcaps. Lights popped on here and there, small bulbs behind filthy windows. He wondered if Kate's world was like this: darkness, then pinpoints of light. He hoped her worst enemy was isolation. The Dunnes could handle isolation.

Only fifteen minutes passed before grim-faced Matty Boland returned. Eddie watched him cut across the beams of car headlights, his head down. He opened the driver's door and leaned in. A swath of grease cut across his cheek.

"We didn't find her, Eddie," he said.

Eddie felt the blood drain from his face. This was okay. This was fine. It meant they still had hope. Hope was everything, all they had.

"Tunnel thing was mostly bullshit," Boland said. "Only one tunnel, built for midgets, looks like. We got five live Russkie types, and a body we want you to look at." Then, as an afterthought, he said, "Male DOA."

They followed Boland through a tin warehouse building filled with deep shelves made from fresh lumber. On the shelves were hundreds of used auto transmissions. Cops from Auto Crime examined them for hidden serial numbers. They entered a new metal shed and climbed down through a trapdoor to a tight wrought-iron circular staircase, almost as narrow and twisting as the staircase up to the crown in the Statue of Liberty.

Down one level, the floor of the mobile home was intact, carpeting almost new. It had not been heavily used. The entrance to the tunnel in a side wall had been covered by a blue plastic shower curtain. Climbing in required a two-foot step up from the floor and good flexibility. The damp smell of fresh dirt prevailed. A draped body lay halfway into the entrance.

"We think they killed him here," Boland said. "One of the teams grabbed two guys running toward a pickup truck with a camper. The back hatch of the camper was open. They were getting ready to drop him somewhere else."

The body was partially wrapped in a brown woolen military blanket with writing in the Cyrillic alphabet. The face remained uncovered; no reason to protect the public down here. He'd been shot once in the center of his forehead.

"Sergei Zhukov," Eddie said.

The stippling around the entrance wound indicated it had been at close range. A harsh fluorescent ceiling light glared off the fake wood paneling and cast all faces in the same pallor as Sergei's.

"Is this legit?" Danton asked, handing Eddie a ring. "It was in his pocket."

It was a Claddagh ring—a common Irish gift—two hands clasped around a heart. This one was inscribed on the inside "To Kate from Dad."

"I gave it to her when she graduated from Sacred Heart," Eddie said, fighting to clear his throat as he stared at the ring. He'd bought it for her in Ireland, in a small shop in Galway, right after they'd walked through Claddagh, a small fishing community on Galway Bay and the Atlantic, the place that gave the symbol its life.

"This is a setup," Howie Danton said. "They put the ring on this mook to take the focus off Borodenko. He gets rid of the problem child, Sergei, plus he gets to blame him for Kate. It's this guy's MO. He plants more shit than Johnny Appleseed."

As they rode back to One Police Plaza, Eddie tried to get his mind around this. What did it mean for Kate? If she was dead, they could have just disposed of her body. Borodenko had ample means for causing bodies to evaporate, either Sergei's or Kate's. So why go through all this trouble, planting the ring on Sergei? Why would it matter who got blamed? It meant Kate had to be alive. That made sense, didn't it? *Didn't it?*

"Quit mumbling to yourself," Babsie whispered, squeezing his hand.

Too tired to con himself anymore, he began to wonder what he might have to say to his granddaughter. No harm in just thinking. Besides, it was good to think about the worst case, defusing God's sacred element of surprise. He'd talk to Grace about angels, because if there ever was a time to believe in sweet angels, this was it. The rest sent shivers. Aunt Martha and the One Holy Catholic and Apostolic Church would insist on a High Mass after a nightmare wake. He'd just hold Grace through all the ceremonial weeping and gnashing. That was best. Hold her. And when the smoke of the incense cleared from the air, he'd ask Babsie to move in with them. He'd get the best lawyer money could buy to fight his son of a bitch of a son-in-law. Then he'd spend his nights in Brighton Beach, with blood on his hands. As many nights as it took.

That's the worst-case scenario, he told himself. Paulie said the worst case never happened when you stacked the odds in your favor. He always said that only losers believed they had to play the hand they were dealt. Eddie Dunne needed to turn the odds in his favor. Lie, cheat, steal, it was all recommended in Paulie's book. Eddie didn't have an ace up his sleeve, but he had a key in his pocket.

WHEN BOLAND PARKED behind One Police Plaza, he was still arguing with Babsie over possession of Kate's Claddagh ring. Babsie wanted to take it to Yonkers as evidence of the kidnapping, but Boland insisted on vouchering it under Sergei's case. "Evidence should be recorded in the jurisdiction where it is first discovered," Boland said. "Maintaining a consistent chain of evidence is vital in this case because it has worldwide implications." Worldwide implications, Eddie thought. One child from Yonkers was all he'd asked them to save. The world could take care of itself. And yet the shit kept piling higher.

A mayoral press conference was scheduled for noon to tell the city it could breathe easier. The immediate cause for celebration was finding the body of Sergei Zhukov, the El Greco diner killer. Beyond that, but unmentioned, the feds had removed boxes of paper evidence from the sunken trailer, and left behind a tiny electronic ear. Success bred success. Matty Boland would run home to shave and dig the Armani out of his closet. He could smell the money the rank of First Grade would bring. Eddie wondered if Boland would sound so triumphant if his child were still missing. But we've been through all that, he told himself. Human nature, the old story.

Pissed-off, Babsie drove home to Yonkers. Eddie went alone to Coney Island, once and again, his second home. When he was a cop, Eddie, like every cop he knew, lived two lives. Cops who couldn't handle separate lives didn't make it. He'd always kept his family away from his job and from Coney Island. Too dangerous, he'd told them, but the truth was, he couldn't risk bumping into a bimbo or bartender who knew him only as crazy in Brooklyn. No sense in exposing a persona he loved when he was in it, and was ashamed of when he wasn't. But he'd put himself in a position where he couldn't share a huge part of his past with the people he loved most. His life had been a lie then. It was a lie now.

He'd lied about Freddie Dolgev's keys. In his pocket was a key to an expensive French lock similar to those on the Mazurka nightclub. Dolgev's key ring had held a set for Coney Custards: freezer padlocks, an equipment closet, and custard machines. Freddie'd probably done maintenance work for the privilege of living in the dank apartment upstairs. One key was missing from the Coney Custards set; it was the one key Eddie had held out. It was marked simply *Z* and imprinted with the same logo as the dead bolt on apartment A. While Boland stood shoulder-to-shoulder with the mayor today, Eddie would be illegally entering the domicile of one Zina Rabinovich.

The law had had its chance, Eddie thought. All

the warrants, affidavits, bugs, wiretaps, searches and seizures, all the surreptitious entries made righteous by words on legal paper added up to zero. He'd learned more from a Gypsy car thief.

Eddie parked two blocks west of Coney Custards and walked down the boardwalk. Gone were the Irish bars, all the wild Gaels dead or in Florida. Only a few Coney Island landmarks were still around: the Cyclone, the Flume, the Astrotower, the Wonder Wheel. Gone were the Mile Sky Chaser, the Thunderbolt, and Luna Park, a simulated city of Baghdad. Kate would have loved Luna Park.

In-line skaters rumbled past him. Bikers, walkers, and joggers were pounding the boards. Everyone out soaking up the warm sun. Eddie figured it had been nine days since his daughter had felt the sunlight. They wouldn't risk exposing her to the outside.

Looking ahead, he could see bright-colored flags and box kites flying. A clown danced around a helium tank, ready to twist skinny balloons into dachshunds. He wondered whatever happened to the fire-eater, the sword-swallower, and the guy who pounded nails up his nose. As the world got crazier, the sideshow became tamer, unable to keep pace.

On West Nineteenth, Eddie cut down the street and ducked into the hallway. He scaled the narrow steps two at a time. At the top of the steps, he let his pulse quiet down as he listened at both doors. Nothing. He waited calmly, hearing the sounds from the street, the clatter of the ice-cream business below. Then he knocked hard on Zina's door. He listened for movement. One more knock, then he used the key.

Zina's apartment was the polar opposite of Freddie's sparse abode. New furniture filled her dark living room, making it claustrophobic. Underfoot, plush carpeting, pillows strewn about the floor. Gauzy veils hung from lamps. Shelves held more candles than St. Pat's. Dark fabric draped the walls, along with what looked like strips of palm, but wider than the leaves passed out on the Sunday before Easter. The room reminded him of a harem scene from *Arabian Nights*.

What he was looking for was an address book or notes. As far as he knew, Zina hadn't been back since they'd arrested Freddie. Any memo or scribbled notation would have been written prior to her having been warned. The living room was an easy search. Not a piece of furniture had a drawer. He moved pillows around, peeked behind the wall hangings, under cushions. Two minutes and done.

In the kitchen, a terra-cotta Mexican tile floor held the weight of new chrome appliances, a gourmet stove, and a small center island with a grill and sink. Pots and pans hung from hooks on a form that circled above the island. Next to the wall phone, he found a calendar with notations. He copied all verbatim: "2:30 hc appointment; S's b-day; SI noon; ? Celltech." He recorded everything as it was written for March, April, and May.

Kitchens are an underrated source of information, Eddie thought. He remembered an organized-crime case he'd worked before he came to Coney Island. They'd used binoculars from outside a window and found a phone number written on a message board. The number turned out to be that of a Genovese capo. That number led to others, then pictures. It was a case their squad called the "Big Lie." They put twenty-five organized-crime figures on the stand. They all denied consorting with known criminals—one another—because it was a violation of probation. Despite undeniable proof, they all denied it, because the capo couldn't afford to have his probation revoked. Per terms of the deal, they all pled to perjury and did minor time. Except the capo, who walked.

Zina's kitchen drawer contained loose change, fast-food coupons, appliance warranties, old watches, new batteries, and a flashlight. Jammed in the back of the drawer was a file box that held unpaid current bills. He pulled her Visa bill, noting the account number and all of last month's charges. He copied down all her recent long-distance telephone calls with date, time, and duration. The only other bill was from Celltech Labs in Lewes, Delaware. He remembered the Celltech notation on Zina's calendar and made a note to check it. Six minutes and done.

An unmade canopy bed dominated the bedroom. A leopard-skin bedspread sprawled halfway across the floor. Eddie checked the nightstand: two pairs of drug-store reading glasses, a dozen pens, hand lotion, a small cache of clippers, tweezers, nail files, and a book of love poems. He hadn't thought she was the grooming or the reading type. Under the bed was an open box, in which were the sex toys he'd expected to find in the nightstand: vibrators, lubricants, and assorted gadgets, both strap-on and handheld. While down on his stomach, pushing the toy box back, he felt the plywood floor buckle slightly. He froze as the air in the room changed.

Eddie turned his face to look. The floor creaked again.

A guttural shriek pierced the room; then a metal bat glanced off his face and slammed against the floor. He yanked his arm out from under the bed and tried to push away. The second swing caught him square on the left elbow, the next across his legs as he rolled to get away. Another blow on his sciatic right hip. On his back, he rolled to his left and brought his knees to his chest. As she stepped forward and cocked to swing again, he kicked forward, springing out with both feet, using his full length. His right foot caught her on the thigh and drove her into the wall. She bounced off, keeping her balance, but Eddie was already up, reaching for the aluminum softball bat. He snatched it out of her hands. Cat-quick, she squatted to the floor and came up with a black revolver.

"Bastard," she said, pushing the gun at his chest with both hands. "Drop the bat."

She kept the familiar black gun pointed at him as she backed away. He felt his empty holster. The gun must have fallen out during batting practice.

"Zina," he said. "All I want—"

"Is your precious daughter, you fuck. Your precious fucking daughter. I am so sick of it. Don't say another word."

Zina wore black jeans and a white T-shirt with a Key West logo. Her black hair hung straight to her shoulder blades. Bangs covered her forehead down to her eyebrows. She was olive-skinned and large-nosed, with a complexion more heavily pockmarked than was evident in the booking photo. But her body could stop a regiment—muscled, lithe, and shapely. Eddie knew hers was the face in the sketches.

"Is Kate okay?" he asked. "Just tell me that."

"Put the fucking bat down."

"We can work this out, Zina," he said, putting the bat on the bed, hands up. Mr. Full Cooperation. "Just tell me how she is."

"Don't waste your breath, Dunne. Just take your fucking shirt off."

"It doesn't have to be this way."

"Just take your fucking shirt off. Let me see that flabby old body."

Eddie unbuttoned his shirt. He knew she was looking to see if he was wired. He threw the shirt on the bed in front of her to see if she'd flinch. She didn't. Too focused, or too crazy.

"We can both win here, Zina."

"Yeah, yeah, I know. You got some line of shit. I know all about it."

"What do you know?"

"The pants, too. Take the pants off."

"Where's my daughter, Zina?"

"You don't even know how funny that is, you manipulating fuck. Scumbags like you don't deserve children."

"Tell me what you want from me," he said.

"All of it."

"Money? You're talking money?"

"You think this is about money?"

"Money can solve it," he said.

"Pants off. Didn't you hear me, you stupid fuck?"

"You can have everything I own," he said, hopping on one leg while he pulled his pants off, but turning as he did so, trying to shift gradually to her right side.

"Got a fast million, fast Eddie?"

"A million? I can do a million."

"How about three million?"

"I can get three."

"Stop moving," she said, pointing the gun at his crotch. "You move any closer and I blow that off."

"Let's go get the money," he said.

"When I'm ready, asshole."

Eddie held his pants by the cuffs, the belt end down. She stepped back quickly, not sure what he was getting ready to do.

"You're not stupid, Zina. We can have a business arrangement. You take the money; I take Kate. All cash, nothing marked. You go your way; I go mine. Not another word about it. Pure business."

"Just cops all over it."

"No cops. I won't go to the cops. I want her back, Zina. I'm not stupid enough to bring those Keystone Kops with me."

"Give me a break."

"No cops, I swear. Anywhere you want to meet. Name the spot. Just me and the money."

"I'm getting outta here, now. Don't try to follow me. I see you follow me, we'll fuck her up."

"Talk to me," he said. "Make me understand it."

"You can't understand," she said. "Guys like you are incapable. You think it's all so easy. Women are so fucking easy."

"Right. I've been an asshole about women all my life. You can start getting even with me now, Zina."

"You think women can't outsmart you or hurt you. I can do both."

"I believe you."

"Believe this. You keep fucking with me . . . somebody's getting hurt. I know how to hurt you."

"I deserve to be hurt, not my daughter."

"You deserve to suffer."

"I should be suffering," he said. "Make me suffer more. Go ahead. Beat me, humiliate me. Punish me. I deserve it. You've got the gun."

"If it was up to me . . ."

"Who is it up to?"

"One more word," she said, walking backward now. Eddie knew she wasn't going to shoot him. Borodenko wanted him alive.

"Call whoever it's up to. The phone's in the kitchen. Call him."

A gunshot inside a house booms like an M80 firecracker in a metal trash barrel. The muzzle flash happens so quickly, you think you imagined it. But the echo of the boom lingers. Only now, as the acrid smell of cordite burned his nostrils, did he understand the slight motion she'd made just before the boom, when she'd pointed the barrel to his right, over his shoulder. The bullet went into the back wall, above the window that looked out at the Cyclone.

"That's for telling me the phone's in the kitchen," she said. "In my own house. The balls on you."

"You're right—I'm an obnoxious bastard. But call the boss. Tell him I'm ready to get the money. He'll be proud of you."

"You think any fucking man gives me orders?"

"No, I'm sorry. You're in charge."

"Fucking A," she said, dipping the barrel of the gun down to point at his crotch. She opened the door behind her. "You follow me, your daughter dies. If I see anyone else, any cop tailing me, she dies."

"Let me get some money for you right now. Good-faith money. No strings attached. I owe you big-time for keeping her alive."

"You're even stupider than I imagined," she said, halfway out the door. "You don't even know who's keeping *you* alive."

"Is it an Irish thing, or what?" Babsie said. "You only look contented when someone kicks the shit out of you."

A cracked molar made it uncomfortable for Eddie to talk. His tongue rubbed raw every time he swallowed or spoke. In the hours since colliding with Zina Rabinovich's bat, his left elbow had worsened, the forearm and wrist more swollen, stiffness extending down to his fingers. The fact that he knew Kate was alive numbed all the pain.

"Legally," she said, "Zina could have killed you."

"Or had me arrested. But she didn't do either."

He was starving despite the bad tooth and the fact it was Wednesday night at the North End Tavern. Wednesday night meant franks and beans. It was the slowest night for customers, because, according to Kevin, people wouldn't pay for food that reminded them of bad times. "Depression food," he called it. Stubborn Martha always countered that if that were true, all-night diners and dirty-water hot dog carts would have gone out of business years ago.

"I'm bringing Zina in," Babsie said. "Maybe Kevin can pick her out of a lineup."

"She'll just lawyer up and disappear on us. Hold off for now."

"So you get another chance at her? You've had beaucoup chances, Eddie. Time for bravado is long gone. Time to look out for little you know who."

"She's not after Grace."

After taking the beating from Zina, Eddie walked it off on the Coney Island boards. He sought out the old-timers, people whose entire lives revolved around cotton candy, french fries, and now the gold mine of video games. The boardwalk held no secrets. In short order, Eddie heard all about the deaths of the old couple who had owned and run Coney Custards for decades. They'd passed away within weeks of each other and left the business and the building to their pompous ass of a son. And that was a crying shame. The son, too good for the Coney life, preferred to sip martinis in the upscale bar and marina in Great Kills Harbor that his parents had worked themselves to death to buy for him. He'd hired Zina to run the ice-cream business. The consensus on Zina was that she was an unstable lesbian, a woman anyone with good sense avoided. He already knew that much.

"Whoever Zina wants," Babsie said, "she'll come after you, and Grace will get caught in the cross fire. With any luck, it'll be just you and Zina, *mano a mano*. The way it was destined to be."

"A little melodramatic."

"I'm just trying to fit in," she said. "I've doubled the guard on Grace starting tomorrow morning. In case you can't leap this tall building in a single bound."

Working off Probation Department sentencing reports,

Babsie had constructed a background on Zina Rabinovich. Zina was the third daughter of a Russian shoemaker and a seamstress, and their first child born in America. Zina's mother died a year later in Coney Island Hospital during the birth of their fourth child, a boy. The father, who refused to speak English, worked hard but never made enough. Her oldest sister committed suicide at sixteen. The second girl vanished. Social Services said they'd all been physically and emotionally abused. After she left school, the only records of Zina were criminal: five times grand larceny auto and a variety of assaults.

"You're sure you never met Zina before?" Babsie said.

"Before Parrot identified her last week, I'd never even heard the name."

"Never ran across her? Not even as part of an investigation?"

"She's in her twenties, Babsie. She would have been in diapers when I was a cop in Brooklyn."

"Then why does she hate you so much?"

"I have no idea."

Eddie looked over at Grace, who was busy placing a chair at each end of the shuffleboard table. Ever since Kate disappeared, Kevin had worked tirelessly to keep Grace busy. Every time he saw her eyes start to glaze over in a thousand-mile stare, he concocted a game of something. Wednesday was easy, shuffleboard night. Kevin had bought an old-fashioned shuffleboard table that ran the length of the back room, taking up the space of three booths. Franks and beans night was always slow, so their new tradition, a shuffleboard challenge, had become a marathon. Kevin would string the game out as long as she wanted to play. Anything for Gracie. If she asked him to turn cartwheels, he'd say, "No problemo." It wouldn't be pretty, though, two-hundred-pound Irish cartwheels.

"I want to get a look at Zina," Babsie said. "And I mean now. I'll hold off on the lineup, but I want to eyeball her myself."

"Staten Island, tomorrow," Eddie said. "It's on her calendar. Last Thursday, I tailed Mrs. Borodenko's Mercedes there. I didn't know it was her at the time, but Zina was the woman driving. They had lunch in Jimmy's Bistro on Hylan Boulevard. Might be a regular thing."

"Long way to go for lunch," Babsie said. "You sure there's not a little secret something going on between these two? A little candlelight and wine hanky-panky?"

"Definitely the wine. Boland says that Yuri hired Zina to keep his wife away from booze. She can't get a drink in Brighton Beach anymore. Bars aren't allowed to serve her when Yuri's not there. Going to Staten Island, far away from anyone who knows them . . . maybe they're thinking a drink that no one sees never really happened."

"If that were true, my ex-husband would have worn a hood."

Babsie asked to see the notes he took in Zina's apartment. He took another opportunity to change position, shift some weight off his right hip. Between the alleged sciatica and the baseball bat injuries, Eddie had all he could do to walk around looking like he was less than eighty years old.

"How did the nuns let you get away with this handwriting?" she said.

"They didn't. That's why my knuckles look like this. I tell everyone it was from fighting, but it was Sister Mary Elizabeth's metal ruler."

Babsie copied down the information from Zina's calendar and bills. Eddie arranged himself in the booth, trying to find a comfortable position. He'd never realized how hard the wooden benches were.

"What kind of company is Celltech?" she said.

"I would think something scientific: biology, computer? Your guess is as good as mine."

The one thing he wasn't guessing about was that Zina was the only known link to his daughter. If Yuri Borodenko were here, he'd go to him and make a deal. Yuri was a businessman. Without him, Eddie needed a way to get to Zina without igniting a psychotic reaction. He knew that a single spark was enough, and she could blast off to the moon.

"Okay, say Zina was too young," Babsie said. "Is it possible you screwed her older sisters or her mother, in any sense of the word?"

"I wasn't quite the wild man you think. Besides, I would have recognized something about her. I'm good with faces, Babsie. People I haven't seen in forty years, I recognize immediately. I'd know who Zina was. Some family resemblance."

"What about your ex-partner?" Babsie said. "He was quite the swordsman."

"Paulie was in that precinct for a long time. He probably screwed half the female population, in every sense of the word."

"Exactly what I've been saying. Since the day they identified his head, I've been saying the same thing, Eddie. This is all about Paul Caruso."

"Then why isn't it over? If Zina already killed Paulie, it should be over."

"Zina didn't kill Paulie," Babsie said, flipping through

her notes. "Zina never left the country. She doesn't even have a passport. Sergei Zhukov killed Paulie."

Babsie told him that one of Boland's feds had reached out for Sergei's travel activity for the past two years. He'd racked up some major mileage, mostly Moscow to New York. But on April first, he had flown from JFK to Rome. He returned to New York five days later, on the afternoon of April sixth, traveling alone.

"If Sergei returned on the afternoon of the sixth," Eddie said, "he had nothing to do with Kate's kidnapping."

"The guy already had enough on his plate that day."

According to Babsie's notes, Sergei returned to New York on Monday, April sixth, on Delta flight 149. The flight left Rome for JFK at 9:55 A.M. Sergei, however, had arrived in Rome only two hours before that on a connecting flight: Alitalia 7708 from Palermo, Sicily.

"Lukin told me that Borodenko called on the morning of the sixth, looking for Sergei. He asked Lexy Petrov to find him."

"Sergei was busy whacking Paulie," Babsie said. "In the late hours of April fifth, a guy answering his description was seen coming out of Paulie's villa. Sicilian authorities said the place looked like someone had taken a serious beating inside. Paulie's car was later found at the airport in Palermo. My guess is that Sergei wasn't supposed to kill him, but it got out of hand."

"Paulie was an old man," Eddie said. "Twenty years ago, Sergei would have had his hands full."

Grace yelled for Eddie's help. Some type of infraction of shuffleboard rules by Uncle Kev-o. Behind the bar, B. J. Harrington told her to quiet down. He was reciting "The Shooting of Dan McGrew" for the regulars. Eddie told her to handle it herself.

Eddie said, "I've been assuming they brought Paulie's head over on one of Borodenko's freighters, with or without the body."

"Time frame doesn't work. Witnesses saw Paulie in Capo San Vito on the fifth. The head shows up on your lawn on the eighth. Not enough time for a sea voyage. Sergei beat him to death, dumped the torso in the Mediterranean, and carried the skull on the plane like a painted coconut."

"Why?" Eddie asked.

"The head? To prove he did it."

"No, why beat him in the first place?"

"Money," she said. "If it's not revenge, it's money. The Caruso brothers screwed Borodenko out of money. You're in the mix because Paulie gave you up to save his own ass. Sergei was beating the shit out of him, so he told him you were involved. That's why Sergei brought that picture of you in front of the boat. To identify you."

"You're working your way back around to the Rosenfeld shooting, aren't you?"

"If the shoe fits . . ." she said. "Didn't Anatoly Lukin tell you that Borodenko was collecting old debts?"

"But Zina was maybe ten years old at the time of the Rosenfeld murders, and Borodenko was still in the Russian army."

"People don't forget that kind of money," she said.

"Forget what money? It's an urban legend."

"Whether it exists or not, Eddie, it's like pirate treasure to these people. Maybe Zina thinks she found the map."

"It doesn't matter."

"What doesn't matter?" she asked, her eyes widening.

"None of it; nothing that happened fourteen years ago,

or last week. None of it matters. Not as long as we get Kate back."

At least Babsie was right about Paulie Caruso. If his life was at stake, no telling what story he'd have told to save himself. Paulie the Priest knew how to survive. "Always have a story ready" was his mantra.

"All I'm trying to do," Babsie said, "is figure out how Paulie fits in. Whenever you're dealing with cops like Paulie, it always comes down to the same root causes: women, booze, or money."

"Sometimes all three."

Her eyes darted around in herky-jerky, unfocused movements. It was a trait Eddie recognized from her older brothers. Another Panko thinking hard. "What about the blonde in the picture?" she said. "The one with you and Paulie in front of the boat?"

"You mean Lana," he said. "What about her?"

"Was she local talent?"

"If you consider the Ukraine local."

"Let's go to that boatyard tomorrow, before we go to Staten Island. See where Paulie kept the *Bright Star.*"

"Boland already thought of it. All the boats in the marina were searched when Misha's body was found there."

"I want to see it for myself."

"Sheepshead Bay, Babsie. You're talking a good hour out of our way. I don't want to get stuck in traffic somewhere on the Belt Parkway and wind up missing Zina. I can't risk that."

"We'll leave here early. I want to get a picture of that place in my mind."

"You need to picture everything?"

"Everything," she said. "Right now, I'm picturing you, and you're starting to look like a grandfather."

The shuffleboard game came to a stop as Grace began sobbing. Deep, racking, uncontrollable sobs. "The last few days," Babsie said, "the slightest thing has set her off." Kevin picked her up and walked toward the kitchen. Eddie started to go to her, but Babsie stopped him.

"Let your brother do it," she said. "Give him a couple of minutes to calm her down."

Babsie was paying attention, thinking for him again. God knows, he needed somebody to do it. Eddie knew that Grace had been sleeping with Babsie the last few nights. This woman, he thought, saving my ass, time after time. Right under my nose since high school.

"I've got a big, big favor to ask," Eddie said.

"Big, big," she said, frowning. "Two bigs. So okay, I'm worried, but curious."

"Tomorrow," he said, "if we find Zina, I'm going to make a deal with her. I'm going to offer her money. She mentioned three million dollars."

"Where the hell you getting that kind of money?"

"I've got some cash socked away, almost fifty grand."

"That's impressive, but a long way from three million."

"It'll be a fake boodle; it'll look like three million. Real bills outside. In the center you use bill-size colored paper; the edges are perfect. We did it on narcotics buys all the time. You wrap the stacks very tightly. The trick is in binding them as tightly as you can."

"What if she sees it's a fake boodle?"

"She won't."

"You're guaranteeing that? She's gonna ask to count it."

"The top stacks will be real. I won't let her go any farther until I have Kate."

Behind them, the click of the shuffleboard disks resumed. Babsie said Kevin would have made a great father. Eddie thought, Isn't that the way it always is? Who the hell is responsible for deciding who should be parents? She reached over and put her hand over his.

"Eddie, listen to me for a second. Let's let Matty Boland know about this. God knows I hate the prick, but we need a backup here."

"That's why I'm asking you."

"But think about the consequences. Say, for whatever reason, Zina goes totally ballistic and it's just me and you."

"That's the way I want it," he said. "That's the big, big favor."

"And if you're wrong?"

"Then I kill her," he said.

"Jesus," she said, looking up at the original tin ceiling of an Irish bar that had seen better days. "And you have the balls to call me melodramatic."

# CHAPTER
# 38

THURSDAY, APRIL 16
10:10 A.M.

ON THE MORNING of the tenth day, Eddie Dunne sat on
the hood of Kate's Toyota, looking up at his house and
waiting for Detective Babsie Panko. His body, which
had never let him down before, now shouted messages
of surrender to his brain. His left forearm was still
swollen, the stiffness in his fingers getting worse. But
even if he had time, he wouldn't go to the hospital;
they'd just sling it and hand him a painkiller. A few
years earlier, he'd broken the radial bone in his elbow
while sliding headfirst into third base in a bar league's
softball game. It felt like that again. Nothing broken
ever heals completely.

He'd been waiting for Babsie for almost an hour.
She'd worked into the night on Zina's Visa card and
phone bills. Then, a little after 7:00 A.M., she ran out the
door, saying she wanted to talk to the DA in White Plains.
Not a word from her since, and they needed to get moving soon if they were going to have time to visit the
Sheepshead Bay Marina. For a woman who grew up a
mile from the Bronx, Babsie didn't have a clue about how

long it took to get around the city in the middle of a weekday.

With the warmth of the spring sun boring through the trees, Eddie could recall the sight of Eileen at her kitchen window, singing in that thin soprano common to churchwomen. As a young girl in cuffed jeans and tight pink sweaters, the former Eileen McGuire sang the words to every doo-wop song by the Dell Vikings, the Dell Satins, or any of the street-corner wonders of the fifties. Somewhere along the way, the joy diminished and the hymns and the sadness engulfed her. It was no secret that she considered the life choices of her husband to be more than she could bear. In the end, she sang the same sad stanzas over and over, without realizing she was doing it.

With a screech of rubber, Babsie's Crown Vic came around the hedges and barreled up the driveway. She looked frazzled, her hair wild. Eddie made the mistake of looking at his watch.

"Just get in the car," she said.

"We don't have time for the marina."

"We have time. Get in."

Eddie insisted on taking his car. He had his reasons. The Yonkers Police Department's Crown Vic had no official markings, but it looked so much like a police car, it might as well have had the bubblegum lights on the roof. Then he whispered to her that he didn't want to use her city-owned car to transport the money. Using his car would give weight to her "story" in case his plan went sour.

"As far as I'm concerned," he said, "you don't know anything about the bag in my trunk. Whatever I do will be a complete surprise to you."

"Let me see this fake boodle," she said, sighing theatrically as she grabbed her cell phone, notes, and camera and shoved them in her purse.

Eddie opened the Toyota's trunk and unzipped a blue canvas duffel bag. Babsie whistled, then picked up what appeared to be a tall stack of older hundred-dollar bills. She held it between her thumb and fingers, fanning the ends with her other thumb.

"This might work," she said. "How did you get them wrapped so tight?"

"Kevin and I used to deliver advertising flyers; the machine is still in the basement of the bar. It cuts, wraps, and binds stacks of paper with this reinforced wire ribbon. You need heavy-duty scissors to cut these bindings."

Babsie began the trip in silence, rearranging her purse. Eddie told her the rawness in his tongue had eased, toughened from a night's reprieve of scraping across a cracked tooth. Then he explained the layout of Jimmy's Bistro, particularly the parking lot. He said he thought he'd be able to approach Zina outside, if Babsie could flash her identification and pull Mrs. Borodenko aside for a few minutes. This would give him time to show Zina his good faith, now bundled tightly in the trunk. The next move would be hers. Babsie nodded, as if to say, Whatever you want.

"I called Celltech this morning," she said.

"You didn't use your nurse connection?" Eddie asked.

"It wouldn't have worked. They never give out information on DNA tests without a court order."

"What DNA tests?"

"That's what I'm getting a court order to find out," she said. "We know that Zina submitted two samples for comparison, but they won't tell us the names without a court order."

"What's the basis for the order?"

"We have reasonable cause to believe that evidence regarding our homicide victim, Paul Caruso, is in the possession of Celltech labs."

Eddie knew the circumstances surrounding the murder of Paul Caruso gave them the legal footing for the court order. A torn photo, similar to one recently removed from the residence of said Paul Caruso, had been found in a premises under the control of Zina Rabinovich, the individual who had submitted the DNA for testing. Ms. Rabinovich was known to have criminal ties to the alleged murderer, Sergei Zhukov, who was in Sicily at the time Mr. Caruso and the photo disappeared. It wasn't a tremendous reach.

"At this point," Babsie said, "we know Zina submitted a VNTR pattern request. That's a parent-child pattern analysis to determine paternity. If one sample turns out to be Paulie's, then it's evidence in a murder investigation."

"How soon will they know?"

"Couple of hours, at most. Our people already completed Paulie's pattern, to back up the dental record identification. Soon as the court order is signed, Celltech can compare the two. How the hell long could that take?"

"If it is Paulie, fatherhood or not, it links Zina directly to his murder."

"Then she's a collar," Babsie said. "So take your best shot at her today."


Toby Davis, the caretaker of the Sheepshead Bay Marina, knew Eddie Dunne the moment he walked through the door. Although his eyes were failing, the grizzled old sailor, who'd won a Purple Heart at Iwo Jima, said Eddie's name before the door closed behind him. Mr. Eddie. Eddie introduced Babsie as a friend. Babsie corrected him, emphasizing she was a detective investigating the murder of Paul Caruso. It surprised Eddie that Toby didn't mention his daughter, but the old man probably never knew his last name. Paul Caruso had owned the boat, rented the slip, paid all the bills.

"Shame about your partner," Toby said. "But he lived a lot longer than I ever thought he would. His momma raised one insane child."

Babsie showed Toby the picture of Paul Caruso, Eddie, and Lana standing in front of the *Bright Star.* Toby held it up close to his face. He knew the guys, he said, but he didn't recognize the woman. Eddie didn't know whether he was being discreet or honest.

"Toby didn't think much of us as sailors," Eddie said.

"Sailors?" he said. "You two wouldn't make a pimple on a sailor's ass. When the *Bright Star* left the dock, I had to put the Coast Guard on alert. Every night, I went home thinking, Tonight's the night those crazy sons a bitches gonna burn down my marina."

"One fire and you're an arsonist," Eddie said.

"On my dock, miss. They start a bonfire on a wooden dock. Now what the hell kind of senseless boys do that?"

Babsie asked the old man what ever happened to Paul Caruso's boat. He didn't have to look in the file. Toby remembered boats, not blondes.

"The *Bright Star?*" Toby said, playing to Babsie. "It was like putting a three-year-old behind the wheel of a race car in the Indy Five Hundred. A thirty-five-foot

Grand Banks. Beautiful craft. Mr. Caruso thought it was like driving a car. He'd forget it didn't have brakes. We had to put two layers of extra tires around their dock. *Whomp,* the whole place shook when they pulled in. Never saw anything like it."

"Lucky they didn't kill somebody," Babsie said.

"How we all survived, I'll never know. God takes care of beautiful things, and He took special care of this boat. Mr. Caruso asked me to sell it shortly after you two got tired of it. I jumped up, got right on the phone. We found it a good home with a young New York City fireman. Local boy named Stark. Mr. Caruso gave him one hell of a deal on it, too."

"We weren't that bad, Babsie," Eddie said.

"Miss," Toby said, "when I came to work in the morning, I never even glanced over at the *Bright Star.* I was afraid what I was gonna see. Beer cans floating in the water, brassieres flying from the outrigging, bare asses on the foredeck."

"Does Mr. Stark still keep it here?" Babsie asked.

"For a while, he did," Toby said. "One summer, he was here almost every day, scraping and painting. Looked better than new when he finished. He renamed it *Stevie's Dream.* Now he keeps it at a private dock behind his house, over near Gerritsen Beach."

Toby said that Stark had reupholstered everything that could be reupholstered. He redid the teak and replaced almost everything in the galley. He said that Stark still brought it in every year for engine work. Usually around this time, late April, early May.

"The day that boat left here," Toby said, "both me and it were smiling."

\*     \*     \*

Despite making great time on the Belt Parkway, they got to Jimmy's Bistro in Staten Island as the valet was parking Borodenko's Mercedes.

"Today's the day they had to get here early," Babsie said.

"We should have been waiting."

"Okay, my fault," Babsie said. "We'll grab them on the way out."

Valet parking complicated Eddie's plan. They hadn't used it the last time he'd followed them here. His idea was to approach Zina as they were getting in or out of the car, but now the valet would deliver the car to the front door of the restaurant. A good chance there'd be a crowd waiting under the awning. Too many people within earshot might spook Zina.

"We're not even sure Zina is in there," Eddie said.

"She's in there. It was on her calendar. We'll just wait."

"I need to know when they're leaving," Eddie said. "Why don't you go inside and eat. Get a table close to them. They have no idea who you are."

"Looks pricey, Eddie. I don't think I have enough money on me."

"I've got nine bucks left," he said. "Everything else is tied up. I'd give you my credit card if I had one."

Babsie said she'd use her own, then slung her purse over her shoulder. The big leather bag bulged with equipment—her camera, her cell phone, her gun, her case folder. All he'd brought to the island was nine bucks, an aching body, and a half-assed plan. He couldn't blame her if she cut her losses with him. Why should she believe that he had a snowball's chance in hell of ever getting anything right? Ten minutes later, he heard the ringing of "When Irish Eyes Are Smiling."

"Your friend Zina," Babsie said, "is uglier than her booking photo."

"What she lacks in looks, she makes up for in muscle."

"The other one just came back from the ladies' room. She's a little wobbly."

"Probably shit-faced," Eddie said.

"She looks like a bulimia case with a Jackie Onassis wardrobe: raincoat, scarf, and oversized sunglasses. Can't see her face. Okay, okay, glasses off, rubbing her face. Pretty. Very pretty girl. What is she, about twenty, twenty-one?"

"Maybe a year or two older."

"She's wearing a dress that looks like something Joan Crawford wore in *Mildred Pierce*. Not that I'm an expert or anything, but it looks old to me."

"Save the fashion commentary," Eddie said.

"Okay. Two bottles of wine on the table. Bottle of red, bottle of white. Zina pouring red. I'll tell you right now . . . Zina looks like that badass Indian in *The Last of the Mohicans*."

Babsie said she'd schmoozed the maître d' by telling him he reminded her of a young Al Pacino. "Works every time in marinara joints," she said. She refused three booths, until he placed her at a small table in the back. Situated behind an ivy-covered partition, it offered a workable sight line to Zina's plush curved booth.

"I saw this in a spy movie," Babsie said. "Peeking through the ivy. *Casablanca* maybe, something in black and white."

Eddie heard a breath. She said she'd blown out the candle and set it in an opening in the ornate brick lattice-work. The candleholder held down enough ivy to provide a less obstructed view. Then another voice: a waiter, giving the luncheon specials. Eddie wanted to ask how much it would cost if they just called it lunch.

"You're paying for this," Babsie said. "Fifteen bucks for a goddamn house salad. Two fifty for goddamn iced tea. I gotta take this menu to Martha and Kevin."

Eddie heard the clink of china and silverware in the background. Jerry Vale sang "Innamorata." Babsie bitched about the prices. What a great surveillance tool a cell phone was. Eddie never would have thought of using it this way. Wearing a body mike and lugging an expensive receiver were the old way. This was so easy. Half the people in the place were probably yakking away on them anyway, so the cover was ideal.

Babsie said, "You were right about Zina being the one in those sketches. That schnozz is unmistakable."

"All you have to do is tell me when they're leaving."

"Oh, Jesus . . ." Babsie said.

"Oh Jesus what?" Use whole sentences, he wanted to tell her.

"Zina just leaned over and kissed her."

"Really?"

"Not *just* a kiss . . . a big wet tongue."

"Bullshit, not in public."

"I told you this was a romance," she said. "This is why you can't let guys do surveillance work. They miss the nuances."

Eddie heard a click and a motor whine. Sounded like a camera, but she wouldn't be using a camera.

"I'm taking a few pictures," she said.

"That was pretty loud, Babsie. Anybody around you?"

"Empty tables and the back door."

"Careful," he said.

The camera clicked and whined four or five times. Babsie laughed softly.

"You need to see this, Eddie. Zina's treating her like she's a prom date. Doing everything but pinning on a corsage. You want to know how to treat a woman? Watch her. The little touches, fixing the scarf around her neck. Brushing the hair off her face. Two women going to lunch are not this touchy-feely. We've got a major romance going here."

"I believe it. Now put the camera away."

"I just did," she said. "And my salad is here."

Eddie waited twenty minutes, listening to Babsie chew and brag about how she'd predicted it would be hot and heavy at Jimmy's Bistro. Women had a sense of subtle behavioral details; guys only saw the obvious. The world according to Babsie.

"Another bottle of red," Babsie reported. "That didn't take long. And they just got their entrées."

Hopefully, it was Mrs. Borodenko chugging the wine. He didn't want Zina drunk. No telling what she'd be like drunk. Eddie tried to figure out how this romance affected the life of his daughter. If it did at all. According to Boland, not a word about Kate had been mentioned on any of the bugs they had in Borodenko's businesses. The cops working the plants felt that the kidnapping was outside of the Borodenko criminal empire. Yuri himself was the only one who ever referred to Kate; every day, he asked if she'd been found yet. It could be bullshit, but he appeared to be out of the loop. Zina might be more of an independent contractor than he'd thought. Wrapping the alcoholic Mrs. Borodenko around her finger. Using her. This would account for Sergei's trip to Palermo. Eddie needed to connect and deal seriously with Zina before Yuri killed her.

"I think Al Pacino gave me up," Babsie said.

"Who?"

"The maître d'. He's over at their booth now, and Zina is looking my way. Pissed-off. Here she comes."

Eddie heard rustling sounds. He could hear Babsie clear her throat. Then he heard another voice: Zina's.

"I have no idea what you're talking about," Babsie said.

"Give me the fucking camera." It was Zina. No doubt about it. That voice was etched in his mind.

Eddie sprinted stiffly across the parking lot. His right hip ached as he bounded up the steps. When he found Babsie's table, she was sitting back, smiling up at Zina. The way her hands were in her lap, he knew she had her gun under the table and was pointing it at Zina's stomach.

"Eddie Dunne, shit," Zina said. "I knew you didn't have the balls to handle it on your own."

"I need to talk to you for a second," Eddie said.

"Get your fucking hands off me," Zina said.

Babsie identified herself to the maître d', who was running in circles around them. She dropped the camera down in her purse with a big satisfied smile. Zina told the maître d' she wanted the film before they left. Two burly guys in tight suits converged on them from the bar. Eddie whispered he had the money in the trunk.

"Three million," he whispered.

"You ain't got shit with you," Zina said. "Except this old whore with a badge."

"Okay, last words before the fight," Babsie said.

She was already up, swinging her leather bag over her

shoulder. One burly guy maneuvered his body between the two women. The maître d' asked Babsie to leave, then explained to Zina he couldn't take the camera. Babsie was a police officer on an official investigation.

"Not so fast, bitch," Zina said, reaching around. "I told you I want that film."

Zina grabbed Babsie by the hair and yanked her toward her. Burly guy number one tried to pry Zina's fingers loose. Babsie ducked and spun, swinging the purse low, as if it were a fifty-pound sandbag. She caught Zina behind the knees. Zina buckled backward, then went down flat. Babsie followed with all her weight as her knee slammed into Zina's midsection. Zina gasped, trying to catch her breath, fists flailing at Babsie's face. Both burly guys reached for whatever they could grab—arms, legs, shirts. Eddie planted his foot on Zina's sternum, grabbed Babsie under the arms, and pulled her up.

The bigger burly guy wrapped Eddie in a bear hug, squeezing his sore left elbow against his ribs. The maître d' Babsie called Al Pacino helped the wheezing Zina to her feet. A clump of Babsie's grayish blond hair clung to the fingers of her right hand. Quick eye contact with Eddie—Babsie saying she was okay. Zina bent over, trying to catch her breath, pointed a finger at Eddie, then made a gesture. She held her palm flat, indicating about three feet high, then ran a finger across her throat. "Gracie," she rasped.

"You come near that little girl," Babsie said, "and I'll blow that ugly head off."

Eddie struggled to get out of the bear hug. He looked around for Mrs. Borodenko, but the pale blonde was standing only a few feet to his right in her Joan Crawford dress. Her eyes were puffy and red, as if she'd been caught in the middle of a drunken crying jag, and she was looking right at him. Staring at him.

"Forgive," she said in a breathy Russian accent. That sad, pretty face. A face from another time. She touched his arm as Zina pulled her toward the door. "Forgive."

# CHAPTER
# 39

"SORRY," BABSIE SAID.

*Sorry* was a word he didn't want to hear again. It never changed anything; time never rolled backward to accommodate your regret. If it did, Kate would be home, Eileen still singing doo-wop. He was sorry for all the pain he'd caused, all the mistakes he'd made. What good did it do? He wanted to put a blinking purple neon billboard in the heart of Times Square, announcing that no one ever had to apologize to him again. Babsie certainly didn't have to.

"It wasn't your fault," Eddie said. "It was a stupid plan. Never had a chance. The woman is a psycho. You can't pin your hopes on the reaction of a psycho."

"The camera was a mistake," she said.

"Babsie, forget what happened."

"I just keep thinking . . ."

"I love you," he said for the first time. "From the first moment of this, you've been my heart, my head, everything I could have ever wanted. In my eyes, there is nothing, absolutely nothing, you could ever do wrong."

Little else was said on the way back to Yonkers. The

thing about apology is that no amount of it eases anyone's pain, thought Eddie. And no amount of money was ever going to get Kate home. He'd fooled himself into thinking this was about money. He wanted to believe it, because it was a tangible way to fix everything. But if it had been about ransom, Kate would have been home long ago. Cash and carry. This was something else. Some Zina Rabinovich–conjured vendetta. Zina was using Mrs. Borodenko to carry it out, and nobody in Borodenko's organization had the guts to tell Yuri his beautiful wife was hollow. Everyone knows what happens to the messenger. Eddie Dunne was not afraid to be the messenger.

"Let me have the camera," he said.

"Let's go home," Babsie said. "Ten days you've been at this. Not sleeping, not letting up. You're emotionally exhausted."

It was too late for exhaustion. It was the last round: Go for the head. He'd decided to peel the veneer off the beautiful Mrs. Borodenko. He intended to broadcast throughout the Russian community the relationship between her and a homicidal lesbian. He had no doubt it would plunge a dagger through Borodenko's macho self-image and bring him rushing home to repair the damage. It could also backfire, but he was down to last chances. Ten days had gone by. Ten days.

Babsie's cell phone rang. He heard only her part of the short hi-and-bye conversation. She answered no questions, gave no advice. She just listened to the dictates of a legal system in full gear. The ball was rolling with or without her.

"Celltech called back," she said. "The DNA sample sent to them by Zina matches ours. They're both Paul Caruso."

"Let me know when you're ready to pick her up."

"Don't worry," she said. "The thing of it is, Paulie's DNA didn't match Zina's. She's still looking for her father."

They stopped at a one-hour photo on Central Avenue. Eddie picked two pictures from the sample sheet. The photo shop was glad to see Eddie. He ordered a hundred blowups each of two pictures in which you could clearly see the faces of both women as they leaned across the table for an eyes-closed, mouths-open, tongues-engaged kiss. No mistaking it for platonic.

He dropped Babsie off at home. She went right to her car and backed down the driveway, on her way to Christ the King. Grace would never be out of her sight until Zina was in custody. Eddie opened a stack of bills from the very top layer of the boodle in his trunk. He folded them and stuck them into his pocket.

On the way back to the photo shop, he thought about the face of Mrs. Borodenko. Before today, he'd seen her only from a distance. Though pale and drawn, she was stunning. As she stood next to him asking forgiveness, her face had flushed pink from the wine and the turmoil around her. Thick blond hair, cut short and blunt, and white-blond eyebrows framed those sad blue eyes. Once-in-a-lifetime blue eyes.

Eddie paid the photo bill with two musty hundred-dollar bills. He stacked the photos on the seat next to him as he drove to Brooklyn, but he kept picking them up and looking, bothered by this face. He thought he was past the age where you believe that one woman is more beautiful than a million others. That was Hollywood hype. After all, he'd spent his life in a city where you saw dozens of beautiful women every day, on every block, all incredibly attractive in their own way. By the time you got home, you couldn't remember any of them. But beauty excuses nothing.

Borodenko had been so proud of his new wife, showing her off at their wedding at the Mazurka. That night, Anatoly Lukin had told him the Russians were all about show; that was their weakness. He told him about the Potemkin villages of the eighteenth century, where Prince Potemkin created an illusion of prosperity in the Crimea to please Catherine the Great. As the czarina rode through the poor villages, Potemkin lined the streets with scrubbed-up children wearing expensive formal clothes. The fronts of the houses had been painted and fixed up. Immediately behind the facades were decay, poverty, and despair. After the czarina passed through, the clothes were retrieved from the children and delivered to the next village. "Nothing has changed," Lukin had said. "It's still all about show." Eddie Dunne would shine a spotlight on the dark corners of Borodenko's house.

Thursday night was the big bar night in Manhattan, the night all the workers hit happy hour with the office gang, figuring they could sleepwalk through Friday. In Brooklyn, however, Thursday night was for the regulars, just the audience Eddie was looking for.

Eddie started with the place he knew would cause the most controversy. He went right to the Mazurka, then straight to the lounge. The bartender was a thick-necked Russkie with a crew cut. Eddie showed him the picture of Zina and her boss's wife in full lip lock. The kid looked at it, then back at Eddie. Eddie dropped a hundred-dollar bill on the bar. The bartender said something in Russian to a waiter picking up a drink order. The bartender tried to return the picture, but Eddie backed away.

In the Mazurka's men's room, Eddie posted pictures above each urinal. The ladies' room received twenty copies on the sink. In the kitchen, he stuck pictures on the wall near the spot where waiters posted their orders. The manager caught up to him as he was coming out of the kitchen.

"I'm leaving," Eddie said as the manager took a quick look at the picture, then called a guy sitting near the door. The bouncer looked like he might be an off-duty cop. "Pass these around, Officer," Eddie said. "Take some back to the station house."

For the next two hours, he put pictures in every bakery, grocery, shoe store, and bar. By the time he got to the Samovar, he was down to just two dozen pictures. Lexy Petrov was behind the bar, pouring a drink, and didn't see Eddie sit down. Eddie handed a picture to the young man sitting next to him. Lexy turned to see him and snatched the picture out of the kid's hands. He ripped it up and threw it in the trash.

"Not your property, Lexy," Eddie said.

"We have enough pictures," Lexy said. "A trash can full."

Eddie reached over the counter and grabbed Lexy by the shirt collar. He pulled him forward and whispered in his ear.

"*Stukatch,*" Eddie said in Russian. A most shameful word. "Should I tell them, Lexy? Tell them you're the FBI snitch?"

It was more than an educated guess on Eddie's part. He'd given Boland Lexy's taped confession and the pipe he'd used to bash in the skull of Evesi Volshin. As he poured a club soda, Lexy laughed as if Eddie had whispered a dirty joke. Eddie saw there were other pictures torn up in the trash can. He figured people had brought them in from other restaurants or a telephone pole. He sipped his club soda and wondered if this would work. Would it cause enough of a problem to make holding his daughter no longer worth it? He had to convince them he was determined to make their lives miserable. That he was still crazy enough to hurt them.

"How about some of that good vodka, Lexy?" Eddie said. "Those bottles you keep below the bar."

"Drink yourself dead," Lexy said, slamming a bottle of Stolichnaya in front of Eddie.

Eddie sniffed it. He loved the smell of vodka. Don't let anyone tell you it has no smell. He emptied his glass, tossing the club soda, ice and all, on the floor behind the bar. The first drink in four years spilled hot over his tongue. The burn. He loved the burn. He loved the taste. Eddie was a guy who truly loved the taste of booze. And the life. He loved the drinking life.

On the TV above Lexy's head, the evening news blinked silently; closed captioning flashed underneath. Eddie figured that more closed-captioned programs were watched by drunks on bar stools than were ever viewed by those hard of hearing. In bad lighting, a street reporter stood on a dock, the wind blowing her hair. Although he could not hear any sound, it was obvious she was yelling. Shouting over the wind and the sound of a tow truck behind her. No doubt the motor whined as the cable of the truck tightened and shivered in the glare of the setting sun. At the end of the cable, a set of wheels appeared, then the vehicle being pulled out of the soupy black waters of the Arthur Kill. As soon as it began to emerge, Eddie knew Parrot was dead. Madame Caranina should have foreseen it: No one who touched Eddie Dunne got out alive.

As the rear end of a van rose, grayer than the water, he knew it was heavily coated with primer. Painted on the side would be SAMMY SOSA and the flag of the Dominican Republic. The caption on the TV screen read "Seven unknown dead inside van pulled from water in Elizabeth, New Jersey." They'd like that, Eddie thought, to be labeled "unknown."

He poured another Stoli. Around the bar, the faces of old drinking buddies all turned toward him. There is no truer love than the love shared by drunken friends. He'd read that on a cocktail napkin. Funny line. All his old Russian drinking buddies, staring silently, waiting for him to self-destruct.

Not that he blamed them for not talking to him. If he had a few more drinks, he'd challenge them. They'd expect that. Booze made him talkative, aggressive, crazy. Crazy was the goal tonight. Before the night was over, he'd hit someone. Maybe take on the whole bar. Why not? "No fools, no fun," his partner, Paulie the Priest, had always said. God, he loved the taste of booze.

Ludmilla, waiting for Lexy to fill a drink order for one of her tables, moved close to him.

"Go home," she said, sliding the bottle away from him.

"The fun is just starting, Ludmilla."

"You're finished. Go home, protect your family." She stepped even closer to him and lowered her voice. "That woman in the picture, Zina, is very sad person, but dangerous," she said. "You know what *subotnik* is? Gang rape. Russian gangsters gang-rape her when she was just a girl, acting tough. They laugh about it. They say what the lesbian needs is good Russian dick. Now who knows what she thinks in her mind."

"I don't care what happened to her, Ludmilla."

"Zina's troubles come worse because of Sophie. Sophie, she has her problems, too. Drinking and such. Not all to blame, Sophie. The way he keeps her locked up in that house."

"Sophie is Borodenko's wife?"

"Yes. Sophie Ross, the model. Very famous in my country. She sent Zina asking questions."

"She sent Zina where?"

"In here, all around the streets. Asking questions about her family, and what happened. Questions about you and your partner."

"Me and my partner?"

"About the robbery. Her mother and father were killed in that robbery. You caught the men. The father was that *mafiya* lawyer, Rosenfeld. I know you remember her mother, Svetlana. Svetlana Rosenfeld."

"Lana," he said.

"Sophie looks just like her mother."

Back out on the sidewalk, Eddie saw a black Lincoln parked across the street. He waited for Matty Boland to call him over. Boland was all smiles.

"You got the Brighton Beach phone lines buzzing," he said. "We could have tracked you every step of the way tonight."

"I figured you were here to see this asshole Lexy."

"That useless piece of shit? He gave us enough to get started, not much more. He's not the wheeler and dealer he pretends to be."

"All show, like the rest," Eddie said.

"Not all of them. Just between us, we got word on one of Borodenko's freighters. Flying a Syrian flag, but it has a Russian crew. It's coming up the Pacific, outside

Mexico right now. It looks like a major drug ship. Remember, you said they weren't into drugs?"

"I've been wrong about a lot of shit."

Boland wore a dark baseball cap, J. CREW across the top. He took it off and ran his fingers through his gray-flecked hair. Eddie noticed a copy of a Russian-English dictionary on the seat next to him.

"You know what your name is in Russian?" Boland asked.

"Fucking Eddie Dunne," he said.

"You've heard that before. We heard it a lot tonight. What I came to tell you is that you can stop with the pictures. We just got the word Yuri Borodenko is pissed, really pissed. That's what you wanted, right?"

"Part of it."

"He'll be home tomorrow. He's in the air right now."

"That's the other part."

"Heard you were hoisting a few in the Samovar tonight. I expected you to be in a lot worse condition than this."

"I quit again," Eddie said. "But I've never been in worse condition."

# CHAPTER
# 40

---

**THURSDAY**
**11:00 P.M.**

BABSIE CAME TO HIM as he sat on the edge of the bed. She pulled the nightgown over her head and rolled back the covers. He loved that she was proud of her body, the fullness and strength of it. No charge for extra curves. They made love quietly but with an emotion born of a grief carried too long. He needed to be touched, needed to feel something, needed her, and she knew it. Afterward, he held her, her head resting in the hollow of his shoulder.

"I've loved you since high school," she said softly. "Is that lame or what?"

"I was way too dumb for you then," he said as he rubbed his fingers across her back.

Eddie thought of an old Irish saying: "Better wed over the mixins than the moor." According to Kevin Dunne, it meant your chances of being happy in life were greater the closer you stayed to home. Babsie made him understand that. Ten days together and already they were finishing each other's sentences, laughing about the same stupid stories. What made it possible was the lifetime before these ten days, the shared childhood, which provided the foundation. The different paths they'd traveled since added the mystery. Everything Eddie had ever wanted was right here, on the hill where he'd grown up. It had just taken him so damn long to realize it. If God would keep Kate safe, he'd never ask for anything again.

"I have something to tell you," he said.

"Not now."

Babsie knew he'd been drinking, and she feared the Irish melancholy. She'd spent too many nights in bars with micks who sang songs of marching off to war. Eddie wasn't like that, but something was pulling him down. Best to wait until morning. Morning makes everything seem less ominous, she thought.

"I don't want any secrets," he said. "I know I'm putting you on the spot. You're still an active cop."

"Wait six months, until I retire."

"Some things can't wait, Babsie."

Eddie Dunne's secrets frightened her. He'd lived recklessly for longer than anyone she'd ever known. Since her divorce fifteen years ago, she'd avoided emotional ties. Her big family and her job were enough. She hoped this feeling for him wasn't some repressed high school crush. The good girl finally snags the dangerous boy. But she was too old and too smart for that. She loved him, plain and simple. These ten days, being near him, had resurrected feelings she hadn't had in years. Still, the little warning buzzer in the back of her head kept saying that Eddie Dunne might be more of a problem than any woman could bear.

"You know that torn photograph you put together?" he said. "The three of us in front of Paulie's boat. Me,

Paulie, and Lana. I told you the woman in the center was named Lana, right? And she was Paulie's girlfriend."

"Why am I not surprised there's more to Lana?"

"Everything I told you was true, Babsie. But I left out that Lana was a nickname for Svetlana. Svetlana Rosenfeld. Lana was Marvin Rosenfeld's wife."

"Jesus . . . Rosenfeld's wife. Don't tell me any more."

They lay there quietly, listening to the sound of Kevin's old car whining on the climb up Roberts Avenue. The steep hill required a good car. A better car than most of the locals cared to spend money on. They could walk or grab the bus to anyplace important. Kevin Dunne refused to pay more than five hundred dollars for a hunk of metal on wheels. He said that it was better the car growl than his stomach.

"I haven't been in love in a long time," Eddie said. "I've forgotten how to handle it."

"It's okay. Telling me says good things; you trust me. I guess that's a good thing. Okay . . . go ahead, tell me about Lana. Was it a full-blown affair?"

"He named the boat after her. Svetlana means 'bright star.' Paulie Caruso had a lot of women in his life, but he was crazy over this one."

"How long did this go on?"

"Two years, maybe a little longer."

"While she was married?"

"She was thirty years younger than he was."

"That's no excuse."

"I didn't say it was."

Kevin's car doors thumped twice. They both listened to the keys jingling as he and Martha went in their house. All sounds in the night were important now.

"The robbery was a setup, wasn't it?" Babsie said.

"So was the big shoot-out in the park. It was all a setup."

She thought of getting dressed and leaving. Maybe if he had a night to mull it over, he'd decide his secrets should remain with him. But Babsie made up her mind right then. She'd gone this far. Whatever it was, so be it. They'd be her secrets, too.

"How much did you know?" she said.

"It took me a few weeks to catch on. Remember you said you thought it was strange we just happened to be driving by the Rosenfeld house at the exact time of the robbery?"

"The first thing that occurred to me."

"Most cops say the same thing: too much of a coincidence. But I wasn't surprised. We drove by that house all the time. Sometimes ten, twenty times a tour. Paulie was always trying to get a glimpse of Lana. Like he was sixteen years old."

"Vestri and Nuñez were patsies," Babsie said. "Set up to be killed, weren't they?"

"Paulie's brother Angelo engineered the robbery. He arranged for Nuñez and Vestri to do it. Paulie had all the inside information. He knew where the safe was. He knew there was a ton of money in it, although I don't think he ever imagined how much."

"Paulie knew the exact day and time Vestri and Nuñez would be there," she said.

"Probably down to the minute. After the robbery, Nuñez and Vestri went to a prearranged spot in Marine Park. They were probably thinking they'd meet one of Angelo's men, switch cars or something. When Paulie followed them, he hung so far back on the Belt Parkway, I thought he was going to lose them. But he knew exactly where they were going. He drove to a spot hidden in a grove of trees. There they were. The shoot-out happened fast. As soon as we got out of the car, Paulie fired the first shot, but they already had guns in their hands."

"When they saw Paulie, they knew it was a setup. They had to be stupid not to smell something strange about Angelo giving them this big a job."

"Stupid, sure, that's why they were picked. But they did better than I did, because I didn't smell anything. None of it seemed forced or manipulated. Paulie was patient. He waited until we came up in normal rotation for that divisionwide burglary assignment. I fully expected him to ride by the house that day. It's what he did every chance he got."

"How much did the Carusos get?"

"Millions."

"How did they get the money out of the park?"

"I'm not exactly sure. After we shot Vestri and Nuñez, I left to look for a telephone to call for an ambulance and the bosses. We had no radio in the car. I know, I know . . . part of the setup. I had to drive out of the park to find a phone. When I got back, ten or fifteen minutes later, I noticed Paulie had grass and twigs clinging to his pant legs. I asked him what had happened. He said he went into the woods to take a piss. He either took the money out of the trunk and hid it or passed it off to someone waiting."

"When did you figure it out?"

"It took me longer than I like to admit," Eddie said. "Maybe I didn't want to believe it. That night, we were heroes, our pictures in all the papers."

"I can't believe you didn't tell somebody about it. It's murder we're talking about here, Eddie. Why didn't you just leak it to IAB?"

"You're not going to like this."

"Oh no."

"Tell me if you don't want to hear it, Babsie. I'm serious. It implicates me."

He could feel her body tensing. Gone was the soft, warm drowsiness. He understood that it was natural for her to start thinking like a cop.

"In for a penny, in for a pound," she said. "I already know more than I want to. If you don't tell me, I'm always going to wonder how bad you really are."

Eddie said, "After the big press conference the next day, we're leaving police headquarters in Manhattan. We get in Paulie's car to go back to the precinct. Cops and brass are walking past us as we're parked there. Uniforms all over the place. Paulie tosses me a stack of bills, mostly fifties and hundreds. I say something like "Oh shit," and I shove it under my coat so no one will see it. I don't look until we're back over the bridge. Total of ten grand. He says he grabbed two stacks off the top, one for me, one for him. No big deal. He says no one has any idea how much money was there. The money was just going to Uncle Sam, and he'd never miss it."

"You kept the ten grand."

"I kept it. Eileen was sick; I owed everyone. It didn't seem like that big of a chunk of the four point two million we turned in. Remember, at that point I still thought it was a good shoot. I thought we were heroes. The only other choice I had was to turn on my partner. And, yes, as weak and wrong as it sounds now, I kept the money."

"Paulie was slick," she said. "He put you in a position where you were in it together. You couldn't go against him because you were equally guilty. No telling how much the bastard really grabbed."

Babsie thought, Five minutes after I tell this guy I love him, he drops a piano on me. That has to be a new record. What the hell is the rest of our life going to be like? But she had to admit, she thought the story was going to be worse.

"Next question," she said. "How did Zina find out about it?"

"Listen to me for a second," he said.

"Oh, Eddie. Don't do this again."

"I didn't know this until tonight," he said. "Mrs. Borodenko's maiden name is Sophie Ross. She's a model who grew up in Russia."

"I know that."

"She's also the daughter of Marvin and Lana Rosenfeld, Babsie."

"I thought their kid drowned in Russia."

"That's what I thought. Ludmilla told me tonight that Sophie's grandparents created that story to avoid a custody battle with the Rosenfelds. They hid her in some small village in the Ukraine."

Babsie could put the rest together herself. After Sophie moved over here, she somehow found out about her mother's nights on Paul Caruso's boat. She sent Sergei looking for Paulie. Paulie the Priest filled in the rest.

"One thing bothers me, Eddie. You said Paulie really loved Lana?"

"Like crazy."

"He put her in a hell of a dangerous position for someone he loved like crazy. In the middle of the robbery, with two nut jobs like Vestri and Nuñez."

"That will always bother me, too," he said softly.

"What happens now?" Babsie said.

"This puts me more in the middle than I thought. Maybe Sophie blames me for what happened to her parents. I need to confront Borodenko, get it settled once and for all. Whatever he wants. Then I'll beg him to save Kate. She had nothing to do with this."

"I meant what happens between us," she said.

"Wait until this unfolds," he said. "Whatever you decide then, I won't blame you."

# CHAPTER
# 41

"KNOCK, KNOCK," Grace said, as they walked down Roberts Avenue.

"Who's there," Babsie said.

"Banana," Grace said.

"I've heard that one a hundred times," Babsie said. "Don't you know any other jokes?"

"Okay, let me think."

Matty Boland had called early that morning. Yuri Borodenko had been burning up the telephone on the flight home from Moscow. Whatever he'd said, the offices of both the Mazurka and Flushing Salvage were buzzing with activity. Babsie knew the investigators working the plant could hear only one side of the telephone conversations, mostly a series of grunted replies that meant Yes, Yuri; yes, Yuri. Both operations were fully in motion before dawn. So many half-assed mobsters were on the road, the task force couldn't follow all of them. That was part of the plan, Boland figured. Lose the Keystone Kops in the clown chase. In the confusion, one trusted associate hides the evidence, or plants the bombs. It would all be over before 2:00 P.M., when Borodenko landed at JFK. Boland told Babsie he'd prefer it if Eddie wasn't there.

She'd let Eddie sleep. He needed it, and she needed time to think about her own moves. Fifty years old, might be a little late for a new life. She'd been independent for too long. She owned her own house, had a good job with a decent pension right around the corner. Now this Eddie Dunne thing, happening too fast. The trick was not to jump too far. Eddie was great, but maybe she needed to keep an escape route open. She remembered an old Yeats poem an English teacher from Sacred Heart used to spout when he got his load on. Something about "never give all the heart." Always keep a little of yourself back. Good advice. Now how the hell do you do it? she wondered.

"I know a joke," Babsie said. "Your teacher's name is Rita, right?"

"Mrs. Coughlin is my teacher, but her first name is Rita."

"Knock, knock."

"Who's there?" Grace said.

"Rita."

"Rita who?" Grace said, starting to laugh already.

"Rita good book and you'll learn something."

Grace laughed as if she were going to bust. Babsie never saw a kid who liked to laugh like this one. She brought out the comedian in everyone.

"I'll say that to my teacher today."

"Yeah, it'll go over big. Tell her your grandfather told you that one."

"Babsie, can I call you Grammy?"

Grace called her Grammy at the light at Palisade as a car came screeching around the corner. Babsie heard it before she saw it. Her instincts kicked in and she pulled Grace close to her. It was an old loud Camaro, coming straight at them. In one move, she scooped Grace under her arm and jumped backward, trying to put a parked car between them and the Camaro. She landed hard on her ass and elbows, her arms wrapped around Grace. The Camaro banged over the curb and stopped inches from the building. Zina had the window down, and the gun pointed. Babsie scrambled between parked cars and out to the road. The Camaro backed up, but Babsie had passed behind it and was running toward the North End Tavern, lugging Grace and her backpack. She could hear the loud Camaro engine accelerating behind her.

The first gunshots shattered the glass of McGrath Electric. The front doors of the North End Tavern were wide-open, blowing out the night's beer stink. Babsie made it in before bullets shattered their glass. Kevin Dunne came running from the kitchen, wiping his hands on his apron. Babsie told him to stay the hell away from the windows and call 911. Babsie ran to the cellar steps, opened the door, and told Grace to get down there and stay. She slammed the door behind her. Martha came out of the kitchen and stood by Kevin, ready to give a piece of her mind to whoever had had the nerve to break her windows.

"Martha," Babsie said, "go downstairs with Grace."

"I'll do no such thing," she said.

The first grenade hit off a coat hook and bounded toward the empty booths. Babsie screamed at them to get down, but they stood there as if they were posing. The explosion rocketed up and out, debris releasing in a wide swath. Martha shrieked as Kevin fell to the ground holding his face, blood spurting through his fingers.

The next grenade came seconds later, as Babsie screamed at the police dispatcher: "Ten-thirteen, ten-thirteen." The dispatcher calmly asked, "Location?" The caller ID was unable to get an address from a cell phone. Babsie, who'd lived there all her life, didn't know the street number. "The North End Tavern," she yelled. "Palisade and Roberts. Ask one of the cops."

In the quiet after the second blast, she could hear Martha calling Kevin, repeating his name over and over in a detached and eerie voice. Babsie crawled through chunks of wet plaster and glass around the side of the line of booths until she reached a spot where she had a straight view of the front door. Water pouring from a broken pipe slapped off a table.

On her stomach, Babsie anchored her elbows on the floor and pointed the gun barrel at the light shining from outside. Zina would appear backlit, a decent target despite the smoke. The smoke was too thick to see the front clearly; she couldn't tell exactly where Kevin and Martha were. Just hang on for two minutes, she thought; the cavalry will be here. Two minutes. Her right hand was tightening up; her elbow felt swollen and numb. Eddie hurts his left; I do my right. Aren't we a goddamn pair?

Babsie heard footsteps walking on the glass, and no more sounds from Martha. The footsteps were slow and deliberate, not moving in a straight line. Pausing, moving, pausing, moving. From her shooter's spot, Babsie could see the front, but her view of the cellar door was from under a table. The heavy clouds lingered—the second grenade must have had a smoke component. Finally, she heard a siren in the distance.

The door to the cellar opened. From where she was, she could see only Grace's feet.

"Grammy," Grace called.

Babsie's hands slid on the wet glass and chunks of plaster. She rolled under the partition that separated the tables from the bar. The footsteps quickened.

"Honey," she said. "Go back where you were."

"I'm scared, Grammy."

Babsie got to her feet and ran toward the cellar door. Zina fired and missed. Babsie got to Grace first, picked her up, slammed the cellar door behind her. She ran down the steps as quickly as possible with wet shoes and the weight of a child in her arms. She knew if she could clear the steps and turn left, she'd be out of the line of fire; then she'd have the advantage. But the door opened as she was halfway down the shallow wooden steps that Kieran Dunne had built out of World War II ammunition boxes. She heard the gunshot, and made up her mind that a little bullet wouldn't be much more to carry. Then she heard a scream of pain. She turned, to see Zina clutching her thigh, then turning away, disappearing. Another shot was fired, then two more. Babsie hid Grace in a jumble of beer kegs and boxing gloves. She went back up the stairs quickly. Two more shots. Babsie kicked the cellar door open and moved into the open in the combat stance she'd been taught. Under a clock that Kevin had reclaimed from the demolished Yonkers Savings Bank stood a blood-soaked Martha Dunne, pointing a gun toward the front door. It was a gun so new, the price tag dangled from the trigger guard.

Zina was gone.

When Eddie arrived, only the medical personnel had finished their work. The Yonkers PD and FD, the NYPD and

ATF, and the FBI traipsed through the crime scene that had been the Dunne family bar. A tiny piece of shrapnel had pierced Kevin's throat; only the quick action of two Yonkers cops kept him alive. They'd carried him to their radio car and raced to St. John's Hospital.

A Yonkers Crime Scene team marked shell casings and traced the various blood trails. Kevin Dunne's blood was confined to one area at the window side of his prized mahogany bar. The telltale blood splatters that had dripped from the fleeing Zina Rabinovich indicated her route: from the cellar door, passing through the blood of Kevin Dunne, finally ending at the curb on Palisade Avenue. Technicians thought she'd been hit twice. A district attorney drove down from White Plains to decide how to handle Martha's unlicensed handgun problem. Martha was at St. John's with her husband.

"Kevin is going to be fine," Babsie said. "They got him there in time."

"How bad was it?" Eddie asked. He'd slept through it, not hearing of it until B. J. Harrington called him.

"Kev won't be singing 'Molly Malone' for a while," Babsie said. "Two or three little entrance holes. The one in his neck caused the major bleeding. It punctured something. He lost a lot of blood, but they got that under control. The rest is just sewing."

"My God," Eddie said, holding his face in his hands.

"He always wanted a battle scar anyway," Babsie said. "Now he's got it all: a war story to tell, a scar to point to. Couple a days, he'll be back here in bandages, holding court. A year from now, we'll be begging him to stop telling the story."

They were sitting in the "cheaters' booth." The one farthest back in the bar. It had been untouched. Grace sat on Babsie's lap, holding tight. They were waiting for her teacher from Christ the King to pick her up.

"Maybe we should keep her home," Eddie said.

"No," Babsie said. "She'll forget about this when she's with her friends."

"All because of me," Eddie said, looking at the ruined framed photographs, the plaques, the huge green-and-gold Sacred Heart banner that stretched almost the length of the shuffleboard table.

"Martha told me you'd say that," Babsie said. "Because you think the world revolves around you. She told me to tell you not to flatter yourself, that this was God's will, nothing more."

"I'm going to rebuild all of it," Eddie said. "I'll find somebody today to come in and clean up. Then we'll get a contractor in here. I'll make it better than it ever was."

"It's gonna cost," she said.

"I can find the money," he replied.

A pretty blond woman with a turned-up nose walked to the back with one of the Homicide cops. Eddie thanked her for coming.

"Ready, Grace," Rita Coughlin said.

"Go ahead, tell her," Babsie said.

"Knock, knock," Grace said, taking her teacher's hand.

After they left, Babsie went into the ladies' room to wash up. Her elbow continued to swell, her right hand getting stiffer as time went on. Eddie wanted to get to the hospital to see his brother. She could get it X-rayed at St. John's.

When she came out, Eddie was looking up at the walls. He'd taken down the picture of himself, the framed cover from *Ring Magazine,* and thrown it in the trash. Babsie heard a phone ringing.

"That's mine," she said. "Where the hell is it?"

She kicked stuff around the edge of the partition, where she last remembered having it. Investigators had moved the debris around, looking for shell casings and grenade fragments.

"That might be the hospital," Eddie said.

"Help me look," she said. The caller was persistent. Eddie dropped to his hands and knees to help her. They found it on the ninth or tenth ring.

"Boland," Babsie mouthed to Eddie. Then she turned her back on him and walked out of his hearing. Glass crunched under her feet. Her voice was a soft but intense murmur.

Eddie stayed on his knees amid the glass and wet plaster, examining the broken bits of his brother's dream. Sooner or later, the sins of Eddie Dunne devour everyone who loves him. Each one a victim of his careless life; all paying for the years he forgot about them, simply because the wine was flowing and the women were willing.

Babsie put the phone in her purse. Her complexion had turned a flushed red.

"Come on, get up," she said. "We're going to Coney Island Hospital."

"They find Zina?" he asked.

"No," she said. "They found Kate."

# CHAPTER
# 42

## FRIDAY
## 11:30 A.M.

EVEN A LAYMAN could tell that the scene in the Emergency Room of Coney Island Hospital was more frantic than usual. Men and women in blue scrubs carrying stethoscopes hustled past men and women in blue uniforms carrying guns. Word spread quickly that the shattered redhead strapped onto the gurney was the Yonkers kidnap victim, a nurse, the child of an ex-cop. A powerful emotional bond exists between cops and nurses. Constantly thrown together in the worst situations, they learn to protect and care for one another. Babsie could hear Kate's name being repeated over and over again in hushed, worried tones.

"No witnesses yet," Babsie said. "The squad is widening the canvass."

"It doesn't matter," Eddie said. "She's alive."

They'd found her on the boardwalk on her hands and knees, struggling to get to her feet. The car from the Sixtieth Precinct, making a routine patrol of the boardwalk, had spotted her at 4:30 A.M. At first, they figured she was a drunk who'd wandered out of a Coney Island saloon. But apparently, she'd stumbled for blocks. Traces of fresh blood were found in several spots going back toward the Abe Stark ice-skating rink, a dark and desolate area of the boardwalk. It appeared she'd been dropped off there and had been moving toward the lights. The cops requested an ambulance for an unknown white female. Later, they were apologetic. They said they didn't recognize her from the picture. It wasn't until hours later, when the ER nurse asked her name, that the wheels began to spin.

"As soon as they get her stabilized," Eddie said, "I'm going to have her transferred to St. John's Riverside."

"Let her get strong first," Babsie said. "They'll take good care of her here."

The preliminary diagnosis was indefinite. She was badly dehydrated. The skin on her forearms and wrists was rubbed raw. Her right wrist might be broken. She'd been heavily drugged, and she kept slipping in and out of consciousness. Her legs, back, and rib area were badly bruised, particularly her left side, down her hip and left leg. A rape kit had been ordered.

"She'll be fine," Eddie said. "She'll be fine."

He believed it, too, but regretted saying it aloud. He knew how quickly things could turn from fine to tragic in a hospital. Don't let God hear you saying everything will be fine. That's all He needs to shove it back in your face. But God did this. God brought her here. And Eddie was grateful. Not overconfident, just grateful. A fighting chance is all I ask for, he thought. Give her a fighting chance.

"She didn't escape on her own, Eddie," Babsie said. "Not the shape she's in."

"No. Borodenko did this. That's why he had all his

hoods on the road. He wanted her found and released before he got home."

"Don't mistake good business for an act of kindness," she said.

"He could have killed her and dumped her body at sea, Babsie. He could have easily done that. It would have been safer."

People wearing rubber-soled shoes squealed past, some glancing over. He stared back into their faces, looking for the messenger, expecting the messenger, the solemn-faced one who says, "We did everything we could, but . . ." God, he hated the smell of hospitals.

According to Babsie, the Yonkers Police Department had mobilized all available detectives to search for Zina. They'd issued a countywide alert for the car and the woman. Police departments, hospitals, clinics, toll bridges, bus stations, and airports all got the word. Matty Boland was coordinating the New York City end of it. He'd sent two teams of investigators to West Nineteenth Street. They'd found it in flames.

"Zina might be in that fire," Eddie said.

"That bother you?"

"You kidding?" he said. "The crispier the better, but we can't count on it."

"I get the feeling you're on Borodenko's side all of a sudden."

"Right now, maybe I am. Everything I did to find Kate amounted to shit. Then bang, she's here. I have no idea why he'd let her go."

Helpless was the worst feeling for guys like Eddie Dunne. He stood against a wall in a long corridor that led to other long corridors, holding a torn and bloody green flannel shirt in his hand. Babsie wanted to bag it for evidence, but she let Eddie hold on to it.

Babsie said, "Don't forget Borodenko was behind all this grief in the first place."

"I'm not so sure."

"What's that supposed to mean?"

Eddie fought to keep his focus, but his world spun in slow motion, as if all energy had drained out of him. The spaces between objects in the corridor seemed random and changing. He could hear Kate calling him, her voice a soft reverberation, like a whispered echo, but so real, the hairs on the back of his neck rose. He knew this was in his head. She was in the room down the hall. If he walked twenty steps down the corridor, he could see her, tubes crisscrossed over her face, machines beeping, nurses prepping her for surgery. She was fine. A nurse came out of the room, walking toward them.

"Five minutes," the nurse said, holding up her spread hand. "Try not to excite her."

His beautiful daughter had aged terribly in twelve days. She looked like her mother in those last mournful moments of her life. Her eyes, so dark underneath, appeared sunken in bruised half-moons. Eddie put his hand on hers, trying not to disturb any of the attached lines. She squeezed his hand immediately; then she squirmed, trying to get her arms up in the air. She was trying to tell him something. But her eyes spoke for her, wide and unblinking, staring directly into his face.

"I love you," he said, fighting for his calmest expression, wanting to transfer hope, to let her draw a sense of serenity from him. "It's all over. We'll have you home soon. Grace is fine, can't wait to see you. We're all fine. Kevin is fine. Everybody is fine." He talked in a rush, knowing that words were too weak to climb the wall of her anguish. Saying them was the only thing.

Babsie held up a picture of Zina.

"Was this the woman who kidnapped you?" she said. "Just nod if you can, Kate."

"Not now, Babsie," Eddie said, but Kate was nodding furiously.

"It was this woman?" Babsie said, confirming her answer.

Kate went on nodding and trying to raise her left hand. She got it up a few inches and held her fingers in the V sign.

"Two?" Babsie said. "Two people?" She could see in Kate's frustration that there was more. But with tubes down her throat and her mouth covered by a square patch of blue material to secure the tubes in place, she couldn't speak. Enough, Eddie thought. She's too fragile.

"Let's do this later," Eddie said.

"She's stronger than you think," Babsie said, overruling him as she'd done for eleven days. "Two women?" Babsie asked as it suddenly came to her. "Two women." Kate nodded. Two women.

She kept reaching for Babsie's notebook. Babsie put the pen in her left hand. She held Kate's arm as the young woman scrawled letters over the page sideways. Four shaky letters, but unmistakably the word *ship*.

"A ship?" Babsie said. "They kept you on a ship."

Their five minutes ended in three; Eddie wanted the questions over with. Kate's heart rate set off alarms. "Let her calm down," he said. He and Babsie went back to the hallway. The hospital PA system reeled off a series of names: doctors summoned here and there. He recognized none of the names from his days and nights in this hospital. Times change, he thought. Your past evaporates in change.

"I thought your pal Boland had the Coast Guard looking at Borodenko's freighters," Babsie said.

"Doesn't matter now."

Babsie grunted something clearly sarcastic, then walked away, talking on her cell phone, ignoring the sign that prohibited that practice. A wheelchair was ordered for the cardiac unit; a priest was summoned to the OR.

Doctors had assured Eddie that barring unseen complications, she'd be fine. Everyone is fine. The next twenty-four hours are critical—another old hospital saw. We all resort to clichés at a time like this. How about closure? he thought. Why doesn't this feel like closure?

"Believe it or not," Babsie said, snapping her phone closed, "Martha went to pick up Grace from school. You might have to rethink some of your opinions of that woman. She's a tough old bird."

"The cops still with her?"

"Of course. Martha just thought a family member might reassure Grace. It was a nice idea, Eddie."

"How's Kev?"

"Critical, but stable. He knows about Kate, and that perked him up. Probably gonna downgrade him tomorrow."

"The next twenty-four hours are critical."

"Always are," Babsie said, searching his face for whatever that meant.

"We're never going to feel safe until we get Zina," he said.

"When Kate gets a little stronger, she'll be able to tell us more. You're right, though. We don't want to push her right now. Let's hold off until she can handle it. Until then, we'll put a couple of cops here, around the clock. I'll get Yonkers to supply a body."

"Sophie Borodenko knows where Zina is hiding," Eddie said.

"Like she's gonna implicate herself and tell us? Yuri's calling in all his lawyers now. *If* she's not *already* on a plane to Moscow."

"Let's go over there."

"Borodenko's house? He has no reason even to let us in the door."

"He'll let us in. I'll tell him who killed Sophie's mother."

"Nuñez and Vestri," Babsie said.

"They pulled the trigger. I know who killed her."

# CHAPTER

# 43

"I WONDER HOW MUCH bootleg gas it took to start this bonfire," Babsie said.

Thick black smoke drifted up through the upper scaffolding of the Cyclone roller coaster. Police diverted traffic on Surf Avenue into one lane, steering them around fire hoses strung through an empty lot and down to the boardwalk. Eddie slowed down to see the blaze that fully engulfed the two-story frame building on West Nineteenth that housed Coney Custards. The entire building was too far gone, swallowed up in flames. Firefighters stood back and dumped water on it, trying to protect the surrounding buildings.

"Yuri destroying the evidence," Eddie said.

"That's why he's not going to let you near his wife," Babsie said. "He'd burn down half of Brooklyn to protect her."

The front door of Yuri Borodenko's home had the same ornate carvings as the door of the Mazurka. Eddie pressed a button and the chimes rang out a few notes of a song he didn't recognize. Before he could ring again, a voice came

over an intercom. Eddie pressed another button and gave
their names. He said he needed to speak with Mrs.
Borodenko. He had important information about her parents. They waited over five minutes, then an Asian man in
a white Nehru jacket invited them in. A set of Gucci bags
was stacked just inside the door.

"Women's luggage," Babsie said.

They were led into a room lined with books. The
books were arranged too neatly to have been read by anyone. Borodenko came in immediately through another
door. He was much shorter than Eddie had thought, but
he'd only seen him seated. The Russian introduced himself. Not a bodyguard in sight. There had to be video security throughout the house; thugs close by, ready to
pounce. Babsie sat on a red leather sofa. Eddie refused a
seat, wandering around instead, looking for the portal
with the hidden rifle pointed at him.

"You have information for me," Borodenko said, getting right to the point.

"First, I want to thank you for finding my daughter."

"Your daughter?" he said, looking surprised. "Your
daughter is in the hospital, am I correct? I heard on the
television. Doing well, I hope."

"A little rough right now, but it looks good."

"I'm happy for that, Mr. Dunne. But don't thank me. I
had nothing to do with your daughter's return. From what
I've heard, you worked tirelessly to find her, as I would
in your position. I cannot imagine what lengths I would
go to in order to save my wife or child. The most extreme,
I can assure you."

"I'm not here to hurt Sophie, if that's what you're
thinking. Or to rehash these past twelve days."

"Very noble of you. I'll pass your thoughts on to her."

"I need to talk to Sophie in person," Eddie said.

"That's not possible. You'll just have to forgive my wife's absence. Rest assured I will relay your message."

"Then ask her where I can find Zina Rabinovich."

"Sophie doesn't have that information."

The room was far less gaudy than Eddie had expected. It could have been the library of an Ivy League dean. A huge red-and-black Oriental rug centered the room. Dark wood all around. The paintings on the walls appeared to be the work of Russian artists. Eddie recognized an oil by Konstantin Lomykin, a favorite of Lukin. Snow-covered roofs in Odessa, the scene as desolate and sad as a hollow in Appalachia.

"I know who Sophie is," Eddie said. "I know all about her."

"And just what do you know about my wife?"

"I was the detective handling her parents' murders."

"I've read your reports."

"Then you haven't read the truth."

Borodenko was less imposing than Eddie remembered. He'd gotten paunchier, and balder. The cardigan sweater, though a soft expensive wool, gave him a frumpy look. His face showed the ravages of the long trip from Moscow and a marriage to a troubled woman half his age.

"Being that you know the tragedy of Sophie's parents," Borodenko said, "it surprises me that you would embarrass her with those photographs."

"We had a potential tragedy going here ourselves," Babsie said.

"I needed a way to force you home," Eddie said.

"Those photographs did not get me home, sir. My travel arrangements were made days earlier."

"Do you want to know why Sophie's mother died?" Eddie said.

Borodenko picked up a silver humidor from the table. He opened it and offered its contents to both of them. Eddie expected cigars, but it was filled with cigarettes— unfiltered cigarettes in a cream-colored paper. Borodenko lit one and walked to the window. The ocean looked as calm as a lake, not a ripple of white anywhere except at the very edge of the shore.

"Sophie's parents were killed during the act of robbery," Borodenko said.

"Nuñez and Vestri, the two men who committed that act, went there with specific orders to kill them."

"Give me one reason why I should accept your version of the truth."

"*You* don't have to accept it, because I'll only tell *her* what happened," Eddie said. "Are those her bags near the door?"

"Sophie is going away for a short time. She has had a rough period recently and needs rest and medical attention."

"She's well enough to travel?" Eddie said.

"Yuri," Sophie called out.

Yuri Borodenko crossed the room and put his arms around the slender woman. Sophie was wearing a dark business suit, but she looked to be still in the process of getting dressed—no jewelry, no makeup, her hair still wet from the shower. Borodenko spoke softly to her in Russian, obviously imploring her to go back to her room.

"My wife is not prepared for this, Mr. Dunne. She is being treated for severe depression and is taking medication."

"No, Yuri, please," she said, pushing him away. "I want to say how sorry I am for the trouble I have caused. It's all my fault, all this trouble. All of it."

She was glassy-eyed and slurring her words slightly.

Yuri said, "My wife is a victim, Mr. Dunne. She has listened to an adviser who preyed upon her like a vulture."

"Zina only wanted to help," Sophie said. "First, let me explain everything to you about Zina."

"You have nothing to explain," Borodenko said sharply; then he spoke to her again in Russian. When he was finished, he said in English, "We are not doing this. This woman is a detective sitting here. We are going to postpone this discussion until I have time to have a lawyer present."

"Nothing any of us says will leave this room," Eddie said. "You have my word."

"I want to speak," Sophie said, pointing to Eddie. "I don't care of the consequence."

Even mob guys can be whipped, Babsie thought. Yuri doing everything but licking her shoes. And she didn't like the way Eddie was letting Sophie work him. Both males circling around her in some middle-aged dance of seduction. Babsie didn't want to hear the blonde's story, or Eddie's latest tale. She'd had enough sad stories in her life. But what pissed her off most was the fact that Eddie had the balls to commit her to legal silence.

"After my parents were killed," Sophie said, "my grandparents took me to Russia with only one small suitcase. They were frightened and only trying to protect me, but I had no pictures, no mementos, nothing of my parents. After I married Yuri and came here, I tried to find out things about them, some old friends with stories or someone with pictures, but no one will help. Yuri won't help because he says it will upset me."

"I hired Zina to help you."

"You hired Zina to guard me, but she did help. But Zina was afraid of Yuri, so I couldn't tell him what we were doing."

"You could have told me," Yuri said.

"Zina worked like crazy," Sophie said. "She found newspapers with pictures, and old friends who knew my parents. We met them in restaurants or Zina's apartment. Like a storybook, everything unfolded for me. Every week new people or mementos, always some memento of my parents' life. That's how I found out about you, and Pavlo going to the boat with my mother."

"Why kidnap my daughter?" Eddie asked.

"Mistake," Sophie said.

"My wife was not part of that," Yuri said. "These are thirdhand rumors she speaks of. She had no knowledge."

"She was driving the BMW," Eddie said.

"I have caused problems," Sophie said.

"We call them felonies," Babsie said.

"This interview is over," Borodenko said, grabbing his wife by the arm. She was stronger than she looked, and, combined with the power of tears, she made Yuri release her.

Sophie said, "Zina went into your house only to get mementos for me."

"What mementos?" Eddie said.

"She found nothing."

"She found Kate," Babsie said.

"She didn't know anyone was at home. Everything was bad after that, it happened so fast. Zina said Yuri would kill her so nothing mattered. I was afraid of what she was doing next."

"You could have stopped it anytime," Babsie said.

Tears ran down Sophie's face. "I wanted to. I wanted Yuri home so bad, but I couldn't tell him what had been done. Zina became crazier, saying she loved me."

Yuri held his wife.

"Enough," he said. "We'll set an interview at a later time."

"Just tell us where to find Zina," Babsie said.

"Not to hurt her," Sophie said.

"I think we've said enough," Borodenko said. "Sophie has a flight to catch. If you have matters concerning us, take them up with our lawyer. We will cooperate fully."

"You sent Sergei all the way to Italy for mementos?" Babsie asked.

"Am I wrong for wanting to know answers?" Sophie said. "Would you leave such questions unanswered?"

"What questions?"

"My father, Marvin Rosenfeld, had a defect," she said. "Zina found his first wife. She was surprised of my birth, due to doctor saying my father had medical defect. He was not able to have children." Sophie shrugged, as if any further medical explanation was beyond her.

"It was *your* DNA that Zina sent to Celltech," Babsie said. "You thought Paulie Caruso was your father."

"None of this matters," Borodenko said. "Zina Rabinovich is the criminal here. She is the one who sent Sergei to Italy. I fired her immediately when I heard. This woman clouded Sophie's judgment with alcohol and drugs. My wife had no idea Mr. Caruso would be murdered."

"I knew of Pavlo's time with my mother," Sophie said.

"Many people knew of them together. Zina said we'll have a medical test for proof. A little teeny bit of blood, she told Sergei, was all that was needed."

"Mission accomplished," Babsie said.

"Then Pavlo told Sergei of you and my mother," Sophie said.

"Your mother was killed because of me," Eddie said.

"I don't believe this," Sophie said.

"It's true," he said. "I met your mother my first week in Brooklyn."

"When was this happening?" Sophie said.

"Latter part of 1974."

"A love affair?" Sophie said.

"For a few months. Then she broke it off, never gave me a reason. Later, I heard she got married. I'd see her shopping on Brighton Beach Avenue, but she didn't know me. She'd look away."

"Pavlo said about the boat."

"I didn't speak to Svetlana again for years. In the early eighties, Paul Caruso brought her to a party we had on the new boat. He introduced her to me as Lana, the love of his life. 'Nice to meet you,' she said. And it went like that, until one night we were alone together."

Babsie Panko turned away and walked to the window. It was her turn to shake her head and stare out at the ocean. Yuri Borodenko nodded, beginning to understand. Eddie knew Yuri could see the whole robbery plan unfolding in his mind, the Caruso brothers at the helm. Sophie flopped down on the red sofa, sitting in the spot Babsie had vacated.

"Paulie was obsessed with your mother," Eddie said. "I knew that when he found out about us, there would be hell to pay. But I never thought he'd do this. I still can't believe he let them kill her. Not in a million years."

"From jealousy?" Sophie said.

"From a sick, vindictive mind," Eddie said. "I should have seen it coming."

"She wouldn't blame you," Sophie said. "I know what her heart was like and I saw your gentleness and kindness. I saw that when I watched you with your little one. Your granddaughter. I knew you couldn't have hurt my mother."

"You've said enough, Sophie," Borodenko said.

"Such a sad, beautiful love story," Sophie said.

"Beautiful?" Babsie said.

"Tell me something about her," Sophie said. "Please. Give me one memory of my mother. One special thing, please."

"Are all Russians this nuts?" Babsie said.

"Lana liked to sing," Eddie said. "She'd sing in my ear in this soft, whispery voice. I taught her to sing Irish lullabies. We were on a blanket in the marina, but she liked to pretend we were in the South Seas. And when she sang *too-ra-loo-ra-loo-ral* in that whispery Russian accent, I didn't know whether to laugh or cry."

"I will learn this song," Sophie said.

"That's just peachy," Babsie said. "Just tell us where to find Zina."

Sophie took a folded piece of paper from her pocket. She handed it to Eddie.

"Is this a joke?" Eddie said, looking at the note.

"No, you will recognize it," Sophie said.

"Maybe you should look harder for a relative of your father's," Babsie said. "They have professional services that do that now. Might save you a lot of trouble in the long run."

"I don't need such services," Sophie said. "Zina did DNA test with Kate, with different laboratory. Eddie Dunne is my father."

# CHAPTER
# 44

THEY CROSSED the Verrazano Narrows Bridge in the thick of the homebound traffic. Everybody was escaping for the weekend except Eddie Dunne's two-person contingent. A sea of taillights stretched out ahead of them on the Staten Island Expressway, but he swung off just past the bridge toll plaza, taking Fingerboard Road to Hylan Boulevard, which extended in a series of traffic lights through small, townlike neighborhoods. His third trip down it in eight days. This time, he'd go past Jimmy's Bistro to Great Kills Harbor on the south shore of Staten Island. If he had been more patient on either of the first two trips to Jimmy's Bistro, he would have tailed Sophie and Zina right to his daughter.

"Sophie is a collar," Babsie said coldly.

"We'll talk to the DA."

"What's to talk about? She's part of a kidnapping."

The note Sophie had given him contained only the name of a boat and the marina. She said the marina belonged to a friend of Zina, someone whose parents had once owned Coney Custards. Zina had kept Kate on the boat ever since that first night in Freddie Dolgev's apart-

ment. Sophie said Eddie would recognize the boat. It had
been a special gift from Zina. Six months earlier, she'd
bought it from a man named Stark in Gerritsen Beach,
then changed the name back to the original *Bright Star.*

"You put me on the spot back there," Babsie said,
"telling them that everything said would stay in that
room. That wasn't right. I can't go along with that, and
you know it."

"So I lied. I would have done whatever it took, Babsie.
Why don't we forget my sins for now and focus on how
we're going to get Zina off that boat."

"With lots of backup, that's how," Babsie said, dialing
her cell phone. "I'm calling Boland."

"Let me take a run at her first."

"She sees you, it's war. She sees an army, maybe she
gives up."

"I can handle her."

"Eddie, Sophie's been your daughter for about an
hour. Think about the one in Coney Island Hospital who's
had to put up with you for the past thirty-four years. Kate
doesn't need you to get blown away right now."

"So I just forget about Sophie?"

"Yes. Your role here is to not risk your life to please an
overemotional Russian barracuda. You don't owe Sophie
a thing. What is it with you guys? Is it the sound of the
door slamming that causes male amnesia? You walk out
of the house and—bang—you forget all about the family. The next pretty blonde gets all the quality time."

"This has nothing to do with pretty."

Babsie was already talking to Boland, giving him the
address, the Sophie story, the whole megillah. Eddie
wondered when the balance of power in this relationship
had shifted to Babsie. He was suddenly stunned by how

little control he had over his life. He'd always thought of himself as a tough guy, doing it his way, but now he realized how dependent he was on the opinions of women.

"Boland has two guys from the task force working out here," she said. "Apparently, they have a big Russian enclave near Great Kills. They'll meet us at the marina. He's also notifying Emergency Services, and the One-two-two. He says we're going to need bodies out here for crowd control."

"It's going to look like St. Paddy's Day with all the uniforms."

"Better safe than sorry," she said. "Harbor Unit is going to be there in case she pulls a *Miami Vice*. But there's no way *I'm* getting on any boat in this skirt."

"They'll need me to identify Zina."

"I can handle that. Let's be clear about one thing. This woman hates your guts, and mine. She tried to kill me and most of your family nine hours ago. And she kicked your ass already. Remember that debacle? This time, you and I are going to let the young studs handle it. The best thing we can do here is nothing stupid."

The setting sun, a bright orange ball burning through a purple-green haze, reflected on the dark Atlantic. The joint effort of nature and escaping gases of New Jersey blended into a spectacular, if not pristine, sunset.

"I didn't see the barracuda you're talking about," Eddie said.

"Sophie plays men," Babsie said, her voice softer. "And she's good at it. She does this Poor Little Buttercup routine and every guy wants to protect her. She plays Borodenko, and she played you. I figure she played Zina until she got her doing her bidding. But she wants everyone to think Zina was the aggressor. It's everyone's fault except poor sweet Sophie's. But I see big holes in the princess's fairy tale. Other people had to be involved in this. Who guarded Kate? There had to have been someone here watching her. And who dropped Kate off in Coney Island last night? Not Zina, I bet."

"So we can't even give her the benefit of the doubt?" Eddie said.

"Have you gone nuts, too? That shit never works when you're dealing with people like this. I know you want to mellow out in your old age, but sometimes you have to drag out your old ass-kicking personality. Give this woman a hard look, Eddie. And save the benefit of the doubt for the people who love you."

They followed a line of traffic into the marina parking lot. Some people were coming early for the restaurants. Others, in SUVs and pickup trucks, looked like they had supplies to load onto their boats for the weekend. Sunny skies and temperatures in the low seventies were predicted for Saturday. Eddie spotted the task force car parked behind the marina building. He recognized the two guys from the Flushing Salvage raid—one agent, one NYPD detective—going into the marina office. Eddie parked next to them. They were about fifty yards from the water.

"We have to figure a way to control this crowd before it gets out of hand," Babsie said, getting out of the car. "If she starts with the firepower, we could have a massacre. Let me talk to these guys. Maybe we can start isolating the area around the boat. Try not to turn into Mister Rogers while I'm gone."

Eddie got out of the car with her, then stood with his arms resting on the roof of the Camry. The flat-roofed one-story marina building blocked most of the pier. He could see a clear line of about thirty boats. Any one of a dozen of them could have been the *Bright Star*. He knew it wouldn't seem the same—nothing ever looked as good as its memory.

The Harbor Unit was already in place, cruising the row of boats. Two radio cars from the precinct went past the parking lot, pulling right up to the edge of the docks. Uniformed cops got out near the dock, looking around for whomever they were supposed to meet. No one ever tells the precinct guys enough.

When he thought about it, Eddie could see Lana in Sophie. Beyond the beauty, he could see mannerisms: the slow, crinkly smile; the way she held her fist close to her waist, with the thumb on the outside; how her eyes became damp at the mere mention of the word *love*. He knew Babsie was right about Sophie. As the days passed, he would have come to the same conclusion. But after he saw Kate this morning, it was as if all the air had gone out of him. He'd collapsed emotionally, ready to blow kisses to the crowd, forgive those who'd trespassed against him. Sophie took advantage of that. Or maybe, just maybe, Babsie had a point about the *pretty blonde* thing.

Precinct radio cars were following one another around, looking for a leader. They should decide in advance on one radio frequency for these things, then everyone is on the same page. Another uniformed cop approached, walking from the south, possibly private security trying to figure out what was happening.

The big blue Emergency Services truck arrived. One of the feds put his fingers in his mouth, whistled, and waved them over, the same way it was done before the invention of the telephone. All the cell phones, all the pagers, but a good whistle still works best.

The Emergency Services boss got it organized quickly. He sent the plainclothes cops up to the docks to move people quietly away from the *Bright Star.* Emergency Services crews strapped themselves into riot gear and dragged out the big shields as several other precinct cars cruised past. Babsie came running across the grass. Even in a skirt, she ran like an athlete.

"Zina's car is in the parking lot," Babsie said. "The marina manager says she's on board the *Bright Star.* We're going to freeze the area first. The place is filling up fast."

"You don't need me."

"You got that right. We have more cops here now than we have in the whole city of Yonkers."

People who'd been in boats walked quickly to their cars. Uniformed cops had been dispatched to all corners of the marina to hold back the new arrivals. Other cops watched the parking lot as the ESU guys lumbered toward the boat.

Babsie hustled back to the group. Zina was her arrest, and she wasn't going to miss out. Eddie wondered about Zina's bullet wounds. How bad were they? Unless Zina was sick or dead, she had to be noticing the massive troop movement around her. Dead would make things easier. Sick, she could be dangerous, probably suicidal. She'd try to bring everyone down with her.

Eddie sat on a picnic bench, thinking that he and Paulie the Priest wouldn't have called anyone for this. In those days, there was no one to call. You just fired up a cigar and kicked the door in. But that was before crack cocaine, suicide bombers, and a gun in every home.

He picked up Kevin's cell phone and called the North End Tavern to get an update on his brother and to hear Grace's voice. But he'd forgotten the line was temporarily disconnected. He started to call his house, when he heard an explosion on the dock. A puff of smoke rose from the deck of the *Bright Star.* Tear gas, or something similar. Somebody was on the bullhorn, telling Zina to give up.

A uniformed cop walked away from the dock, limping slightly. Eddie wondered if this was the start of one of those "injured on the job" scams. That pissed him off—some bozo seizing the opportunity to get three-quarters pension for a knee he'd hurt playing tennis. Not only was it a sleazy move; it cheapened the debt rightfully owed to those cops who were actually hurt in the line of duty. To some scheming leeches, three-quarters pay, tax-free, was like winning the lottery. The leeches hired lawyers and made a career of their fight to screw the city. We *are* the city, Eddie thought, his blood pressure rising as Matty Boland arrived in the Lincoln Town Car. He cruised past the limping cop, heading toward the smoke.

The guy on the bullhorn made further pleas in a heavy New York accent, all apparently unanswered. Eddie dialed information to get the number of Coney Island Hospital as the big shields edged closer to the boat. Eddie had no doubt that Zina Rabinovich would fight to the death. He wrote the hospital number on the palm of his hand.

He began dialing as the limping uniformed cop came toward the radio cars parked nearby. As he came closer, Eddie saw the guy was wearing a light blue uniform shirt. Not our job, Eddie thought, must be private security. NYPD cops had quit wearing the light blue shirts a few years ago. So much for his faked injury tirade. This guy was a square badge, getting the hell away from the impending fireworks. He was hauling ass, even with the limp. Couldn't blame him. No sense getting killed for minimum wage.

But as he got closer, Eddie could see the badge wasn't square. It looked like an NYPD detective's gold shield. The light blue shirt must have been the only thing in his locker today. The guy was highly decorated, an impressive display of ribbons and commendations on his chest. He was coming right at Eddie, moving fast. Then he started to run.

Eddie stood up quickly as the guy pulled a machine pistol from under the uniform jacket. The first blast took out the Camry's headlight. Eddie dived behind the car. Bullets thunked heavily into sheet metal. He squeezed his legs up behind the front wheel well. He reached for his service revolver, but he didn't have it, or a prayer. He got off his knees and ran to the marina building. Three steps into it, he felt as if he was slogging through heavy mud. Bullets kicked the ground around him. Then the Lincoln Town Car cut across the lawn and gravel flew. A heavy thud from the Lincoln's bumper sent the cop airborne. His hat flew off and hit the ground in front of him.

Even with the dust and cordite in the air, Eddie knew it was Zina. Matty Boland jumped out of the Lincoln, his gun drawn. Zina scrambled on hands and knees toward the machine pistol. Boland fired twice, the second shot smashing into her skull at an angle and sending chunks of bone and blood flying as she kept crawling on her belly until she reached the gun. Steps away, Boland fired five times, one shot hitting her in the face, just below her eye.

Eddie kicked the machine pistol farther away, but her crawling had ceased. Paulie the Priest would have put a few more rounds into her just to be sure. With lesbians, he'd say, you can never tell.

Up close, Eddie could see the uniform was old, faded, and far too big for her. The sleeves and pants had been crudely altered with safety pins. Eddie knew this particular uniform had been purchased in 1966 from an authorized police tailor on Kingsbridge Terrace in the Bronx. Inside both the jacket and pants, stamped in white ink, would be the last four numbers of Eddie's NYPD tax registry number. The gold detective shield with his number was a fake. A good fake. The black name tag with white lettering read DUNNE. Zina must have taken it from the back of his closet when she grabbed Kate. He never knew it was missing.

"How did you know it was her?" Eddie said.

"The Medal of Honor," Matty said. "I saw it when I rode past. You and the Priest were the only guys I ever worked with who won it. I thought, Who is this guy? Then it came to me. The ribbon had to belong either to you or Paulie Caruso."

Babsie came sprinting from the dock. Other cops, half her age, tried to keep up. Matty Boland knelt down and opened the jacket. Zina had strapped a massive arsenal to herself, including hand grenades, ammunition, and three other handguns. Eddie picked up the dusty uniform hat. Inside, under the plastic, was a picture of a ten-year-old redhead with more freckles than Howdy Doody.

# CHAPTER

# 45

## SUNDAY, APRIL 19
## NOON

THEY WERE SITTING on a park bench in Yonkers, looking down at the grass infield of Lennon Park. Two dozen little girls were playing soccer, kicking the ball in whatever direction appealed to them. The ball would suddenly appear before them and—whack—they'd kick it away, almost in self-defense. Most of them were content to get in a kick and jump back. They'd been playing for almost twenty minutes and the ball had not approached either goal. The goalies, their interest lost, gazed up at the crowd.

"If I had legs like that," Babsie said, pointing to Grace, "I would have kissed this job good-bye and tried out for the Rockettes."

She looked over at Eddie. "What the hell's so funny?" she said.

"I was thinking you'd make one hot Rockette."

Eddie had been at Coney Island Hospital earlier that morning. Kate had made remarkable strides. Her stomach had been pumped. Doctors weren't sure exactly what drugs she'd ingested. They went ahead and flushed her system as well as they could. Her main problem, serious dehydration, had responded well to the IV fluids. She looked much better. The bruises, abrasions, and broken bones would heal with treatment and rest. Kate said she'd been slapped a few times, but her injuries came from struggling. Her doctor, the son of a cop himself, predicted she'd be home by Tuesday. As soon as the soccer horn sounded, they were going to take Grace to see her.

Kevin Dunne remained in the hospital, a long road ahead of him—at least two surgeries and lifelong speech therapy. Martha was at the North End Tavern, supervising the cleanup crew and drawing new construction plans. Eddie promised to supply the labor.

"I filed the warrant for Sophie," Babsie said.

"We'll never see her again."

"Not without an army of lawyers. She was already on the Concorde when Zina was trying to kill you. Probably eating shrimp on the Riviera before we got home to Yonkers. Must be nice to be rich and beautiful."

"You *are* beautiful," he said.

"I'd rather be rich."

Bit by bit, it was all coming back to Kate. Eddie filled in some holes for her. She said she was first held in the apartment above Coney Custards. She remembered the smell of sour milk and the sound of the machines. The following night, they moved her to the boat, where she was guarded by two or three different people. She said that after the initial struggle with Zina, Sophie was the only one who had actually hit her. She'd come in drunk or high, start sobbing, then slap Kate around, yelling at her in Russian.

"Kate said she could smell mothballs," Eddie said.

"Your old uniform."

"I was so close to her that first day, Babsie. The day I met Lukin on the boardwalk. Just a few blocks. I could see Coney Custards. She was upstairs. If I'd walked a little farther, maybe I would have heard her voice, a scream."

"No second-guessing. You promised we wouldn't do any second-guessing."

Kate had told him that when she was on the boat, she could hear a band practicing nearby. They played the same songs, in the same order, every day. Kate memorized them. One of the nurses had kids in New Dorp High School. She called the director of the music program and read off Kate's list. It was the New Dorp High School marching band Kate had heard.

"So the love story of Zina and Sophie starts to go sour on April sixth," Babsie said. "Kate surprises Zina when she's breaking into your house. Zina panics and snatches her. To make matters worse, later that day Sergei shows up with Paulie's head and reports everything Paulie blabbed about the Rosenfeld millions, plus the romance between you and Lana. That day changed everything for them."

"April sixth was a bad day for all of us."

"But from that point, Zina knew she had to go for broke. It was about winning Sophie, and she'd stepped over the line. She gets Sophie in this emotional state about her mother, then tries to keep her in a sick dream. That's why Zina gets up the next morning and shoves Anatoly Lukin under the train for his part in the murder of the Rosenfelds. Now she's Sophie's secret hero. Couple of days later, she ices Angelo Caruso for his part; poor Ann Marie is just there. And that leaves you, but she can't kill you, because you've become the central figure in an imaginary romantic triangle."

"As I said before, you can be a bit melodramatic."

"It slipped into a sex game," Babsie said. "Zina wore your uniform. Sophie wore the old dresses from thrift shops, like the ones she thought her mother wore. They had the original *Bright Star* as the setting. If she had known that story earlier, the one about Lana singing Irish lullabies, that would have gone into the script, too. Kate being there probably added to the excitement. Maybe that saved her life."

"What about the DNA? The possibility I was Sophie's father."

"That was an afterthought. Secondary to the wine and weird sex."

"Did you have these erotic ideas in Sister Mary Elizabeth's class?"

"Sexual role-playing is big these days. We locked up a high-priced hooker on Central Avenue a few months ago. She had a closetful of costumes. She had nurses' uniforms and nuns' habits for every order you could think of, including some that would make you hide your knuckles."

"It was Paulie the Priest who saved Kate's life," Eddie said. "Zina would have killed her without blinking. But when Paulie told them about me and Lana, it raised the possibility that I was her father. Sophie couldn't let Zina kill her sister."

"So tell me the truth about the fight at the Caruso graduation party," Babsie said. "That whole choreographed *Raging Bull* thing, that was bullshit."

"Finally, you're right about something. That night, I hit Paulie Caruso harder than I'd hit anyone in years, and I meant it. He was spitting his teeth out in his hand."

"You went there hunting for him," Babsie said.

"I wasn't invited."

"How did he find out about you and Lana?"

"Tailed her is my guess. He had to've known for a while, but I never noticed any change in him. Most guys, there'd be a fistfight, and it'd be over. Paulie internalized it, brooded. Even the day of the robbery, I never had a clue he was pissed. Then immediately after the press conference, he starts treating me like garbage. Didn't want to be near me. It took me a couple of weeks. Then I went after him."

"Ever consider turning him in? You could have made a deal for yourself."

"I needed proof. The only evidence I had was the ten grand Paulie gave me. He would have denied it. I would have gotten locked up; he would have walked. Unless I could get an admission on tape."

"That's the reason you went there," she said.

"On the day of the graduation party, I wired myself up and drove to Howard Beach. Paulie was in the backyard. I came in through the garage, as always, through the basement. Angelo was down there cooking, checking the gravy. He had a few vinos in him and was singing and stirring the gravy. It was just me and him down there, and he said to me, 'How does it feel to be a millionaire?'"

"Paulie never told him he kept your share."

"I played along. I asked what Paulie was going to do with his. Angelo tells me he's taking care of washing Paulie's share. 'Two point eight million is not easy to keep in your sock drawer,' he says."

"No wonder Paulie could afford the Italian villa. He had almost six mil, his share and yours."

"Paulie only gave Angelo one share to wash. I told Angelo that all Paulie gave me was ten grand. He can't believe it. We go outside and he's arguing with Paulie in

Italian. He tells Paulie that he's giving me his share. That's when Paulie tells me he knows about me and Lana. He says he had Lana whacked because of me. That's the word he used, 'whacked.' That's when I hit him. Twice, hard. He goes down, blood and teeth everywhere. The wise guys grab me."

"And they feel the wire."

"One guy does and rips my shirt open. I take the wire off, hand it to Angelo, and tell him I was only getting him proof that Paulie screwed me."

"He bought it?"

"Not right away. But he made a few phone calls and found out I wasn't working for any DA's office."

At the foot of the hill, a weekly gathering of the same ruddy-faced old men had begun. One by one, they shuffled down through the park, coming from Sunday Mass at Sacred Heart in tan raincoats and gray tweed overcoats. From youth to death, they trod the same weekly path to the front door of Morley's Bar and talked stiffly of politics and local history until Morley legally unlocked the door and the hops and malt commenced to unlock the tongues.

"You think it was true," Babsie said, "that Paulie really had her killed?"

"It could have been a macho thing—he had a problem with that. Then again, he had a wild mean streak."

A collective girlie scream rose from the field below as the ball neared the goal.

"So what do you think?" Eddie said. "Too much baggage for you?"

"You? A cruise ship has less baggage than you."

"I was a bad drinker, Babsie. Virtually everything in my life that I regret, I did when I was drinking."

"Give me some time to think, Eddie. I'm still pissed off about Friday in Borodenko's house. You should have told me you had an affair with Lana. To me, that goes right to the heart of trust."

The bells of Scared Heart church rang behind them. They both looked at their watches, although they knew exactly what time it was. They'd heard those bells all their lives.

"My mother used to tell a story about you when you were a kid," Babsie said. "She stopped in church during the middle of the day one time. It was like a Tuesday afternoon. She goes in to light a candle. She thinks the church is empty, but then she hears this low murmur coming from the little altar on the side. She sees Father Prendergast. He must have been in his nineties then. He's saying Mass on the side altar, and you're the altar boy. Only the two of you in the entire church."

"He was dying then," Eddie said. "But he had some good days, and he'd want to say Mass. I was probably in the eighth grade. A little bigger than most of the others. They'd send someone to get me out of school."

"My mother said that you helped him to a chair, right in the middle of the Mass. He sat on the side for about fifteen minutes. And you knelt in front of the altar and waited."

"He had spells; then he'd get better. I missed him when he died."

"My mother said it was the sweetest thing she ever saw in her life. You helped him when he forgot where he was. Just the two of you saying the Mass. She said you weren't as bad as she'd thought."

"Well, actually, I missed the money. I always stole five bucks from his wallet after Mass."

"You're so full of it," she said.

"Now I want those days back," Eddie said. "I don't deserve it, but I want it all. I want the clean sheets, family dinner after Mass on Sunday, school plays, Monopoly on the floor, soccer games. All the things I thought were boring years ago."

"No more cocktails and showgirls?"

"Just you."

"No more secrets," she said.

"Absolutely no more secrets. I swear."

Eddie looked back down at the soccer field. The screaming got louder. Grace's team made a goal, or thought they had.

"You weren't as bad as you think," Babsie said. "I'll tell you this. If Paulie Caruso did that to me, no way would I have let him keep all that money for himself. No way I'd let that bastard walk away with my share. I would have burned it or given it to charity . . . anything but let that scumbag have it."

Eddie nodded. His brow furrowed, he kept nodding, deep in thought.

"You took the money," Babsie said. "Don't tell me you took the goddamned money. Oh shit. That's why that fake boodle in your trunk looked so good. It wasn't fake."

"I didn't say I took it."

"Jesus, Eddie. You are so goddamned high-maintenance. Does it ever end with you?"

"Babsie, listen to me. I never said I took the money."

She sat there breathing hard. This was exactly what her father had warned her about when she'd tacked his picture on her bedroom wall in freshman year. Look at those eyes, her father had said. All those eyes will ever see is trouble, because that's all they'll ever look for.

"I love you," he said. "And I understand the responsibility that goes with it. I promise you, no more secrets. I meant that."

He was willing to give up the money to save his daughter, Babsie thought, at least that's in his favor. She looked down the hill past the Toyota, at the girl who called her Gramma. Grace loved him. God, she loved him. Kids are never wrong.

"Keep me in the dark on this, Eddie," she said. "The new rule is we both get to keep one secret. This is yours."

## ABOUT THE AUTHOR

ED DEE retired as a lieutenant after twenty years with the NYPD's Organized Crime Unit. Then he earned an MFA in Writing at Arizona State University. His debut novel, *14 Peck Slip*, was a *New York Times* Notable Book of the Year.